Günter Grass was born in Danzig in 1927.
He is Germany's most celebrated contemporary writer.
Though best known as a novelist – author of The
Danzig Trilogy (*The Tin Drum, Cat and Mouse* and *Dog Years*)
and *The Flounder* – he is also poet,
playwright, sculptor, graphic artist, essayist and
political spokesman.

Also in Picador by the same author

The Rat
The Tin Drum
Cat and Mouse
Dog Years
The Flounder

Günter Grass

From the Diary of a Snail

Translated from the German by
RALPH MANHEIM

published by Pan Books

First published in England 1974 by Martin Secker & Warburg Limited
This Picador edition published 1989 by Pan Books Ltd,
Cavaye Place, London SW10 9PG
9 8 7 6 5 4 3 2 1

Copyright © 1972 by Hermann Luchterhand Verlag

English translation copyright © 1973 by
Harcourt Brace Jovanovich, Inc.

ISBN 0 330 30557 3

Originally published in German under the title
Aus dem Tagebuch einer Schnecke

Extracts from this book originally appeared
in *The American Scholar* and *Fiction*

The Author and the Publisher regret that
certain passages have been omitted for
British legal reasons.

Made and printed in Great Britain by
Richard Clay Ltd, Bungay, Suffolk

(*Reproduced from* The Complete Graphic Work of Albrecht Dürer *by permission of Thames & Hudson Limited*).

Melencolia I by Albrecht Dürer

Editor's Note

The 1969 election campaign in West Germany, which for the first time after the Second World War brought the S.P.D., the Social Democratic Party, to power and Willy Brandt to the Chancellorship, forms the background to this book. In almost one hundred election speeches, Günter Grass campaigned for the S.P.D. against the Christian Democratic Union (C.D.U.) and its Bavarian sister party, the Christian Social Union (C.S.U.), and the incumbent Chancellor of the West German Federal Republic, Kurt Georg Kiesinger.

1 Dear children: today they elected Gustav Heinemann president. I meant to start with Doubt, whose first name was Hermann and last name was Ott, but Gustav Gustav comes first. It took three ballots to elect him. (He has two doctorates; that's why the backbenchers who call themselves sewer workers and sit at the Rheinlust Tavern, betting rounds of beer on the outcome of the ballots, call him twice Gustav.) But when I reckon it up with care and enter all the delays (and not only the breakdown of the computer on the first ballot) in my waste book, I see that this day was twenty years in the making, even if he, Gustav Gustav, could scarcely have suspected what he was being simmered for or how tough things—and not only the beef—are in Germany.

Place: the East Prussia Hall next to the Radio Tower. Outside, staggered barriers to ward off demonstrators of the A.P.O., or extraparliamentary opposition. Inside, the Christian Democrats and Neo-Nazis exchanged winks of complicity: their candidate's name was Schröder. (Gustav Gustav, who knows his parliamentary backbenchers and likes to sit with itching thumb over a game of skat, joined the sewer workers now and then, but never long enough to develop beer buttocks.) Smell: nondescript. Ballpoint at the ready. Rumors: How many Liberals willing to be bought off? Rumor reads the future of the current Berlin crisis from pretzel sticks strewn at random. In the lobby the draft promotes rumors about a deputy by the name of Gscheidle, who with bandaged head is rolled in to vote. The TV camera comes to rest on him. Forecasts that fear to cross the threshold. The unhurriable process of calling names, casting ballots, counting: from Abelin to Zoglmann . . .

I was sitting on the visitors' bench. (Not far from me Frau Heinemann crumples her handkerchief.) Making slight slits as usual when something is hanging in the balance, I succeeded in evacuating the hall: even the chairs moved off without a murmur.

I can do that, children; I can think things so hard that I see them.

Even before it came in, its characteristic sound: foamy crackling. Then I saw it moving through the deserted East Prussia Hall. I tried to adjust my breathing to its haste but, breathless, had to give up.

Or similar happenings in slow motion: when Anna and I settle our marriage accounts in retrospect.

It pushed itself through the picture, never to be encompassed in one glance; even as a fragment it remained part of a will, which preceded the will to further will and, impelled by will, distended space on a wide screen.

Four children seldom united in one photo: antithetical twins, Franz and Raoul, eleven; a girl, Laura, eight, in pants, and Bruno, always motorized, four, who, contrary to all expectation, did not decide to stop growing at the age of three.

When, with its extended tentacles, the snail sensed the approaching finish line, it hesitated: it didn't want to get there, wanted to stay on the road, didn't want to win.

You talk Swiss German with Anna—"*Mer müend langsam*

prässiere" and Berlinisch with me: *"Was issen nu wieda los?"*

Only a "naked snail," a slug. My tedious principle. Only when I promised to set it a new goal, when I cut the future into slices for it to feed on successively, did it cross the imaginary line and leave the East Prussia Hall without waiting for the applause of the majority, who had instantly returned, or for the silence of the minority. (Here are the figures: with 512 Social Democratic and Free Democratic votes against 506 C.D.U. C.S.U. N.P.D.* votes and five abstentions, the *Bundesversammlung* elected Dr. Dr. Gustav W. Heinemann President of the Federal Republic on March 5, 1969.)

Since then he has been straightening out our screwed-up history and its holidays. (When he came to see us on Niedstrasse the evening before the election, he brought good cheer with him but nevertheless pulled out his wallet and showed us the hatred of his opponents: tattered newspaper clippings; the nagging old sores.) Homeless. I've already told you: a naked snail . . .

It seldom wins and then by the skin of its teeth. It crawls, it goes into hiding but keeps on, putting down its quickly drying track on the historical landscape, on documents and boundary lines, amid building sites and ruins, in drafty doctrinal structures, far from well-situated theories, skirting retreats and silted revolutions.

"What do you mean by the snail?"
"The snail is progress."

---

* C.D.U., Christian Democratic Union; C.S.U., Christian Social Union, sister party of C.D.U.; N.P.D., National Democratic Party, the Neo-Nazi Party.

"What's progress?"

"Being a little quicker than the snail . . ."

. . . and never getting there, children. A little later, when the trial meetings had been agreed on and the flights had been booked, when the student Erdmann Linde had moved into our Bonn office and started mapping out our campaign trips with varicolored pins, when the first campaign speeches had been stuffed with medium-term odds and ends and our aims had been (more or less) established, when I had taken to shuttling back and forth between Berlin-Tempelhof and Cologne-Wahn, setting out light and coming home with a bulging traveling bag (presents), when I had begun to be here today and gone tomorrow, but on the move even when here, a mobile, regionally dispersed, almost intangible father—all four of you at once and each of you extra specially fired questions at me, and with questions loaded me into the airport-bound taxi: When, why, how long, against whom?

Bruno has been thinking it over; he knows against whom. Before I say, "So long now," he says, "Be careful, or the *Wahlkampf** will gobble you up." The fact is that from Friday to Monday he sees his father and draws pictures of him on board a whaling ship. Firm and resolute in the bow, swathed in oilskins, wielding a harpoon. "Thar she blows! Thar she blows!" Battling the whale, far far away in danger, home again after a narrow squeak . . .

"Where are you off to again?"

"What do you do when you get there?"

---

* *Wahlkampf:* "election campaign." *Walkampf* (same pronunciation): "fight with the whale."

"Who are you fighting for?"
"What'll you bring us?"

Once I've started out, all this, divided into sixteenths by the jolting of the rails or kept in lane by the Autobahn, acquires a date, puts out stimulus words and takes on meaning.

For me the election campaign began in a drizzle on the lower Rhine. In the Kleve town hall I spoke on "Twenty Years of Federal Republic," a speech which afterward lost weight in some towns, put on topical fat in others, and never came to a full stop. A few days after Kleve, on March 27, I received a letter from Nuremberg, signed by one Dr. Hermann Glaser, an official in the municipal bureau of cultural affairs. (Which may have had something to do with my choosing Hermann as Doubt's—properly Ott's—first name. From Glaser's letter I learned how soon the Nuremberg authorities had started to prepare for the Dürer year 1971. I was asked to deliver one of a series of lectures. On April 24, Dr. Glaser wrote to thank me for my acceptance. He hoped, I read, that the election campaign would bring me to Nuremberg. Later on, we visited Erlangen, Röthenbach, and Roth. But not Nuremberg, because we usually avoided big cities and covered only small towns (like Kleve), also, children, because Friedhelm Drautzberg, who drove our Volkswagen bus, kept away from Dürer's native place to avoid a former fiancée who lives there, and not infrequently justified his detours to himself and me.

Glaser in my ears: throughout the election campaign I argued with that man, who, like Doubt, bore the first name of Hermann. Even in pauses, standing after my own speech or callus-assed from seated discussions, I quoted Dürer's journals: the pinchpenny; called Glaser's attention to Pirckheimer by pointing Doubt's index finger. While following a conveyor belt through the Oberhausen steel mill, I saw severe drawing, rigid even in its draperies; and while we were visiting the Kathmann poultry farm in Calveslage near Vechta and the gadgetry of the General Electric plant at Constance, I casually viewed the cabinet of engravings that accompanied me on my journey. (His signature hewn in stone, dangling from branches roots rooftrees. His playfully tail-wagging, sleeping poodle in the Passion woodcuts, usually in the foreground. His love of muscles and women's double chins.) First jottings in Gladbeck: slag hellebore moondust. After Dinslaken a paraphrase: angels in nightgowns. In Giessen, recipes for ink: black gall. I thought I was still searching, but I had already made up my mind: for I carried a glossy picture postcard through Upper Swabia and Lower Bavaria, through Friesland and Franconia; but it was not until a few days after September 28 (when Willy Brandt had got down to business and had stopped playing irresolutely with matches) that I wrote to Dr. Glaser: "My lecture will deal with Dürer's engraving *Melencolia I*."

"What's that?"
"Is that what you get when you write books?"
"Does it hurt bad?"
"Is it like the S.P.D.?"
"What about us?"
"Will we get it, too?"

Since the jottings for my Dürer lecture are entered in my waste book among notes that refer to Hermann Ott or Doubt, which record your exclamations or my own, try to capture the land snail's mode of locomotion and hold fast the effluvia of the election campaign in shorthand, Doubt in his cellar, you growing children, Anna, and I are getting more and more mixed up with Melancholy: already my spirits are growing heavy-gray; already you've spent a whole Sunday playing Melancholy and "there's nothing to do"; already Anna has developed a faraway look; already the horizon is curtained off by the perpetual rain of Dürer's hatching; already progress is infected with acute stasis; already the snail has found its way into the engravings. In short, the draft of a lecture, which thanks to Dr. Glaser's prepaid time I won't have to deliver for another two years, is expanding into the Diary of a Snail.

Be patient. My entries come to me on the road. Since in my thoughts, words, and deeds I am categorically earth-bound and even aboard a Super 111 am at best an unauthentic flier, nothing, not even an election campaign, can speed me or any part of me up. Accordingly, I request you to dispense with cries such as "Faster!" or "Get a move on!" I mean to speak to you by (roundabout) bypaths: sometimes offended and enraged, often withdrawn and hard to pin down, occasionally brimful of lies, until everything becomes plausible. Certain things I should like to pass over in circumspect silence. I anticipate a part of the part, whereas another part will turn up only later and partially. And, so, if my sentence twists, turns, and only gradually tapers to a point, don't fidget and don't bite your nails. Hardly anything, believe me, is more depressing than going straight to the goal. We have time. Yes, indeed: quite a lot of it.

We're having tripe, which yesterday after my return from Kleve and while slimming my speech for Castrop-Rauxel and fattening it up again, I simmered for four hours with caraway seed and tomatoes. Seasoned toward the end with garlic. The stomach walls of the cow hang like too-often-washed Turkish towels from the butcher's hook, in little demand except as dog food.

Cut into thumb-long strips.

Now they're steaming in a bowl.

Anna and I like them. Why shouldn't the children like them?

Now strife is floating on the soup.

Franz Raoul Laura Bruno. This knot that was tied in our bed: something that reaches out and grabs things.

The four-stage rocket rises while skin forms on the tripe broth, which demands to be stirred.

Well-rehearsed interruptions all around.

Sound that no button can turn off.

Only sign language remains.

Because, since no one and everyone wants to be first, lest anyone be first or last, the several-times-repeated cry of "You get the rag!" rises shrill and victorious over the tripe and the spilled H_2O.

The family tug at the missing tablecloth, unable to separate the too-dense fabric of their voices or the cause—was it the spilt water?—from the effect, the tripe that insists on backing up: sudden insight.

"Pig!"

"Pig yourself."

"Look who's talking."

"Superpig!"

(None of them makes it mildly Swiss like Anna—"You really are a piggy-wiggy"—they all talk like their father.)

Blubber. Bellow. Stink. Waterworks.

Harmony—or a desire to eat tripe in peace and to remember past occasions on which tripe was eaten, until nothing was left in the pot and we gently grazed our sorrow with friends: pacifist cows . . .

Where do wars start?

What is the name of misfortune?

Why should anyone travel when home sweet home?

(And no one out of malice or caprice, but only because the glass was smaller than the water or the H_2O or his thirst—and because the tripe in its broth: reasons.)

"All right. Now Laura may say something."

"First Laura, then Bruno."

"Where are you off to again tomorrow?"

"Castrop-Rauxel."

"What are you going to do there?"

"Talktalktalk."

"Still the same old S.P.D.?"

"It's just beginning."

"And what'll you bring us this time?"

"Myself, among other things . . ."

. . . and the question: Why those streaks on the wallpaper? (Everything that backs up with the tripe and coats the palate with tallow.)

Because, sometimes, children, at table, or when the TV throws out a word (about Biafra), I hear Franz or Raoul asking about the Jews:

"What about them? What's the story?"

You notice that I falter whenever I abbreviate. I can't find the needle's eye, and I start babbling.

Because this, but first that, and meanwhile the other, but only after . . .

I try to thin out forests of facts before they have time for new growth. To cut holes in the ice and keep them open. Not to sew up the gap. Not to tolerate jumps entailing a frivolous departure from history, which is a landscape inhabited by snails . . .

"Exactly how many were they?"

"How did they count them?"

■■■■■■■■■

It was a mistake to give you the total, the multidigitate number. It was a mistake to give the mechanism a numerical value, because perfect killing arouses hunger for technical details and suggests questions about breakdowns.

"Did it always work?"
"What kind of gas was it?"

Illustrated books and documents. Anti-Fascist memorials built in the Stalinist style. Badges of repentance and brother-hood weeks. Well-lubricated words of repentance. Detergents and all-purpose poetry: "When night fell over Germany . . ."

Now I'll tell you (and go on telling you as long as the election campaign goes on and Kiesinger is Chancellor) how it happened where I come from—slowly, deliberately, and in broad daylight. Preparations for the universal crime were made in many places at the same time though at unequal speeds; in Danzig, which before the war did not belong to the German Reich, the process was slowed down, which made it easier to record later on. . . .

2 About mountains of eyeglasses, because they strike the eye?

About gold teeth, because they can be weighed?

About loners and their private eccentricities, because multi-digitate numbers arouse no feelings?

About over-all figures and bickering over decimals?

No, children.

Only about habituation in its peaceable Sunday best.

It's true: you're innocent. I, too, born almost late enough, am held to be free from guilt. Only if I wanted to forget, if you were unwilling to learn how it slowly happened, only then might words of one syllable catch up with us: words like guilt and shame; they, too, resolute snails, impossible to stop.

As you know, I was born in the Free City of Danzig, which, after the First World War, had been detached from the German Reich and, with the surrounding districts, placed under the tutelage of the League of Nations.

Article 73 of the Constitution read: "All citizens of the Free City of Danzig are equal before the law. Exceptions to this law are inadmissible."

Article 96 of the Constitution read: "Full freedom of faith and conscience is guaranteed."

But (according to the census of August, 1929) the roughly 400,000 citizens of the Free State (among them I, barely two years old, was enumerated) included 10,448 Jews, few of them baptized.

By turns, the German Nationalists and the Social Democrats formed coalition governments. In 1930 the German Nationalist Dr. Ernst Ziehm decided in favor of a minority government. From then on, he was dependent on the twelve votes of the National Socialists. Two years later, the N.S.D.A.P. (National Socialist German Workers' Party) organized a parade that passed through the inner city in the morning and through the suburb of Langfuhr in the afternoon until, grown tired under placards and banners, the paraders crowded into the Klein-Hammerpark Garden Restaurant. The concluding speech featured the motto: "The Jews are our misfortune." Some of the newspapers called it impressive.

Social Democratic Deputy Kamnitzer protested in the name of the Danzig citizens of the Jewish faith, but the Senator of the Interior saw no breach of the law, although a photograph of a placard reading "Death to the Crooks and Profiteers" lay on his desk. (Since there are crooks and profiteers among Christians and atheists as well as Jews, it was argued that the threat applied not only to Jewish crooks and profiteers but also to the crooks and profiteers of other denominations.)

Nothing special; a parade for a purpose among other parades for other purposes. No dead or wounded, no property damage. Only increased beer consumption and merriment verging on the staggers. (What they sang then: "Cornflower blue"—what they sing now: "A day like this, so lovely, lovely . . .") Lots of young people in their Sunday best, flowery summer dresses: a folk festival. Since everyone knows, fears, and wants to avoid misfortune, everyone was glad to hear the misfortune called at last by its name, to know at last where the high prices, unemployment, housing shortage, and private stomach ulcers came from. At the Klein-Hammerpark under the chestnut trees it was easy to say all that out loud. There was (is) a Klein-Hammerpark everywhere. Consequently, the meaning was not: the Danzig Jews are our misfortune. But the Jews in general, everywhere. Wherever a handy name was sought for misfortune, it was found: in Frankfurt and Bielefeld, Leipzig and Karlsruhe, Danzig and Kleve, where I recently arrived in the rain and signed my name in the Golden Book at the town hall.

A small town not far from the Dutch border, which, saturated with history and swan lore, was destroyed shortly before the end of the war, and even today, rebuilt in its original small-checkered pattern, looks as if it were about to fall apart. (Little industry—children's shoes and margarine. Consequently a lot of commuters. By the end of the campaign we had climbed from 25.9 per cent to 31.1 per cent: a town with a future . . .)

In the afternoon, when I tried to have a discussion with the students at the girls' high school, disguised schoolboys from Erkelenz or Kevelaer occupied the platform, declared themselves by sheer schizophrenia a majority, and (amid the smell of floor polish common to school buildings) proclaimed in chorus: "We've been betrayed by rats. By Social Democrats!"

After the discussion—I tried to chip the paste off the usual historical collages—a few of the executioners asked me for my autograph.

Again, nothing special: a brief scuffle. Rival claims for the microphone. The normally gentle Erdmann Linde joined in. An S.P.D. treasurer was knocked down. (I heard his wrist had been broken.) Nothing remains but the chant: "We've been betrayed by . . ." for the question of betrayal is as old as the desire to hear misfortune called by its name.

In Kleve, a small town on the lower Rhine, and in the neighboring communities of Kalkar, Goch, and Uedem, there lived, in 1933, 352 Jews, united in the Kleve community. Too much misfortune for the townspeople to put up with.

It all begins, children, with: the Jews are. The foreign workers want. The Social Democrats have. Every petit bourgeois is. The niggers. The left-wingers. The class enemy. The Chinese and the Saxons believe have think are . . .

Signposts with changing inscriptions but identical destination: destroy unmask convert smash eliminate pacify liquidate re-educate isolate exterminate . . .

My snail knows this rustproof language, the flashing, twice-tempered words, the Freisler finger on Lenin's hand.*

How inoffensive or terrifying are the successive speakers at the microphone when they reel off the destroying angel's small print—hard total pure sharp—and pledge allegiance to what can do without: the unconditional uncompromising unswerving irresistible betterment of the world—without mercy!

Every day now (sometimes to my consternation) I hear about this kind of thing. They crowd around. And I discover with what a prodigy of deception hate fosters beauty in youthful faces. Something for photographers. They are only a few; the majority look on with sickly alarm. They want to abolish something, anything, the system, for want of anything better, me.

Later, over beer, they're pleasant and in a relaxed kind of way even polite. They didn't really mean any harm. Every-

---

* Roland Freisler, ferocious president of the Nazi People's Court that judged political crimes.

thing—"you know, the whole lousy business"—including themselves strikes them as boring or ridiculous. They sulk because nothing's going on. They're sorry for themselves. Homeless because their homes are too good. Embittered, coddled children, who twine their troubles into a litany: parents, school, conditions, everything. (When their spokesman has to speak without a microphone, I see that he's inhibited and stutters.) Their sheepish self-pity makes me more ironic than I mean to be. I talk, talk beside the point, talk to no purpose, listen to myself talk until they're sick of me and take their surfeit home.

Where are they headed? What crusade will enlist them? "What should I do, Franz? Tell me, Raoul, what?" Just put up with it? Keep putting up with the same rubbish?

Later on in Delmenhorst, a pretty girl student called me "Social Fascist!" several times in crescendo, till her eyes glittered and her face was covered with spots. But my snail can't be insulted. When it's overtaken by rhythmically moving parades, it never speeds up; not long ago, it outdistanced a protest demonstration with banners and placards by ante-dating it.

In March, 1933, when parades of the SA and the Hitler Cubs had become a daily occurrence, the organ of the Jewish community published an article celebrating the founding of the community fifty years before. The writer spoke of the period before 1833, when there were five isolated communities in Langfuhr, Mattenbuden, Schottland, Weinberg and Danzig. Gustav Davidsohn, chairman of the Schottland community, had managed to unite the dispersed groups and inaugurate the building of the Central Synagogue, an edifice that conformed alarmingly to the "historical" variety of Danzig architecture. But since the new synagogue with its organ was regarded as a

sacrilege by an Orthodox minority, the Mattenbuden synagogue was kept open. Synagogues were also built in Zoppot
and Langfuhr, for the community was torn by strife. Even in
the days when the Jews were respected citizens of Danzig,
there had always been open quarrels between Orthodox and
Reform Jews, between Zionists and German Nationalists. Dividing lines were drawn: well-to-do citizens bent on assimilation
were ashamed of the impoverished arrivals from Galicia,
Pinsk, and Bialystok, who spoke Yiddish without compunction
and in spite of all the charities did for them remained embarrassingly conspicuous.

Persecution of the Jews had become common practice in
revolutionary Russia, and by 1925 some 60,000 Jews from the
Ukraine and southeastern Poland had come to Danzig on their
way to America. While waiting for their visas, the emigrants
were lodged in a transit camp on Troyl, an island otherwise
used largely for storing lumber. Three thousand Jews, Polish
subjects for the most part, remained in Danzig, failing to
suspect what was in store for them.

"What about Doubt?"
"Yes, what about him?"
"Did he have any brothers, or maybe a sister?"
"Or did you just make him up?"

Even if I've had to make him up, he existed. (A story told
me years ago by Ranicki as his autobiography stayed with me,
leading a quiet life of its own; patiently, it insists on an invented name, established origins, and a cellar to take refuge in
later on.)

Only now, children, can Doubt come to the surface, pre-
dominate, take on body, cloud the atmosphere, pour vinegar

on hope, behave bravely and amusingly, be outlawed—only now, in short, is it finally permissible to speak of Hermann Ott.

Born in 1905, the only son of an engineer at the Praust pumping station, he graduated in due time from the Sankt Johann High School. Since 1924 he had been studying, not engineering (hydraulics, for instance), at the Danzig Engineering School but biology and philosophy in faraway Berlin. Only in vacation time can he be seen idling on Langgasse or visiting the Schopenhauer House on Heilige Geistgasse. Obliged to earn his own keep—his father, Simon Ott, had been willing to pay only for hydraulics—he has taken an office job at the Jewish transit camp on Troyl. This is where he is first given the name of Doubt, or Dr. Doubt—the young student is as handy with the word "doubt" as with his knife and fork. He makes himself useful to the camp management and to Rabbi Robert Kaelter by keeping accounts of the receipts and expenditures and calculating the food requirements, which vary from day to day; but when not at work he professes doubt as a new faith. His listeners are Galician artisans who are amused by his categorical Why, which even calls the weather and the chosenness of the people of Israel into doubt. ("*Och Zweifelleben, wie bekim ich blojs a daitscheches Visum?*" asks the tailor from Lbov. "I doubt," says Hermann Ott, "whether a German visa will be of much use to you in the long run.")

In 1926 the transit camps on Troyl were discontinued; the nickname Doubt remained, although Hermann Ott, whose family hailed from the village of Müggenhahl in the Werder, could demonstrate his strictly Mennonite origin. (His grandmother Mathilde, née Claasen, successively widow Kreft, Duwe, Niklas, and Ott, was said to have performed valuable services for the drainage system in the Vistula estuary; but I've already written too much about active grandmothers.)

3 All sorts of things take refuge in my waste book: found articles, nailed moments, stuttering exercises, and angry exclamatory dashes.

In Kleve, for instance, where I thought of visiting the barrows in the nearby Reichswald, I noted: the island of Mauritius, about which I shall have something to say later on, has been made known by a postage stamp. Must describe Doubt. Autographs on beer mats. Bettina, though patient with our children, has recently become cross with me because her boy friend has "politicized" her.

Or in Rauxel: when the twins are twelve in September, I will not buy Raoul a record player. What did Doubt look like? Tall gaunt stooped? Here we speak in the auditorium of the Adalbert-Stifter High School. Bettina is reading Hegel in a study group.

Or in Gladbeck: Doubt was of medium height with a tendency to corpulence. In the hall pollsters with questionnaires, researching on how and when I make a particular hit with women. One record player downstairs for everybody is plenty. Ride down into the "Graf Moltke" mine. Back on the surface, they make me a present, on the loading platform, of a tin of snuff. Have to repeat the act of snuff taking three times for TV. Chipped beef and schnapps with shop stewards. Bettina's conversation with me has become strictly impersonal.

Or in Bocholt, where the textile crisis (Erhard calls it a

"healthy shrinkage") feeds discussion: no way of proving what Doubt looked like. At the St. Paulus trade-union house schoolboys are bringing out the red flags. Let's stick to gray tones from now on! Besides, Bettina has our old record player, and Raoul can borrow it. My hotel is called the Archangel. The loving cups of the marksmen's societies displayed in glass cases. The word "snail-fug." A Catholic shop steward takes me aside. "I'm fed up! Welfare commissions, pure hokum! Katzer has hornswoggled us. . . ." he says.* He's old tired finished washed up.

And in the Marl, known for its intricate architecture, Doubt looked different. Breed an iron-eating snail. Have to talk more softly to get through because of all the loudspeakers. In the meantime, member of a jury at a poster contest for schoolchildren: despite increasing gray tones, the next decade promises to be colorful. Costume rental: Doubt.

And in Oberhausen, where the local Social Democrats ill-advisedly stage a "Merry Evening" in anticipation of May Day. Meet a lot of people. At the control desk of the rolling mill. Furnace tap, often seen in films. But the noise-silenced work, usually described as a dynamic process, obeys no aesthetic law. I imagine fast-moving things, I want acceleration, I think in hops, skips, and jumps; but the snail is still reluctant to hop or to be accelerated.

Another entry here: pea soup with old man Meinike. (When I listen to old Social Democrats, I learn something, though I can't say what it is.) How he thunders on, points ahead, says forward, keeps evoking the past, falls silent, blinks watery eyes, suddenly pounds the table to impress his son.

Nothing doing, Raoul: no record player. When he went walking on the walls of the former Rabbit Bastion, Doubt wore

---

* Hans Katzer, Minister of Labor during the so-called Great Coalition, 1965–1969; also chairman of the Social Committee of the C.D.U./C.S.U.

checked knickers. Bettina also says "We" when she means "I."
Several suicides at Bonn ministries: civil servants and secretaries. Barzel* disavows Kiesinger. Wonder if Dr. Glaser in
Nuremberg has any feeling for the *Melencolia*. Doubt did not
wear glasses. . . .

"You mean you know him?"
"Is he a friend of yours?"
"Was he always gone, too?"
"Did he look like his name?"
"Well, sort of sad. Sort of funny . . ."

He looked sad funny nondescript. Think of him as a man
with everything out of kilter: his right shoulder sagged, his
right ear stuck out; he also blinked his right eye and lifted the
right corner of his mouth. This unbalanced face, alien to all
symmetry, was dominated by a fleshy nose with a left deviation. Several swirls of hair made a part impossible. Not much
chin, always prepared to retreat. A lopsided young fellow, with
a tendency to fidgets and knee flexing, eccentric and given to
rasping sound effects, weak in the chest. No, children, better
not think of Doubt as sickly and blinking. In photographs
representing the faculty of the Crown Prince Wilhelm High
School, he, who began to teach there in March, 1933, towers
almost embarrassingly over his colleagues, who may be described as of medium height. He taught German and biology
but might almost have been taken for a hulking gymnastics
teacher, though—apart from bicycle trips to the Werder and
through Kashubia—he practiced no sport. A man with physical strength that he made no use of. Later on, when a gang of
Hitler Youth beat him up, it didn't occur to him to resist. A
man who inflicts pain only in shaking hands. Who in sitting

---

* Dr. Rainer Barzel, Majority Leader of the C.D.U. in the Bundestag.

22

down worries about the chair. Diffident strength on tiptoes. A fussy giant.

No, children, better not form any picture of Doubt. He was made up of contradictions, never looked any particular way. (Possibly the body of a weight lifter supported the lopsided, and under pressure of thought, grimacing face of a bookworm.) Even I, who have known him for years, am unable to define his appearance, to give him a snub nose, an adherent left ear lobe, or nervous sinewy hands.

Imagine Doubt any way you like. Say: extreme ascetic pallor. Say: awkward reserve. Say: rustically robust. Say: nothing striking.

Only this much is certain: he did not limp. He did not wear glasses. He was not bald. Only recently on my way from Gladbeck to Bocholt, as I was trying the snuff received from the Graf Moltke mine without benefit of TV and solely for my own enlightenment, I saw him and was sure that his skepticism peers out of gray eyes.

In other words, he's still peering, and maybe he blinks after all. Doubt not to be dispelled.

I've known him longer than myself: we kept away from the same kindergarten.

When Doubt tried to cancel himself out, I put him under contract: dependent, he gives me orders.

Sometimes he attends my meetings: that heckler in Bocholt the other day; that tumultuously silent fellow in Marl. Now stillness is descending on my hotel room: Doubt arises . . .

I don't know whether the withdrawn man whom I call Willy and whose past can never end will soon (as I hope) stop playing with matches and prolong the trajectory from Bebel*

---

* August Bebel (1840–1913), German Social Democratic leader.

to the present day by a snail's measure of justice. (I am almost inclined to think that when Doubt was sitting in the cellar later on he invented this precise construction of interlocking refuges as a game against time.) Bonn, Kiefernweg. Spent an hour with him today. I'd have liked to swipe his matches, because people are imitating his game, and it's getting to be a paralyzing fashion. (To say that he was taciturn this morning would imply that one had known him to be talkative.) He listened, took notes, and went right on with his matches. It became clear to me that the man won't fight until the state he's in has worn itself out. (What makes him hesitate? His adversaries' hatred, the servitudes of power?) Before leaving, I succeeded in making him laugh, I don't remember how: between melancholy and Social Democracy there are sometimes desperately funny short circuits.

Even before the elections, when in March, 1933, the article celebrating the fiftieth anniversary of Danzig's Jewish community concluded with Goethe's words, "Persevere in defiance of all the powers," the twenty-eight-year-old Hermann was teaching school; at the same time he was signing letters as assistant secretary of the Schopenhauer Society, an association of elderly and basically conservative gentlemen, devoted more to local patriotism than to any learned pursuits. One of Ott's functions was to guide visitors to the philosopher's birthplace in Heilige Geistgasse. There he muddled dates and quotations and (in passing) explained Schopenhauer's melancholia as the heritage of a family of Hanseatic merchants.

In addition to the organ of the Jewish community, there was in Danzig a Zionist monthly that found readers also in Dirschau and Gdingen. *The Jewish Nation* was edited by Isaak Landau. And simultaneously with the community organ's article on the founding of the synagogue, which, except for the quotation from Goethe, abstained from any reference to politics, Landau ran an article about the incipient persecution of the Jews titled "The Situation in Germany."

In consequence, the journal was suspended for three months. Frightened by anonymous threats, Landau left the Free State on a bicycle borrowed from Ott. Near Klein-Katz he slipped across the border to Poland and sent the bicycle back by train from Putzig before continuing on his way to Palestine. Landau also sent a picture postcard featuring the lighthouse on Hela Peninsula. Between salutation and signature it expressed the hope that there would be no lacking of lighthouses in the future.

"I doubt," said Hermann Ott, "that this will be the only flight."

A little later a number of Jewish students at the engineering school had to abandon their studies because their National Socialist fellows made work in the drafting rooms and laboratories impossible for them.

"How did they make it impossible?"

"By chicanery."

"For instance?"

"Pouring ink on their drawings."

"Just dumb tricks?"

"It's possible that some of the SA students thought they were only playing dumb tricks."

"What about the students now? Would they?"

"I don't know."

"Tell me the truth. Would they?"

"Some might."

"The Maoists?"

"It's possible that some Maoist students think they're only playing stupid tricks."

"But if they're against the system and for justice?"

●●●●●●●●●

Let's try to be broadminded. The violent and the righteous are hard of hearing. Only this much, children: don't be too righteous. People might be afraid of your righteousness; it might put them to flight. . . .

After a Jewish instructor at the engineering school was forced out of his job—as a German subject he was handed over to the German authorities in Marienburg and sent to a camp (the word "concentration" was not yet in use)—Ott was horrified by a case of radically logical flight. A seventeen-year-old boy hanged himself in the gymnasium of the Crown Prince Wilhelm High School—from the horizontal bar—after his schoolmates had forced him (only a dumb trick) to display his circumcised prepuce in the toilet.

A few of the guilty students were expelled. But in the presence of the assembled faculty Hermann Ott expressed skepticism: "I doubt that anything can be accomplished by expulsions as long as certain of the teachers see fit to assign generalizations such as 'The Jews Are Our Misfortune' as subjects for essays."

Doubt meanwhile taught fifth-form students—who subsequently in North Africa, on the Arctic front, or as members of submarine crews, found no occasion to become middle-aged or skeptical—the "skeptical view" of Schopenhauer, the lover of poodles. (Of morality and dignity nothing remained but neck stiffeners and powder puffs.) "I doubt," said Ott to his fifth form, "that you're listening to me."

In April, 1933, the Ziehm minority government dissolved the Volkstag. In the elections of May 28, the National Socialists won a bare majority of 50.03 per cent. (In the Reich only 43.9 per cent of the electorate had voted for Hitler in March.)

Someone called Rauschning became president of the Danzig Senate. The unions had already let themselves, without appreciable resistance, be "co-ordinated" with the National Socialist industrial organizations; a disgrace which to this day inspires the German Trade Union League with virtuous protestations of "Never again!" and tortuous confessions of guilt, especially on May Day. . . .

"Didn't they go on strike?"
"There was no general strike."
"Would they now if something like that? . . ."
"I don't know."
"Honest and truly. Would they?"
"I really don't know. . . ."

. . . and at the weekend I bring little certainty home with me in my suitcase: fug-saturated shirts and this pit lamp from the Graf Moltke mine in Gladbeck, given to me along with the snuff by Dziabel, chairman of the shop committee.

Forward—that's the name of a Social Democratic weekly. The schoolbooks used to call a general, Blücher by name, Marshall Forward. In the Hitler Youth they used to sing (I, too, sang): "Forward, forward, the ringing trumpets blare. . . ."

A stupid word that has often enough accelerated regression. An inflated, and for that reason quickly deflated word, whose air is enthusiasm and whose pump is faith. A word that leaps over tombs and mass graves, translated into all languages, a catchword familiar to all loudspeakers, which is examined only in retrospect (conversations between refugees). Let's look and see whether forward isn't already behind us. Interrogate the rundown heels of our shoes. Clear-cut decisions, but the signposts contradict each other. In the midst of progress we find ourselves standing still. The excavated future. The mysticism of statistics. Gothically ornate ignition keys. Automobiles wrapped around trees . . .

Later, Franz, when you're disillusioned,
when you've learned—the hard way—the refrain of the
                      "It's no use" song,
when you've sung it in company,
forgotten it out of spite
and learned it again at night school,
later, Franz,
when you see
that this way and that way and even this other way won't
                      work,
when things start going bad with you
and you've spent your portion of hope,
when you've forgotten love in the glove compartment
and hope, the well-meaning boy scout
whose knee socks are always slipping,
has lost itself in ashen grayness,
when knowledge lathers in chewing,
when you're through,
when you've been knocked cold:
flattened shredded desiccated—
a man about to give up—
when at the goal, though first,
you recognize applause to be
delusion and victory a punishment,
when your shoes have been soled
with melancholy
and your pockets bulge with slag,
when you've given up, at last given up,

given up once and for all, then—Fränzeken—
after a pause long enough
to be called embarrassing,
then stand up and start moving,
moving forward. . . .

. . . for when we—all of us cubical men—started to meet at
my house on Niedstrasse a year ago, to besiege our long table
and exasperate each other, we put down between overloaded
ash trays, a wee little beginning; it was lame from the start. We
all insisted that our wee beginning must regard itself as an
experiment, because each man at the table, though each in his
own specific way, harbored the intention of giving up very
shortly if he hadn't done so long ago, at the latest when the
Great Coalition was ended; only Jäckel senior spoke with the
assurance of a historian and called the situation normal.

Hard to let each other finish speaking. That bored poking
about with pipes and appurtenances. Evasions into the vesti-
bules of academic intrigues. Compliments to Anna, who "looks
in" rather absently for a moment. Precautionary omissions
and enjoinders to come to the point.

And so we spoon-fed our wee beginning. It was given paper
and parenthetical wisdom to eat. In three pages (no more) we
registered the pusillanimity (from which we dissociated ourselves) of the Social Democrats, their internal squabbles that
paralyzed the party, their provincial complacency, their fuzzy
image making, their cumulation of offices and jurisdictional
disputes, their right-wing opportunism and left-wing arrogance, their leadership torn between procrastination and ambition, their lack of determination (despite undeniable instances
of zeal and ability) to win the impending Bundestag elections.
The impetus—this was our panacea—must come from outside.
Under certain circumstances (which remained to be created) a

number of small but active groups succeed in shaking the weary party out of its resignation. Provide a spur. Play the pacemaker. Prepare the terrain. Found (Social Democratic) voters' clubs. Catch and channel the wave of protest . . .

Our arrogance was rich in cynical sound effects. Desperate long-distance runners trying to outdistance each other by the length of a joke. Lying gasping on our faces, impelled only by the crawling instinct to look for starting holes. Rubbing pepper into a snail's creeping sole.

Right now I have no desire to brush in atmosphere or doodle little men, although outside, while chairs were stiffening our bones, drama was stalking on a wide screen. Dutschke* in the lead, the student demonstration advanced tight-linked and conflict-oriented, heroic and beautiful (in the segment captured by the camera) against us puny revisionists; and for us, promoting revisionism. Accustomed to noise, we sat on the fringe, pedantic harpers on words, who want everything, even the vaguest things, named with precision.

After Gaus had had his outburst, after Sontheimer had been incapable of any decision, after Baring had regarded his contribution as not negligible, after I had been irritatingly pigheaded, and all of us had once, Gaus several times, been right, Jäckel senior spoke as a historian and called the date of the elections a goal toward which we must move progressively step by step.†

---

* Rudi Dutschke, the leader of a militant Berlin student group, shot and critically wounded in 1968.

† Gaus, Sontheimer, Baring, Jäckel senior: fellow Social Democrats

4 . . . or should we throw up the sponge? And simply clear out? Sell our possessions and emigrate, no matter where? "My visa has come!" cried the snail and took its house with it.

Hermann Ott was also said to have considered emigrating in those days: to Canada (where he had Mennonite relatives), to London (drawn by insular skepticism). Doubt planned several new existences that canceled each other out. Consequently, he stayed where he was and planned his staying.

We planned to open an office in Bonn, where the organization of local voters' clubs would be planned and the use of my time meaningfully scheduled: from March to the end of September, with planned intermissions.

One of the three office rooms was assigned to our planned (but still unnamed) propaganda organ. We planned large and small ads and as our first sign of life a press conference in Bonn, which was to be held on Monday, March 25, at the Tulpenfeld Restaurant, and adequate word of which, as planned, got around.

For mid-April we planned Sontheimer's speech at the Godesberg party congress. (It's in the minutes. Was received with applause.) We planned posters, leaflets, moderate chain

reactions, and a lentil dinner with press and Wischnewski.*
(Reported in fifty papers, because lentils are news.)

We also planned names—Baudissin, Lenz, Böll,† and heaven knows who else—and had, a procedure built into the plans of every true planner, to prune, to make new plans, or distil and clarify old ones.

Our elaborate dice game was rejected (too expensive) before it could be developed into a political war game and amuse anybody. The carrier pigeon campaign planned for the Ruhr district came to nothing. We had also—it goes without saying—planned a movie, and in addition we planned to . . .

Listen, Raoul, your plan appeals to me, even if it won't work. Put it aside. Don't get mad right away. Fly off the handle slowly. And don't say: "Why do these things always happen to me?"

I've told you a hundred times that your big and little mishaps don't mean that the world or neighborhood is against you.

I've taken you and your cuts in the head to the doctor on Sundays.

I've shown you how to lard a leg of mutton with garlic.

I often see you coming in too much of a hurry and catch you when you jump.

I anticipate you, help you to blow off steam. (You and your mother are too much alike for proximity at table.)

Before anger makes you feather-light, hold on to me, for instance; I'll brake you (and Doubt will brake me).

How politely indulgent you are when absent-mindedness makes me say "yes," though I've previously said very plainly: "No record player."

---

* Hans-Jürgen Wischnewski, leading Social Democrat.
† Wolf Graf von Baudissin, writer and political figure; Siegfried Lenz, Heinrich Böll, German writers.

Your order is a chaos full of hard work.

Even if it spills over, I like you to pour me wine.

Your plans appeal to me. Come, let's make plans!

For the fun of it the way I'd like my funeral to be planned: merrily and insidiously.

Whom shall we invite?

Not just friends.

What will there be to eat afterward (before, as we've planned, my taped voice welcomes the guests)?

Leg of mutton larded with garlic—as your father has taught you.

But I'm still more or less alive. My plans are simmering on a low flame. For the present I'm busy preventing. And aiming at small gains. Making gray holes in the blackness.* Covering dyed-black-in-the-wool election districts: Catholic-pagan picture-book regions, where the organization of voters' clubs—you know our plan—is made difficult by people's fear for their reputation and clientele, their fear of the priest, the school principal, the neighbors, philistine fear in regional costume.

Or when in the afternoon (after visiting factories) I sit with shop committees and listen as work and working conditions are described to me as a curse dispensed on a smooth-running conveyor belt: injustice guaranteed by contract.

Or in discussions, when the sons of the bourgeoisie start exculpating themselves by trying to redeem the world with a microphone. When grimly I try to pull the weeds of German idealism, which spring up again as inexorably as rib grass. How they persist in pursuing a cause—even the cause of socialism—for its own sake. . . .

---

* "Blackness" refers to the C.D.U., the Christian Democratic Party, *i.e.*, the clerical party.

Or the faithful under their cheese domes, how fresh they keep themselves. Raoul, let's go on being heretics. Come, let's make plans. But now let's see what Doubt is up to. . . .

He changed schools. I found that out from Dr. Lichtenstein, now living in Tel Aviv, who collected all the documents: dry decrees and Senate minutes, the stilted euphemizations of a crime that from the outset gave promise of growth and brilliant future. (I had taken the final draft of my manuscript with me on my visit to Israel from November 5 to November 18, 1971. Erwin Lichtenstein informed me that his documents on "The Exodus of the Jews from the Free City of Danzig" were soon to be published in book form by Mohr in Tübingen. Frau Lichtenstein, née Anker, said to Anna: "We were newlyweds then.")

Beginning in March, 1933, the Jewish stores in Danzig were boycotted; Jewish members of the judiciary were, for no stated reason, transferred to subordinate positions; Jewish doctors, even irreplaceable specialists, were dismissed from the hospitals and expelled from the Medical Association; the employment of Jewish artists at the Forest Festival in Zoppot was forbidden; all Jewish employees at the Danzig radio station were given notice; The Bar Kochba Gymnastic Society was barred from using the municipal gymnasiums; and life was made intolerable for Jewish children at the city schools: they were obliged to sit segregated. When the "German salute" was given, they had to stand at attention but were not permitted to raise their right arms like their schoolmates; the same applied to Jewish teachers.

Erwin Lichtenstein said in Israel: "At that time I was a young fellow, syndic of the Jewish community. We were opposed to Jewish schools. Only the Zionist People's Party had been petitioning for them for years. Now the Senate forced our hand. . . ."

In March, 1934, the Jewish community was obliged to set up an eight-class elementary school. At first, rooms in the public school on Rittergasse were made available. Later on, the school moved to Heilige Geistgasse. When pupils started coming from as far as Praust, Tiegenhof, and Zoppot, additional private rooms were rented on Brotbänkengasse. (Samuel Echt, a high school teacher, directed the Jewish elementary school until shortly before the outbreak of the war when, reduced in numbers by emigration, it was moved back to Rittergasse. When Echt emigrated, Aron Silber became principal.) At the same time, a private high school was founded.

In Haifa Anna and I visited Ruth Rosenbaum. In the presence of her eighty-nine-year-old mother, who lives halfway up Mount Carmel with a view of the sea and a houseful of momentos of Danzig, the daughter had her doubts: "Must my name be mentioned?"

Because Ruth Rosenbaum was unable to obtain a position in the municipal schools, her mother had put ads in the community organ and the *Voice of the Nation*. Eight Jewish children of secondary-school age replied. Ruth Rosenbaum started giving private lessons in her father's house at 5 Dominickswall. (Thirty-seven years later, she said: "I had no idea what it would lead to.")

She was twenty-six. Soon she was the principal of the Private Jewish High School, which is still referred to by former pupils (Eva Gerson in Jerusalem) as the "Rosenbaum School." The school grew and was later moved to the villa of a former brickyard owner (1 Eichenallee, at the corner of Grosse Allee). From spring, 1934, to February 15, 1939, it was directed by Ruth Rosenbaum. Today, in Haifa, she gives private lessons (English and French) and would prefer not to be mentioned.

In addition to Ruth Rosenbaum, Romana Haberfeld, who had been obliged to leave the Viktoria School the previous year, Brünhilde Nachmann, and Herren Ascher and Litten, engaged at a later date, there were also non-Jewish teachers who had been dismissed from municipal high schools for statements critical of National Socialism: Elfriede Mettner, Herr Martens, and—why not?—Doubt, under the name of Hermann Ott.

Ranicki, who did not study biology, but whose story has stayed with me, may now ask questions. Did Ott have a special liking for Jews? He liked to argue with Jews (Herr Litten, for example) about words and their meanings.

Did this Ott apply in writing for the position at the Rosenbaum School? He wrote: "I doubt whether, apart from my pedagogical activity, I shall be able to develop a special interest in the problems of Judaism; all religious usages are intensely alien to me."

Did Ott then apply for political reasons? Not really. True, he was against the Nazis and, sharing Schopenhauer's opposition to Hegel, against Communism, but he also spoke skeptically of Zionism.

In that case, why couldn't this Ott have gone somewhere else?

My dear Ranicki, because only at the Rosenbaum School is Doubt conceivable, hence real.

Hermann Ott went on teaching biology and German. He brought his nickname with him. (Ruth Rosenbaum probably doesn't remember him, though he must have been industrious with her in the school garden, because in the third-form diary we read: "Today part of the school garden was closed because wasps had built a nest there. In the evening Herr Martens and Herr Ott smoked out the nest.")

Ott found appreciation as a teacher; but his honorary activity as assistant secretary of the Schopenhauer Society came to an end because—according to a letter from the president —immediate contact with Jews is incompatible with the values of purebred German philosophy.

There were merry goings on at the Rosenbaum School. Purim festivals were celebrated. Purim plays were rehearsed. In the third-form diary we read: "Meier Isaaksohn played the merry rabbi. The Chassidim weren't bad either. We had Hamantaschen to eat afterward. . . ."

For another Purim festival Ruth Rosenbaum's father, Dr. Bernhard Rosenbaum, a lawyer by profession, wrote a play in rhyme titled *Amalek,* dealing with the projected massacre of the Jews in the Persian Empire. (The wicked Haman persuades King Ahasuerus to promulgate a law setting aside a day on which all the Jews are to be killed. But Queen Esther's uncle, the aged Mordecai of the house of Kish, persuades the queen to intercede with Ahasuerus and beg mercy for her people. The wicked Haman is hanged. And the day of the projected massacre is celebrated as Purim forever after.)

In the third-form diary we read: "It was quite a job learning all the parts. At the last minute Fritz Gerson who was to play Haman fell sick. Susi Strassmann came forward and said she knew Haman's part. . . ."

No, children, absolutely unpolitical. Ruth Rosenbaum said in Haifa: "Politics stayed outside. My father screened us off. As teachers, we were fortunate; we had a chance to experiment and at last to do something about school reform. I introduced courses in handicrafts, for instance. And we made no distinction between majors and other subjects."

Doubt must at that time have resumed his collecting of snails. References are to be found in the entries concerning hikes—the third form did a good deal of hiking: "Soon after Purim we went on an excursion to Freudenthal. We took the train to Oliva, and from there we hiked. Herr Ott took his specimen box. . . ." Or: "Excursion to Lappin. The bridge to Podfidlin was closed, so to cross the Radaune we had to walk to Oberkahlbude. We were very near the Free State border. We had a wonderful time on Ottomin Lake. We helped Herr Ott collecting. On the way to Prangschin someone took our picture. . . ." Or: "Train to Brentau. Then we hiked, mostly through the woods. Herr Ott was delighted because he found some strawberry snails. We sang songs in German and Hebrew. That made the time pass quickly. . . ."

It may have been these excursions that led Hermann Ott, in addition to his philosophical essays which for the most part picked bones with Hegel and drew inspiration from Schopenhauer, to write articles about the local landscape and customs, which slightly abridged but never distorted appeared in the *Danziger Volkszeitung,* an obscure Social Democratic paper. The readers of the *Volkszeitung* learned where snails were to be found: along the Radaune, around Ottomin Lake, between Tiegenhof and Neuteich, behind the dikes where the Kashubians bake bricks, where beach grass grows, on the way to Fischerbabke.

Now that Doubt has become conceivable and active as a teacher at the Rosenbaum School, he turns out to be more versatile than I had originally planned; it seems that he also wrote "brief comments" for the *Volkszeitung.*

5 On my return from Snailville I strike myself as fast-moving. It lies to the south of Upper Dawdle on the road to Creepy Corners, and along with the townships of Sluggish Falls, Dally-in-the-Woods, and Backlog, belongs to an election district where the Socialists have been making progress since Bebel, but getting ahead only very slowly and relatively. (Since we have been suffering from consciousness, a false consciousness has come into being.)

You can see, children, that I had to make special preparations for Snailville, a small town whose architecture and homey atmosphere remind one of Burgsteinfurt, Weissenburg, Säckingen, and Biberach; it was necessary in particular to adapt my standard speech—"Twenty Years of Federal Republic"—to the Snailville mentality by making certain cuts and adding historical passages, because several days before my arrival—coming from Marl, we still had May Day in Dinslaken ahead of us—a debate had taken place behind Renaissance windows in the Snailville town hall and had been followed by a vote. By fifteen black votes to six on our side (and two Liberal abstentions) the town council had issued a proclamation indirectly aimed at us. Here it is:

"Citizens of Snailville! Changes against which we have long been warning you are threatening to materialize. As we learn from the leaflets of radical innovators, the thousandth anniversary of our formerly diocesan city is to be celebrated under the scandalous slogan: 'Let us not fear the great leap!' The innovators are planning to mask their true intentions behind sports contest. Hopping races are to be held not only in the schools but also—provocatively!—outside the Town Hall. We see through their devices! It has also reached our ears that a proposal to rename our beloved Snailville is in the offing. 'Snail's Leap' is the name they have in mind for our city. We call upon all citizens to thwart this sacrilege. No leaping for this town. Though we do not reject progress out of hand, we distrust haste. We have always arrived in good time. Often, we have owed our survival to arriving too late. It is imperative that we halt the speed-up that is threatening Snailville and cancel certain measures already under consideration. Nip them in the bud! Our fortune is our perseverance. We do not hurry."

(Since then I have visited other towns equally concerned with preserving their home-grown stasis, jumbles of narrow, winding streets clogged with through-traffic, towns that seemed to be preserved in exhaust fumes and might have been called Snail Bend or Slugheim.)

The night when I addressed the numerous citizens who had gathered in Snailville's historical Market Hall on Vogteiplatz, I managed in my exordium to interpret the snail in the city's coat-of-arms as a symbol of progress. Obviously, I recommended no leaps and above all no "Great Leap Forward." I also steered clear of such words as "expansion," "areas of concentrated effort," "crash program," "infrastructure," and "planning." But when I had elucidated the fundamental difference between conservative clinging snails and progressive mobile snails and, holding fast to my image, reduced all motion to snail measure, an increasing number of my listeners resolved to be clinging snails no longer and showed a willingness to interpret their city's heraldic animal (in the spirit of my gastropodological disquisition) as a Roman snail edging inexorably forward on its creeping sole. "Progress is a snail," I said. (And when I termed Willy Brandt's slow, steady ascent a "snail's career," I was rewarded with amiable, startled applause.) No enthusiasm, but at least they listened when, in the light of its century of toil, I spoke of the Social Democratic Party as a snail party. My speech ended with an appeal to my audience not to shut themselves up in their shells, but, snail-wise, to persevere in their journey and let their tentacles reach out into the future.

Of course, the ensuing discussion, even when such questions as sliding-scale pensions and the city-planning bill came up, revolved exclusively around interpretation of the snail as such and—as one would expect in Germany—the snail principle. A speaker from the extraparliamentary opposition—even Snail-ville has its A.P.O.—went along with me rather hesitantly, characterizing the "Long March through the institutions," often invoked by the student-protest movement, as a snail program. When, with Trotsky, I offered him the handy word "permanent," he consented to see the revolution as dialectical confirmation of the snail principle. (I dropped the magic word "Hegel" and permitted myself two long quotations from Engels, only the first of which was my own invention.)

A successful meeting. In autographing paperbacks brought by members of the audience, my Magic Marker dropped decorative snails on the paper (along with my signature) for the benefit of young ladies of voting age. Later we sat in the Vogtei Tavern and praised Snailville's Riesling. Since a good many listeners (and voters) had come from Upper Dawdle and Dally-in-the-Woods—a bus had been chartered in Backlog—the Social Democratic candidate, a high school teacher whom I would have liked to call Hermann Ott, spoke of a meeting that would have lasting repercussions, though there was reason to doubt that its success would have time to show up in the election returns. (On toward midnight I even managed to enlist the collaboration of several local citizens, including the head physician at the hospital and the curator of the Museum of Local Art and History; since then Snailville has had its voters' club.)

A town, children, of medieval stamp, which industry dares approach only hesitantly. In the afternoon I visited a factory where stop watches are assembled and chatted with the shop committee in a room whose walls were decorated with framed photographs of famous sprinters—including such celebrities as Harry and Fütterer. Their dedications praised the Snailville stop watches and termed their reputation "international."

(When the time came, we registered a 4.8 per cent increase in the Social Democratic vote. We did not leap but slithered from 20.3 per cent to 25.1 per cent: Snailville is getting ahead.)

While our race was going on,
the public aged and died.
No witness at the finish, no applause, only our own sounds.
Be patient, I'm clinging forward, I'm coming.
Many overtake me and later fall by the wayside:
Object lessons in unsteadiness.
I lie behind myself.
My track dries away.
On the way I've forgotten my goal.
Now I shall withdraw;
what's left of me is fragile.
I hear that it's windy outside
but promising in the short run.

In Jena, children, he saw the emperor Napoleon on horseback and in the unity of horse and rider found something that he called *Weltgeist;* it has been galloping ever since, whereas I put my money on snail consciousness.

In Dinslaken, Adolf Mirkes, president of the leather workers union, one of the big wheels of the German Trade Union League, spoke. Then I made my May Day speech: "Against the big wheels . . ."

For a century on gliding foot, in principle lagging behind the charger, in practice ahead; nevertheless, the stallion was still the favorite.

First, an accordion band played. I like that. But it's not enough. Too much long-drawn-out harmony. For on jobs where piecework prevails, where output is everything and overtime is profit (for whom?), anger accumulates: it finds no speech; no one gives it the floor; no trade-union paper converts its sediment into printer's ink. A helpless marking of time, which is graded in well-insulated seminars: deficient inadequate false consciousness—measured by the runaway nag, the *Weltgeist.*

When a Swabian handed the idea on to the Prussians, Professor Hubris entered the civil service.

Everywhere they want to change other people's consciousness before their own: sons of too-good family who go into ecstasies about the proletariat, as if the Mother of God had appeared to them in person; soured pedagogues who stretch their idealistic soup with a shot of Marxism; daughters of the upper classes on the lookout for an exclusive left-wing tennis club; more recently, professional soldiers of the Cross, who dispense the blood of Christ in Hegelian bottles.

When the *Weltgeist* entered into the union bureaucrats, they started talking in a high-riding style that soared over every hurdle. For where is the lathe or milling-machine operator who can understand one word when questions of work and pay are Hegelianized?

In Dinslaken I spoke about boring trade-union papers that

43

bury issues—worker participation in decision making, for instance—under mountains of verbiage, about the arrogance of unreadable scribbling.

My unchanging theme, since this abuse is long-lived and perpetuated by back-slapping cliques. Wherever I go, the members of the shop committee nod: "Just what I've been saying all along."

They pound the table: "Exactly. We need a paper that's readable, a paper with something in it." I'll have to repeat myself, hammer away, make up a jingle. ("What will become of progress, my dear colleagues, if the unions try to undercut the pace of a snail!" Doubt smiles, as if he were trying to split a thread.)

It seems that he collected snails as a child, alongside the fields or in the vegetable patches of his native Müggenhahl, and later on, when his family had moved to the Lower City, on the walls of the former Rabbit Bastion, Bear Bastion, and Promenade Bastion, and in the meadows near Kneipab, to have kept them in terrariums, and observed them with a mania for detail.

After the First World War, when the demand for hay fell off, only vegetables were grown in the low-lying fields around Müggenhahl, which were traversed by drainage ditches. The whole Hundertmark region was transformed into a produce garden, especially productive in hotbed lettuce. With vegetable raising came garden pests: taut-skinned garden slugs, slate-gray with blackish lengthwise bands, and the mostly grayish-brown field slugs with netlike markings. It may well have been the periodic campaigns of annihilation waged on the garden and field slugs by the Müggenhahl schoolchildren, who counted them gleefully as they gathered them in pickle jars, poured boiling water on them, and were paid for their yield—ten pfennigs for a two-quart jar of slugs—that moved young Hermann Ott to side henceforward with all snails and slugs (and later on with all those facing destruction like common field slugs); in any case he never killed the snails he collected except for purposes of observation.

In high school Hermann Ott was permitted to bring his collection to class. Regarded as an expert, he gave lectures. Every weekend he bicycled to the Werder, where amid gnome-headed willows he searched the banks of the drainage ditches for dark shiny snails and smooth agate snails. Near the Nassenhuben steam pumping station, a crumbling ruin since electric pumping stations had been built for the drainage system, he found his first slender sinistral narrow-whorl snail: a rare find.

In his days as a student in Berlin his collector's zeal waned; possibly his ponderous, circuitously philosophical sentence structure took the place of snail collecting. The little word "why" became for Hermann Ott a specimen box in which he collected everything that set itself up to be a datum or valid hypothesis or, once proved, had gone into retirement, preparatory to mounting each item on a pin and subjecting it to the acid test of doubt. (It appears that even before his university days snail collector Ott had learned from Schopenhauer to put observation first and knowlege second and to avoid the Hegelian method of proving preconceived knowledge by the results of observation. Ott took over considerable remainders of mockery. He laughed systems to pieces and made all absolute pretensions run the gauntlet of his wit. In addition to Hegel's traditional titles—"Protestant Jesuit" and "Mystification Artist"—new names were given him by Ott: Consciousnessmonger and Speculatius. When in the early thirties he described the *Weltgeist* in a similar paper as a four-footed spook that must have sprung from the head of a speculating horse trader, those intimate enemies, the left Hegelians and the right Hegelians, attacked him in unison; for right and left alike, they were determined to see the *Weltgeist* mounted and galloping—and pretty soon it was indeed galloping full tilt.

"Who's Hegel?"

"Somebody who sentenced mankind to history."

"Did he know a lot? Did he know everything?"

"Thanks to his subtlety, every abuse of state power has to this day been explained as historically necessary."

"Was he right?"

"A lot of self-righteous people think so."

"What about Doubt?"

"Everybody laughed at him."

When Hermann Ott was teaching biology at the Rosenbaum School and had resumed his observation of snails, he seems to have written an article on totalitarianism under Hitler and Stalin. Because it was not published in the *Danziger Volkszeitung,* only the title has come down to us: "On the Consciousness of Snails—Or How Hegel Will Be Overtaken."

6 When a bill to speed up the snails was introduced—by humans—the fishes voted against it, the birds (with the exception of the chickens) abstained, the clinging limpets were absent, the required two-thirds majority was not attained, the snails continued to be pacemakers, and the other items in the reform package, including a bill providing for the progressive taxation of inertia, were referred back to committee.

After that, the usual protestations were heard: we can't move any faster; we're slow only by comparison; actually, we hurry; we're always on the move. Everybody knows what unsteadiness leads to. Our ponderation should be rewarded.

After brief discussion (and hearing the testimony of mutually contradictory experts), the House decided unanimously (for reasons of political stability) to keep up the subsidy for the busing of snails on special occasions.

When history demands. When the cloak of history swishes past. When history rolls over us. When history confronts us with great tasks. When history, which (as Hegel says) is concerned only with state-constituting peoples, measures us by the sacrifices that we . . .

From the terrace through the glass door, you saw us sitting there for hours on hard chairs that deny the head an elegiac

posture. Prussian chairs. We call it a work session. (Because
so many things have a weary taste, we also call it, in quotes, a
salt mine.)

You'll read about it later on. Then be indulgent with us,
children, for having to be so hard on ourselves and others, for
being so desperately sure of ourselves, for our lack of enthusiasm, for presenting such a sorry picture. We had so little; only
the meager pleasure of knowing better and the handy smooth-
ness of much-used objects. You saw us sitting there. . . .

Whenever Sontheimer, Baring, Gaus, Jäckel senior, and I
run into Ehmke and Eppler (who are both members of the
Cabinet), quadragenarians start tearing each other apart; each
of us recognizes his own decrepit pragmatism in the others and
wants to demolish it. We like each other only in part. Doubt,
whose name was Hermann Ott and who put observation first
and knowledge second, might have been our chairman. No
article of faith that Gaus didn't drown in whisky. No thesis
from which Sontheimer couldn't wring a reservation. Nothing
that Ehmke didn't know better. And even Eppler, whose hair-
line gives promise of high-rising idealism, gets nasty as soon
as someone wants to cure the Third World with the principle
of hope.

I won't give you a lot of portraits. Still others sat at the long
table, trying to be useful. No heroes; only a meeting of
quadragenarians.
They examine each other with the passionate interest of
coroners, soon bored with so much reasonableness. Then (by
way of distraction) they auscultate the notorious younger
generation, also the older gentlemen above and around them
when they boil over and in apoplectoid fits of enthusiasm join

the youngsters in invoking ultimate goals. ("Disgusting, that new-fashioned Schiller collar!" "All those blue-eyed boys—revolting!") Always cool-headed and concerned with the medium term. Hitler's onetime cubs have left their joyous dawns behind them. Let's not be tragic heroic self-pitying. Their emotions die young, of definition. Sentimental? At the movies, if ever. Never admit a weakness. They're sitting pretty, they've been relieved even of the problems of aging—so it seems—by the new wave of thirty-year-olds. "That's all behind us. We've always been old."

This much is true: early-acquired senility prevented us from starting innocently at scratch. Even in our dreams we sighted no new land.

Since we distrust ourselves above all—even Ehmke does that whenever he allows himself a breathing spell—we see no reason for distrusting others less. Tricky players who never weary of catching each other cheating. Incurably industrious. We seem to be trying to compensate by overproduction for the reduced achievement of a few decimated war years. Each one of us has at some time missed something that throws up bubbles because it cannot be made good. Consequently fidgety. Knee flexors skirt chasers wolves, but always under control. Jäckel senior, who as a historian seems eminently grown up, squelches anyone indulging in infantile outbursts with seamless silence. Never, never again shall we be permitted—we never were—to be infantile.

Those, children, are my friends, if quadragenarians can be blind enough to see each other as friends. Hermann Ott, surnamed Doubt, was thirty years of age in the summer of 1935, when he made friends over a garden fence in Müggenhahl with Isaak Laban, vegetable dealer and German Nationalist, who must have been in his bald mid-forties. Instant strife:

both knew better. Friendship fed on contradictions. Maybe I could find a garden fence to chat across with Drautzburg, or Erdmann Linde, or Marchand. . . .

Where I spend the night. Where I find a piece of candy on the pillow. The modern, air-conditioned Hotel Steinsgarten in Giessen. Menu with historical abstract. To one side of the entrance a brass plate: "Academy for Organization." Pretty soon I laughed on the wrong side of my face.

Curdled assent.
No lowered thumbs: a grin's enough.
Everything, the burgeoning smile,
astonishment, consternation, fright,
the hard lines of grief
everything curdles—even shame.
A pennyworth of *Schadenfreude*
accomplishes all this.
Or the fear of being recognized.
Or the embarrassment of a naked face: a grin as clothing.

When yesterday (in the discussion period) the old man tried in jumbled words to talk about his bygone days—unemployment, relief, inflation, Reichsbanner against SA and Red Front—group laughter crumbled, then firmed into a grimace. (More than a grin.)

When after a cry of "That'll do, Grandpa!" the old man flew into a rage—yes, Raoul, he yelled, he was beside himself—quite a few were embarrassed and left, but it took them a long time, even in their sleep, to smooth out their grins.

Façades, it is said, can do it.
Victors—but also the vanquished—congeal.

50

That replaces commentaries on TV.
Embarrassment has found its mimicry.
When we hear of death (its multidigital figures),
when defeats (those old friends) greet us,
when we are alone
trapped by a bit of mirror,
we abandon our faces: to grin is human.

Giessen and Wiesbaden, where the A.P.O. shouted for Heintje,* are behind me. Two days of twaddle. But as a reward I can travel by train and scribble in my waste book: *dafür* ("We are for it"), our campaign paper, has come from the printer's. Too late for general May Day distribution. Only Drautzburg supplied with 4,000 copies for Oberhausen Frankfurt Koblentz. Yesterday at Böll's. Frau Böll brought in a bottle of schnapps, because there was nothing else in the house: sons drink it all up. Cab driver says he'll vote for us this time, offers his services ("When you make it") as a Minister's chauffeur. Kashubian merriment with countryman Ehmke. Looks gluttonously at photographs, thinks he looks terrific in all of them. ("Man alive!") My conversation with the shop committee in Giessen keeps running after me as I pace the floor at the airport, whistling away my fatigue: men who like to huddle together. Every word meets resistance. They seem bowed down by their own weight. Distrust as consensus. Intermittently comradely crude: "Hey, Heinz, is that all the noise you can make?" Their handshake: firm but not demonstrative. They regard me as a "world-famous writer," pretty well informed, even about sick and retirement pay. After a while, they address me as fellow worker. (Here again, when spoken to in private, some of the top white-collar workers

---

* A popular child singer on radio and television.

admit that, "to tell the truth," they ought to be unionized.) At lunch in the canteen the gentlemen from the laboratories sit separately, because their white coats might catch dust from the molding-shop workers. (Shop committee and management agree: no class problem!) Pickled herring and potatoes for all.

Meanwhile, relapses. Meanwhile, Doubt, who recently (and tentatively) has been wearing the round-windowed spectacles of those condescendingly bright students who brandish the word "irrelevant" as though wishing with Heidegger to say "forgetful of being." Now he's in charge of the third form. One of his students (Blaustein) dies of appendicitis. At the end of the term the third form of the Jewish Private High school puts on a play: the Ring of the Nibelung. Fräulein Mettner directs the rehearsals. Betty Anker plays Kriemhild, Simon Kurzmann Siegfried. Hermann Ott lays out a small maze in the schoolyard. (No, children, Doubt doesn't wear round-windowed spectacles after all.) A photograph in the third-form diary shows a robust woman with a watering can and a low chignon: Ruth Rosenbaum. Herr Ott argues philosophical questions with Herr Litten, who teaches Hebrew. The janitor's name is Rosinke.

Meanwhile, sent back page proof of *Local Anaesthetic*. Drafted a new speech. Titled, because Raoul sometimes calls me that, "Reflections of an Oldtimer," it will burden our morose mamma's darlings with the troubles (such as rent payments) of those living on retirement pensions: how drained and embittered they are, how irksome to a society dominated by the myths of youth and productivity. (If in doubt, children, vote for the old folks and against the privilege of the young.)

....

A Sunday morning. Lilacs in the front yard. Anna, Franz, Raoul, and myself at the Nationalgalerie: a fresh look at Corinth, then Beckmann. Later, beer and pop at a garden café in Kreuzberg. To catch my breath. And not look too closely, just to blink. To be driven by Anna. The small change of pleasure. (Apart from his friend Isaak Laban, whom could Doubt pick quarrels with? The janitor? Herr Radischewski, the coach of the Bar Kochba Gymnastics Association, who has recently been teaching gymnastics at the Rosenbaum School?) Franz and Raoul daub "I love peace" on everything in sight and while daubing fight to the verge of fratricide. Tomorrow, Bonn . . .

We've opened our office there. Our letterhead: "Social Democratic Voters' Drive." Beside it, a rooster's head that I drew in 1965, still crowing Es-pay-day;* the snail as emblem would have shattered against the cult of progress. Snails admire roosters.

At work in three rooms: the students Erdmann Linde, Wolf Marchand, Holger Schröder, and, temporarily, until the Volkswagen bus gets here, Friedhelm Drautzburg, who is to drive himself and me through sixty election districts. The bus was bought secondhand, but holds up.

Our secretary, Gisela Kramer, works out our schedule with Eva Genée, my secretary in Berlin, and is setting up a card file. Gisela Kramer isn't a student, so the language and problems of young men who as students belong to a privileged class (from which circumstance they suffer aggressively) are still strange to her. "At the bank where I worked before," she says, "people were polite."

Our office is on Adenauerallee, which was formerly called Koblenzerstrasse. The tobacco shop around the corner has

---

* The initials S.P.D. as pronounced in German.

recently been carrying "Black Twist." The Rhine (not visible) is said to flow parallel to our street. The flower shop downstairs helps to propitiate Gisela Kramer when the air upstairs is offensively word-polluted. Bonn (as concept and as city) remains unfathomable.

Where to begin? The university arrogates in a sphere of its own. Behind leaded-glass panes pensioners spew venom. Parliamentarians arrive with a change of shirts. Everywhere branch offices and phantom addresses. And through this conglomeration the railway draws its line: gates usually closed. Across the street the Moritz Arndt House. No government quarter, instead malignantly scattered government eighteenths. Only the climate unifies Bonn. We are not at home here.

Wolf Marchand, who is supposed to be writing a thesis about Josef Roth,* has shelved it. He's the editor of *dafür,* our campaign paper. He duns contributors for still-outstanding articles for number two and looks for a nonexistent distribution network for number one: the S.P.D. communicates only internally; toward the outside world it is sullen and speechless. Marchand's speech is stilted. Germanic philology has made him ironic. He would like to be unsure of himself but lacks the means of expression. Even in doubt he's a stylist.

Erdmann Linde is supposed to be in charge of the office. Since he has an artistic nature and tends to improvise like Paganini, our office runs satisfactorily as long as we have to improvise. He, too, is sensitive, but in a different way from Marchand, who suffers from not having finished, whereas Linde accuses himself of not having begun. (Yet he's president of the Young Socialist League in western Westphalia and saturated with card-file-deep information about the member-

---

* Austrian novelist and essayist, 1894–1939.

ship.) He organizes my tour, choosing election districts where the S.P.D. vote languishes between 20 per cent and 30 per cent. He also thinks I should visit districts where a direct mandate might be obtainable (by the skin of our teeth): Verden Erlangen Krefeld Mainz Augsburg. . . .

Actually, I'd like to be nice, to polish up virtues and display them in a pleasing light—Marchand's polite letters, Erdmann's relaxed way with children—but Doubt advises me to be hard on friendship and look without tenderness into the question: Why do so many students have stomach ulcers? He himself, he tells me, was not spared at the Rosenbaum School, and his friend Isaak Laban called him "a question mark in knickers." (In an excerpt from his waste book he writes to me: the thick skins of the sensitive and the thin skins of the insensitive call for the same kind of cold cream: cosmetic friendships that without mirror or reflection have no substance.)

Erdmann Linde likes to shroud himself in melancholy. I like this dejected air of his. He can discuss organizational questions with such beautiful gloom. When so-called practical problems lead him to look me full in the face, I see the Jesus-like twenty-nine-year-old Dürer of the self-portrait he painted in 1500, when the Christian world was expecting its doom: the same vulnerable ego. On Sundays Erdmann Linde visits race tracks in the Ruhr. Galloping, not trotting, I think. He knows quite a lot of horses' names—April-Shower Teja Green-for-Hope Satellite—and bets his money cautiously and sometimes profitably.

Friedhelm Drautzburg studied law and passed his first state examination; that's enough for him. (Believe me, children, under Maria Theresa he'd have been a pandour; you'd see him on TV dashing across the fields as the Empress's courier.) He,

55

too, has his ambition; he gets engaged at brief intervals in order to win over as many girls as possible to the revolution, to give them a "left swing," as he puts it. Since, like me, he has a mustache, he was able later on, when we were traveling together, to relieve me of a good deal of handshaking. At the moment, he's doing up packages in the office, giving advice, telephoning a good deal, keeping his left-swinging dates on a short-term basis, and waiting for our Volkswagen bus, which a Munich publisher has donated for the sake of the cause: "But please don't mention my name."

In the meantime, until the bus gets here, Holger Schröder travels with me. Since we take a good many trains, I'm thankful, when it comes to making connections, that Schröder combines timetables with devotion. This proverbially stiff law student from Hamburg, whose soul, I can state with certainty, is not that of an artist but that of a detail-crazed bureaucrat, has a hard time of it with Linde, Marchand, Drautzburg, and himself.

Doubt advises me to stop here. He, for his part, he assures me, will refrain from exposing the tensions between teachers at the Rosenbaum School. It was hard enough, he tells me, for the youthful Ruth Rosenbaum to run the school. You can imagine: her father's towering personality, Romana Haberfeld with her long experience, and such eminently respected teachers as Messrs. Ascher and Litten . . . (The third-form diary reports incidentally: "We were happy about the snow. But in threatening one of the boys who was about to throw a snowball, Herr Dr. Ascher slipped and broke his leg. . . .")

At the end of the university term Karlheinz Bentele, a Swabian from Lake Constance joined us. He was the youngest. His enjoyment of food saved him from turning into one more high-tension pylon. Intelligent and rotund, he exuded good humor that no one dared to dampen. Bentele was the only one of us, I think, to put on weight during the campaign. He ate and ate, while the rest of us . . . (Incidentally, the reason for our quarrels and other parlor games is to be sought in the jackhammer on Adenauerallee, which behaves day after day as if it were engaged in building the Bonn–Bad Godesberg underground railway. Vrroom! it goes, vrrroom! Marchand and I exchange knowing nods: like in Döblin, *Berlin Alexanderplatz* . . .)

In the meantime, Doubt's friendship with Isaak Laban, the vegetable dealer, has made progress: their arguments are no longer confined to the garden fence, for Laban, who was wounded in the arm at Verdun during the First World War and earned the Iron Cross, has been wearing mourning since the death of President Hindenburg. Laban is a member of the League of Jewish War Veterans. Even when bundling onions or laying out hotbeds, he talks patriotism. Doubt says: "When everything goes to pot, the Jews will be the last sincere Germans." (Herr Ascher also has the reputation of being an unconditional patriot and German nationalist.) And Drautzburg, children, never doubted that he was far to the left of me.

Let's see if this works: some men in their forties and a few in their late twenties sit down at a table, find each other repulsive, saddle each other with responsibility for the present and future, devise appropriate adjectives for each other, and carry motions: to establish voters' clubs in fifty election districts during the pre-electoral period; to concentrate on young people, career women, educated senior citizens, and on those Catholic workers who are beginning to break away from the C.D.U. and Katzer's social welfare committees. Though lacking an ultimate goal, we do have a campaign goal: to substitute a Socialist-Liberal coalition for the Great Coalition. A majority of eight seats would do; twelve would be better. And not to let ourselves be paralyzed by Bonn and all it stands for; a timid resolution. Everything is clear or looks it. Nau has confirmed the printing schedule. Hermsdorf has nodded in the presence of witnesses. Wischnewski thinks he understands us. Ehmke is acting as if he invented us. Willy sends regards. The S.P.D. is determined—or rather, is determined to be determined. And we have Uncle Herbert's blessing (so far).*

In our office we behave as if only snails were left in the world. Each of us announces barely perceptible steps forward. And Erdmann reports success at the races: "At least I broke even!"

At least, children, I'm losing weight.
It wears you out, but at least it's fun.
At least we've got Heinemann now instead of Lübke.†
At least the city planning bill is expected to.
Snail language: at least.
(Because all, simultaneously but at different rates of speed or slowness, postpone decisions until the results of the latest studies, if not at hand, have at least been announced. . . .)

What you might call engrained. His sense of order: his eraser always lay next to his pencil. Doubt (like Gaus) must have had the kind of intelligence that can't fall asleep because even his yawns demand to be framed in a proposition, a polished sentence, which brings Gaus (and Doubt) wide awake.

---

* Herbert Wehner, Deputy Chairman, Social Democratic Party, and Minister of All-German Affairs, 1966–1969.
† Heinrich Lübke, predecessor of Gustav Heinemann as President of the Federal Republic of Germany.

7 He collected only land snails and confined himself to the Central European varieties. Of course Doubt esteemed marine snails and surprised his pupil Fritz Gerson, who had also started a collection, by his knowledge of exotic species, such as the Kamchatka sea-ear, the Caribbean fighting snail, or the Australian knight's helmet, which attains a length of as much as two feet and is mentioned both by Tasman and by Captain Cook. But he collected only in the swampy meadows of the Werder country, under cushions of moss and layers of fallen leaves in Sakoschin Forest, in the dense weeds and bushes on the banks of the Radaune, in sandy areas, amid the crumbling walls of abandoned sugar mills and between the hotbeds of the Müggenhahl produce gardens.

He recorded every important find in a notebook, which also assembled his why sentences and, in keeping with the Lichtenberg* (not to be confused with Erwin Lichtenstein, who lives in Tel Aviv) tradition, was called a waste book: "chrysalis snail. Oliva forest, eastern slope of Swedes' Trench. Damp warm habitat under beech leaves. 9 A.M., April 12, 1935."

Or anecdotes: "Spent two hours with Fritz at Isaak Laban's, turning over vegetables; afterward drank currant wine. We laughed at the battle order of Laban's tin soldiers (Königgrätz) and vexed him with snail jokes about the performance

---

* Georg Christoph Lichtenberg, 1742–1799, German satirist and aphorist.

of the German athletes at the Berlin Olympics. After a brief
shower, we started back. Near Praust we found a great slug
measuring six inches in the creeping state. We got off our
bicycles. I touched its mantle. Even in retracted state it
measured three and a half inches. Fritz picked it up. Back
home he pontificated on the basis of his reading: Max Stirner's
views on philosophical anarchists, then Zionist maxims. Fritz
pooh-poohed my misgivings, which he called pathological,
pessimistic, and liberal."

Fritz Gerson was . . . But even now, before I make him
into a character and call him Doubt's favorite pupil, I have to
revise him radically: when in Jerusalem in November, 1971, I
spoke with his sister Eva, who shortly before the end graduated
from the Rosenbaum School and was able immediately afterward to leave for Palestine with a youth certificate. The fact is
that Fritz Gerson (known as Fritzchen) was born on October
14, 1920. (When, in the company of Doubt, he found the
great slug on Prauster Chaussee, he was not yet sixteen.) He
left the Rosenbaum School after the fifth form. In 1937, wishing to embark on a business career, he was apprenticed to
Simon Anker, a grain merchant, though Walter Gerson, a
lawyer, had thought of having his musical son become a piano
tuner. The family lived on Hermannshöferweg in Langfuhr. In
Jerusalem I saw photographs: Fritz and Eva in embroidered
Russian peasant smocks. Fritz in a sailor suit. Also a picture of
his girl friend Lotte Kirsch, whom he wanted to marry. Eva
Gerson said: "It's true the other way round. I belonged to the
Zionist Youth Organization, Fritz was unpolitical. He never
considered Palestine. He wanted to go to America. . . ."

If Doubt and I nevertheless make Fritz Gerson into a favorite pupil and snail collector, and incidentally a Zionist agitator,

it's only because Fritz Gerson left so many questions unanswered—and because Doubt as a young teacher insists on a favorite pupil.

There he sits with a flawless part in his hair, smiling characteristically. Doubt's nose was about as long as eleven average-sized dashes. He was incapable of opting for anything, with the possible exception of himself. It's hard for Doubt (and our kind) to be for anything: that, children, is why we made an effort and called our campaign paper *dafür* ("We are for it"), though all of us (including Gaus) had spoken long and convincingly against this very title.

Doubt collected snail shells in labeled glass tubes and larger specimens in mustard glasses that he bought cheap from the Kühne Mustard Company. A bureau (inherited from his parents) housed his snail-shell collection in six shallow drawers. On shelves stood glasses in which slugs were preserved in 160° proof alcohol. But he was more interested in the living snails that he kept in four, later seven terrariums. Lime-impregnated earth, in some of the terrariums mixed with peat, rested on a layer of mixed gravel and crushed stone. For the zebra snail and for heath snails that seek dry ground, Doubt had prepared sandy soil. Over the earth he laid moss, dead leaves, stones, and rotting wood. In each terrarium one or two earthworms kept the soil loose. He introduced plants that snails do not ordinarily eat: moneywort, tansy ivy. He fed the snails dandelion, soaked bread, and butter fungus, also lettuce, which he bought cheap from Isaak Laban. Insect larvae were given only to the subterranean reddish glossy snails: sluglike with vestigial shells, they are more mobile than other varieties, almost fast-moving.

■■■■■■■■■

What concerns us here is the mode of locomotion: we attach a pedometer to the leg of progress.

(His favorite pupil seems to have been unsteady, given to enthusiasm over his own ideas.) In Jerusalem I asked Eva Gerson about her brother's character and tastes. "We hardly knew each other. Nothing in common. It was only when I came to Palestine that we started to miss each other and write letters. But after two letters the mail stopped. . . ."

Doubt concentrated on the snails' propulsion; Fritz Gerson observed their reproductive process. Selecting specimens of the hermaphrodite Roman snail, which lift themselves up by pressing their creeping soles together and thrust calcareous darts (known as love arrows) into each other's soles, he had managed to photograph them in the process of insemination and ovulation.

The series of photos was shown in biology class. (In Jerusalem Eva Gerson showed me the blue biology notebook she had taken with her to Palestine: a record on the time-consuming crossbreeding of various species of fly.) Also in biology class Doubt set the creeping soles of his specimens of the brick-red rufous slug, striped glossy snails, and red-brown hairy snails on a glass plate. Thus all the students were enabled to observe how snails advance with a wavelike motion on a viscid mucus secreted by the forward edge of the foot.

"What kind of a snail are you?"
"What kind do you want to be?"
"The kind with a shell or the naked kind?"
"Go on, tell us."

I am neither a common garden snail nor a keeled slug.
Don't count me among the eight-toothed, rye-kernel-shaped,

narrow-mouthed, and occasionally sinistral Helix family, which belongs to the order of the pulmonate land snails.

I am not one of the finely grooved door snails that cling to damp walls and tree trunks.

I do not live in brackish waters. Nor am I to be found in oceans, on reefs, in surf or shallow water, or on sandy deep-sea bottoms among the limpets or the pelican's feet or the tritons.

I am not the edible Hercules'-club.

Neither a whelk nor a checkered turban shell.

Pleasant as it may be to be called a moon shell, and much as I would like to tell you how the Phoenicians obtained their purple, about the mountain of shells that was found near Taranto, or the process by which the mantles of the princes of the Church are dyed cardinal-red, I am not an exploitable purpura.

No one will find me among the 112,000 species of mollusk, 85,000 of which are classified as snails or slugs (gastropods).

I am the civilian snail, the snail made man. With my forward, inward drive, with my tendency to dwell, hesitate, and cling, with my restlessness and emotional haste, I am snail-like.

Still indeterminate, I am gradually evolving into the snail principle.

Even now I am a fit subject for speculation.

(It would actually seem that when Hegel spoke of the *Weltgeist*, what he actually had in mind was not someone on horseback but a mounted snail.)

Who will film me and show for the length of a feature picture how I move on my creeping sole through the Bergisch Land, to one side of the Ennepe Valley, past the Ruhr, from Unna via Kamen to Bergkamen?

"You're on time," said Dr. Krabs, the district syndic (and party secretary). "The comrades weren't expecting you so soon."

■■■■■■■■■

Like Drautzburg—who is finally going to drive us in the Volkswagen bus to Westphalia and the Ems country, through the Spessart to Franconia and across the Rauhe Alb to Bavarian Swabia—like Friedhelm Drautzburg, who became engaged often, quickly, with alacrity, Doubt, too, tended to let relationships turn into betrothals, several in quick succession and each one total: in matters of love, Hermann Ott was unencumbered by doubt and almost idiotically credulous.

It seems that while still a student in Berlin he was twice engaged: once to a student of applied art, whose attachment to cats must have been too exclusive; and once to a waitress who had struck his fancy at Aschinger's but apparently lost much of her charm off the job. (But it is also possible that Doubt discouraged both girls by talking too much Schopenhauer, just as Drautzburg met with little appreciation as a suitor when he served up academic hash as the main course. Love doesn't like to be questioned about vocabulary.)

While teaching at the Crown Prince Wilhelm High School, Hermann Ott got himself engaged to the daughter of a crane operator at the Schichau shipyard. Since crane operator Kurbjuhn was organizer of the National Socialist German Labor Front shop cell, this engagement went out of existence when Doubt started teaching at the Rosenbaum School.

There he was regarded as a useful though crochety pedagogue. It is not clear whether Doubt tried to propel his relationships with the female teachers engagementward. I should like to think of a friendship between him and Elfriede Mettner or Fräulein Nachmann. I picture him on excursions to Heubude beach with the principal: collecting snails in the sand dunes. But when I sat face to face with Ruth Rosenbaum in Haifa, my picture fell apart and I began to cross out considerable sections of my manuscript.

(Her memory is uncertain. Even her creation, the school on Eichenallee, has become something small and abstract in her mind.) I ask her: "Did the faculty take part in the political conflict of those days?" Ruth Rosenbaum assured me that only educational reform had seemed important. Her father had held a protective hand over the school.

Dr. Bernhard Rosenbaum, deputy chairman of the Jewish community, was a moderate Zionist in the position of having to defend the interests of a community whose Conservative wing regarded itself as progressive compared with its Orthodox wing.

When the boycott of the Danzig Jews became increasingly official and the Senate prohibited ritual slaughtering, certain members of the community suggested as a compromise that the animals should be anesthetized before slaughter, but Rosenbaum rejected this proposal and submitted doctors' affidavits to prove how quickly and painlessly the cutting of the carotids drains the blood from the brain of bovines, sheep, and poultry. He invoked a decision handed down by the German Bureau of Public Health in 1930 and cited Aryan witnesses, but the Senate maintained its decision.

Doubt seems to have had his troubles at that time. He was opposed to ritual, including Jewish ritual. Because (as Ruth Rosenbaum says) there was no room for political argument in the school, Doubt quarreled over the fence with Isaak Laban, who as a German Nationalist and Orthodox Jew was doubly obstinate. (When Gaus is looking for a fight, he, too, can always find a victim among his superenlightened friends, someone he can cheerfully slaughter. Ritualized reason.) In the conceivable correspondence between Bernhard Rosenbaum and Hermann Ott, however, the controversy over the prohibition of ritual slaughtering had only a marginal place. Walking (along the Radaune) and corresponding (because they felt like it), the lawyer and the teacher preferred fundamentals: why that man Moses had led (chased) his people around in a circle, and what had made him think up laws . . .

Still, the fact remains: Doubt had become engaged in April, 1937, to a librarian at the municipal library. As she watched him collecting and sorting, Erna Dobslaff promised her financé to get used (in time) to snails.

8 No sooner—so it seems—had Moses left the dividable sea behind him than he began to scold quite a good deal. At first too loud—for his intimates—then, suddenly, though the occasion would have justified a boulder-splitting blast, gentle for the benefit of the people, then again wielding his tongue like a crowbar, as if to pry the names of the accused from his periods: "It can, it will, it must!" And so he flung himself and all those who had to listen into a bath of hot and cold words. Disorganization, epidemic sloppiness, the pedantic orientational disputes of the vanguard, and the grumbling of the unequally slow straggler groups had made his anger eloquent. He even injected a cough into his syntax. He broke misleading guideposts over his knee. "I am not the way, but I know the way. You don't like me, but you can make use of me. When I'm gone, then you can, oh, yes, then you can. You make me laugh: Ha! No, gentlemen of the self-styled vanguard, when I'm tired, it doesn't mean I'm asleep. Anybody who wants to go back from here will have to be able to divide the sea. . . ."

You laugh, children, when you hear him on TV, hurling words, biting questions into bits, spinning sentences into mazes. Go ahead and laugh—sometimes I laugh, too—but don't laugh *at* him.

First he sifts his speech through the assembled shop committees in an undertone. (That was last March in Bochum, I'm entering this belatedly.) Even when seated, he's running back and forth, a rare phenomenon, behind bars. Many come—because you never can tell—to watch him from a distance. Suddenly, after a soft-spoken invocation of imperatives, he strikes terror by spitting out the word "coldly," chops his sentence like cordwood into logs of equal shortness, mounts a heaven-storming ladder, which he (presumably immune to dizziness) lengthens and again lengthens, climbs down—in mid-sentence—hesitantly, as though in love with the altitude, then, back among his logs of equal shortness, piles up a pyramid of subjunctives, lets it slowly (for the benefit of those taking notes) collapse, laughs—why does he laugh?—and stands there alone with his laughter.

Alone in having been right and having been wrong. A man you'd like to do something nice for, if you knew what. He loves something unflinchingly, we wonder what. He has a good deal behind him that would like to shine through but isn't allowed to. (Unjust to himself and others.) Everyone, even his enemies, is grateful to him, but only after the fact. Sometimes he holds out his death as a threat. He carries the indispensable with him in two briefcases. Sudden departures are his stock in trade. Often he wakes up before he falls asleep and eats his breakfast before anyone else. (Pain? I don't know.) He bites on something that has disguised itself as a pipe. Looking down from the platform, I fear, he sees more dead than anyone can have friends. (No one relieves the chairman, who has been sitting there for hours; he does not go to the toilet.) After discussions he sums up what the others had wanted to say. Occasionally of late, he has succeeded in being cheerful, as though smiling for no reason. They say that to amuse himself he's been looking around for a successor. (Gaus, who is reputed in our circle to be close to him, turns into a self-conscious son whenever he speaks of him.)

Much has been written about him and his past. He has been quite a number of things: Marxist sectarian, anarchist, Communist, Stalinist, a renegade to the point of self-abandonment. And now he is a deliberate Protestant Christian and Social Democrat. He is said to be thin-skinned and vulnerable, and—like all converts—an assiduous believer. I don't know him—that is, not well. I've been against him and for him. Arguments at a distance and close by. (Such persistence in remaining strangers becomes a bond.) He once gave me some tobacco. I watch him as he keeps trying to teach chaos perspectives. (One would like to help.)

Now he has finished speaking. After a moment of shock the shop committeemen take refuge in applause. Again (and as usual) he looks past the assembled shop committees and sees something. (Even those who wouldn't want him as an uncle call him Uncle Herbert.)

"Who else?"
"Who's it going to be now?"
"What about Willy?"
"You saving him for later?"

Along with *Zenobiella umbrosa,* a snail having regular stripes and, seen through a magnifying glass, a fine granular surface, and the lapidary snail, which climbs smooth beach trees in the rain, we have the common amber, or Bernstein snail,* a pulmonate land snail, named after Eduard (Ede) Bernstein, who edited Engels' posthumous papers and later came into conflict with Marx. The Bernstein snail lives in the vicinity of water. At the time of the Anti-Socialist laws Bernstein lived in

---

* Bernstein: amber. This snail (*Succinea putris*) is known in English as the amber snail.

Zurich and edited *The Social Democrat*, which was distributed illegally in Germany. On September 28, 1936, four years after Eduard Bernstein's death, Doubt recorded the finding of several specimens: "Near Krampitz, where the lake flows into the Radaune. Their water-logged bodies cannot be drawn back into the shell. Host of a distoma that lives and pulsates in the tentacles, attracts birds (thrushes) and is thereby transmitted by them." At the turn of the century Eduard Bernstein became known as a revisionist. His book: *Evolutionary Socialism* . . .

"Always about other people."
"We know all that. We know all that."
"Tell us something about yourself. About you. What you're like."
"But tell us the truth. Don't make it up."

At the Erfurt party congress in 1891 the Bernstein snail, a land snail belonging to the order of pulmonates, was named after Eduard Bernstein (the seventh child of a Berlin locomotive engineer), because snails and revisionists . . .

"No! Something about you!"
"What you're like when you're not making yourself up."
"What you're really like."
"Really and truly."

To begin with, mostly evasions, zigzags on paper. I'd better stick to snails and Bernstein, how he infuriated St. Lenin with his book—. . . *a Criticism and Affirmation*—because Bernstein's refutation of the theory of pauperization, the denial of the existence of an ultimate goal, and especially his insistence on an evolutionary, inherently slow, phased and altogether snail-like process. . . . "About yourself! Not that other stuff. What you're like and how you got that way." . . . just what

I'm doing . . . impressed me and (all in all) turned me into a Bernsteinian. It's permissible to call me names. I am a revisionist.

All right: about myself. It won't be much of a picture. Of all flowers my favorite is the light-gray skepsis, which blooms all year round. I am not consistent. (No use trying to reduce me to a common denominator.) My supplies: lentils tobacco paper. I own a beautiful blank recipe pad.

In addition to telling stories and telling stories against stories, I insert pauses between half sentences, describe the gait of various kinds of snails, do not ride a bicycle or play the piano, but hew stone (including granite), mold damp clay, work myself into muddles (aid to developing countries, social policy), and cook pretty well (even if you don't like my lentils). I can draw left- or right-handed with charcoal, pen, chalk, pencil, and brush. That's why I'm capable of tenderness. I can listen, not listen, foresee what has happened, think until it unhappens, and—except when knotted string or scholastic speculations are being unraveled—have patience.

But this much is certain: I used to be able to laugh a lot better. I pass some things over in silence: my gaps. Sometimes I'm sick of being alone and would like to crawl into something soft, warm, and damp, which it would be inadequate to characterize as feminine. How I wear myself out looking for shelter.

Where does the peeling of a personality begin? Where is the tap that holds back confessions? I confess that I'm sensitive to pain. (If only for that reason, I try to avert political situations that might expose me to intolerable pain: slugs shrink when touched.)

You often see me absent in mind, dispersed. I'm always dispersed, though I go on for pages collecting myself, sorting myself out, and totting up my balance, arrears and all.

Where am I now? Wherever my tobacco crumbles, has crumbled, or is planning to crumble.

In among the kitchen herbs, for instance. Believe me, children, if one of those quarrelsome ideologies that are always pulling out the carpet from under each other's feet, could manage, with their little articles of faith and ultimate goals, to raise so much as a sprig of fuzzy-soft salvia, it might (possibly) lure me to the table. But my palate has been tickled by neither rosemary nor basil, thyme nor even parsley. What they've served me is tasteless. My spoon goes on strike. Marx boiled to a mash or—as more commonly—watered down, yields at best a foreboding of slobgullion, that dog vomit which promises equality and slobgullion freedom to all.

Or look for me over white paper, as with charcoal I cast fleeting shadows, with pencil drive birds out of bare hedges, allow my saturated brush to hop about in the snow, or my pen to spin out its nervous gewgaws. I draw what's left over. Recently, I've been drawing snail shells and snails in two-way traffic. The progress of my snails can be seen in tracks that dry away quickly. A rich, that is, broken line, one that splits, stutters in places, here passes over in silence, there thickly proclaims. Many lines. Also bordered spots. But sometimes niggardly in disbursing outlines.

It's true: I'm not a believer; but when I draw, I become devout. The portrayal of the Immaculate Conception demands a hard pencil that makes silver-gray credible. Gray proves that black is nowhere. The Mass is gray. Mysticism: when spiders dive into glasses and die after excreting their gray. But I draw less and less. It doesn't get quiet enough any more. I look out to see what the clamor is; actually it's me that's clamoring and somewhere else.

■■■■■■■■■

For instance, on campaign trips in our Volkswagen bus. Mostly through regions where the Social Democrats live in a nervous, uneasy diaspora: yesterday Lohr and Marktheidenfeld, today Amberg in the Upper Palatinate, tomorrow Burghausen on the Austrian border, the day after tomorrow Nördlingen and Neuburg (evening meeting at the Kolpinghaus).

I am a Social Democrat because to my mind socialism is worthless without democracy and because an unsocial democracy is no democracy at all. A bone-dry, inflexible sentence. Nothing to cheer about. Nothing to dilate your pupils. Accordingly, I expect only partial achievements. I have nothing better to offer, though I know of better things and wish I had them.

Often on the road in Central Franconia or Münsterland, I think of dropping out: What do they need me for? This creeping, medium-term approach! These reformists! Look what fun Enzensberger* is having: hops off to Cuba without a care in the world while you knock yourself out trying to drum up enthusiasm for the activation of pensions for war victims or to get people to recognize facts that had whiskers fifty years ago. (A rotten business.) I talk and talk; I listen to myself talking about things already talked to death, such as worker participation in decision making. I'm with it, but I'm also far ahead, exploring realities that pant for a different kind of justice. I spin thoughts, chase after the thread, tangle myself up, lie my way out, and settle the dispute over the apple with its legend. Then, children, I make words, soak wallpaper off the walls, break open floors, rip the linings out of coats, knock on mortar, make façades laugh, cut the fingernails of the dead and the living. When, for instance, Doubt in his native Müggen-

---

* Hans Magnus Enzensberger, poet and political essayist.

hahl traced the line of local mayors back to the sixteenth century and unearthed a decree of 1595 imposing penalties on those shirking the *corvée* . . .

"Not about him. Maybe later."
"More about you. What you used to be like."
"Before you were famous."
"Were you always gone and someplace else?"

Yes, but with less baggage. Though sometimes older than I'll soon be, I could run off in the middle of a sentence without looking back. I was fairly skinny and had a habit of squinting at an imaginary point. And even earlier, my father and mother never knew who or where I was, even when I was sitting right there at the table, making faces like Franz. Never again will I be able to read as I did when I was fourteen: so absolutely. (To demonstrate her son's absence to my aunt, my mother, once served me a cake of soap instead of a plum bun. They both had a good laugh.)

When I was fifteen, I wanted, in thoughts, words and works, to murder my father with my Hitler Youth dagger. (From generation to generation the intention remains the same, only the weapon changes.)

When I was sixteen I loved an unfinished girl—to be filled in as desired—from a distance; ever since, I have been able to wish and imagine until she knocks, comes in, and starts a fight.

When I was seventeen—held together only by my sword belt—I learned under my steel helmet to know fear, later (by way of compensation) hunger, and soon thereafter the vast wild-animal corral known as freedom.

From eighteen on, I tried to survey that corral and discovered how intricately subdivided it is and how seldom reason and intellect are neighbors: the greater the intelligence, the more devastatingly its stupidity can run wild. It is seldom the fools, and often the shrewd and knowing, who try to make the world pay for their defeats.

After that, I spent quite a long time living very little but only writing; I was a storehouse for dispersed fragments, also for duly entered losses. To my storehouse came: decimated age classes, fathers' debts of guilt, and sons' I.O.U.'s, demobilized clowns who had collected their comic effects in file cases, long-forgotten fairy tales that now bore witness to harsh truth, batteries of perfume bottles, collections of torn-off buttons and other objects which—a pocket knife for instance—had for years been searching for their loser. I noted them all and tried to return them to their lawful owners.

When I was thirty-two, I became famous. Since then, Fame has been with us as a roomer. He's always standing around, he's a nuisance, hard to get away from. Especially Anna hates him, because he runs after her, making obscene propositions. Inflated and deflated by turns. Visitors who think they've come to see me look around for him. It's only because he's so lazy, and so useless when he besieges my writing desk, that I've taken him with me into politics and put him to work as a receptionist: he's good at that. Everybody takes him seriously, even my opponents and enemies. He's getting fat. He's beginning to quote himself. I often rent him out at a small fee for receptions and garden parties. Amazing the stories he tells me afterward. He likes to have his picture taken, forges my signature to perfection, and reads what I scarcely look at: reviews. (Yesterday, in Burghausen, shortly before the meeting, a not untalented crook tried to sell him his life story—twenty years in Siberia.) My Fame, children, is someone I ask indulgence for. . . .

■■■■■■■■■

"But aren't you rich when you're famous?"
"How rich?"
"Isn't it nice to be rich and famous?"
"What can you buy with it?"

Since I've been famous, neckties, caps, handkerchiefs, and
whole sentences complete with instructions for use have been
stolen from me. (Fame is someone it seems to be fun to piss
on.) The more famous a man gets, the fewer friends he has. It
can't be helped: Fame isolates. When Fame helps you, he
never lets you forget it. When he hurts you, he says something
about the price you have to pay. I certify that Fame is boring
and only rarely amusing. (Recently, when Laura wanted six
autographs to trade for one of Heintje's, we all decided to be
pleased with her deal.)

But I am fairly rich. By scraping everything together I could
buy one of the smaller, as good as deserted churches here in
Berlin, and convert my church into a hotel, which might, in
emulation of the papal bank, call itself the Holy Ghost Hotel. It
would serve all the dishes that I myself cook and eat: leg of
mutton with lentils, veal kidney on celery, green eel, tripe,
mussels, pheasant with weinkraut, suckling pig with lima
beans, fish, leek and mushroom soups, on Ash Wednesday
hashed lung, and on Whit Sunday beef heart stuffed with
prunes.

For this much can be said: I enjoy life. I'd be glad if all
those who so persistently try to teach me how to live enjoyed
life too. The betterment of the world ought not to be the
monopoly of embittered people with stomach trouble.

Aside from that, children, I'm an accident, who has accidentally survived, accidentally manages to write something,
but might also, just as accidentally, have founded an expand-

ing industry—shipyards, for instance. Well, maybe next time. Then you can be my partners and look on at launchings, to see my ships founder. Anna could say: "I baptize you. . . ." I could write (what?) a book about it. . . .

"Is that all? Isn't there some more about you?"
"Ships—I can see that. But all that other stuff . . ."
"Come on, tell us some more."
"Short stuff. What you like. What you don't like."

All right. Short sentences to remember and forget.
I smoke too much but regularly.
I have opinions that can be changed.
I usually think things over beforehand.
In a devious way I'm uncomplicated.
(For the last four years I've been putting words and sentences between parentheses: it has something to do with growing older.)
I like listening from a distance when Laura keeps hitting the same false notes at the piano.
When Raoul rolls me a cigarette, I'm pleased.
When Franz says more than he meant to admit, I'm surprised.
When Bruno tells jokes wrong, I can laugh the way I used to.
I particularly like to watch Anna starting to make over a dress she has just bought.
What I don't like: people armed with the word "trenchant." (Those who don't think but think trenchantly also take trenchant action.)
I don't like bigoted Catholics or orthodox atheists.
I don't like people who want to bend the banana straight for the benefit of mankind.

I am repelled by all those who are able to prestidigitate subjective wrong into objective right.

I fear all those who want to convert me.

My courage is confined to being as little afraid as possible; I do not give demonstrations of courage.

My advice to all is not to make love in a hurry like cats. (That goes for you, too, children, later on.)

I like buttermilk with radishes.

I like to bid high at skat.

I like broken old people.

I, too, repeat my mistakes.

I was pretty well badly brought up.

I am not faithful—but attached.

I've always got to be doing something: hatching out words, chopping up herbs, looking into holes, visiting Doubt, reading chronicles, drawing pictures of mushrooms and their relatives, alertly doing nothing, driving to Delmenhorst tomorrow and the day after to Aurich (East Friesland), talktalktalking, nibbling at the dense blackness wherever I see gray spots in it, marching forward with the snails and—because I know war—resolutely keeping the peace, which, children, is another thing that I like.

"Can I ask a question?" says Franz in conclusion.

Bruno refers to grown-ups as "blown-ups."

They're boring, says Laura.

In a not unfriendly kind of way Raoul calls me "old-timer."

9 While Bruno sits huddled by the front garden gate, waiting for the daily crash, Laura paints dream horses, Raoul remodels an immersion heater, Franz is with Jules Verne, I am on the road, Anna is writing letters, and Bettina is drying her hair (at the same time reading Hegel), the two Volkswagens approach. In another moment they will collide at the corner of Handjerystrasse and Niedstrasse, wrench Franz out of his book, divert Raoul from his scrap iron, remove Anna from her letter and Laura from her horses, lure Bettina to the window and Bruno to the scene of the crime, while I remain on the road. I have always had a passion for simultaneous events. This has given Doubt and me a good deal of trouble, because everything that the two of us have thought, heard, tasted, sensed, or missed, has come jostling to the door, demanding first admittance and has been—as you are, children—simultaneously present.

While one event was taking place, another, along with the denial of a previous event was occurring, and the German Democratic Republic was being recognized by Cambodia. All of which is spoken of. Are there any questions?

At press conferences, within whose horseshoe-shaped tables I sat immured in March and April in Gladbeck, Dorsten bei Marl, and Oberhausen, in May in Kamen, Saarbrücken, Esslingen, Lohr, and Nördlingen—others were held in Wiesbaden, Burghausen, and elsewhere (including Snailville). I was questioned about the atomic arms pact, preventive arrest, what I thought about the Russo-Chinese border dispute on the Ussuri, my attitude toward worker participation in decision making, committed literature, the Catholic Church, Heinemann's relation to the Bundeswehr, the foreign minister's relation to his son Peter,* my opinion of the Great Coalition (and naturally about my estimate of the outcome of the elections) and the use of garlic in cooking.

My answers were short or long-winded, quotably sarcastic or embarrassed and evasive. (On demand, I told anecdotes: the things that happen to you on a trip.)

In Burghausen, while I was giving a press conference at the Lindacher Hof, shots were being fired outside (the weather was fair): while pursuing his divorced wife, the worker Norbert Schmitz shot down the tailor Josef Wohlmannstetten, then, himself pursued, fired at the police—who, while he was still pursuing his divorced wife, had approached in a radio patrol car and reached the scene when Wohlmannstetten was already bleeding—and while I was answering timely questions at the Lindacher Hof, was shot several times in the right thigh by the policemen.

What comes over the ticker: a flood of news items. How they are selected and dished out in the right proportions; whose opinion is reflected in the headlines and what commentary draws the teeth of the news items or grinds them to a cutting edge. I answer and put down stepladders for further questions.

---

* Willy Brandt, whose son Peter aroused controversy as an actor in the film based on Günter Grass's novella *Cat and Mouse*.

But in Amberg no one wants to know what will come after de Gaulle. After May 9, however, the economic Hamlet question: To revalue or not to revalue? Schiller and Strauss in the spotlight.* Kiesinger's "Never!" What the experts and other extras say. A play with choruses. The classical warning of the sixty-one professors: "If the mark is not promptly, then the wage situation may well . . ."

Whole strings of questions: What I think of Kiesinger's National Socialist past, Wehner's Communist past, the students in general and the radical students in particular, the Pope and the pill, postwar German literature, and Axel Cäsar Springer,† the order to shoot at those trying to escape over the Wall, and, as a married man, of my wife.

I answer (when possible) and roll cigarettes. Doubt rustles in my inner lining and suggests misgivings. It's risky to vary my Giessen answers in Wiesbaden. When the going gets rough, I make up questions that someone allegedly asked me in Kamen and answer them truthfully. (But Doubt despises me when I resort to trickery. A carping schoolteacher: that's what he is!)

Sometimes the editors of local school papers are present. They ask why I wear a flowered tie with a striped shirt, whether it isn't high time I came out in favor of recognition of the German Democratic Republic, and what's the point of it all (not just life). (The editors of school papers don't like to write: they bring tape recorders.)

Press conferences, says Erdmann Linde, are important.

A press conference gets around, disseminates photos with

---

* Karl Schiller, then Minister of Finance, advocating revaluation of the mark; Franz Josef Strauss, party head of the Christian Social Union.

† Director of the largest and most influential newspaper chain in Germany; also controls publishing houses.

candidates in them, remains suspended like an incomplete sentence, and costs nothing.

At press conferences I meet friendly, browbeaten, heart-breakingly dependent journalists. (Often they write better than the owners of the regional papers permit.) Some of them give tips.

Because I collect fug, the local political situation, different in each town but everywhere equally entangled, is given me carefully wrapped to take home: presents with a local smell.

Gratefully, from place to place, I praise the specific quality of the beer, the native white wines.

"Any more questions?" Lambinus, chairman of our local organization, who is sitting next to me, asks the assembled journalists from Lohr and Marktheidenfeld, and folds the dated bill.

After I answer a last question: "Have you been in Mark-theidenfeld before?" with an unequivocal "No," the conference is considered closed; after that, Franconian wine is drunk, and local scandals and entanglements discussed on a purely social level. (How beautiful Germany is. So transparently impenetrable. So eerily innocent. So different and the same wherever you go. So self-forgetful.)

Before we break up, someone begs leave to ask (off the record) a personal question: "What are you writing about just now?"

"About things that are simultaneously current—and between times about an ancient head of lettuce . . ."

On Saturday when we go to our weekly market in Friede-nau, we buy dill and cucumbers, halibut and Havel eel, pears and chanterelle mushrooms, haunches of hare and Vierland force-fed ducks, wherever we please. No one points a finger at us and asks: "Why from her? Don't you know that she? Better not buy from him or her. Not if you know what's good for you."

We buy wherever eel and dill, hare and cranberries whet our appetite. Aside from that, Anna and I are especially fond of some of the market women: our herring girl, for instance, who is always cheerful, always laughing, even in the bitter east wind. It hasn't always been this way in Berlin and elsewhere: where I come from, toward the end of October, 1937—I was ten years old and didn't understand—the Jewish vendors were driven out of the Danzig market. Only on Häkergasse, in a place apart, were they allowed to lay out their zippers and thread, their charcoal and dried fruit, their potatoes and vegetables. The idea was for everyone to see which Aryan housewives continued to buy from Jews. The *Danziger Vorposten* wrote: ". . . we well understand the indignation of our fellow Germans who followed the purchasers, for the most part women, back to their homes with cries of 'shame!' "

When Hermann Ott, as usual on Saturday, went looking for his friend Isaak Laban, the vegetable dealer from Müggenhahl, whose loyalty to the Kaiser was still undiminished, in the big covered market next door to the Dominikanerkirche, he found in Laban's place a young peasant woman selling fresh Werder butter, pot cheese, and eggs. A wooden slate informed the public that her name was Erna and that she came from Käsemark. When Ott asked about Laban, her predecessor, she folded her arms: "Who cares about the Yids?"

The neighboring market women showed the gaps in their teeth. Soon Ott was surrounded by their jeers, and, still jeering, women, elderly gentlemen, and young girls followed him to Häkergasse, where he found Laban. In the midst of gleeful yapping Ott remained cool and fish-eyed. He greeted Laban, who had assumed his sergeant's posture acquired in the First World War: "Nothing special to report, sir." With ironical allusions, Ott struck up a conversation with his friend and without haste chose a head of lettuce from among the products of Laban's hotbeds. They had found their tone. Laban inquired about Ott's snails. And Ott reported that the opinion was going round among his yellow slugs and his reddish-lipped strawberry snails that another race, which was also slow and hence related to the snails, would soon have to think about emigrating.

Laban rearranged his lettuce heads, considered the yapping that had developed into a wall, looked into the hate-splotched faces, and said, "Come to think of it, they may be right." Ott paid, and Laban returned pfennigs.

When the schoolteacher started for home with his head of lettuce, a "shame!" as broad as it was shrill accompanied him to the streetcar stop on Holzmarkt. Before he climbed aboard the trailer of the Number 5 that went to the Lower City, a lovable little grandma pulled a hatpin out of her pot-shaped felt and thrust it once, and once again, into the green lettuce. "Shame!" she shouted, and wiped her hatpin on her sleeve. When he got home, Doubt didn't mention the incident to his snails.

Even before the Jewish vendors were removed from the Danzig, Langfuhr, and Zoppot markets, members of the Jewish community had begun to say, "If there's no more justice, we'll have to go shopping at Semmelmann's."

Josef Semmelmann and his wife Dora manufactured and sold luggage, first in Neufahrwasser, then at 61 Breitgasse in the Old City. A prosperous business: Semmelmann's luggage was suitable for overseas travel.

On the Saturday when on Häkergasse Doubt, for a few pfennigs, had bought a head of lettuce, which shortly afterward was twice stabbed, the "people" took to violence in

Danzig's business streets and markets: the notions displays, dried-fruit crates, potato baskets, and vegetable stands of the Jewish vendors were plundered, overturned, and trampled. The windows of several Jewish shops in the Old City were smashed. Despite ample proof of their guilt, the looters of two jewelry shops made no acquaintance with a judge. (A report, signed Luckwald, sent to Berlin by the German Consulate General cited riot damage and mob excesses.)

Which would lead one to believe that the men of SA-Sturm 96, with headquarters on Reitbahn across the street from the Central Synagogue, had left only riot damage behind them. No report, not even that of League of Nations Commissioner Burckhardt, tells us that after Herr Semmelmann's trunks and suitcases had been slashed and his steam press and leather stamp converted into scrap with crowbars and sledgehammers, he himself was beaten with rolling pins: removed to Marien Hospital, he died of a heart attack on November 20, 1937. It soon became apparent that a good many people decided too late to go shopping at Semmelmann's: suitcases were in short supply.

Coming from Franconia, we have to pass through the Westerwald. It's raining, and whistling doesn't help.

Nothing moves. And contrariwise.
The little word "pointless" comes puffing from our pipes.
Nature and its peepholes blocked off by crosshatching.
You'll never get through. Things'll take care of themselves.
(Doubt whispers nasally: footnotes about free will.)
Don't listen. The same boring drivel.
Everything is exhausting, especially jokes, remembering, telling, listening when you've heard them before. I can't laugh

85

and wiggle my ears at the same time any more. Two wind-shield wipers stand in for Melencolia's hourglass.

Drautzburg and I are driving in an air bubble. No protest, no objection, nothing touches us.

(Not until after Limburg does the rain start dripping on yesterday's newspapers: Barzel says thinks would say . . . A name for everything that's absorbent but can't, under pressure, hold water: now he expresses serious misgivings, now he takes off his glasses and pours oil on parentheses; now, glasses on again, everything flows off him.)

Road under repair, heavy two-way traffic. Seen from the air, our Volkswagen bus in the middle of the Westerwald is no exception: air bubble on the road.

Drautzburg claims we have a destination.

"A bit late," he says. "Got to make up time."

I don't drive. I say, "It's raining."

I'm tired—"So take a nap."

For thirty miles I sleep myself back to the Vistula lowlands, across wheat fields and drainage ditches, beside which stand willows making faces; in so doing, I refute the contention that a body can be only in one place at any given moment and at the same time avoid a region that figures in the well-known soldiers' song and is rich in precipitation. (Our radio says something about a North Atlantic low-pressure zone.)

When we get there, the rain is a thing of the past: despite the weather the hall is chock-full! When wet coats moisten the air in closed rooms, it becomes easier to talk of dry matters: progress and such. Nobody gets thirsty. Less doubt . . .

"When will I get my horse? You promised. A promise is a promise. All you talk about is whatsisname and S.P.D. A couple of horses. Aren't there any where you've come from?"

....

In Delmenhorst: Young Communists liquidating each other with words traps. (I am the guardian of a sacral object: the microphone.)

In Wilhelmshaven I've got an authentic cousin: ("The time at Aunt Martha's . . . the gooseberries . . . the time at the shooting match on Bürgerwiesen . . .")

In Emden the Bronshalle holds more than 900 people. A successful meeting, as we read the next day in the *Ostfriesische Rundschau.* Slept soundly and without schedule at Heerens' Hotel. Morning walk (after buying tobacco) around Emden, lyrically brick-red and windswept: so spick and span and freshly aired, it cheers you up and tempts you to stay on. (But Drautzburg doesn't feel like getting himself engaged in this town.) We leave at dawn, planning to be in Hohenlimburg by noon and Iserlohn (Sauerland) in the afternoon. On lush green, subsidized green, horses to the right and left of us, horses at last!

How she glues a jealous ear to the tuned-down radio and listens all by herself (nobody else allowed) to her Heintje, who, like her, wants a horse.

How she starts running round again, waving her arms.

Frightened, she frightens us.

With three brothers, she doesn't want to be a girl.

(The masculine overpressure compresses her voice; I call her Squeaky. Later on, gentle as she is, she will be allowed to be properly and successfully gentle.)

An April face. Simultaneously laughing and glowering: variably cloudy.

On the stairs, all about the house, to every chair and table, to everything that has four legs and can count, she says in a loud voice: "I want a horse. A real horse. Not just brothers all over the place. A live horse. In my room. Just one. I don't mind if he's little. A horse—only this big—that'll lie in bed with me."

We try in vain to substitute for a horse.

She refuses to eat, everything is "Ugh."

Always in pants. Straddling chairs. Envious because Bruno has (and displays) something she hasn't got.

(O nature! O ye hermaphroditically self-sufficient Roman snail . . .)

I've given her a mirror, but she doesn't want to see herself.

After three days of campaigning in East Friesland, I'd have liked to have shown my daughter these sprightly horses and, at the hotel (between loving cups), the photographs of Oldenburg equestrian societies. I don't know much about warmblooded, cold-blooded, and half-blooded horses. Anna wants me to buy Laura a parakeet. For all Erdmann Linde's patient instruction, I can't tell the difference between a gallop and a trot.

Oh, yes, I forgot: In mid-May (after an afternoon meeting in Duisburg) I flew from Düsseldorf to Belgrade to open a book exhibit. Three days later I flew to Hamburg where, in a Liberal environment (with a view of the Süderelbe), I attended the inauguration of a voters' club. The next day I went (by train) to Münster to promote, against the opposition of a no-longer-so-young Young Socialist, the founding of the Münster Social Democratic Voters' Club in a remodeled mill. (Talkingtalking and for hours reducing Doubt, who feels frustrated, to silence.) The day after that, I went to Bremen, to speak to 500 librarians about the condition of our army libraries ("What do the soldiers read?"). Next day flew back to Berlin with my presents and told you, children, what Belgrade is like . . .

■■■■■■■■■

On the road we stop to rest. (Drautzburg also wants to know what it was like down there.) Between destinations we sit down, aliens in an alien meadow. It buzzes as meadows do in early summer. A photographer, who has come along for *Quick* magazine, takes pictures of us sitting alien in the buzzing meadow.

"So what about Yugoslavian Communism?"

Now we're reading the paper: "It is unlikely that in the present legislative period the city-planning bill . . ."

Drautzburg says: "On a day like this I could get myself engaged."

I remind him of the drawbacks of the three-field system.

Despite the emptiness of the meadow, he is projecting a large family. Sweet how they all give each other a hand, how they get along even on Sundays. It's fun to project high-rise housing in an empty meadow.

"I'm sorry," says Drautzburg, "but we'll have to be going."

We take everything with us: the *Quick* photographer and his pictures, my remarks on Yugoslavian Communism, our scarcely read newspapers, simultaneous actualities, Drautzburg's large family, our alienness; and we also take with us the experience that meadows buzz in early summer. (Doubt—I feel sure—would have found a few Roman snails.)

10 At the time when Doubt's head of lettuce was stabbed and luggage maker Semmelmann was beaten to a pulp with rolling pins, 7,479 Jews were still living in Danzig. A little later, twenty-four Jewish physicians were forbidden to practice; many emigrated, including Dr. Citron, a general practitioner, who summer after summer had relieved Doubt's hay fever. (Only Drs. Walter Rosenthal and Kurt Jakubowski were permitted to go on treating non-Aryans.)

It's chronic, nothing can be done about it. Hermann Ott claimed that his hay fever depressed him and made him euphoric at the same time. As soon as summer came on, Doubt began to define himself as suffering.

Beginning in August of the following year, attacks on the Mattenbuden synagogue and the shattering of windowpanes at the Borussia Lodge at Olivaer Tor became a daily occurrence. After Herschel Grünspan, an East European Jew, had murdered the German diplomat vom Rath in Paris, synagogues were set on fire throughout the Reich, Jewish shops plundered, many Jews murdered or driven to suicide, and several thousand Jews sent to concentration camps. (In his waste book Hermann Ott confined himself to Lichtenbergian shorthand on the subject: "The Reich Kristallnacht is a spacious metaphor."

In the diary of his (in the meantime) second form, someone wrote: "After reading Selma Lagerlöf's *Memories of My Childhood*, we wrote the author a letter and sent her a Danzig picture album. Herr Ott and Fräulein Mettner helped us to arrange a Lagerlöf celebration."

The so-called Kristallnacht of November 9, 1938, had its parallel in Danzig: the synagogues in Langfuhr and Zoppot were set on fire. Only the Central Synagogue on Reitbahn remained unscathed—this because several members of the Jewish War Veterans' Association, including World War veteran Isaak Laban, stood guard and with lawyer Bernhard Rosenbaum's help obtained police protection when SA men tried to break down the main gate. (The next day Rosenbaum and his wife, in need of a rest, left for the south of France. In Nice he fell ill, and since it now seemed unlikely that he would ever return to Danzig, he wrote to the Jewish community resigning his position as deputy chairman. But his daughter stayed, and Hermann Ott also went on teaching, though fewer and fewer pupils attended the Rosenbaum School. By the end of November there were barely 4,000 Jews left in the Free City of Danzig.

He apparently regarded them as sisters. How Melancholy and Utopia call each other cause. How the one shuns and disavows the other. How they accuse each other of evasion. How the snail mediates between them: punctilious, indifferent, and cynical as go-betweens can be.

On December 17, 1938 (during Advent), when Doubt began to suspect that hermaphrodite snails contained substances with therapeutic qualities applicable to the treatment of melancholia (and probably of utopia as well), the Jewish community decided to leave the Danzig Free State and to emigrate. (Herr Segall, the Zionist, did not speak; he appealed.) All those members of the community who had assembled in the Central Synagogue signified their approval by rising. Some of the old people were said to have fainted.

As though progress had stasis as an echo. As though melancholy were the inner lining of utopia. As though the sprinter were impeded by an unsalable millstone. As though the world, and not just Doubt, suffered from chronic hay fever.

Since the Danzig Jews had to pay for their journey in hard currency, real estate was assessed: the Jewish cemeteries in Langfuhr and Stolzenberg, the damaged synagogues on Mirchauer Weg, in Mattenbuden and Zoppot, the unscathed synagogue on Reitbahn, the Borussia Lodge at Olivaer Tor, and the empty lot at 7a Husarengasse were assessed at roughly 500,000 Danzig guilders; but after negotiations with National Socialist district leader Kampe, in which Erwin Lichtenstein, the young syndic, was obliged to participate—"Was my husband pale when he came home!" said Frau Lichtenstein in Tel Aviv—the purchase price was reduced to a mere 330,000 guilders. The contract specified that the synagogues should not be used for profane purposes but torn down. And so they sold their synagogues and with the proceeds defrayed the costs of an uncertain emigration.

Heavenly Jerusalem! What sources can Doubt have consulted? Dürer's slow-as-molasses journey to The Netherlands? "I presented the factor of Portugal with a small carved Christ child; I also presented him with an *Adam and Eve*, a *St. Jerome in His Study*, a *Hercules*, a *Eustachius*, a *Melencolia*, a *Nemesis*. . . ." Or did he learn from the despondency of the princes in the German tragedy and discover the snail in retrospect as a baroque allegory?

On the night of March 2, 1939, Hermann Ott went to the customs depot on the Mottlau to witness the departure of 500 Danzig Jews. The onlookers included: friends and relatives of the 500, high police officials, British Consul General Shepherd, who had helped to make the arrangements and at the same time warned the emigrants not to try to enter Palestine, then a British mandate, illegally. Only the two authorized Jewish physicians, two male nurses, savings-bank director Bittner, who had been appointed Commissioner for Jewish affairs, several police officials, and Heinz Kaminer as representative of the Jewish community, were allowed to accompany the 500 to the port of embarkation. (Since seven of Doubt's students and Isaak Laban, the vegetable dealer, were among the 500, Hermann Ott had asked permission to accompany the departing group; his request was rejected, no reason stated. The emigrants were to be transported in buses across the Free State border to Marienburg, then in a sealed train via Breslau, Vienna, and Budapest to the Black Sea port of Reni. There (so it was said) the *Astir*, an 800-ton freighter, would take them aboard. No official mention was made of a destination.

In his speculation on the hermaphroditic nature of Melancholy and Utopia, Doubt let himself be guided by the example of two Roman snails, which, after an exchange of semen, fertilized themselves spontaneously. Tables and graphs arguing (schematically) the end of the sexes, redemption.

After the 500 had embarked and their escort had returned to Danzig, Heinz Kaminer reported to the heads of the community: by means of wooden partitions the freighter *Astir* had been equipped to carry passengers. The men had been quartered in the bow, the women in the stern.

Fritz Gerson, who had observed how the Roman snail reproduces, contradicted Doubt, calling his transference of hermaphroditism from the realm of nature to the area of mythology sloppy and unscientific.

When the emigrants gathered in groups outside the buses, Hermann Ott said to his pupils: "Drop me a line en route or when you get there." And Simon Kurzmann, whose steadiness at school could be taken as an indication of reliability, promised to send news.

In justification, Doubt cited his hay fever, which also defied scientific treatment. He said, "In antiquity, by the way, Saturn —bilious, bitter, and just—presided over Melancholy and Utopia."

While saying good-bye to his friend, Hermann Ott took refuge in jokes. But when asked whether he had left his World War medals (the Iron Cross, First and Second Class) in Müggenhahl, Laban replied with unruffled dignity: "Why should Laban part with his decorations?" Just before Laban got into the bus, Doubt seems to have stuffed a small package in his jacket pocket: "My snails send their best regards."

Melancholy and her obverse admit of transplantation: when more and more Central European Roman snails were found in the gardens and vineyards of Mount Carmel (above Haifa), this supplementary (and likewise illegal) immigration was attributed to Hermann Ott's gift to his friend. (Later on, Laban opened a vegetable stall in Haifa. He seems to have listed his wares in chalk on a wooden blackboard: "Spring potatoes from Müggenhahl! Onions, carrots, lettuce—like fresh from the Werder!")

Even before the departure of the 500, the Rosenbaum School was closed. A circular explained that the enrollment had dropped from over 200 to a mere thirty-six and that more pupils would be emigrating shortly. (Ruth Rosenbaum went to France a little later, proceeding to Israel only after the war.) At the end of February eight students (the last) had managed to obtain their secondary diplomas (which were certified by the Senate). (When in Jerusalem I asked Eva Gerson for details, she said: "The Nazis on the examining commission, including Schramm and other bigwigs, were rather impressed by our performance.")

The remaining pupils gathered in Hermann Ott's apartment at 6 Rabbit Bastion. They drank tea, argued a little, and joked about the attendant circumstances of a house search that had thrown Doubt's apartment and snail terrariums into chaos. Doubt impersonated the policemen: how carefully, with curved tweezers, they had searched his snail shells for elements of "Zionist conspiracy." Sensational headlines were thought up: "How World Jewry Hides Its Protocols!" Or "The Jewish State in a Snail Shell!" Altogether, Doubt's remaining pupils spoke a jargon fraught with symbolism; the freighter *Astir*, which nothing had been heard of for weeks, was referred to as the "snail ark" and looked for (in the school atlas) on the Mediterranean.

When at the end of March it became necessary to evacuate the Central Synagogue on Reitbahn (as per contract), Doubt and his remaining pupils helped to pack the ritual objects, which were soon sent to New York, where they became the Gieldzinski Collection in the Jewish Museum. (In 1966 the scrolls of the Torah were destroyed when fire broke out in the library.)

What else do you want to know, children? Fritz Gerson stopped observing the mating habits of the Roman snail. His family was waiting for immigration certificates for Palestine. Eva Gerson, who had left immediately after graduation, was supposed to send them from Tel Aviv.

How the sisters live separately. How Melancholy and Utopia write each other letters. How they revile each other as the cause. How they love each other and find no words. How in Jerusalem I read old letters and how photographs tell me nothing.

When his student gave up Roman snails, Doubt interrupted his speculations and made himself useful. He helped with preparations for sending children to England. In May, seventy-four, in July, first six, then sixteen children left the Free State. When, on August 23, 1939 (a week before the outbreak of the war), twenty-six more children set out for England, an article in the organ of the Jewish community concluded with the words: ". . . and when you are out in the world, remain true sons of Jewry, to whose sufferings you owe the privilege of going out into the world."

"Did they have to go to school, too?"
"Did they all learn English quick?"
"And what about their parents?"
"Where did they go?"

Only a few of the more than a hundred children were to see their parents again. A few days ago, an English journalist who is doing a story for the *Observer* accompanied me on a campaign trip to Paderborn, Meschede, Schwelm, and Ennepetal. Back in the Volkswagen bus after visiting the Stockey & Schmitz factory, he intimated in subordinate clauses that he (like myself) had grown up in Danzig and (like myself) had been just twelve when the war broke out. This English journalist was your age, Franz and Raoul, when he left Danzig in one of those four groups of children. He couldn't remember a schoolteacher by the name of Ott (known as Doubt); but he could still see the city—gables, churches, streets, porches, and chimes, gulls on blocks of ice and over brackish water—in chiaroscuro, like broken toys. Are you listening?

11 "Oh, pretty well. Always a trickle of local progress. In Meschede a schoolteacher from the N.P.D. And while playing skat in Ennepetal . . ." I come in with my bag, utter subordinate clauses that cheat Anna's "How was it?" out of an answer, and see you all bewitched in front of the television screen.

Laura is expecting a four-legged marvel and Bruno a very special motorcar, Raoul is on his way out, Franz is making faces.

Four individual children in attitudes that are sometimes transposed. Prayers following the Offertory, preceding the Consecration. You see traffic jams on the Autobahn. Apollo business. Regularly Vietnam. Advertising with its mouth full of happiness. Inaugurations of house and garden shows. Landscape in the background. Episode featuring a dog. The bloated bellies of the Ibo children. Dead fish in the Rhine. Speakers who sum up not yet concluded developments. Someone who is sad and plays the guitar. Laurel and Hardy. Students and police. Serenely spouting bishops who infallibly miss the point. Vocational guidance and so on.

Whenever I try to explain something (which is only a picture), the four of you listen or don't listen or listen to something else, each in his own way.

I try to speak (graphically), as far as possible addressing each one of you and Laura in particular.

You show fourfold patience when I get tangled up in all the details and exceptions that demand to be taken into consideration: ". . . because, you see, the antiaircraft guns are not only of British and Soviet origin, but also of Swiss. . . ."

Suddenly, in the middle of my increasingly lurching sentence it's time for "Bonanza," "Flipper," "Sandman East.". . .

"May we?"

"It's going to start in a minute."

"You can watch, too."

"When it's over, you can tell us some more about Biafra and stuff."

The snail doesn't hesitate before thresholds. (No educational search for ground water right now.) Arrives by fits and starts and looks to see what the lilacs are doing out in front. They're going by. Anna is still asking: "Well, how was it?"

Fragmentary as usual. Above Meschede roosts a Benedictine abbey, built of concrete and weighing seven millions. The Ennepe is a little river. Drautzburg sends regards. Yes, every evening jam-packed. Always the same questions: revaluation of the mark, preventive arrest, abolition of capitalism. They didn't let us into the Honsel Works—aluminum. (No campaigning in the plant.) In Essloh, on the other hand, dropped in on a weird character. Makes tools, crowbars for instance, in a real old-fashioned blacksmith shop. No, my voice is holding up. Otherwise the usual. Skat in Ennepetal, at the Hotel Weide. The comrades are cautious players: small winnings.

Just the usual remarks: "What's been going on around here? Did Raoul? Any mail from Prague?" Anna wants to know more, everything. "What about Cologne? How was it with Barzel?"

I don't really know. I ought to have known that he and how he. Let's see now, what was it like?

If he were an opponent and not an imitation. If he were a distinct individual and not multipliable ad libitum. If he existed as somebody and not as a reaction to something. But he exists only as a paraphrase. Even when I want to say that he's a Christian Democrat, I have to say that he seems to be one. Since he doesn't want to be regarded as conservative and lacks the obstinacy of a reactionary, he is made into something. He doesn't make himself; it or somebody makes him. What the interests demand. What the situation calls for. He always acts accordingly. His behavior has made his name useful: someone barzels, acts barzelish, is an exponent of barzelism. Not an opponent you can count on, children; a means that aspires to power, but will never amount to anything but a means of achieving power. No, it's not uncanny that Rainer Candidus Barzel should abuse his opponents; what's uncanny is that everyone wants him to. He himself would rather not; it, the abuse of opponents (a universal need), makes use of him.

And I didn't make it. Here in Cologne, where he was born in 1840 and his father (a Prussian sergeant) coughed his lungs out, later in Brauweiler, where as a child he heard the cries of the prisoners chained in their cells, then in Wetzlar, where his mother cut bread very thin.

It started with Bebel, when he was still young, wearing the green apron of a journeyman turner. His comrades took up a collection for his train fare, when at the age of twenty-eight he set out to make his first speech in the North German Diet. (On the relations of the South German states to the North German Federation. Violent protests on the right.)

When Bebel was jailed in a fortress—he was often in the clink and so was Wilhelm Liebknecht—his wife, a milliner from Leipzig, ran their small business.

From 1878 to 1890, when the Anti-Socialist laws were in force, the party operated illegally, public meetings were forbidden, and when Bebel traveled through Swabia, Saxony, and the Rhineland selling the products of his trade, he also traveled as the chairman of the spied-on, split but continually reconstituted Social Democratic Party. By day he took orders (banisters and door handles), and in the evening (shadowed by a gendarme, who had to be shaken off) he met with frightened or quarreling comrades.

Socialism, children, began with a quarrel. Then, as today, it was about the classical question: Reform or revolution? Wherever I go—Gladbeck, Stuttgart, Delmenhorst, or Giessen—Bebel is still around, and the quarrel of the snails who want to jump has kept fresh.

But the little turner from Cologne straightened it all out. Maybe that accounts for the phrase so often heard among Social Democrats. "Don't worry! We'll turn the trick."

Bebel "turned" Nuremberg, Eisenach, Gotha, and, beginning with Erfurt (1891), several party congresses, on the agendas of which the revisionism controversy figured prominently.

Grown up in casemates. Protestant apprentice. Itinerant artisan, prison inmate, and agitator. His speeches in the Reichstag (on colonialism). Even if the German history textbooks have passed him over in silence, he has outlasted Bismarck, who has left only statues behind him.

Bebel wrote letters to London, Zurich, and London. Because it wasn't so easy to explain to manufacturer Engels how difficult socialism is in practice. (And how sad it makes you and how funny it looks to say revolution and to practice reform-ism.) But Marx kept carping; he was more intelligent, he was far away, thought more clearly, had the last word and applied his absolute measure. Only Engels understood (in letters) and sent ten English pounds for the forbidden newspaper.

Bebel died in Zurich in 1913.

For some years now Willy Brandt has been wearing Bebel's pocket watch, which still keeps good time.

■■■■■■■■■

Look here, Franz. You read everything that comes along: Jules Verne and Che Guevara, Anne Frank and Donald Duck. May I (not now, after a while) slip you August Bebel? *My Life*. A slow book. A snail biography . . .

What we read in books: how the black crowd have always gone by different names. How they kept at it and popped up again. How their perseverance redoubled. How they lent the Nazis their respectability. How for small advantage they con-doned the great crime. How they can't remember. How they call themselves Christians when they're Pharisees. How they turned the Church into a branch office of industry. How they frightened parents (with fairy tales) and tried to keep children stupid (in schools for midgets). How bothersome (and incom-prehensible) they find democracy. How coldly they made use of their power until they had to share it. Now they're nervous and afraid of losing. (The man with Bebel's pocket watch is at the door.)

   "Do you think you'll swing it?"
   "Do you really think it'll be okay?"
   "Do you really think they'll vote for Willy?"
   "Or do you only hope so?"

102

Because they may lose votes at the center, the black party dreamed up Kiesinger with whom they (because he has learned how it's done) hope to win votes on the right.

12 I've come from the lowlands where they sweep up little mounds and redistribute them: above all, no high ground; it might offer a view.

In Mainz a Young Socialist tore up his party card. He did it slowly.

Over the plain, sometimes concealed by hedges, the snail makes its way and sees no end in sight.

Drautzberg says, "He was simply disgusted. That's why he. Just had to."

I say, "And now he's fed up because, though he tore up his card very slowly, his satisfaction didn't last long, just a momentary tickle."

In the lowlands, slowness is customary. Nevertheless, the snail finds spectators. Among the sedentary it's a sprinter: at last something is happening!

Consequently, he made a big noise in the papers with his torn party card.

Everything is clear, even the increased clouding-over of lenses.

Since I was sitting behind him on the platform when he slowly tore it up in front of the platform, I saw his hitherto timid back straighten up: an angry snail who didn't want to be a snail any longer.

Drautzberg says: "You're too hard on him. He was a left-wing student; he'd had it; he thought it stank, and had to express himself somehow."

I say, "He expressed himself all right. And got himself applauded." One of these days I'll tear something up, too—but what?

The next day, Trier. They've put up scaffolding around the Porta Nigra. (Oh, to be a stonemason again and patch up façades.) The day after, Burgsteinfurt. Tried to be forceful and, relatively speaking, held up my end. But the next day church steeples were the only benchmarks on a flat surface. (You, too, find everything flat and impalpable.)

"Can we model?"
"Make something with clay?"
"Any old thing."

But put newspapers underneath. Not that one. There's something in it, something I have to go on reading as it drags on and gets thinner and thinner.

Gray wet clay.
The clay sweats and smells old.
Clay breathes at me: Do something!
A lump in space, unformed but offering potentiality.

"What should we make?"
"Go on, tell us!"
"Something round?"

For instance, an ark in the form of a snail shell, floating between horizons and finally arriving: at last we shall receive tidings.

．．．．．．．．．

On the evening of June 29—after twelve families had been admitted to Bolivia as settlers and a group of fifty Jewish emigrants from Danzig had been allowed to take up residence as artisans in Shanghai, a place that required no visa—a radio dispatch made the rounds: "The freighter *Astir* has landed 742 passengers on the coast of Palestine."

It was not until the beginning of August that Hermann Ott received a letter from his pupil Simon Kurzmann, who in the meantime had found work as a longshoreman in Haifa: "Am now loading Jaffa oranges . . ."

Kurzmann wrote that not only the 500 from Danzig had been taken on board at the Black Sea port of Reni, but also 250 Rumanian and Hungarian Jews, and in Varna another fifteen from Bulgaria. "Which naturally resulted in plenty of friction, especially when waiting in line for meals and while dishwashing . . ."

The former pupil's report listed items connected with the emigrants' rationed diet. Herr Ott was informed of a burned cooking pot, rancid coconut oil, maggoty cheese, potato soup, ship's biscuit, and the daily sugar ration: two lumps. The lighting system broke down, and Kurzmann's description of an attempt to repair the generator was as long drawn-out as the proceedings themselves. An account of a fire in the stern took up space. A gasoline lamp had exploded. When the water gave out, they had had to pour milk on the flames: ". . . luckily it was sour and had flies in it. But only a few bad burns. On the other hand, plenty of bones were broken in a storm off Rhodes. . . ."

Kurzmann's letter gave only a bare outline of the *Astir*'s wanderings: "From Istanbul we went to Cyprus. We cruised offshore for a few days and had no idea what was going on. Then we had to go back to Greece to take on coal in Zoa. From there we headed straight for Palestine, planning to attempt a landing near Tel Aviv. Off the coast we were spotted by an English reconnaissance plane. We went on with blacked-out lights, but then they sent up flares and stopped us with bursts of machine-gun fire. Police boats came alongside. We had to anchor beside the Haifa breakwater. When I saw the mountain behind Haifa, I thought: That's where I want to go. But only the seriously ill were allowed ashore. One of these was Isaak Laban, who had been having diarrhea since Zoa. When we had taken on food and water, the *Astir* had to put to sea again. We passed Rhodes in a storm and put into the port of Labire. There the crew walked off because they hadn't been paid. The food went from bad to worse. We all had lice. The worst was the rats. A good many of us got diarrhea. We staged a hunger strike, but after a day and a half the captain made us call it off. Finally a motorized sailboat arrived; we were supposed to attempt a landing with it. But on the second day the tow rope that attached it to the *Astir* snapped. The boat's engine spluttered, and we had to put into Herakleion in Crete to have it repaired. That took a few days. The Greeks in Crete were tops; they gave us plenty of cigarettes. Then we put out to sea again. When we were transferred to the sailboat thirty sea miles off the coast, no one could sit or lie down. We stood in two tiers, and there was no chance of anybody falling down. The women and old men were on the upper level. The trip to the coast was supposed to take five hours. Suddenly the engine spluttered and stopped. . . ."

You can imagine, children. Ott's former student's letter included a lengthy account of the heat, the smells, and the increasing difficulty of breathing in the lower tier. Kurzmann wrote of fainting spells, fits of coughing, vomiting, and exhaust fumes. Finally, at daybreak, the captain let first the women and old men, then the others go up on deck. When some of them tried to drink sea water, they had to be sent back below. The coast was in sight. First the captain went ashore in a rowboat. On his return he spoke of Arab villages and a Jewish settlement farther to the south.

Kurzmann wrote: "Later an English officer came on board and authorized us to land. About ten Arab boats shuttled back and forth. In landing the passengers, the Arabs stole plenty. They even hit people for refusing to hand over their knapsacks. I lost everything. Too bad about the box of amber I collected on Heubuden beach. After an hour's march, we came to an English army camp. Up until then we hadn't had anything to drink. Next day we were taken to Sarafand and Haifa. I stayed in Haifa because it's a seaport. Isaak Laban, whom I met recently, has opened a market stall. He sends regards and thanks for your little present. . . ."

Ott passed this report on to the heads of the Jewish community. Excerpts were read to the assembled community in the gymnasium on Schichaugasse, which had been converted into an emergency synagogue. It was further announced that the Danzig Jews who had emigrated to Palestine had formed an organization. The "Irgun Olei Danzig" had resolved not to forget the Jews who had remained behind in Danzig.

The names of respected citizens belonging to the executive committee were read: Benno Eisenstadt, Dr. Leo Goldhaber, Dr. Josef Mestschanski, Isaak Pape, Dr. Josef Segal, Frau Sarah Sternfeld, Dr. Walter Schopf . . .

In March, 1967, a few months before the Six-Day War, I flew to Israel to deliver a lecture: "On Habituation." At the Dan Hotel in Tel Aviv, I was welcomed by a group of elderly ladies and gentlemen, whose still-broad speech identified them as former Danzigers. It was then that I got to know Dr.

Lichtenstein and his wife, whom I'd be glad to have as an aunt. (In Beer Sheba I met two former students of the Private Jewish High School. Their speech retained little trace of broadness or nostalgia. But one of them thought he remembered Hermann Ott. "We called him Dr. Doubt. . . .")

On the way to Burgsteinfurt I stretched out in the Volkswagen bus, made sight slits, and ceased to hear the midday news in brief. Instead, as I approached the house at 6 Schichaugasse, I heard arguments and counterarguments. . . .

Some 2,000 Jews were left in Danzig. Between the Zionists and the executive committee of the Jewish community a quarrel broke out in the summer of 1939—not a bad quarrel, rather the kind that would have been normal in normal times—because the Zionists wanted to hold their annual Herzl Memorial meeting at the Schichaugasse gymnasium, and on this occasion to sing "Ha-Tikvah," the Zionist anthem.

The heads of the community forbade the meeting. Everyone felt put upon by everyone else. Dr. Itzig, the chairman, resigned. From then on, the already feeble community was further enfeebled by political strife, which had been carefully avoided since 1933. Most of those who had remained behind were old and ailing, impoverished, or chronically poor, people attached to their furniture, hopes, and habits, whose only source of assistance by then was the Middle Class Kitchen on Schichaugasse.

Hermann Ott helped to purchase supplies: carrots and cabbage from Müggenhahl. Not only the old people without means of support, but also the homeless eastern Jews were kept alive by this kitchen. They couldn't afford any expensive certificates and foreign visas. Many went back to Poland and were put to death later in the gas chambers of Auschwitz or Treblinka.

Since the Rosenbaum School no longer existed, Ott taught at the Jewish Elementary School, whose principal, Samuel Echt, had left for England with the last group of children; from August until the first days of the war his position was filled by Aron Silber, one of the teachers.

Doubt—the nickname followed Hermann Ott to the Elementary School—tried to keep out of the controversy between Zionists and Orthodox Jews. Nevertheless, disputes arose in his conversations with Fritz Gerson, whom Zionism had rendered contentious. Because Doubt could approve neither the nationalistic arguments of the Zionists nor the passive resignation of the Orthodox Jews, his pupil regarded him as wishy-washy, if not cowardly. While Fritz Gerson was abruptly breaking off his friendship with his former teacher, two German battleships were putting into Danzig harbor. (Doubt seems to have predicted, in a conversation with Leopold Schufftan, the aged cantor of the emergency synagogue, that the tumult of war would soon drown out the internal quarrels of the Jewish community.)

When the guns begin to speak. In Danzig, where the first heavy-caliber word struck home, the lodgings of many Jews were searched on September 1, 1939. The Stutthof concentration camp sprang up (and rapidly grew) between the Vistula estuary and Frisches Haff; Leopold Schufftan, among others, was sent there; he died on October 8.

A week after the outbreak of the war, David Jonas, the new chairman of the Jewish community, wrote to Erwin Lichtenstein, the former syndic, who had succeeded in leaving for Palestine just in time. Jonas reported that the remaining

110

Danzig Jews had been evicted from their lodgings. Some committed suicide when they received an official order to move to the Jewish old people's home on Milchkannengasse.

Up to the middle of September, Hermann Ott is believed to have remained quietly in Müggenhahl, where he still had relatives. His pupil Fritz Gerson, however, left Danzig a few days before the outbreak of the war, without taking leave of Doubt, and joined his parents and his uncle in Polish Bromberg. The next day the family fled southward. On September 11, near Zakopane in the foothills of the Carpathians, further flight was blocked by the German armed forces. Along with six other Jews, the lawyer Walter Gerson, his son Fritz and Walter Gerson's brother-in-law were shot and buried in a forest (near Rabka). (His stride, I believe, was about the same length as Raoul's: when he walked, he ran.)

In Jerusalem Eva Gerson showed me a photo of her eighteen-year-old brother: wavy hair, full lips, bushy eyebrows, slightly slanting eyes. And I read a Red Cross letter written by his mother on May 13, 1942, in Rabka: "Dearest Evchen, glad to have good news of you. Heartiest congratulations on your twentieth birthday. Hoping and praying, love and many kisses, Mama." Martha Gerson survived until summer; then she was shot and buried in the woods along with ninety-five Polish Jews.

Doubt received news of his student's death from Dr. Jakubowski, the last Jewish doctor still practicing in Danzig. Because mail (though often circuitously) still found its way to its addressees (also because Hermann Ott has meanwhile been thinking of flight and begun to take on a reality conforming to the story told me by Ranicki, who represented it as his own story), Doubt tried to write a letter to his student's sister in Palestine. When he read it over, he had doubts about the wording: too much about snails and melancholy. . . .

The day after Anna and I visited Eva Gerson in Jerusalem, I was to read passages from the manuscript of this book at the university (Canada Hall). That was on November 9, 1971, thirty-three years after the Kristallnacht. Some young people belonging to the extreme right-wing Betar Organization tried with noise and prayers to prevent me from reading. They shouted: "The Germans are murderers!" As you know, children, I went ahead with my reading. You are not murderers.

Hermann Ott helped to fit up the warehouse on Mausegasse, which was to become a ghetto for the last Danzig Jews, but at the same time his thoughts of flight took on complexity. To master glazier Friedeberg (a former chairman of the community) he said: "In the event that I should one day prove to have disappeared without saying good-bye, please do not doubt that my departure was a necessity."

". . . and now after twenty-five years. From rubble and ashes we. From scratch. And today we are once more. Without false modesty. As the whole world is forced to. No one expected it. We can hold up our . . ."

Yes, indeed. Story on story, and cost a pretty. Money in the bank all the same. Everything runs, flows, conveys, and lubricates itself automatically. Not only the victor powers, God himself comes to us for credit. We are again, somebody again, we are . . .

And wait for the echo. Hoping it will run backward and be merciful: we are, are again, again are . . .

And pray on bended knee to the growth rate, which is in

heaven. And now admit that what we hear is time, not the creaking of growth, but only time on its creeping sole.

Over everything that high-rises and costs a pretty, over debit credit surplus value, over everything that idles and lubricates itself out of habit, glides the snail, leaving its track behind: a mucus membrane that crackles as it dries, remains transparent, and makes us, just as we are, are somebody again, silent and plainly visible.

Providently, Doubt bought razor blades (Rotbart brand), more than a hundred of them. Now he nods absently and glances at what I have brought home from Mainz, Trier, and Burghausen: footnotes for progressives.

13 It's Sunday. And on Sunday, Franz, when we're bored with each other, your boredom, which you never get tired of dragging around the house, is especially entertaining. You step on your toes, you bash your knees on nonexistent opportunities, your eyes take aim at the void, and you say: "Nothing doing around here. What can I do? Tell me something exciting or funny, or sad, if you must, some old story, something you were mixed up in or even if you weren't, but something real, not just invented, without any statistics in it or S.P.D. and stuff. Tell me something about somebody hiding —for real, because he had to, like Anne Frank: that was exciting and funny and sad. It was real, too, and not the least bit boring. . . . Is it still Sunday?"

One Sunday, Franz, on an ordinary boring Sunday, a day so motionless that even the snail seemed to be in a hurry, Hermann Ott was busy in his apartment at 6 Rabbit Bastion, surrounded by inherited furniture. He was evacuating his terrariums in preparation for his flight. (That same afternoon he deposited his lapidary snails, which require sandy soil, in places he thought they would like; in the Oliva mixed forest, in the Brösen sand dunes, in the meadows behind Kneipab. . . .) None of the snails was allowed to accompany him on his flight.

＊＊＊＊＊＊＊＊＊

"So where did he go? And what did he take with him?"

Decisions didn't come easily to Doubt. What with his love of old engravings (for hours, too many hours, he leafed through his portfolios) he might easily have delayed his flight too long. After a first and second review Doubt narrowed down his selection. In the end he took an English hand-colored engraving of a snail carrying its house—and a reproduction of an engraving the original of which you can see in the print room at the Dahlem Museum. Here it is on a picture postcard.

"What's wrong with her? Apartment hunting?"

No, not given notice and evicted. But you're right. She looks like a living eightball, a bump on a log.

"Look at those hips. And the way she sits there."

This much can be guessed: broad-assed, she's stewing over some loss. She's out of sorts, down in the dumps, a state often attributable to constipation, flatulence, or absence of orgasm. What that is I'll tell you some other time. (Raoul joins us and casts a glance.)

"Sure is a sourpuss."

You might think the poor girl's golden hamster had run away or that she was watching TV: some quiz program or the "Cultural Review." Nothing has run away. No commercial flickers. Boredom, yes, but the basic kind that can't be diverted. Franz's would be gayer in an engraving.

"Well, what about her? Tell us."
"Maybe she's only art or some such junk."

She goes by different names. The word *Weltschmerz* is untranslatable. *Schwermut* (heavy-heartedness; melancholy) is also indigenous, and so is German *Grübelei* (brooding). It's not the usual grief people get because someone has died or gone away. Nor is it anything like your unbelieving father's cheerful pessimism. This way of sitting signifies neither despair nor grief. True, I say: peevish morose disgruntled. True, I interpret: she's sulking, eating her heart out, stewing in her juice; but my findings are too familiar to provide this orphan with a name.

She nests in railway stations: under cold smoke, undecided before ticket windows, dispersed on waiting-room benches, formerly among refugees with their battered cardboard boxes. She clings to obsolete timetables and blighted hopes. She hides in moods. She looks familiar to us and sits for many. She lives in slums, in garden suburbs, in bungalows and villas, also in castles that are hard to heat. We meet her under bridges, amid shattered pillars, on junk heaps, and wherever else poets find their rhymes. I won't exploit the autumn and turn over dead leaves, but this much is certain: fed up with everything, she finds all soups equally tasteless. Everything sounds hollow in her ears, and she tots up a hollow list: absurdity, the eternal cycle, the futility of all effort and the recurrence of the same, forever the same puppets, the monotony of it all and the venality of words, tearing down and building up, the infinite and the finite, determinism and wildly stuttering chance, and, of course, production and consumption, this immutable, already programmed destiny, this snail existence, which, like a roller coaster, gives an illusion of speed but merely turns on its pivot like a compass. . . .

....

"Things really are pretty stinking."
"Think so?"

Saturn is her planet.
She peddles sprouting potatoes and hair in the comb.
On Sundays she commands us to remember the way to school and back.
She collects buttons, defeats, letters, and (like Doubt) empty snail shells.
She keeps a dog that has no appetite.
When visitors come, she warms up gruel.
She colors the mood of mariners (sailor with harmonica) and likes to blow the foghorn.
To the phonograph-record industry she has sold the rhyming phrases: to-part-from-you-my-sweet and never-more-to meet.
She's not afraid of kitsch or jokes.
Her sister's name is Utopia, a gullible little thing; always on the road.
On her, however, everything weighs, even—as you can see—the wreath of fame.
Power is known to her and so is vast, self-canceling knowledge.
At meals she lets her spoon dangle.
Open turnip pits, boiling laundry, semen after ejaculation, also iodine, lavender and vinegar, wet clothes, lilacs in the evening, and mouse droppings carry her smell.
Like foretaste, she dreads the aftertaste of love. After overlong overloud laughter, after too much pork with dumplings, after booze, after man and woman have copulated successfully and the moment of happiness has passed, after a rousing speech, after a seemingly endless leap, immediately after victory, she turns up with her antiques: scales hourglass bell, and—as you see here—nicked sword.

Her bric-a-brac can be varied. (I intend to vary it later on.)

Her name means "black bile." (In former days the doctors prescribed a decoction of hellebore; today they prescribe Tofranil or the couch—in the hope that she'll get it off her chest.)

When his mother died in 1514, Albrecht Dürer engraved the *Melencolia* on a copper plate. Many say: a German work. Everyone recognizes himself.

With Dürer's *Melencolia* and little other baggage, Harmann Ott started on his flight.

"What about you, Franz? If you had to escape, what would you take with you?"

"I dunno. Maybe my microscope."

Both of us, and Raoul, too, thought there would have been room for a microscope in with the bric-a-brac in Dürer's engraving.

"Suppose I had to clear out; what should I pack?"

Raoul suggests the kitchen herbs. Franz regarded my typewriter as appropriate escape luggage: "Without it you'd go broke."

And with precision he shows me where, in the picture—on her lap instead of the compass—my Olivetti might be reduced to silence.

A beautiful Sunday. (Friedenau is also included in her territory.)

Franz asked: "Do you like prunes?" Afterward, I cracked pits: that faint trace of prussic acid. . . .

But then Bruno came in, and life started up again.

He imitates me. He stands on a chair, throws out his arms and cries: "S.P.D. Get your S.P.D.!"

He campaigns the way I ought to campaign in Bavaria: "Or would you rather have Huber? The same old Huber?"

Bruno is a terse speaker. "Too much talk is stupid. That's all!"

He gets applause. Success. We all laugh.

"Do it again, Bruno! More election campaign!"

But he doesn't want to; he's already won. Now he's got another idea; he's sick of talktalktalk. "Maybe yesterday, later." (Except that I'll be on my way to Andernach, Mayen, Bad Neuenahr. To talktalktalk amid pumice and basalt tomorrow, later . . .)

"And Whozit, what's her name again?"
"And what about Doubt, hasn't he left yet?"

Shortly after Hermann Ott left his wait-and-see station in Müggenhahl, he took his fiancée Erna Dobslaff to the movies. No sooner had he left her after escorting her home than he was followed by a gang of Hitler Youth, stopped at the corner of Straussgasse and Weidengasse, forced into a doorway and wordlessly beaten up with sand-filled leather gloves. (His assailants seem to have been students of the Petri High School, among them Squad Leader Fenske.)

His late mother's sister came from Müggenhahl to take care of him. From time to time, the librarian Erna Dobslaff looked in and attempted suasion. On recovering, he applied for reinstatement in the municipal school system. Three weeks later his application was rejected, no explanation given. Doubt made no further applications.

He was still needed. When at the end of November the Agency for Palestine in Berlin authorized the departure of fifty Danzig Jews, Hermann Ott helped with the preparations. To save them from being sent to Stutthof, it was decided to include the last remaining young people in the departing group. After many detours they reached Vienna by train. Marched to Bratislava, they were interned in a camp manned by Slovak Hlinka Guards. Later on, the Danube steamer *Uranus* took the emigrants to the Hungarian border and then back again to Bratislava. Apart from the fifty from Danzig, there were 650 Jews from Vienna and 300 from Germany aboard the *Uranus;* they could scarcely move. Transferred to three small steamers, they reached the Yugoslavian port of Kladovo in mid-December. There they remained for nine months.

Shortly before Christmas Ott was summoned to police headquarters. The brief and businesslike interview dealt with his activity as teacher at the Private Jewish High School and with letters Ott had written to someone in Nice in southern France. The content of all the letters (and of the answers to them) was known to the investigators. When Ott described his letters and those of his correspondent as scholarly in orientation and began to elucidate his work on Melancholy and Utopia with quotations from Aristotle and Ficino, not forgetting to mention the snail in its role as mediator, the two police officials took turns in slapping his face. When given leave to go, he heard: "We'll meet again, buddy."

"Why didn't he leave sooner?"
"When he'd already packed."
"He was nuts to wait so long."

Doubt does not flee so quickly. Only yesterday, when I visited the Meurin Pumice Works in Kruft and worked over an election district that extends to the Eifel and is correspondingly black, I pondered, between a side trip to Mayen and a conversation with the Benedictine monks in Maria Laach, whether it was worth while to give you unpleasant details of Doubt's engagement to the librarian Erna Dobslaff, or whether it mightn't suffice to tell you that shortly after his interrogation by the police Hermann Ott broke with his fiancée on political grounds. She appears to have said, "It is our good fortune to live in great times. There's no room for people with a snail philosophy." At that time there were still 113 registered persons at the Jewish Old People's Home in the Aschenstift. The warehouse later fitted out as a ghetto held eighty persons. Jewish furriers were quartered in a few overcrowded private houses. (There being no further need for it, Doubt seems to have thrown his engagement ring into the Radaune.)

At the monastery only incidental questions about literature: "May we ask what you are writing about at the moment, assuming that you find time to write?"

I owned to the almost-socialist monks that I was busy telling you in a roundabout way how things came to be as they are, why I have to be away from home so much, and how many defeats Doubt had to swallow before he began to consider flight.

"But those fifty?"
"Are they still there? What's become of them?"

You want to know what became of the Danzig Jews who with about a thousand others were held up in Kladovo. Along with 400 Yugoslavian Jews, they were interned in Sabac. When a small number of immigration certificates arrived from Palestine, only one couple, Aron and Feiga Schermann, out of all the fifty were released and allowed to proceed.

"And the rest?"
"Are they still alive?"
■■■■■■■■

On October 12, 1941, long after Doubt's flight, the German army occupied the Sabac camp. Before over a thousand inmates of the camp, among them the Danzig group, were shot by German execution teams, Israel Herszmann, an engineer who like Hermann Ott had lived in the Danzig Lower City, escaped. By way of Dalmatia and Italy he reached Switzerland, where he was interned in Bellinzona until December, 1944. Not until the fall of 1945 was Herszmann able to board a Haifa-bound ship in Marseilles. Doubt's flight covered less ground.

Laura wants to know all about it: "Those people that were shot, were they really dead afterward?"

Franz and Raoul don't like it when their sister "keeps holding things up" with her questions.

She tends (like her father) to look for things on bypaths: "Where Herszmann is now, in Haifa, if that's what you call it, have they got real goats?"

My daughter's hand in mine.
Looking for goats.
We find abandoned snail shells.
Do you see any?
Not yet.
Are there any here?
Sometimes.
We hear them tinkling on the slope: there and there.
We like goats.
We only collect snail shells.
We used to be goats.
We are curious and scary.
My daughter's hand in mine.
This way we feel safe.
We have salt with us.

■■■■■■■■■

"Yes, Laura. More than a thousand. They were all dead afterward."

On March 28, Doubt received a second summons from the police. On a Sunday he evacuated his terrariums and found new homes for his snails, and on Monday, two days before he was to report, he packed a few personal belongings in a straw-colored linen suitcase. Along with his waste book he placed a reproduction of Dürer's engraving on a layer of undershirts and socks. Next, he put in his cable-stitched knitted jacket. He found it surprisingly easy to part with his books, his drawings, and his snail collection, for he removed only the English hand-colored print of a grove snail from its frame, and laid it between sheets of cardboard on top of his pajamas. What else? A hundred and twenty-five razor blades. Toothbrush and tooth-paste, Nivea cream, styptic pencil, nail scissors in a toilet bag. Beside these toilet articles, as though picked up at random, Aesop's Fables. He closed his suitcase.

Doubt left no letters of farewell. He took no photograph with him. Only identification papers and his savings-bank balance, which he had withdrawn on time. (Raoul always wants to know how much. About 2,500 marks.) He tossed the key to the house door into the janitress's mailbox. In the court, where his bicycle was waiting, he replenished the air in the tires. He strapped his suitcase to the baggage carrier, made his way without meeting anyone through the entrance hall to the street, checked his trouser clips, mounted his bicycle, and rode through the Lower City, across Milchkannen Bridge and Green Bridge up the Long Bridge, then through Heiligegeisttor on the right bank, by well-calculated detours through the narrow streets of the Old City—past the Sawmill and the Convent, through Böttchergasse and Weissmönchenhintergasse—and only now, after any conceivable pursuers have given up between St. Catherine's and the Big Mill, past the Central Station, across Irrgarten Bridge and without looking back (from Olivaer Tor on) down Hindenburgallee to Langfuhr. In Hochstries he turned left and via Brenntau, Mattern, Ramkau, Gross-Mischau, Zuckau, Seeresen pedaled against a light head wind and between rows of trees already in bud, to Karthaus.

Doubt had no destination, but an adequate supply of fear. (Kashubia—chief city and district capital Karthaus, now Kartuzy—is referred to in guidebooks as the Kashubian or Kassubian Switzerland). Fear is a reliable traveling companion. (Characterized by gently rolling hills, Kashubia extends from Dirschau on the Vistula to Stolp in Pomerania, from Putzwiger Wiek and Hela Peninsula to the Berent district.) As he rode, Doubt laughed because he was afraid. (Travel folders tell us that Kashubia's numerous lakes abound in crabs.) Between Zuckau and Seeresen Doubt rode through a shower, which, however, lured no rufous slugs to leave the ditches for the road to Karthaus: too early in the morning. (For you, Raoul, because you are interested in genealogical ramifications and chaotic borderlines, I write informatively: the Kashubians or Kassubians, who today are said to number 300,000, are old Slavs who speak a dying language larded with German and Polish borrowings.) Soon dry, Doubt noticed shortly before Karthaus that he was riding on a flat rear tire. (My family on my mother's side is Kashubian, which makes you, Raoul, like your sister and your brothers, one-quarter Kashubian.) Doubt pushed his bicycle as far as the town. (Karthaus is situated between two lakes, Krugsee to the southwest and Klostersee to the north. The reason for its name is that in 1381, at the behest of a world-weary Kashubian count, Carthusian monks built a monastery there, the Marienparadies charterhouse—a name that makes you stop and think.) Doubt knew Karthaus. The monastery church with its coffin-lid roof cast, and still casts, its reflection in the lake. (In 1818 Karthaus became a Prussian administrative district.) In the interval between the two World

Wars, when the district capital reverted to the name of Kartuzy, Doubt had hiked through Kashubia with students, first of the Crown Prince Wilhelm High School, then of the Jewish High School: weekend excursions across the Free State border. (In Karthaus there was a brewery operated by the monastery, a steam-powered flour mill, a mechanized dairy and four sawmills, which Doubt would be hearing in the distance when the west wind blew. On their last excursion, which took place early in the summer some weeks before the outbreak of the war, Doubt's student Fritz Gerson had found several specimens of *Perforatella bidentata* in a clump of alders by the Radaune. (This will interest you, Raoul: today there's a Kashubian Museum in Kartuzy. We might go there someday and rummage around in chronicles. . . .)

Doubt was acquainted with Anton Stomma; he had often rented bicycles for himself and his students in Stomma's shop. Stomma had also done minor repairs when they had come on bicycles.

He was alone in his shop. Actually, Doubt had only wanted to have his tire repaired. Nevertheless, he removed his trouser clips and let them jiggle on the palm of his hand while Stomma was cleaning rusty bicycle chains in a tub of gasoline. When Stomma asked him if he was planning a bicycle tour to Berent or via Chelmo to Radaune Lake, Doubt replied without having had to to think: "Not really."

They conversed cautiously. Stomma's exploratory question: "Well, what's going to happen now?" Doubt's counterwhisper: "They'll victory themselves to death."

Stomma locked the shop from inside. Back behind the counter, he briefly held a schnapps bottle to his lips: his Adam's apple. Doubt was afraid of being offered a sip. Stomma rammed the cork into the bottleneck with the flat of his hand and observed that he didn't know which was safer:

for a Kashubian to remain Polish or for a Kashubian to get himself Germanized. Doubt owned that he could supply no clear-cut answer to this question. Between remarks about the weather, he emitted signals that he left to Stomma to decode. He was, he declared, working on a piece of scholarship that obliged him to live in strict seclusion for quite some time. "I'm looking for something monastic, something Carthusian."

Stomma didn't want to understand. Doubt had to lay it on thicker. Only when he admitted that he was looking for a discreet host, to whom he could show gratitude later on, when it was all over, Stomma, as though in passing, mentioned a cellar storeroom. Doubt showed interest and hinted at payment. Stomma wanted to know for how long. Doubt spoke of a year.

"And then what?"

"By then they'll have victoried themselves to death."

"And if they don't?"

"Then it'll take a little longer."

"And suppose I decide to get myself Germanized?"

"I could help you fill out your application."

Stomma wiped his hands with wool waste. "Let's hope nothing goes wrong." He took Doubt's suitcase and a first payment. "But it's kind of damp down there and it's full of junk."

Everywhere parts and parts of parts. Nothing whole. Found articles with nowhere to go, as though Raoul had invented a counterworld for the fanatically orderly Doubt: your chaos, in which it is possible to live.

14 Before Doubt goes down to the cellar and starts getting used to it, I catch up on my entries: conversation with Edvard Kardelj* in Belgrade; editorial meeting (*dafür*, number two) in Bonn; skat with Jäckel senior and Gaus; after the meeting in Iserlohn, I meet Karl Schiller, who (with a cold) has been holing up on a farm; conversation with Alva Myrdal at the Hotel Vier Jahreszeiten in Hamburg; on June 17 in Oelinghausen near Bielefeld . . .

I sit and make entries. Overhead, the incoming and outgoing Boeings and Super 111's, on which I come and go: Monday morning go, Saturday come, in order (partly present) to sit on our terrace. . . .

Poking around in my waste book: Behind reflecting eyeglasses Kardelj listened. Discussed aid to developing countries with Alva Myrdal over tea . . .

Across the street, surrounded by a board fence, the no man's land, which for the present, until the builders take over, belongs to rats, pigeons, and children. (Two years later, a playground emerges with climbing poles, barrels to crawl through, slides, and a chicken-wire enclosure for ballplayers.)

---

* Party leader in Yugoslavia and President of the Federal Assembly 1963–1967.

I note the name of the farmer in whose house Schiller and his cold holed up.

Lichtenberg's name for the waste book used by English merchants was *Sudelbuch.* This method of writing casually against time was recommended to me by Doubt. . . .

Half concealed by shrubbery, I observe how our front garden, entertainingly programmed by a former owner, changes from week to week: lilacs hawthorn dogroses. Lily-of-the-valley beside the garbage cans. (From the house I hear Anna and the children, all running at once and mixing sounds. Protests from all directions. I like that.)

Afterthought: on the plane to Hanover played a few quick rounds of skat with three men who had been bowling in Berlin. After I've lost a hearts hand, someone who had doubled says: "Things are moving in Hagen where I come from. This time Willy will make it."

Friedenau has a good deal to offer. Situated under an air corridor, it hides crotchety little Dutch-brick homes behind apartment houses built in the early 1870's, treats itself twice a week to a market where fruit, vegetables, fish, eggs, and kitchen herbs are sold in front of the town hall, presents, outside the post office, a circular park on whose benches old women compare each other, has its corner bars and shaded beer gardens, will be a hundred years old in two years, and manages not to obstruct my terrace, on which I prechew and aftertaste the election campaign. . . .

With a big farmer, it goes without saying. His finely chiseled pride. How he (experimentally) tries on resignation. How he bounces and is concentratedly nervous. They don't let him revalue. He mustn't be proved right. (Is it possible that Doubt in his cellar—weakened by flu and not yet inured to hardship—becomes similarly quiet for lack of an audience?)

In the afternoon, silence. Except perhaps for that dry report, at the corner of Handjerystrasse and Niedstrasse, which Franz and Raoul define with equal dryness: "Man, that's great! Two Volkswagens again." (In Raoul's room, the state of which may have led me to furnish bicycle dealer Stomma's cellar with chaos, a spare-parts depot is in the making: windshield wipers, hub caps, steering wheels, the entrails of disemboweled total-loss wrecks.)

Now at the end of June the lilacs in our front garden are worthy only to be remembered. At the market, as every year, "new dill pickles!" are in the air. (In his cellar, Doubt hopes to be less susceptible to hay fever.) In 1871 a "joint-stock company for land purchase and construction" was founded in Berlin. At that time the future Friedenau quarter was still farm land. One of the builders was called Hähnel; now a street is named after him. (As for Doubt's spring flu, it can be said in retrospect: it was a light case.) In among exactly forty-nine birch trees, the old women sit on their island surrounded by circular traffic and are bitter tired finished. When young girls on their way to the post office take a shortcut through the circle, they are inspected by twelve or perhaps seventeen old women and judged too young, too cuddly. Children never play there, they prefer the no man's land.

On my terrace I wait half concealed for Doubt to turn up. (Johnson used to come by now and then to sit here and be peculiar.) Doubt comes often, I only have to call him. We discuss what's amiss. I advise him not to lie with his head in the damp north wind that blows into his cellar; he advises me to start by introducing Stomma, his host, and his daughter Lisbeth to the children.

Since he is keen on novelties (from my time)—"Anybody who has to sit in a cellar like me takes an interest in gossip"—I tell him in what bar the Friedenau revolutionary group meets, also that a mutual friend has come back from Cuba disillusioned. Doubt smiles a thin-line smile: "Ideological tourism existed even in my day." (My latest entries—the offended, hence elegiac Schiller, skat with changing partners—leave him cold. At the most he takes an interest in Enzensberger's new insights: "And now what? Is he writing poetry again?")

Now we chat about Stomma's lilacs, which are crowding their way between the outhouse and the rabbit hutch. I list the names of Kashubian villages—Bissau Ramkau Viereck Kokoschken—and, after an incoming Super 111 has bequeathed silence, Doubt tells me about something that happened in the summer of the war year 1941: "Imagine: with his daughter's help Stomma is putting up a barrel of pickles." From this he draws a direct inference: "Consequently, there will be more and more people coming home with news from the nearest district capital or from Cuba. Stomma, for instance, has been in Dirschau lately."

I ask, "Where will this barrel be kept?" The barrel with its smell will be kept in Doubt's cellar. "Incidentally," he says, "Kurt Jakubowski, the last Jewish doctor to practice in Danzig, emigrated to Cuba shortly before the war started. I'd be curious to know . . ." I promise Doubt to ask Erwin Lichtenstein, who knows everything.

After that, small talk. We play with the words "dill pickle season."* (And in among forty-nine birch trees the old women in the circle in front of the post office list all the things that are so much more expensive this year: among them, dill pickles. Suddenly, Doubt changes the subject. There seems to be nothing more to say about our mutual friend and his disillusionment over Cuba. He tells me that he plans, while in his cellar, to shrink time with research and to gather insights into

---

* *Sauregurkenzeit:* the summer slack season.

the role of hermaphrodite snails as mediators between Melancholy and Utopia. "It must be possible," he says, "to find an antidote for time in the substance of snails."

Why should I discourage him? There's plenty of room in the cellar. Now he's quoting: Lichtenberg, Schopenhauer, his and my Jean Paul . . .

When the children come in from the front garden and occupy the terrace, Doubt obliterates himself. He fears too much present. Somebody might test his existence with a handshake. He insists on remaining ambivalent and goes as he came. He hadn't said hello and he doesn't say good-bye.

Now I am called into question fourfold: "How was it? Where were you? When you going again? Where to?"

It went off fairly well. I was in the Voreifel, a pretty black part of it. Now I'm going to take a break. Talking all the time drains you. Meanwhile, we've got various things going: twenty-five voters' clubs in as many election districts. Erdmann Linde thinks (and so do Marchand and Drautzburg) that I should rest a while and look on from outside. So Anna, Bruno, and I are driving to Czechoslovakia. We're planning to meet friends in a forest. I'm planning to collect mushrooms, write a new speech, add footnotes to my waste book, and round out my picture of Doubt; as you know, children, I'll never get rid of him.

In Stomma's storeroom bicycles and parts of bicycles were rusting. Frames hung, handlebars up, from a steel cable twenty feet long, as long as the cellar. Below in crates: screws, valves, bundled spokes. Scattered in between: nondescript scrap. In Stomma's storeroom potatoes sprouted, briquettes lay in piles, sugar beets for syrup making were stored, a barrel of pickles took up space. The wired-glass pane of the cellar window admitted a modicum of light from the yard. The trap door over the stairs opened out into the kitchen, which was the same size as the cellar and directly above it. Stomma's shop adjoined the kitchen and fronted on the street side. Above the shop, the kitchen, and the living room (also known as the parlor), which had windows on both the yard and the street, the attic provided two bedrooms for Stomma and his daughter. (The house, yard, and surrounding garden had belonged to Stomma since the death of his wife.) Only the kitchen had a basement.

Stomma's storeroom smelled of axle grease, rust, potatoes, and turnips, of the dampness that seeped through the north wall, and of the beach-grass mattress that Stomma had put down for Doubt on the stamped clay floor under the cellar window. The pissy quilt. From June to early winter the barrel of dill pickles smelled.

(Only once, in the summer of 1941, did Stomma store freshly mown grass for his rabbits in the cellar: Doubt's hay fever burst instantly into bloom.)

Since the clutter in the storeroom included a chair, Doubt had to ask only for a table. Later, he sewed himself a floor mat out of burlap bags. Doubt paid three marks a day until November, 1942, shortly before Stalingrad, when he ran out of money. Soon he knew every crack and crevice in the plaster ceiling, every bump in the clay floor, every incrustation, scab, and fungus growth on the north wall of his cellar.

Stomma's house was situated on the road to Seeresen, at the northeast edge of Karthaus. (When the wind was right, the four sawmills and the bells of the monastery church could be heard in the cellar.) Only at night was Doubt permitted to use the outhouse between the rabbit hutch and the pigsty and to empty his bucket. Adjoining the yard and the windowless back of the house was a vegetable garden with a few apple and sour-cherry trees in it. The front garden on the street side was narrow: gooseberry bushes, sunflowers, one chestnut tree. From the vegetable garden in the rear, rolling potato fields extended as far as the woods. A wooden fence surrounded Stomma's property, bordered to the right and left by the gardens of neighbors, with whom, as usual in the country, Stomma was on the outs. In the yard, behind the rabbit hutch and the outhouse, nettles grew under the lilacs. Stomma had no friends, and no one ever came to see him. He had no radio and no dog. A solitary man who cursed to himself in an undertone.

When Anton Stomma led his guest to the cellar, he said, "There's nobody else but Lisbeth; that's my daughter. She's not quite right in the head. I'll tell her to keep her mouth shut."

The bicycle stayed upstairs. Later, when Doubt ran out of money, Stomma sold it.

No, Raoul, that was before the big bombings. Don't ask, "Then what? What happened then? What happened afterward?" Ask what happened before, what was going on before all that, until something came after and was given a name. Stories that are left to their own gradient tend to be exciting in a banal kind of way. From Dresden, where we had lunch on the terrace at Brühl's and tried to imagine what the city on either bank of the Elbe may have looked like before the fire, we followed "Transit Praha" signposts to the border. . . .

Lisbeth Stomma's story is soon told. She was nineteen when, four years before the outbreak of the war, she took up with an employee of the Polish Railways, who shuttled back and forth between Karthaus and Dirschau—an affair that had its high points in barns and idle freight cars. The outcome was a child, for whose upkeep he paid regularly, though he seldom came to see it. On the fourth day of the war the Polish infantryman Roman Bruszinki was killed in the battle for the Narew crossings. On the very first day of the war, the child, a boy of three, had been run over by a military vehicle, whose horses, like the horses of other vehicles, bolted when the column was bombed by Stukas not far from Karthaus. Lisbeth Stomma had gone out onto the Berent road with the child to look for the uniformed Roman Bruszinski, whom she expected to see in the horsecart of every passing unit.

The child—named Hannes by his mother—was buried in the Karthaus cemetery. Ever since then, wherever she went stood lay, Lisbeth had seen cemeteries in front of or behind everything that she saw or said she saw. She visited every cemetery within reach, in Kelpin and Chmelno, even in Neustadt, as well as the Consolidated Cemeteries adjoining the Schlossgarten in Oliva. When she spoke at all, there was always some incidental mention of cemeteries. She never said, "Then I'll go to the market for eggs." She said, "After the cemetery I'll go to the market for eggs."

In the opinion of the neighbor woman and of the doctors at the district hospital, Lisbeth was mentally deranged but harmless. People referred to her as cracked, nuts, or meshuga. Actually, Lisbeth Stomma was weighed down—but not crushed—by common melancholy. When she came home from her cemeteries, she was patently cheerful. Lisbeth Stomma found cemeteries pleasant, or, as she said later to Doubt, cozy. "Once I get there, it's cozy; I'd never leave if I didn't have to."

Not only Saturn. It's the quaternity: dry moist warm cold. It's the elements: earth water air fire; the cardinal points: north south east west; the seasons and temperaments. It's the four humors which, when not properly mixed, make the bile bitter and black. Yet Lisbeth Stomma remained cheerful in a rather shrill way, as long as no one tried to talk or keep her out of cemeteries, as her father did with a stick.

Doubt, who read the newspapers, said to Stomma after reading him the daily Wehrmacht communiqué: "So much for the military situation. I must admit that the German armies are winning almost convincingly, and you would probably be well advised to hand me, your guest, over to the competent authorities as soon as possible. But aside from that, I'd appreciate it if you'd let your daughter take her daily walk to the cemetery. Where else can the poor thing go? You and I are too this-worldly, too much concerned with survival, to take the place of graves and ivy in her mind."

Stomma respected Doubt's advice, because he looked on Doubt as a Jew and the Jews as shrewd. "All right, she can go if that's what she wants."

Lisbeth Stomma was on her way from or to the cemetery. In cemeteries she carried on short, intimate conversations with the graves. She knew quite a lot of dead people. But it wasn't the curiosity and unrestrained sympathy of elderly women who entertain themselves visiting cemeteries. She offered condolences to none. She disturbed no one but cared for the neglected graves of strangers.

Stomma was a strong man, a bruiser. With one hand he could lift Doubt, who must have been underweight, over his head and sometimes good-naturedly, often painfully, press him against the ceiling. He was kind to his rabbits; when rabbit was wanted for dinner, Lisbeth had to do the killing.

Anton Stomma was born, so he said, in Gussin, Karthaus district, in 1888, the year of the three emperors, when Wilhelm I died, then Friedrich III died, and Wilhelm II mounted the throne. His parents, Josef Stomma and Hedwig Stomma née Bolinski, leased farms successively in Barwick, Adlig-Pomietschin and Lowitz, Lauenburg district, and ruined them.

Since West Prussia belonged to Prussia at that time, Anton learned in school to speak German, but hardly to read or write it. At home Kashubian was spoken, and when visitors came from Berent or Dirschau, Polish. At an early age Anton Stomma began to hate Prussians and schoolmasters: to him all Germans were Prussians. He called the Prussians *Piefkes*. At fourteen, he was apprenticed to a blacksmith in Lowitz but did not finish out his term. Later on, Stomma's father went in for trucking: he and his son carted crushed rock for road building in a two-horse open truck.

From 1908 to 1910 Stomma served in the 141st Infantry Regiment in Strasburg, West Prussia, on the Russian border. There, again, he did not learn to read, but he did learn to dance at village shindigs and to topple and lay village girls while taking them home. (Over and over again he told Doubt about those days, counting on his fingers how many girls from the sugar mill had spread their legs for him. "And the way they puffed and panted!")

Later, in Dirschau, he worked in a garage that repaired military vehicles. Consequently, he became a truck driver in the World War. (When Stomma spoke of the war—and Doubt became familiar with the itineraries of all Stomma's convoys—it was always about heavy ammunition that had to be taken to the front in France or Rumania in spite of enemy fire; for the duration of the war Stomma's hatred of the Prussians was suspended.)

After the First World War, West Prussia became Polish. Stomma bought an old NAG-Siemens cheap, and using it as a taxi earned money in two currencies in Dirschau. But in 1920 he drove his cab, which was losing a front wheel, into a tree, so converting it to scrap. (When Stomma spoke of that disastrous ride to Pelplin and his NAG-Siemens, he always dwelt at length on the hub of his left front wheel and its damaged left-handed thread. Doubt understood: Stomma had loved his car more than anything in the world.)

In the same year, he married Johanna Czapp of Karthaus, whom he had got with child. Lisbeth Stomma was born two months after the wedding. (On photographs that Stomma brought to the cellar Doubt saw Lisbeth at the ages of ten, twelve, and fourteen: a child who might have been called pretty in a rustic kind of way. Wheat-blonde, she wore butterfly bows in her hair. Skinny and angular, she stood by the garden fence against a background of sunflowers; only with the onset of melancholia had Lisbeth grown fat and sluggish.)

During the first years of his marriage Stomma had farmed the potato fields that along with the house on the road to Seeresen had been his wife's marriage portion. Later on, he sold the few acres of land and set up his bicycle shop. In the early thirties, first his two other children, twins, then his wife had died. Lisbeth kept house for Stomma. Lisbeth tended the vegetable garden. Lisbeth went with the railroad man and got pregnant. Once Stomma hit the railroad man as they stood face to face in the parlor. He hit him with a bicycle pump. To her little Hannes Lisbeth seems to have spoken Kashubian and her articleless German: "Don't run out in street! Get me dish from kitchen!"

At school Lisbeth had learned to speak but hardly to read or write Polish. At home Kashubian was spoken, or, when visitors came from Berent or Dirschau, German.

I really ought to go into the statistics of history at this point and say something about the changing linguistic mixture in the villages of Karthaus district. When was Klobschin called

Klobocin, and why was Klobocin called Klobschin? When and how often was the hamlet of Neuendorf, west of Turmberg, called Novawies in Polish? Why does Seeresen, which lies between Karthaus and Zuckau, appear as Derisno when first mentioned in 1241, as Seheressen beginning in 1570, and alternately as Seresen and Serosen in the period after 1789? Why, in the nineteenth century, did it become Seeresen, though concomitantly it appears time and time again in Polish and Kashubian as Dzierzaźno? Such is history as its fallout affects the countryside.

When, in August, 1940, Anton Stomma applied for Germanization as an ethnic German, Doubt helped him to fill out the questionnaires, to unearth relatives of halfway German descent, and to write his *curriculum vitae*. The guest spent many evenings being patient with his host. Every letter Stomma formed cost him a struggle. Doubt's cellar became a schoolroom. Over lined paper his pupil became a child: he dreaded ink blots. A gain of time for Doubt: slowly Stomma learned to write, but to read, to read the *Danziger Vorposten*, he never learned.

15 When in our Peugeot Anna drove Bruno and me across the border to Czechoslovakia near Zinnwald in the Erz Mountains, we saw that the white distress signals—"Svoboda!" "Dubček!"—hastily daubed on hoardings, factory walls, above doorways, and on façades were already gray and faded, corroded by time (ten measly months). It's time that makes terror habitual: time is what we must write against.

An old trick. Before their crime, criminals figure out how long it will take for their crime to be forgotten, overlaid by the crimes of other criminals, reduced to marginal history. Whether they acted with the pomp of vanity or with sickly guile, whether they set themselves up as giants or whistled a leitmotiv for fate to dance to, whether the criminals bore the name of Hitler or of Stalin (whether Ulbricht survived his Stalin or Kiesinger took the seat of his Hitler), time, the passage of time, benefits the criminals; for their victims time does not pass.

We drove past Theresienstadt, a German concentration camp tended as a memorial. (Beginning in January, 1942, the Jews living in the Danzig warehouse ghetto on Mausegasse, old people like David Jonas, the last chairman of a community languishing in terror, were deported to Theresienstadt. There, the old people died off. No outside help was needed. David

Jonas lived to see the liberation and died shortly afterward of typhus.

As a rule, the murderers survive. Quietly at first, then blatantly, they go about peddling the time that has meanwhile elapsed and collecting advances against the time that will shortly elapse. Patterns embroidered on shrouds. Surviving murderers are serviceable models, giving significance to trends. Guilt as the badge of greatness.

Soon the occupation of Czechoslovakia will be explained (to you, too, children) as a tragic but (alas!) for reasons of security necessary event. What the United States government (in Vietnam) calls "pacification," the Soviet government calls "normalization." (Rewritten crimes that have found their rewrite men.)

I shall go backward in time (for you): in March, 1921, three and a half years after the October Revolution, Lenin and Trotsky crushed the uprising of the Kronstadt and Petrograd sailors and workers, who wanted democratic Communism and not party dictatorship, with cannon fire.

Forty-seven years later, when cautiously and at long last the Czechoslovakian Communists began to show that "socialism with a human face" is possible, Leonid Brezhnev sent in military units from five Communist countries, including—and don't forget it—German soldiers in uniforms of Prussian cut.

As far as the Berounka, a tributary of the Vltava, we had to ask our way. Employing the devices of weak peoples whose wits had been sharpened by terror, the Czechs and Slovaks tried to defend themselves against brute force, which is always single-minded. (Road signs were turned around, street signs disappeared.) Stupidity was identified but could not be stopped. Now it lives on the passage of time. A writer, children, is someone who writes against the passage of time.

When, after a number of detours, Anna, Bruno, and I reached Nouzov, which is in the middle of the forest, our friends were already there. We start with an exchange of greetings that goes on and on. We try to laugh, and succeed. We eat bread dumplings and drink Bohemian beer. (I have my typewriter with me and a picture postcard of the *Melencolia*.) The inn where we're staying is an old forester's lodge. We walk in the woods, disperse, meet again, and hold words in reserve. On layers of leaves, on a bed of pine needles. Shouting in the woods. Each on his own. Avoiding clearings. Suddenly sighting mushrooms. (There are charcoal burners in these woods, who live outside of time.) Pick up a cold toad in the ferns for Bruno. Or observe with amazement how enormous and imperturbable ant hills can be. (No sign of Doubt's reddish-brown hairy snails.)

In the afternoon we talk about other things. Pauses for fear of offending. How fortunate that irony has survived (covertly) and is now in supply. In the half-shadow between the children Štěpán and Tomáš, knee-deep in a meadow, Anna: something to imprint on my memory.

I remain on the fringe, because the prevailing mood can't hold me, because I'm still on the move, looking for something with my typewriter. Spreading out papers in a strange room. Not noticing the wallpaper. Getting used to a chair. Weaving in afterthoughts. Getting started.

My speech that I write in Nouzov is titled "Of Limited Possibilities." Anna is sitting in the yard with our friends. They hear me clattering. I oppose skepticism to faith. I contest the permanent and unchanging. My disgust at the absolute and suchlike thumbscrews. Why I'm opposed to the claims of the "one and only truth" and in favor of multiplicity. My language narrows down. (Here, where freedom is a word like spoon.) Someone has always gone before and made preliminary decisions. No zero point from which to start counting. But regressions of history: how Strauss and Barzel might engender a Strauzel—compact blackness. Writing against the new darkening that is already setting in and in defense of something that is limited and therefore reasonable—or trying in the middle of the Bohemian Forest to write about the aid to developing countries bill and Erhard Eppler, a Christian and Social Democrat who lives, as it were, in the subjunctive.

More mushrooms. We find some charcoal in an abandoned kiln. The innkeeper lends us a window grating to use as a grill. Spareribs and bottled beer. We hold our sad barbecue at one end of a gravel pit that has also been used as a shooting range. Bruno collects small-caliber cartridge cases. In the evening a village dance. A good many drunks, getting more and more subdued. Pauses in which to feel strange. The music weighs the Czech soldiers down, nails them to their tables; some of them are crying. . . .

Now it's time for us to leave—in a few minutes. Our friends standing in dispersed order. Long last looks to charge our memories. Little words for the trip. Advice to car drivers, because during the night, while music drowned out all other sounds, two side mirrors, one headlight, one taillight, and our righthand windshield wiper have been stolen. We laugh too loud, hug the children, and say, "Take care of yourselves." Anything else? Anna looks about as if she'd forgotten something. Lost syllables and other arrears. Now we stop talking about time that has passed. (Since all have their parts, I'm left with the role of morale builder.) I say, "Maybe we'll make it. Maybe we'll win, just barely. Then maybe the pressure will let up. I think . . ." And we drive off with too few rear-view mirrors.

They won't have any peace. Power will cover them only partly. Their fears will multiply. Everything will crumble and fray. They will never be secure. Already they're ridiculous in their effort to look respectable.

Just before Dresden a storm overtakes us. Anna stops the engine. The one windshield wiper isn't enough. Bruno is as quiet as the storm is loud. Anna and I can't think of much to say either. At the most, anger borrowed from the elements: "But there must be some kind of belated justice. . . . Brute force can't forever . . . Time mustn't be allowed to . . ."

After the fireworks we talk normally again: "Just barely, Anna. You'll see: this time we'll just barely . . ." But Anna is looking into the missing rear-view mirror.

It may be, Franz and Raoul, that when you're in search of something later on, Communism will give you hope; it lives by holding out hope of the true communism to come.

Some day, because in Germany theory is put before practice, you may try to find a solution in that totalitarian system, which claims to reconcile the contradictions and promises painless transitions. (A pacified existence.)

Faith may give you eyes for an ultimate goal and make you blind to the human beings of the present. (The few thousand incorrigibles.)

You may come to condone injustice as prerequisite to the great, all-embracing justice to come. (Subjectivism can only delay us.)

It may be that the goal will be everything to you and the wishes of a few Czechs nothing. (Petit bourgeois.)

I am entitled to fear that when time has passed, and because lesser undertakings have proved too difficult, you may set yourself the goal of forcing the liberation of mankind by Communism (the true variety): at any price . . .

I say: you may . . .

I say: over my dead body.

On the Autobahn near Senftenberg—we can see the chimneys of the soft-coal combines—I say to Anna: "Somewhere around here I was wounded just before the end."

You can't tell by looking at the country how scared I was. Altogether you can't tell much by looking at the countryside.

At a rest stop we buy blueberries from a woman with a kerchief on her head, who could be my grandmother. Bruno is asleep, curled up in the back seat. We drive off.

I can't say: they should have fired when the five armies invaded their country. (In Israel I heard young Jews accusing their murdered fathers and grandfathers, even the few who had survived: "They shouldn't have waited like dumb sheep; they should have defended themselves. . . ." As soon as the murderers' crime begins to be forgotten, the victims are convicted; they should have resisted. Ideas foreshadow violence. Ideas can be resisted. Consequently, resistance must begin before ideas take power.

After the customs and passport inspection, we understand the lavish precautions: concrete barbed-wire watchtowers mined no man's land . . . This "frontier of peace" fears no comparisons.

■■■■■■■■■

Who likes blueberries? At home, we tell them about Štěpán and Tomáš. We transmit regards and repeat ourselves. Yes, it's a big forest, you can get lost, and in the middle of the woods there are real charcoal burners who make charcoal, and mushrooms and ant hills. . . . (No, there's nothing stirring. The deathly rigidity of commanded order. Even the snails refuse to.) Yes, it was beautiful. The river is called the Berounka. . . .

"And what does Frantiček say?"
"And Olga?"
"And what does Vladimir say?"
"Is he even sadder than he is?"

(What comes now is between lacunae.) As you know, children, a year later—when even more time had passed—Vladimir, whom Anna was so attached to, who was my friend—began to die; and on October 19, 1970, he died at the age of thirty-nine. That very nearly drove us . . . Because of his, Anna is, and I am . . . As for you, we asked for your patience.

Obituary for Vladimir?
What he did missed up on wanted began concealed?
Wherein he failed, what he bequeathed us?
How we were within calling distance of each other?
Exactly when his headache began?
What intervened, separating us from his death?
All that will go into my obituary, later.

16 And what now? Unpack pack. Tomorrow I have to start again, to stop the time from passing. I've brought home a brand-new speech, written in Czechoslovakia. . . .

On our way back we cooked a meal by the roadside: bacon and chanterelles from the Ulm market, which has the cathedral as a stone market cross. I'm speaking not of the top of the steeple but of its edge, which is cracked, flawed, battered, and yellow with age. . . .

Because he was besieged by cold, only cramped, shivery words came to him: Doubt was frozen stiff. But he punctuated even the chattering of his teeth with semicolon after semicolon, because (from mid-November on) he dictated only to the frost. Chilled periods in which Melancholy and her grandiloquent sister strode together over crusty snow. Clanking gestures. The crystal system. A cellar window grows ice flowers: chiseled utopias . . . The cold seeped out of the walls and lay down with Doubt on his mattress. But he didn't fall sick.

Today I come from several directions. I know more now. Hesitation comes more easily.

Before the meeting at the Hotel Hörhammer I visited the site of the former concentration camp. (When I was a seventeen-year-old POW, they brought me here to educate me: we didn't want to understand; we saw the showers and cremating chambers, and we didn't believe.)

With Drautzburg and Glotz, our candidate in the Dachau election district, I went to a museum. I saw groups of visitors hurrying up to large coarse-grained photographs and exhibits in glass cases, and falling back. (Drautzburg, too, was slow to move on.) The visitors' book was put before me. Later I heard that the municipal authorities had been at loggerheads about the expense of maintaining the far-flung site.

More than once I saw myself in different roles. I saw myself at the age of seventeen, hard of hearing and obstinate, and I saw myself at forty-two writing in the visitors' book. I saw the snail amid the preserved installations of the camp. A long-lasting track. Well-wrapped guilt. I'm running way behind myself: tedious . . .

Doubt's memory had become conglomerate. He was no longer able to establish a chronological order between school excursions, Purim festivals, the funerals of relatives, once-current events, his notes on Schopenhauer's prize essay *On Free Will,* and his mutually annulling betrothals. He was no longer able to determine which had been Herr Ott's pupils at the Crown Prince Wilhelm High School and which at the Private Jewish High School. Names that he recited to himself—Schmerling, Fingerhut, Lublinski, Rotkehl, Schapiro, Kurzmann, Mandel—dissolved in mist; only the aggressive seriousness of his student Fritz Gerson refused to evaporate. The moment Stomma mounted the stairs, "Fritzchen" stood gangling—he had shot up too fast—beside Doubt's mattress, displaying his bullet wounds. He inquired about last things as hungrily as if he had been inhabited by a tapeworm, which began to devour Doubt's answers—long-winded circumlocutions around the last things—before they had a chance to appease his hunger. About the meaning of life. About nature and idea. He was also curious about the freedom of the will to resist: "Didn't we want to defend ourselves? Or didn't we want to want to defend ourselves?" Doubt got used to the cold and wrote didactic frost periods in a diary that Stomma had bought him in Karthaus. . . .

No doctrine sustains me. I don't know the solution. I make you a present of Doubt and advise you to lose him. I show you people encountered at random, what weighs on their minds and how they torment themselves. See with what anguish that old woman compares prices. See the old man with a retirement pension waiting for the mail. See how old age hurries past broadly smiling advertisements. . . . Forgive me if in an undertone I advise you: be accurate. Don't say: Other people smell. They only smell different. Don't be afraid of heroes. In the fog, children, sing out: Be afraid!

Are you still listening? You don't want to be snails? You want to reach the goal more quickly and presentably? But you're snails already: I see Raoul hesitating before he grabs or rejects.

I beg you, continue to be sensitive. There is no such thing as a standpoint that demonstrates itself. A snail—always on the move—hasn't got any fixed positions.

He whiled away the time for Stomma, his host, for Stomma's daughter Lisbeth, and himself. A hard job; but who will confess to being a professional whiler away of time? (Ranicki, whose story is here resurrected, knows that.)

For 224 weeks, on 1,568 days, especially on long winter evenings, Doubt demonstrated how much nut-size knowledge a schoolteacher garners up and carries about with him, if only as fugitive's baggage. Everything—the invention of the lightning rod, free will, the function of the chair, what makes the tides, how the pyramids were built, the earthquake in Messina, and Schopenhauer's flight from the cholera—can be told in story form. (During the evening meeting in the banquet hall of the Hotel Hörhammer, I told why, how, and where I had bought a Bavarian necktie with a lozenge design, so infusing some life into dry-as-dust political material.)

When nothing occurred to him, Doubt, concerned for his reputation as a whiler away of time, had to invent something new. Because, when no new stories were forthcoming, Stomma, who remembered all the old ones, slipped his leather belt out of its loops. (Why did Stomma resort to blows? Because he believed in blows—if in nothing else. Because blows were expected of him. Because when striking blows, he felt alive. Because he was afraid.)

With the belt out of his trousers, later with bicycle spokes. "This'll help your memory," said Stomma, laying his guest educationally (and also to redistribute blows he himself had received) over the table. Afterward, Doubt told new stories. (I have it easier: thanks to my frequent changes of scene, my story—about buying a necktie with a blue-and-white lozenge design—can be told over and over again.)

When the snail wanted to fly, he went to Ulm. When he got there, it was market day outside the cathedral. The housewives were all looking at price markers. No one was looking up when the snail, tentacles in the lead, flew from the top of the steeple and headed for Memmingen.

After Doubt had taught his host to write, he slowly dictated Aesop's Fables to him. Sometimes Doubt tried to make up fables. Then he told about the snail, the weasel, the lark that towered over the snail, and the swift horse who, whenever he won a race, wished he were a snail. Stomma wrote the fables in a lined school copybook, but he couldn't read what he had written. Lisbeth Stomma also listened when Doubt whiled away the time with stories; but no one knew for sure what she heard, whether she heard more or something different.

When, after the Balkan campaign and shortly before the Russian campaign, Doubt ran out of Aesop's Fables, he told what Livy, Plutarch, and Herodotus had seen fit to tell. After the fall of Vitebsk and Smolensk, Doubt began telling about Alexander, Hannibal, and Napoleon. When the German divisions had taken Kiev but were stuck in the mud outside of Moscow, Doubt made Alexander and Hannibal perish, kindled the great Moscow fire, and cast a gruesome light on Napoleon's retreat. By chasing the remnants of Napoleon's army—including bands of volunteers from Danzig and Dirschau along with what was left of the Lippe battalion and dispersed Polish legionaries—through Kashubia, where many of them sickened and died in the stables of the Karthaus monastery, he was able to call the lightning victories of the German armies into question; at the same time he entertainingly whiled away the time, which is said to weigh most compactly on rural districts.

When at election meetings I speak of the sandboxes in which people try to win lost wars and recover lost provinces, many listen with tilted heads: sandbox players. Since I come from Danzig and know what I've lost, I have a right to talk this way. Doubt will agree with me: it was lovely in Danzig. The clouds entirely different. The snow much whiter. Boat trips to Kalte Herberge by way of Fischerbabke. Towers and steeples big and little: zinc-green and brick-red. The two timber-frame warehouses on Mausegasse, where silent in their overcoats aged Jews went on hoping . . .

150

■■■■■■■■■

When Doubt had told enough stories, Stomma and Stomma's daughter left him. Now he's lying sleepless in his cellar. He collects fragments, peers into warehouse windows, skates with his pupils to Krampitz, rides his bicycle several times across the Milchkannenbrücke, through the Old City's jumble of streets and—unable to deviate from his course—to Karthaus. A busy dispeller of sleep. Leaping snails can, to be sure, be imagined, but the imagined snail leaps only relatively to the creeping snail that does not have to be imagined. Even if Doubt succeeded (for dear Utopia's sake) in breeding hopping snails, their novel speed would prove only that the intervals they have jumped over have no desire to hurry.

Only toward morning, when pouring rain made its presence felt in the cellar, did Doubt find sleep.

I have the following from Dr. Lichtenstein, who quotes from the diary of Bertold Wartski, a shopkeeper: On August 26, 1940 (a Monday), the last Jewish emigrants left Danzig. Five hundred and twenty-seven persons from the Aschenheimstift on Milchkannengasse, from the warehouse on Mausegasse, and from the overcrowded private houses—on Töpfergasse, Pfefferstadt, Steindamm, Hundegasse, Kassubischer Markt—assembled at four in the afternoon at the shipyard restaurant on Fuchswall. Many of those from the private houses had no ration cards and came without provisions. SS-Obersturmführer Abromeit and his men broke the emigrants down into groups. All were obliged to surrender their money. Then ten groups of fifty were marched down Wallgasse, Schichaugasse, and through the Schichau housing development to the new loading platform in the shipyard area: a long march for the old people.

Many inhabitants of the city, standing on sidewalks or balconies, or looking out of windows from behind flower boxes, took loud leave of their erstwhile fellow citizens. Flanking laughter, malicious jingles, spitting. The young people showed particular zeal. (I wasn't there; but—children—I was thirteen and could have been there.)

The special train consisted of twelve third-class carriages for the emigrants and two second-class carriages, which were occupied by SS-Obersturmführer Abromeit, Commissioner for Jewish Affairs Bittner, two Jewish physicians from Breslau, several Gestapo officials, and medical personnel. At 8:12 P.M. the special train left the city without stopping at the central station. Some 400 Jews—we don't know the exact number—remained in the city. Soon thereafter they were forced to wear the yellow star on their outer garments, but they didn't give up hope.

When we stopped to rest on the way to Dachau, I watched a brick-red rufous slug eating its way into an apple core, as though, defenseless as slugs are, to provide itself with a substitute shell. (Thomas Höpker, who was traveling with us, didn't see me with the snail but wanted to take my picture with a live rooster for a poster.)

"Well? Will they get there?"
"Or will they be?"
"What if they hadn't left?"
"Did they want to or did they have to?"

Recently Doubt and his host have also taken to speculation. Stomma appeared in the cellar and said, "I do what I want!" When Doubt asked, "Which of the two possibilities will you want to convert into action?" Stomma stuck to his contention: "I can do what I want, and nobody's going to stop me."

"Fine," said Doubt. "You can decide of your own free will

to hand me over to the Gestapo with the possible consequence of finding yourself in trouble after a German defeat; or you can decide, again of your own free will, to keep me here as your guest in return for small payment, with the possible consequence of finding yourself in a favored position when the Germans are defeated. Now, my dear Stomma, make your decision, provided you are free to reject the one course without taking the other."

After pausing long enough to run through all the possibilities, Stomma said, "You mean I can't do what I want?"

Doubt lectured: "Your freedom to do what you want is curtailed by the circumstance that of two possible decisions only one can be converted into action. In either case, you're a prisoner to the action that's not performed, hence no freer than I am. Except that you eat better and are able to get some fresh air when you like. As the prisoner of a decision that has not been made, you have at least that much freedom. In point of fresh air, an enviable freedom."

Stomma and Doubt laughed. For the duration of a laugh, they both found it amusing to be dependent on each other. Then Stomma drew his leather belt rather slowly from its loops. Unbidden, Doubt bent over the table. (He counted to twelve.) While Stomma whipped, he had to hold up his trousers with his free hand: even a belt can't do two things at once.

"Well, I guess that'll do."

"What now?"

"What would you like?"

"Maybe you could bring me my . . ."

Stomma left the cellar and in due time descended the stairs with fried potatoes, scrambled eggs, and coffee substitute. Doubt ate standing up. "Well," said Stomma, "is it good?"

After the meal host and guest laughed again. Repeated bursts of merriment, Doubt giggling, Stomma snorting, about the limits imposed on the will. Lisbeth looked on without understanding: she was free enough to want only one thing, to visit the cemetery.

Later on they played morris. Stomma lost, because every time he wanted to make a move he became aware of other possible moves. Bewildered, with an expression closely resembling that of a man thinking, he saw his counters disappearing.

The special train reached Bratislava on August 27, 1940. While the emigrants were boarding the Danube steamer *Helios*, fights broke out among them. Young people took possession of the few cabins. While carrying luggage aboard, Chaskel Neger, who had lived in Danzig-Ohra, fell into the Danube and was carried away by the powerful current. (Later on, members of the Haganah organized a shipboard police force and introduced severe discipline. Because of the overcrowding, one-way traffic was imposed. Uncleanliness was punished by beatings.)

When the *Helios* with the Danzig Jews, the *Schönbrunn* with the Austrian Jews, the *Uranus* and the *Melk* with Prague Jews passed the Yugoslavian river port of Kladovo, the Danzig Jews waved to waving Jews on the bank: these were the fifty who had been stuck there since December, 1939, and who were shot later on with a thousand other Jews. Some who waved from the bank were related to some who waved from the deck of the *Helios:* brothers sisters parents children . . .

"But couldn't they?"
"Couldn't they make some kind of exchanges?"
"Wasn't the captain a Jew?"

Nonstop to Tulcea in Rumania. Here, on September 11, 3,595 emigrants were transferred to the ocean liners *Atlantic, Pacific,* and *Mylos;* the *Atlantic* took on the Danzig Jews. . . .

∎∎∎∎∎∎∎∎∎

"Did they all want to go to Palestine?"
"Or would they rather have gone back home?"

For a long time a good many of them didn't want what they later had to want. The state of Israel owes its existence to a will so strong that even the weak-willed were carried over the threshold: the will to survive.

When, after the meeting at the Kornhaus, I went for a little walk and bought some mushrooms from a Jewish vendor at the Ulm market, he said to me while weighing them: "Trouble trouble. People don't know what they want. Or they can't want what they'd like to want, namely, to buy from me because it's cheaper."

In his cellar Doubt (who had little other exercise) pursued his will. He wanted something, didn't want something. He wanted to want something, wanted not to want something. And his will to want or not want something was preceded by another will that wanted or didn't want to want something.

When Doubt began to go still further back in pursuit of his will, he found before his will another will to will or not to will something, and this again preceded by a will, after which there again trotted a will to will. As far as he could follow himself, will had been sewn—willfully—into the lining even of his will-lessness.

After peeling the onion, Doubt found it hard to determine where he had wanted to ride his bicycle when he took the road to Karthaus; for he assuredly had not wanted to go to Stomma's.

"Pure chance that I'm here."
"How long are you wanting to stay, if you please?"

"It doesn't depend on what I want."

"Dumb Jew! I'll learn you to want something!"

Yes, children, beatings. In the winter of 1941 to 1942 lots of them. But Doubt didn't want to leave Stomma's cellar. He also didn't want to be a Jew. He told his host at length about pure Mennonite ancestors, who in the sixteenth century had come to the Vistula estuary from Groningen in Holland: "Ever since then, there have been members of my family in Müggenhahl and Nassenhuben, Käsemark and Neuteich. We've always refused to do military service. And in 1780 the Prussians even had to make our exemption from military service official. We Mennonites have always had a will of our own. Even if we wanted to shoot now and then, we never wanted to shoot, and we didn't want to want to shoot either."

But Stomma didn't believe him; he wanted a Jew in his cellar.

17 Before Apollo 11 starts on its way and the Church Congress opens in Stuttgart: on November 24, 1940, the *Pacific*, the *Mylos*, and the *Atlantic* put into the port of Haifa. Across from the *Atlantic* lay the four-stacked *Patria* under steam. By decision of the mandate authority, it was to take almost 4,000 emigrants on board and deport them to a British colony. When, on November 25, the forced embarkation began, a bomb exploded in the *Patria*. Members of the Haganah, the Zionist underground organization, had deposited the bomb in order to prevent the deportation. The *Patria* capsized and sank in five minutes. Two hundred and sixty emigrants, including an unknown number of Danzig Jews were drowned. (The man responsible for the crime is still living in Tel Aviv. No trial was held: something went wrong, but these things happen.) The survivors, including some thirty Danzig Jews, were interned in the Atlit camp and were allowed to stay in Palestine. Despite their resistance, the rest of the emigrants were put aboard the Dutch vessels *Nieuw Zeeland* and *Johan de Witt* by British police. On December 26, both ships dropped anchor off Port Louis, the port of the then British island of Mauritius. (Remember that famous blue stamp, children?) Men and women were interned separately in the prison of Beau Bassin. One hundred and twenty-four deportees, among them several Danzig Jews including Wartski, the shopkeeper, died of malaria and typhoid. The typhoid epidemic had started on board the

Atlantic: a cook had died in the toilet. (The quarantine flag, children, is yellow.) Not until August 26, 1945, did the survivors leave the British island of Mauritius and arrive, on board the *Franconia,* at their destination: the port of Haifa.

I won't say much about it. Apollo 11 will be starting off in a minute. The Stuttgart Church Congress is being held under the motto "Hunger for Justice." Everywhere judgments are being made. How am I to explain why the S.P.D. pins will have orange glass heads?

After another total collision at the corner of Handjerystrasse and Niedstrasse, Bruno said to Anna, "If a blue and a yellow Volkswagen crash, will they be green?" When the colors declared war on each other, gray was the peacemaker. Bruno knows the color theory.

Our campaign is going to be orange. Not only our campaign pins but also our placards, posters, and leaflets: fat and frolicsome, rich in calories. Also paper caps and balloons. The dynamics of dynamics. (It ought to work; it's been tested.)

Seriously, orange was the subject under discussion. In Bonn (in May, I think) Marchand, Linde, Drautzburg, and I sat with Wischnewski, Leo Bauer,* and other election campaign specialists at our long table on Adenauerallee. Cool jugglers of big numbers, unblinking appraisers of groups and trends, purposive pessimists, engaged in metabolism: we ate statistics and excreted forecasts. We filled ash trays and from their overflow read the crucial figure after the decimal point. We speculated: Would Schiller and Brandt, or Brandt and Schiller, or only Brandt or only Schiller with or against Leber and Schmidt, bypassing Wehner or in league with Wehner against

---

* Leo Bauer's political career is described on pages 308–9.

or with Schiller, manage to arrive at a decision on the (crucial) question of revaluation?

Apart from that, we had color samples before us. Since blue leaves people cold, red is regarded as out of date, and yellow is controversial, we spoke long and knowledgeably about the tested attraction of orange; for when immediately after the summer vacation the actual election campaign begins, the Social Democratic Party of Germany is to campaign in orange. Emnid, Infas, and Allenbach* have discovered virtues: it's cheerful and sensuous, makes an active athletic modern impression, attracts the young without repelling the old, radiates maturity and health.

The soft-spoken Werner Müller, who always seems rather out of sorts, as though, afflicted with Doubt's hay fever (he lived withdrawn behind a gauze curtain), put forward the opinion that orange appealed also to melancholics. And someone knew what the morose student Schopenhauer is supposed to have said to Goethe (in sharp opposition to Hegel) about orange and its effect on women, old people, and young voters: more than any other color orange has the faculty of shaping the will. (Going Schopenhauer one better, Wischnewski called it life-affirming.) And so a decision was arrived at for which we shall have to bear responsibility before history (that bugaboo). No contrary votes. Even Wehner, it appeared, had not come out directly against orange.

But Doubt, whose opinion and cellar experience are worth at least an aside, gave me (through Gaus) winkingly to understand that, when all is said and done, orange is simply an alias for gray.

In April I had accepted an invitation to read and engage in discussion at the Evangelical Church Congress in Stuttgart. (A

---

* Public opinion analysts.

letter from Professor von Hentig urgently requested my presence.) Anyone who was there will remember how swelteringly in those midsummer days righteousness (and the hunger for it) weighed on the Killesberg. Ten thousand had come: well-wrapped souls, seekers with billeting orders. All were in a sweat: concern and happiness, Jesus and the sorry state of the church, ecumenical considerations and commitment oozed from their pores. Aimless youngsters went about barefoot in early Christian style. The sayings of the minor and major prophets were served up and cleared away. (Though absent, pillars and dwellers on pillars were conceivable.) Signs indicated in which hall the motions of hope were to be brought to a vote. (Resolutions to determine the way to happiness.) For four whole days the controversy over Jesus (born of the Virgin Mary) lingered on the agenda. Syllable-splitting exegetes: everyone had read his Bible, each a different Bible; some had read Marx, each a different Marx. When the church opened itself, it emptied itself. Everything (not only happiness and the Cross) was discussed. The subconscious found expression in chanting. Community was sought in common: evangelical fug.

I read in Hall I, to a working group dedicated to "the Individual and His Fellow Men." Two thousand individuals had come. I read about Scherbaum, the high school student who wanted to burn his dachshund. Since everything was discussed, ritualized protest was also discussed. Large numbers of barefooted and, now that it's too late, Early Christian young people are thirsting for a new myth, yearning to believe something; having glimpsed paradise, they will jump over the barrier of reason. . . .

You see, children, the word "paradise" frightens my snail. Listening to the heralds of paradisiacal conditions, it shrivels up. For it remembers only too well the strict requirements for admittance and the obscurantist house rules. It knows what total banishment awaits those whose conduct is unsuited to paradise.

I have to admit that I was curious: I sent my snail out on reconnaissance. While in Hall I, amid righteously distributed heat, I inveighed against ritualized protest (and also declined to call the self-immolation of the Prague student Jan Palach an edifying example). My snail visited other working groups. Thanks to this division of labor, we were everywhere. . . . (Even with the group industriously discussing "Jews and Christians.")

"And then what? What happened then?" Then Augst happened.

Long before he took the floor in the discussion I'm going to tell you about, Augst, always under a different name, had spoken in other discussions.

I'd known him a long time. In Delmenhorst, Mainz, or Ulm we might have winked to each other as old acquaintances. When he doesn't turn up, I miss him: without Augst something seems lacking.

When at the Church Congress he really did speak (and also act), his action did not surprise me: it had been may times announced. I knew the excitability of quinquagenarians who want to unload and expunge everything, but everything, in a single brimful confession. I know the empty gestures with which they invoke values, their war-album dream of defending lost positions singlehanded (as once upon a time at Mount Cassino or the Kuban bridgehead), I know how they reach into the air for support, how their fluttering voices cry out for "a unified and eternal Germany!" and how the rising heat of passion makes their faces break out in spots.

I also knew, since both are ageless, the younger Augst before the elder began to speak. Both bear witness to the absolute. Both crave annihilation and redemption. Both are determined to squeeze out truth: a difficult and unsuccessful bowel movement. They lack the evenly circulating warmth of conspiratorial communities; the elder Augst lost it at the end of the war; the younger Augst hopes to find it in the wake of a, so he believes, imminent revolution. I heard them singing a duet about ultimate goals and the joy of losing themselves in a common cause; long before Augst spoke . . .

When I spoke against it at the Church Congress, the ritual had already been prepared. Not unsuspecting, no, with a concern that has become habitual, I spoke words of reason, but too late. When Augst took the floor, I recognized him by his headlong, syntax-rejecting speech. Nor was there anything new about his crumpling of notes, his long-winded confusion, the embarrassment he created. The increasing restlessness of the barefooted younger generation was to me an everyday sound: laughter and heckling. (As expected, Professor Hartmut von Hentig admonished the young people; as expected, the young people complied with his request "for a little more tolerance.") It all developed like a Passion play, where knowledge of the action is taken for granted.

Augst stood behind the number two microphone in the center aisle. I leave out the trimmings. He began by attacking the church for rejecting his fellowship. Cramped by his word rubble, he spoke of lost soldierly comradeship. He deplored loss of values. He regretted that no one had taught him and his generation (the war generation) to talk freely, like the young people today, to unburden themselves. He said still more and repeated himself. It is impossible to reproduce what he said,

because he tangled himself up in the underbrush, and his confusion was pathetic. I can only list: whole-hearted commitment, left in the lurch, bear witness, unstinting loyalty, selfless
sacrifice like the youth protest movement, in other words, total,
to make myself heard . . .

Only at the end did his stammered clearance sale get back
on the tracks. He had prepared his conclusion, and he leapt
into it. Without rummaging in his notes, he said, "Now I've
got a provocation for you: I salute my comrades of the SS."

Seated on the platform, I took it down. As though the scene
had been rehearsed, his words found their response; for the
booing of the barefooted young people was also a part of the
ritual, of the Passion. He had struck the sensitive spot. Booing
as obedient reflex. And even my attempt to stop the programmed happening with the usual arguments, with my lack-
luster snail experience, became a part of his Passion ritual.

Others spoke up in their thirst for righteousness. A plea
went out for a naked "New Man." Those on the platform were
frankly embarrassed. Professor von Hentig suffered publicly.
Professor Becker tried to arbitrate. And I didn't jump up
either to stop him. (Later on, a columnist wrote: "That was
direct rank-and-file democracy, a far cry from the usual consumer indifference.")

I've already told you, children. It was very hot at the
Evangelical Church Congress. The subconscious was handed
around like a sudarium. Someone in the middle of the hall
shouted, "Quick! A doctor!"

When the awkward incident was announced from the plat-
from, the meeting was considered closed. For once the youthful

Early Christians refrained—despite their thirst for righteousness—from collecting autographs.

Booed off the floor in his lifetime. Furnished a brief unambiguous explanation. Not even mourning can save its clothes: giggles burst seams, reveal flesh. Where does passing laughter go?

It wasn't the heat. It wasn't a fainting spell. Afterward, many claimed to have seen that Augst had a small bottle in his hand while speaking. Someone had noticed concave facets. A girl student had been struck by the black screw top. Conceivably someone knows still more or something else. There were said to be traces somewhere, but no one remembers: traces of what?

The pharmacist Manfred Augst left a wife and four children. Two small bottles were mentioned in the statement of the Stuttgart police. The unused bottle, it was reported, contained prussic acid.

Augst died on the way to Robert Bosch Hospital. The headlines read: "The Last Argument: Suicide"—"A Lonely Man Takes Cyanide"—"Unnoticed By All: Death"—"Suicide Casts Its Shadow on the Church Congress." In the weekly *Christ und Welt* Maria Stein headed her article: "Ritualized Protest."

Augst was fifty-six. He died on July 19, 1969, after the spaceship Apollo 11 was launched at Cape Kennedy, after it covered (by the following day) half the distance to the moon, after (on the third day) the lunar module "Eagle" (termed Lem) was inspected for the last time, and some two hours before the rocket burn swung the manned spaceship into an elliptical orbit around the moon.

■■■■■■■■■

We saw it on the television screen that evening at the home of Klett, the publisher. (Forward! The goals are painting their faces, putting on red, not orange.) Aboard Apollo 11 all were well. Party chitchat about the Church Congress. (Redemption, merely a question of colors by now.) Maneuvering rockets were fired. In muffled tones a few of the guests discussed the God concept in Karl Barth. Nibbling pretzel sticks. (Who can speak of truth and falsehood when the facts speak in simultaneous translation?) Augst too, of course, came up in the conversation. Nibbling peanuts. (Someone succeeded in jumping over his shadow. Now they're all practicing, and hoping again.) Aldrin, or was it Armstrong, told a joke that people on earth were supposed to laugh at. (So we'll stick to orange.) I looked for an encyclopedia among Klett's books: something about prussic acid. Nibbling almonds. (There's no such thing as pain, only remedies for pain.) So many nice young people. Klett's daughters, the girl student from Prague. Nibble nibble. Then potato salad was served, and Apollo 11 suffered a blip. In a cracked voice that seemed punctuated by headache, Professor von Hentig asked himself and the guests where the limits of education were to be sought. The answers were vague. Only Ehmke knew where. I was reading the encyclopedia. Jäckel senior said, "Come on, let's go."

Potassium cyanide, a salt of prussic acid (HCN) is released by the gastric acids and kills by paralyzing the nervous arrangements of the heart and respiration. Eighty bitter almonds contain 60 milligrams of prussic acid, the fatal dose. (The almond as metaphor: quotations from Celan.) In autopsy, the smell of bitter almonds in the cranial cavity reveals the cause of death. In Augst's case the symptoms of asphyxia by poisoning were listed: forced breathing, diminished breathing, loss of consciousness, convulsions, cessation of breathing.

18   I put it down, creeping sole and all, on the bunker which, off kilter and deprived of its field of fire, has survived amid dunes: unsalable and hard to demolish. (Should I, because this is a slug, a naked snail, design the Atlantic Wall bunker as a home and sketch in every detail? Sight slits, concrete shapes, high-grade German construction?)

While next day I was flying from Stuttgart to Paris with my bag, Aldrin and Armstrong were climbing into the Lem, Collins remained alone in the command module, I made a note in my waste book about my visit to Thaddäus Troll with Jäckel senior, wove inserts about Kiesinger's "No!" to revaluation of the Deutschmark into the speech I had written in the Volkswagen bus, inserted Czechoslovakian afterthoughts (Anna and Vladimir sitting on the stairs talking in Nouzov), and by writing escaped into a snail landscape, but despite my elaborate attempts to get away from him, Augst refused to be avoided. Not until Lamballe, where Anna, Raoul, and Bruno were waiting for me on the station platform and Raoul assailed me with the latest—"Man, the landing craft is blasting off in half an hour!"—did it look as if Augst might let me walk barefoot at low tide, swim on my back at high tide, broil mackerel, steam mussels, go about with sand in my pockets, and take a vacation in Brittany.

■■■■■■■■■

I didn't tell you much. Yes, there were questions—"Did you, were you, did you know him?"—but how could I talk about potassium cyanide and the death of the pharmacist from Tübingen at a time when the moon and on the moon those two men in their enormous shoes had priority?

The owner of the house is in the amusement business and during the summer travels from fair to fair. I think he must operate one of those clicking lottery wheels, because the whole place is full of china goldfish and suchlike prizes. There's a tide table hanging in the kitchen-living room—we cook with bottled gas—of our rented summer cottage.

If Augst had been asked who and what had been to blame for his death, mention might have been made of the weather: the heat was to blame.

What else? And who else?

Conditions in the past and now.

Who in the past? What now?

In the past, teachers, school; now, the system, the systems: Communism, capitalism. At an early age coercion: piano lessons.

And even before that, at the beginning?

His mother, because his father. Then, by extension, not only the weather, but also advertising, the well-known subversive author behind the microphone, the numerous ice cream vendors at the Church Congress. In a nutshell, the society of consumption and the city of Stuttgart.

In other words, dependence on and the repression of all . . . Yes, indeed. The proverbial and fashionable alienation plausible to everyone who owns an ignition key. (Also his

167

needs, pathetic in the first place, which found no, or only belated, and then inadequate satisfaction.)

Weak warped lopsided, nonexistent or repressed, in any case false consciousness.

But what of heredity and original sin?

Yes, of course. His father, because his mother.

And who else? And what else?

The political parties, "they" up top, money, the machine, the geographical situation, the liberals. At an early age, a stomach ulcer and the intermediate examination. Then the lost war, and the whole infamous caboodle: freemasons, Jews, bureaucrats. Later on, women (several, but one in particular). Today, the general glut, the prevailing injustice, the lack of hospitals schools housing laws, the absence of higher values and inner meaning.

In other words, life? Everything? The whole shebang.

Yes. But especially the weather (and schoolteachers) because the heat and all those students and agitators behind the microphones.

In other words, everybody but himself?

The Church Congress and the public.

God, because for His sake the Church Congress and the public, while the ice cream vendors were making their crummy little deals with the heat . . .

Would Augst have said ". . . and my family" if he had been asked about guilt and the guilty? Later on, I asked Frau Augst and Augst's sons. "He was a sick man," said Frau Augst in Tübingen. "We tried everything, but he got more and more depressed. . . ."

How it creeps across the horizon and stretches it: without smoke trail, headed for the Channel Islands or farther.

168

Now at high tide I could simply deny everything. I don't want what I know. Refuse to shake hands with myself. Or drink cider with Doubt. We take a formal tone with one another; each pays his own check. He wants what I don't know.

The village to which we carry the mussels, snail shells, and corroded thoughts that we gather at low tide is called Plurien. Slate covers granite: layers of gray, white joints. Near the church (and the monument commemorating two World Wars) three butchers have set up their stalls: buy tripe for today, calf's head for tomorrow. (How imposingly Madame Hénaff folds her arms outside her *charcuterie*.) When we come from the ocean, before choosing to see the church steeple, we see the white water tower of Plurien.

We two beachcombers, casters of shadows. Back and forth along the bay, waiting much too long before smearing our backs, et cetera, with Nivea. Between low and high tide we talk ideas into the ground. (While the creeks are still running down, the sea starts rising.) "And you call that dialectics?" says Doubt, plodding along.

Why wouldn't I let my snail climb the Plurien water tower as it rises pale against the sky—on the side (for visibility)?

"You see," says Doubt, "I can't believe this vertical nonsense." He's carrying his sunburn back and forth. He's already begun to peel. The children laugh, meaning me. "That's what you get. Why do you drag him out of his cellar?" (As if my tortuous principle had no right to vacation and exercise.)

Now at low tide along the beach: my side to the sea, his to the promenade. At the breakwater we turn back. I now on his, he now on mine. Our friendship is used to mockery. We search in clumps of seaweed, bend down, find something. Not a word about tracks in the moon dust.

Now at high tide our findings are gradually obliterated. Franz and Raoul have left the lunar module with Donald Duck. Bruno, too, has had a soft landing. At the edges of craters in the Sea of Tranquillity Laura finds solemn-looking goats that seem to be made of glass. ("What about snails? Aren't there any slugs at least?") My stage props move and claim to be perceptible. Anna hears how many visitors Dürer's *Melencolia* admits with indifference and feeds with gall-bitter implications.

Someone has put a ladder up against the house and has ventured heavenward.

Likewise ascending from left to right: the scales, the hourglass, the bell on their nails. What weighs, runs, is silent and signifies.

With insufficient exercise a young lady has grown bulky. Now she sits in chronic dejection and offers bric-a-brac (from estate sales).

So far no buyers have come into the picture. Nobody wants to burden himself with significance. What remain true to themselves: white elephants.

(Plurien also maintains an antique shop across the street from the Café des Sports: spinning wheels, Breton milking stools, waffle irons, pestles without mortars—mortars without pestles.)

At last the tourists arrive.

Under the flat roofs of bungalows with Scandinavian furniture, where coolness sets the tone and the modern style does its best to demonstrate that it hasn't had a drop to drink, rare pieces are to be seen in tabernacle-sized niches. We collect systematically at random. Along with our little everyday finds, we pick up Melencolia's household utensils.

Maybe I could start something like this in Nuremberg: "When, ladies and gentlemen, the spaceship Apollo 11 released the lunar module and in it two men with their offerings, not only did Armstrong and Aldrin plant the medallion and the flag and deposit the sensitive instruments of today; scales, hourglass, and bell also took their meaningful places, and with gloved finger one of the men—Armstrong—traced the master's initials, the A and the D, in the moon dust. . . ."

The two of us practiced in the sand: looking for shelter between widespread legs. (Our hide-in-the-cellar morality.)

Or this detail: the notched sword. (Dürer found it in the Emperor Maximilian's armory. He bought it for the price of junk and on the advice of Melencolia—who rests her right leg, which is too short from the knee down, on its two-handed hilt—placed it parallel to the hem of her skirt and beside the dull plane.)

I have known sharp thoughts that, weary of their sharpness, stepped out into the open, several times cleft the air unrefuted, once vigilantly circled the house, met my friend Doubt on the way, and came back in full of notches. (Open a junk business: Hegel for sale.)

But, all right, have it your way: he's back in his cellar again. In 1941, after a hundred weeks of subtenancy, Anton Stomma made his guest a Christmas present of a still serviceable heirloom, which he had accepted from a soldier's widow (in Ramkau) in payment for a bicycle pump. (Bathed in gasoline, it lost its rust, became receptive to the hand, let itself be opened, and, honed on leather, acquired new sharpness.)

By summer, 1941, Doubt's supply of Rotbart razor blades, calculated to last a year, had run out. Since then he had sat, first stubbly, then sparsely bearded, on his beach-grass mattress, plucking and pulling, until Stomma, infected with Christmas spirit, had presented him with the open razor on a bed of evergreen, along with a piece of crumb cake.

Because Raoul insists on the cellar, I'll show you Doubt lying smooth-shaven on his mattress and—his face to the damp north wall—no longer plucking, but scratching, because time has attacked him like scabies: he's flaking and itching all over. To combat the itch of time, he recites everything he can think of: all the medicinal herbs, every species of fern and plantain, all the women he has ever tried to crawl into, all the systems and their philosophers, followed by those who laid the trap of ridicule for them—the independent thinker Georg Christoph Lichtenberg, the memo mill Jean Paul—and finally meets his poodle-loving friend, a sourpuss fundamentally hostile to systems. They exchange observations. They cultivate observation until knowledge, partial knowledge, is achieved. (As Doubt and I walk along the beach at low tide, so—easily imaginable —do he and he sit in Stomma's cellar.) Doubt reports on the unintentional relations between hermaphrodite snails and Melancholy, Schopenhauer on the will of climbing plants, be they peas, beans, or hops, to describe circular movements in the air until they find a solid body to twine around, if they do find one.

No, children, honest to goodness: in the cellar. Doubt is trying to be a tendril. Already his thinking is elliptoid. But no prop is available; for even if we crystallize our hope into a principle, it refuses to serve as a solid body. Whatever may twine in its directions, it won't support so much as a bean.

(Only Baron Münchhausen succeeded in breeding a climbing plant, which after untiring circular movement found the moon and grabbed hold; that had consequences.)

In the meantime, man has set foot on it. I won't laugh; it's your moon. Only allow me to exchange the geometrical object in Dürer's engraving (it dominates the middle ground) for a space capsule. And admit it: it's a pretty boring business, the way it drags along from blip to blip. At the launching the disappointment when everything, as always, goes off smoothly. And the speech balloon language. You can do it better. When Raoul holds his nose and practices the countdown: ". . . six five four . . ." Come on, it's low tide. We'll search the creeks for abalone and the clumps of seaweed for dream snails. Maybe we'll find a whelk—or two. Maybe contradictions will add up to something. Maybe the solution is lying around in the sand. (And the bundle of keys remains to be interpreted.)

When soon after his mother's death Albrecht Dürer began, on a Monday morning composed of sunshine, chatter, and laughter, to engrave the *Melencolia* on copper after preparatory sketches, he found, in the folds of a drapery study, a bundle of keys belonging to Agnes, his cantankerous wife. The intricate key bits amused Dürer; and now we are free to guess what doors and caskets are intended and whether Saturn was the locksmith.

Panofsky and Saxl presume that the bundle of keys means domination and secular power. I translate into the language of daily life: the parents (both of them) have jobs; since they are away from home for nine hours every day, they hang the house keys (usually on shoelaces) around their children's necks. Such children are easily recognized. Everywhere—though nowhere engraved on copper—they play the part of melancholy adults. (Raoul is friends with a few of them on Niedstrasse and meets key children in your no man's land or on Perelsplatz.)

But supposing it's all a lie, simulated in the television studios? Supposing they're not on the moon at all? That the moon dust and craters are a fake? And the Sea of Tranquillity a backdrop? That the Russians and the Amis have a secret agreement to telecast the phony achievements of cosmic *détente?* That the superpowers helpfully make up records for each other, while the little fellows look on with impoverished, well-behaved amazement?

They're still backing and filling about the mark: to revalue or not to revalue! When Barzel says, "In all sincerity." Small potatoes. I cook ray; it has a fresh, pungent smell of iodine. I'm writing in the shadow of the lopsided bunker.

Doubt raises his head. In full ash trays everything is being proved. Every pot found its lid. Called by its first name, the secret cried: Here!

We chatted (over Breton cider) and argued (at low tide on the beach) about the tongs below the hem of the skirt, about the magic number square and the compass, about allegorical interpretation in general. We quoted Benjamin and Proust, the conservative Gehlen and his leftist pupil Lepenies,* Doubt (with special enthusiasm), his poodle-loving Schopenhauer, and I (with special enthusiasm) Lichtenberg, the hunch-backed master of homely truths. We mentioned (in passing) the Emperor Maximilian's circle of humanists and were both familiar with Dürer's statements about the "fourfold com-

---

* Arnold Gehlen, sociology professor with strong rightist leanings; Wolf Lepenies, sociologist, disciple of Gehlen.

plex." We avoided the present, and it punished us with ignorance of the past.

Discussed were: first, the number square as the artist's signature; second, Saturn as principle; third, the European Enlightenment on its way to surfeit with knowledge; fourth, melancholy as social behavior; fifth, Dürer's ailment, the yellow spot; and sixth, although we were trying to avoid the present, the promise of happiness and prohibition of melancholy in Communist countries.

Doubt was mostly against. Concepts irritated him. He rented a loudspeaker car normally used for advertising (Dubonnet, Butagaz) and in Plurien, Plévenon, and Erquy harbor, on promenades and on the beach at low tide proclaimed fundamental doubt: already tar was coming in with the tide, already there was talk of premature departure, already the bathing season was under suspicion of melancholy.

What makes it so humorless and tense? Why does its (promised) happiness express itself so grimly? What has driven the good cheer out of socialism and taught it the (manly) earnestness that vinegars all fun and wants to explain it (as useful)?

We examine the picture postcard of an engraving. After the proportions have been measured and Doubt has knowledgeably mentioned the relations between Albrecht Dürer and Nicholas Cusanus, our beachcomber's humor gets uptight and teeters on the brink. Laughter boils down, thickens. Desperate wit at high tide. (Dangerous to go swimming right now.)

Shooting at a snail. Breathing exercises. Even Doubt is losing weight.

■■■■■■■■■

He gets beatings. In the spring of 1942, lots of them. With the belt, with a bicycle spoke. His tone—that fervid grumbling—was found distasteful. "Nice," he said, "but disappointing." In his cellar, Doubt couldn't hear the wind. "Outside," he said, "nothing is in keeping with the facts."

Or he laughed for no apparent reason. Only after repeated threats and belt loosenings—"What is there to giggle about?" —did he show surprise: "My absolute craving for peppermint drops: Don't you think it's funny?"

Every time Doubt was beaten, he was embarrassed by the pause after the blows. Stomma breathed heavily and sympathetically. Doubt's attempts to fill in the hole: "Please, let's talk about something else, something banal and without ambiguity: the German victories in the Caucasus, for instance."

Mail, forwarded. Suggestions that I should make a definitive statement about everything. "What in your opinion would be the maximal solution of a) the war in Vietnam, b) the population explosion in underdeveloped countries, c) the problem of the two Germanies?" I don't know anything maximal. I'd rather watch Anna, working out her ballets far away on the beach. (All alone with herself. "Don't call, children, don't call.")

Nature, the backward pupil. Don't trust speculative thinkers. Since they don't look, they see everything total and judge it totally. Their racket is totality. There they stand, Germans with a mission, determined to drum dialectical materialism into the ocean as far as the eye can see; it's got to tally with the system. . . .

Out of inclination or just for the hell of it, Doubt in his cellar thought up systems in order to confute them. The honeycomb system, the system with tubes. For his nonstop escalator system he received medium blows. And while Stomma made his bicycle spoke sing, he heard Doubt recant: "It's all speculation." (Later, he wrote in his diary: "There is no system, because there are several. Even snails hesitate to take themselves in an absolute sense.") The partly good-natured Stomma had made him a present of a new school copybook.

Something that (who?) ought to write about: someone has had a strict Catholic upbringing, has in his student years lost his faith but not his need for religion, has done all right for several years as an ironic freethinker, turns (fed up with his irony) Communist against his better judgment, and reverts to being the believer he was brought up to be. (As a parallel, someone converted from Communism to Catholicism: nothing simpler.)

Draw a two-shelled snail.

And on a Monday, children, a Monday like today—the day on which Aldrin and Armstrong have returned to their lunar module and are comfortable again—Doubt won his host over to a system that had Doubt's cellar as its center and was called the "boxes-inside-boxes system." No sooner had Stomma been won over than his guest refuted the "cellar as such" and the system derived from it. (Hard blows for Doubt.) Afterward he made the notation: "Saw the shell in two."

So they've done it. At a seaside café we see little on the screen, and what we do see has the wobbles. The tide said more. We made lovely fresh tracks in the sand. While swimming, I tried to laugh under water. The newspapers offered opinions about the Defregger case: executions, orders from above, and questions of conscience—the war experiences of a suffragan bishop.* We drove to Cape Fréhel, admired the lighthouse, shouted something at the seagulls, stood slanting against the wind. (While we were visiting the medieval Fort de la Latte, I swiped some of the rosemary that grows above the dungeons and torture chambers.) For you I cooked sea bream and blubbery St. Peter's fish. I laid fresh sardines and mackerel on the grill. We ate morays, rays, and octopus. I steamed cockles and mussels in white wine. Praires we ate raw, with lemon. The foot of the abalone must be cut out of its shell-like case, wrapped in a cloth, pounded until soft, well washed, and steamed in butter with garlic and finely chopped parsley. In boiling salt water the giant sea spider was shocked and changed color. Its broth: stock for fish soups to which saffron is added. For you, children, pale-green smelts fried in oil until crisp. In the evening we enjoyed pelican's feet, those small umbilicate snails. (Cook's dialectic: the sea and its offerings.)

Before I grow old and possibly wise, I mean to write a narrative cookbook: about ninety-nine dishes, about guests, about man as an animal who can cook, about the eating process, about scraps . . .

On the last day of vacation, when the suffragan bishop Defregger was still holy and the scientists had already begun to evaluate the rocks brought back from the moon, the French franc was devaluated: which had consequences for us—in the election campaign.

---

* Matthias D. Defregger, one of the auxiliary bishops of the archdiocese of Munich-Freising, officer during the Second World War, at the time accused of involvement in the shooting of Italian hostages during the retreat of the German Army, that is, "passing on orders" that led to the execution.

19 We met him and his wife in the rain a few days before our departure. At the moment he is ambassador extraordinary and is suspected on principle. He, too, wanted to do nothing for a few days, just take a rest and read the Breton Chateaubriand.

His nose might have grown in a stalactite cave. Drips unguarded, needs no nose protector. Bruno made a grab at it, called it funny. (In Sterne it would have been good for a whole chapter. His Uncle Toby would have addressed it as a bug, Lichtenberg, with feeling, as a torn-off fly button.) Bruno is right. As a clown he would have fewer enemies. Even the Bavarians might like him, because his nose—a comical case of sorrowful individualization—is so absolutely predominant.

Always when I see him (and I've been seeing him on his creeping sole for the last ten years) scenes come to me for an old-fashioned silent film with St. Vitus's dance; he appears as a flannel-gray hero (wearing a vest over a discreet paunch); strangely solitary, talkative only by implication, he travels with a patent-leather suitcase, to Russia in the wintertime, for instance. He is always getting into danger: on endless carpets, while buying a fur cap, in stalled elevators, at conference tables that sink through the floor, while tasting caviar which, as samplings demonstrate later on, contains built-in listening devices. But on the screen we see him wordlessly sharing all perils: a snail that knows how to keep moving—especially at the negotiating table.

Today, still quietly on the move; then, impossible to locate on the beach. In the evening we got together in our rented kitchen-living room. I showed what Linde and Marchand had sent: the second issue of *dafür*, our campaign paper. Terse praise, precise objections. He considered helping us indirectly, via the back door which, as everyone knows, can be an entrance as well as an exit.

There is something Leporello-like about his relation to Willy—even when he is soberly interpreting diplomatic notes: he knows all about deviousness (and is consequently regarded as devious).

When I asked him, "How does it look? Will we make it?" he said after a pause, during which I heard the snail creeping across a coalition bulletin: "If Willy, who can't fail to see that de facto there's nothing solid behind him but the wall, I won't say gives up his playing with matches for good but at least breaks it off for the time being; if—which only Schiller can prevent—the party is given credit for Schiller's success, and if the weather on election day, without being too good, is not definitely bad, then just barely, then we might just barely . . ."

Bruno, who was listening to us, manifested his confidence with both hands. (Frau Bahr was glad there was no cellar under our kitchen-living room; as a precaution, I had even looked through the products of my collector's zeal, sea shells and snail shells: There were no keenly listening hermit crabs.)

By the way, children, Doubt bears a certain incidental resemblance to him: in my silent film, I hear the two of them talking about the nature of hermaphrodites, about transformation through proximity.

Unfortunately, my vacation is over: Straubing, Weissenburg, Röthenbach, Erlangen . . . Unfortunately (by Drautz-
burgian detours) Nuremberg gets bypassed.

Bruno likes to say "unfortunately." He got it from Laura.
Laura got it from Franz or Raoul.

But none of you said "unfortunately" as often and as *à
propos* as Bruno does.

"It's my tricycle, unfortunately."

"In the third place, you started it, unfortunately."

"I got an extra stick of chewing gum, unfortunately."

He places that word as a keystone; it can't be refuted, unfortunately.

This one word is the sum total of his politeness. Like the
strong silent men in classical Westerns, who drop their "sorry"
after a crushing straight to the chin, Bruno casually says
"unfortunately" when something tastes good, amuses him, or
strikes him as pretty: "I think it's nice, unfortunately."

The pleasant and its echo.

(As embarrassed victors, after winning the elections, try to
say "unfortunately.")

Even on his birthday Bruno said, "It's my birthday today,
unfortunately." And in introducing me to a visitor (with
flowers for Anna), my youngest son said, "This is my father,
unfortunately."

Sorrow—one need only displace it—cancels itself out; now
I'm going to write about happiness, unfortunately.

In Straubing I was happy. (There black is adorned with gilt
and set in baroque frames.) Loud-mouthed anxiety in regional
jackets. Because the famous Gäubodenfest was in progress, our
candidate expected the hall to be only half full; and at first, to
be sure, there was only a moderate trickle. (Implicit faith
won't do; it's got to be childlike. "Don't worry. By the time

we've finished our beer, they'll be arriving in droves.") When the Kronensaal was full to bursting, Otto Wittmann was fit to be tied; his happiness communicated itself by mere taps on shoulders. Even his party secretary, who had warned him, first against me as an individual and second against holding a meeting with me, seems—as witnesses reported later—to have been pretty well pleased, unfortunately.

So after the meeting we went to the Gäubodenfest. I took several rides on the merry-go-round: a pleasure so roundly and senselessly enjoyable that it's not mentioned in Marx and can therefore be termed "socially irrelevant." (Later, the roller coaster: Drautzburg begged off.)

Craving for calves' feet. Afterward, I with my blue-and-white tie with the lozenge design, was put under a Bavarian hat, equipped with a baton, lifted onto the platform, and, in a beer tent (as spacious as the Cologne cathedral, though not so mystically high), asked in Bavarian to conduct an Austrian march (Radetzky). What happiness to be allowed to have stage fright. The *Kapellmeister* was satisfied, though I had forced the tempo like a Prussian.

Then a Social Democratic schoolteacher, who had come down from the woods (and knew himself to be a damnable anomaly in his part of the country), taught me how to hold beer mugs and set them to the lips. Then I autographed female Bavarian arms (above the elbow) with a soft felt pen: fun for all. Then somebody wanted to tussle with me, but the comrades at the table took care of that most expeditiously. Then we went somewhere else, because the merry-go-round hadn't stopped being roundly unreasonably enjoyable. (Definitely petit bourgeois, unfortunately. Assimilated, pre-empted by the system.)

"And how was it in Weissenburg?"

"There was a new and acoustically perfect gymnasium."

"Were you happy again and stuff?"

"A bit of an aftertaste. The Junge Union—three rows strong—dissociated themselves from Strauss and his Bamberg animal metaphor."

"How will they vote now, if they vote?"

"Black, of course, the way they've learned to. They're just nice kids, worried about their pocket money."

"And how was it in Röthenbach?"

"In the afternoon I delivered my Volkswagen bus speech."

"What's it about?"

"About everything that comes to me when Drautzburg is driving and I'm stretched out in back, wondering what's supposed to be so Christian about Strauss and Kiesinger and Barzel."

"And Erlangen? Nothing doing there either?"

"Nothing, though Drautzburg was afraid the S.D.S. and its radical bees would come buzzing around our ears. But they didn't come. Still on vacation. Soy-bean cutlets . . ."

Today, not sure who would touch it, I cooked it some more; in West Prussia a four-pound chunk of cow's udder was cooked for five and a half hours until firm enough to slice, yet tender.

As a child I ate cow's udder with my grandmother. I was afraid I'd grow teats.

Our candidate in Erlangen is a man named Haack, the gentle, tenacious sort. Might barely slip through for a direct mandate. Voters' club in the making, said (promised) the superlatively pregnant Veronika Schröder, looking past me— but there was nobody there. Or maybe something in the wrong direction. Sometimes her cross-eyed gaze. Sees several realities at once. The Saxon woman from over there, née Hentschke.

The smell, in which bay leaves and cloves, mustard seed and cayenne predominated at first, was pleasant for an hour or so, then became increasingly definite to pungent; aging cheese, stale milk. (Breweries also like to surround themselves with a cheese smell.)

The consequence of cooking cow's udder: a badly ventilated dairy sent its vapors up the stairs and through the house. Too late Anna opened the transom with the broom handle and emphatically turned on the ventilator.

"Ugh, it stinks!"

"I don't want it, take it away."

"Eat it yourself."

"It's foul."

"Like Raoul's feet."

"Look who's talking."

"Ugh!"

After a while I added onions, soup greens, and vinegar. The cheese smell was still present, but less overpowering.

Sour aftertaste (not to mention the foretaste) or not, we'll have to eat it.

Because daily, after an emergency slaughtering in Seeresen, Doubt in his cellar ate pickled cow's udder such as we'll be eating tomorrow.

In exchange for two bicycle tubes Stomma had laid in a supply.

Now it's cooling: well cooked and shrunken.

For a whole week the host served his guest cubes of cow's udder, floating in their broth and, grown unrecognizable, denying their origin.

Doubt said: "Why not? What's wrong with udder? The smell—as if diapers (or even my quilt) had been boiled—is deceptive. What harm can there be in these relatively tasteless blobs? At the worst they suggest flabby but easily digestible veal."

Pleased with Doubt's encouraging words, Stomma ladled out

more and more, and on the following Sunday served him a good thick slice: breaded cow's udder, fried a delicate brown. With feed potatoes, which with udder broth poured over them smelled less like an open potato pit and tasted only faintly of sprouts.

After the meal Doubt, as usual, read the paper to his host. The situation on the eastern front was stabilized. Mention was made of planned retreats and successful defensive actions. After the udder dinner, an atmosphere of stable warmth and shelter, a feeling verging on happiness diffused itself in Doubt's cellar. Stomma made himself comfortable by loosening his belt two notches and recited, with Baltic pronunciation, a few Latin phrases that Doubt, while the Caucasus offensive was in progress, had taught him by way of compensation. (*Cogito ergo sum. Carthaginem esse delendam.*) Then Doubt read crudely amusing items from the feature section of the *Danziger Vorposten*. Something about a butcher who would rather have been a watchmaker but had no hand for small fragile things. Stomma laughed and rubbed his thighs; Lisbeth giggled at entirely different passages.

How they tell each other jokes, sink into gloom, get drunk, brag of dangers, take leaks, fly at each other and rub thighs, naked and magnificently indigent: sometime, I don't know when, I'll write a book—*Father's Day*—located in Berlin, and on Ascension Day devoted exclusively to cubical men. . . .

Or: suppose Doubt had had a sister, whom I am unable to visualize. Suppose Doubt's sister, younger than he, had traced Doubt (to his cellar). Suppose Doubt's sister (who did not exist) had suddenly turned up in the cellar.

Or write a poem titled "Between." (When in Erlangen I, between myself and . . .)

185

········

Always when Doubt read the newspaper to his host, he had to read between the lines. He also made slight changes in the daily Wehrmacht communiqué, calling a retreat not planned but precipitate, seasoning the evacuation of a bridgehead with heavy losses, supplementing U-boat successes with losses of U-boats, not lying but (as we do when we read the *Frankfurter Allgemeine*) reading between the lines of the *Vorposten*. When German victories became more and more nonexistent, when in the winter of 1942 the ground was laid for a defeat that began in January, 1943, and was called Stalingrad, Doubt's situation in the cellar began—with occasional reverses —to improve: Stomma spared his belt, ceased to strike with singing bicycle spokes, served his guest less cow's udder and feed turnips, more spareribs and cabbage. On Sundays a table-cloth. And when Stomma went upstairs, the stable lantern stayed in the cellar. He donated an old sweater against the cold, a tear-off calendar against time; and from February on, he regularly sent his daughter Lisbeth to the cellar to lie down on Doubt's mattress and to take him in. (But melancholy feels only itself.)

When Lisbeth Stomma went down to the cellar to join Doubt, she unbuttoned her smock while still on the stairs. Doubt couldn't summon up the will to say no when between table and mattress, slowly, with forlorn consecutiveness, she removed her clothing piece by piece. Usually she said, "Father wants me to." And sometimes she said, "Father's gone out on his bike. He says to look after you." Only once, so it appears, did Lisbeth Stomma ask first if he wanted to be looked after.

(Whatever evasions he sought, whether on the way to Melancholy's lead chambers or soaring to Utopia's hermaphroditic heights, the truth of the matter is that in either case he wanted

186

to be taken in by a woman.) Doubt let himself be taken and took, just as he had taken the razor, the tear-off calendar, and the matted sweater; but he did not confine himself to taking.

Lisbeth was better-looking recumbent. Plenty of sleepy flesh, blondely downy, and motionless. Above Lisbeth, who never closed her eyes and always saw something different, there hung, pasted on cardboard to the left of the window, Doubt's hand-colored print representing a snail carrying its house, and to the right of the window, likewise on cardboard (and now spotted with mold) his reproduction of the *Melencolia*. Long out of the habit—for he had even given up masturbating—Doubt quickly got back into the habit. Her heavy step on the stairs—as though she were carrying a sack of potatoes—her smell of peat, and already his member answered the call. While she undressed, he unbuttoned. (Evidently, Lisbeth remembered how she had done it and had it done to her by the railroad man: she simply lay down and spread her legs.) So much stored up and premeditated. Doubt crawled into Lisbeth Stomma as though the cellar were not hiding-place enough for him. He left nothing out. His urge refused to diminish. Infinite tenderness, infinite curiosity, as though there were caverns still unknown. It wasn't just the hole he was looking for; he had more to get rid of than juice. But Lisbeth remained dry and didn't close her eyes. She lay mute under his thrusts, which struck the void. She didn't take him in; she just let him do it until he had finished and fell off to one side.

There was no echo, he called out in vain, and it made him sad. Believe me, children: he didn't just pump himself dry. Lisbeth for him was not a knothole or the hollow of his hand. He worked hard (curbed his sorrow), tried again and again, he wanted her hot and overflowing: his program was happiness. He wanted her to say "Yes" and "Now." He tried to awaken love, that brief jubilation with its long aftertremblings; but she stayed at the cemetery and didn't notice him.

It doesn't come, with her it doesn't come.
For her market is black.
Rain flickers, the film is torn.
Come on! It doesn't come.
A gray soap opera, its script walks in sackcloth and ashes: everywhere one-way streets. Nothing coming in the other direction, nothing.
Look at the angel cheated by fate. Without innermost innards. The mythological cunt. True, Saturn came during the night, bucked her and bucked her, but nothing came, nothing: now she's just sore.
And muter than mute.
There's a skeleton in this angel.
Drapery covers the stagnant stench.
(Nobody would want to look reach search under her nightshirt: dry and sore.)
A petrified carp's mouth.
Word balloons from the past and blocks of basalt are piled high.
Hieroglyphics hewn in lava.
Words begotten in Capricorn.
With clammy fingers she holds the compass and cannot
Close the circle.
No cry consents to rise, to be long and sustained.

It went on like that through March, through April. I tried to make myself think that something had to happen: a shock, a thunderclap, a miracle, happiness.

●●●●●●●●●

Back to Bonn from Erlangen at night. Write a gray Mass. Make Doubt my Hosanna. A Mass without a Credo . . .

Accidents on the Autobahn. Mile-devouring chatter with Drautzburg about everything that happens is of interest: about ourselves and the cover story the *Spiegel* (while we are on the road) is doing about us; about *Local Anaesthetic,* which has just appeared and is blocking the road, bait to catch them with; about promises, whether the promised voters' club in Erlangen will actually; about wishes while brushing the teeth: Drautzburg's revolution; and in general (because we are obliged to drive through the Westerwald so late at night) on the widespread case of Lisbeth Stomma . . .

The snail on the telephone receiver. Good bugged connection. Before they call back. Expectations. The line goes dead.

In Bonn, not much sleep. From 10:00 A.M. to 12:00 A.M. on Kiefernweg. In my waste book: he's a new man, laughs even in the morning, talks—which is pleasantly striking—about himself, seems to have noticed the (de facto) wall at his back, wants to fight, doesn't say, "Wait a while," has stopped playing paralyzingly, as though dead to the world, with matches. (A man who has found his will while looking for cuff links.)

20 Someone feels neglected, fiddles with notes, wants to get to the mike and unburden himself.

Now several times Doubt and I. He began to love Lisbeth Stomma on purpose. He wanted to find examples of such love in black and white, missed the books he had left in his flat at 6 Rabbit Bastion, surveyed them in retrospect. There they stood: all lined up, ready for the firing squad.

(Augst says, "Here I am again. Please mention me. As an exemplary case." And Doubt forms sentences with himself.)

Voters' clubs are functioning in more than forty election districts. Erdmann Linde has drawn up a balance sheet. We're said to be doing well at the grass roots. (No inroads, but undecided voters are listening to us; decimals.) Over the phone Laura says, "Tell your election campaign to stop."

For want of his books, he decided to write a book, and asked Stomma for more paper. Because he was in a state of love, he wanted to write about the all, something that does not exist.

If now in Room 18—a quiet room on the court (with bottle-washing machine)—the telephone should ring: "Augst speaking."

190

■■■■■■■■■

When Doubt's rectilinear statement about human existence moved into a snail shell, it felt very tortuous.

He doesn't want to be a footnote; he wants to mount the stage (figuratively) over and over again with his little bottle.

While we were still in Plurien and nature, tides and all, was refusing to have anything to do with dialectics, Adorno the sociologist died. Couldn't stand it. Was taken at his word and wounded by words. Had a disease with a different name. Died of Hegel and the undergraduate consequences.

Overflowing with second and third sentences, but the first won't come. When Doubt grew dejected in love and sluggish in his dejection, he asked Stomma for leave to chop wood at night. "Make too much noise," said his host, and gave him bicycle tubes to mend. "Make less noise."

Maybe confine my writing to footnotes on people: to see the S.P.D. treasurer going from room to room in the party building is to see a Social Democratic principle in motion: the lifelong cashier whom nothing and no one can stop, punctual sobering exemplary even in doubtful cases (resistance). Collected membership dues even when the party was underground. (A snail with arch supports.)

Gray words. Sediment disadvantage buttonhole rocket-launcher necessity. Call Augst's act an act of despair.

"How shall I begin?" asked the cellar bug. "Anyway, not like this." Doubt began to draft letters he could not mail; but he also drafted answers to unsent letters and until the end of the war carried on a lively correspondence, which (in excerpts) is still worth reading.

What I talk about, now three times daily? About sick pay, about the aid to developing countries bill, about high C, the atomic disarmament treaty, about the consolidated school as precondition for student government, always too long about Willy and the new *Ostpolitik*, about Strauss and Barzel under the trademark of Strauzel, about insights that seem to be unsalable, about radicalism in Germany—when left and right slogans become interchangeable—uncertainty about the outcome of the elections, unfortunately not yet off the cuff: still laboriously reading every word.

In the cellar, nothing new. Doubt tried to cry, but the best he could do was blink. Even when he guided Lisbeth's hands, they remained deaf. Nothing, no touch or clasp, occurred to them. Sometimes in his hunger he begged: "Try to be a little affectionate. Just a little . . ." But she seemed to have left everything at the cemetery.

Maybe too sure of myself. Maybe I ought to be more personal. Less talk at one remove: the coal mine modernization bill.

If, for instance, August had liked himself better.

As soon as the damp north wall in his cellar began to dissolve, Doubt was able to think boldly, loftily, and without a net. A snail on a tightrope; how long tension can be sustained.

If August had collected something. Anything at all, maybe beer mats.

"Will you bring me, give me, buy me?"

"What I'd like to know, Franz, is whether you could go for three hours without talking about money."

"I'll do it. How much will you give me if?"

Meeting with no response, Doubt's love for Lisbeth Stomma kept fresh. He dressed it up, called it milk salt meadow oblivion cleft happiness his all. Lisbeth Stomma was absolute, unquestioningly she bore up under his terms of address and costume words: a clothes tree.

Too late now to offer Augst my friendship.

When in his distress Doubt insulted books—"Word coffins!"—Stomma, who couldn't read, beat him.

Someone whom love has made susceptible to jealousy eats his wife's (mistress's) ear plugs, hoping to feed on the substance of her dreams.

At the microphone: Augst. Lisbeth became totally mute.

Help, children! *I* don't talk any more; *it* talks from my mouth: ". . . convinced . . . because . . . nevertheless . . ."

My friends: Whose stomach ulcer will burst next?

And Leo Bauer's ash-gray melancholy when he interprets favorable forecasts—Infas or Emnid—down to the last decimal.

■■■■■■■■■

But only a footnote? (The snail as fortune teller.) Kierkegaard speaks of Hermetism.

When Lisbeth Stomma went mute, nothing changed except that she dispensed with the use of her tongue. She kept going to the cemetery and also to the market, which had less and less to offer. She still went to the cellar and lay down on the mattress for Doubt. But no more talk about happenings amid tombstones.

His six-volume edition of unwritten books.

Well-motivated attempts to save him: I should have asked him to join the theologians and professors on the platform.

Only mutely present; for Lisbeth liked to listen, though on the short way to her Doubt's stories lost their meaning or took on a different meaning; for, said Doubt to himself, there's no such thing as no meaning.

Give names to pauses. Put holes into lines. Boil down the spoken plethora. Say little with precision. Distant horizons made palpable. Give myself a chance. And right now: milk Doubt.

Found a snail shell.
The amply tailored ear—
no use keeping quiet—hears everything.

When shortly after Stalingrad and the defeats in the Lybian desert good manners moved into Doubt's cellar, Stomma began to address his guest as "Herr Doktor." Even when he (more and more infrequently) beat Doubt with his belt, he said, "I'm afraid, Herr Doktor, you've got a little rubdown coming."

I should have invited Augst to help us with our election campaign: "You're needed. It's not entirely pointless, even if it sometimes looks that way. Things don't always have to be so total and absolute."

At Christmas, when Franz was six years old, he stuck a blowpipe in his throat. I first smashed the blowpipe into bits, only then called Anna and the doctor.

She's missing among the signs of the zodiac; no wonder everything happens in such a hurry too late.

After Lisbeth took to lying mute with Doubt, he was able to read more into her: answers to his many why sentences. Now that no "Dunno" came out of her, he made her knowing. He conversed very nicely with the mute Lisbeth.

On the road Augst, as a pharmacist for instance, could have advised me in matters pertaining to Doubt.

Since Stomma insisted on having a doctor as his guest, Doubt, whose knowledge of herbs was considerable, prescribed a potion that, according to Hippocrates, was capable of driving out black bile. It gave Lisbeth Stomma diarrhea. Her black feces were regarded as proof that her melancholia, which throve especially in the wintertime, had passed out of her.

He might have collected medieval recipes: grated china bark, Glauber's salts, pomanders, musk pellets, amber, silvery balls, divers decoctions.

. . . .

When Lisbeth went mute, she became witty. Often Doubt had difficulty in keeping up with her chatter. The mute Lisbeth gave Doubt advice, told him how to interpret the military situation to his advantage; she knew what would keep up her father's fear.

He could have consulted books to find out how happiness or sleep-inducing pomanders were made in Dürer's day: henbane seed, hemlock seed, oil of mandragora, asarabacca juice . . . (Doubt took hellebore, which Lisbeth brewed for him.)

Since Stomma suffered from gout, Doubt prescribed the purgative decoction for him as well; for it is believed in the country that hellebore relieves and arrests joint diseases and deep sorrow, even if it does not eliminate or cure them.

As a pharmacist, Augst could have confirmed this.

Look in Lichtenberg for references to his hypochondria. Why he noted the sentence from Sterne's *Sentimental Journey:* "I was too near myself to say it was for the sake of others."

When Doubt so desired, mute Lisbeth, utterly barred and bolted and with eyes reflecting nothing as she sat at the table or lay dry and unconcerned with Doubt inside her, could be talkative, garrulous, even crude: she told dirty jokes, called Doubt a cunt lapper and mouth fucker, and when he wanted her to be—and in his affliction Doubt wanted her that way—was as lewd a trollop as they come.

No, Raoul. Nobody called Augst up to the platform. We didn't think of anything, just watched him do it.

196

■■■■■■■■■

At the pharmacy in Karthaus, Stomma procured the dried root that grows in calcareous soil on cool mountain slopes. Doubt often took the decoction: their hellebore parties, when they took turns going to the outhouse, were strangely cheerful despite the strenuous violence of their evacuations; for hellebore loosens not only the bowels but also—as Hippocrates tells us—the tongue and senses. Mute Lisbeth was witty, Stomma full of feeling, and Doubt of ideas—he inaugurated his cellar theater.

21 Noted in my waste book before Constance, Säcklingen and Reutlingen: Faster!

> Stalled on its roller skate,
> It threatens deadlines with petrifaction.
> Late it transpires that the orientation,
> still later modified by how many faith units,
> has at last been corrected.
> Everything is subject to progress,
> even the idea of designing hats
> approximating the shape of snail shells.

After visiting a medium-sized factory where felt hats—mostly Bavarian, but also cosmopolitan varieties on subcontract—are pressed, shorn, steamed, dyed, molded to size, creased, provided with silk hatbands on the outside and sweat bands on the inside, and stamped with the name of the contracting firm, I noted that along with the usual models certain others that could have a future are stamped with gold lettering: Jacobin caps, for instance.

For his theater Doubt experimented with head coverings: Stomma's meager stock. With hatters progress takes a pressed form. Doubt took this one and that one: so many roles. (If the elections turn out favorably, it might be a good idea for the visor cap of the Social Democratic past to be reintroduced in a felt version, if possible by Schiller at the Hanover Fair, as proof that the phase of aberrant taste, when even trade-union officials wore employer's headgear, is over.) Doubt, who had brought his duck-pond hat to the cellar with him, declared that the real head was the hat. (Raoul's broad-brimmed variety. He calls himself George Hunter.)

Now in Constance. (Jäckel senior and the student Bentele have come along.) We visit AEG-Telefunken. Late summer. The smell of lye. Lake Constance. (And tomorrow Säckingen. Anna is planning to come over from Switzerland across the Rhine and bring Franz. Hoping for something, in a pinch for words.)

In February, 1943, when the cold not only congealed all movement on the eastern front, but also invaded Kashubia and glazed the north wall of Doubt's cellar, Anton Stomma and his melancholy daughter often sat (wrapped in blankets) on Doubt's mattress, viewing his cellar theater. Between stored potatoes and the last hanging bicycle frames he had stretched a bed sheet: sometimes he played in front of the sheet, sometimes with the help of the stable lantern he produced shadows from behind the sheet. (Few props: an assortment of hats.) His many-sided, ambitious program: after hellebore parties, as soon as the decoction had exerted its purgative and senti-mentalizing effect, Doubt treated his purged audience to sim-plified versions of scenes from classical tragedies and comedies; he made the Prince of Homburg sleepwalk behind the sheet, made him in front of the sheet find Natalie's glove and make a fetish of it, made him haughtily lead the Branden-burg cavalry, made him shake with fear, made him pronounce his own death sentence, made him, already blindfolded, retrieve his life behind the sheet and Natalie in front of it. (The old hats, except for the duck pond, belonged to Stomma and his late wife.)

Commoners, too. Doubt enacted the grisly tale of the infanticide Rose Bernd.* Within reaching distance, engine driver Streckmann knocks bookkeeper Keil's eye out (Streckmann in visor cap, Keil in fedora). With bestial groans the otherwise mute Lisbeth indicated dismay when the newborn child was elaborately choked to death behind the bed sheet.

Was it ambition, or was it a deep-seated inclination in Doubt to play himself? He thought up debate plays, which met with little applause. Philosophical polemics behind and in front of the bed sheet. Socrates was much too long in taking the cup of hemlock. Jokes about dust-eating scholastics and casuists left Stomma cold. Rich in words and poor in action, these plays revolved around totality, the whole, the absolute; only the cholera that carried Hegel off and Schopenhauer's quotation-loving poodle provided distraction. (Hegel wore a Napoleonic paper hat. Under Doubt's duck pond, Schopenhauer growled speculations, which still enjoy currency, to tatters.) In front of the sheet or behind it, Stomma didn't care for it: too much "squabbling" and "jibber jabber."

More successful was the dramatic squabble of the high-bosomed Mary Stuart of Scotland with the flat-bosomed Elizabeth of England. Doubt simplified the poet's language, shone in female parts, and was unflaggingly agitated as Mortimer. Amazing that he, a past master at puncturing pathos, should have been capable of such ecstasy. (He had artfully cut the two crowns out of two cast-off stand-up collars dating back to the

---

* *Rose Bernd*, a play by Gerhard Hauptmann. Streckmann and Keil are characters in the play.

twenties, when Stomma was still a gay young blade in Dirschau.)

A committed theater: courageously Doubt inserted political jokes at the expense of Reichsmarschall Göring and other eminences. A subsidized theater: Stomma reduced the cellar rental by half. A, except for Doubt's prolix sleep inducers, successful theater: loud applause for Count Egmont when he rent the fetters of Spanish tyranny (and what was more, in Stomma's top hat). A direct, action-inspiring theater, for Stomma, carried away, discovered the freedom fighter in his bosom. When Klärchen,* whom, ironically enough, Doubt had endowed with certain dimly discernible features of his Lisbeth, summoned the people of The Netherlands to struggle for freedom, there was no holding Stomma: firmly planted on his legs, he thrust his fists against the ceiling and—he, too—proclaimed freedom. He'd take on the "Polacks" and the Prussian *Piefkes* with one hand: nothing to it. His cry of "Freedom to all Kashubians!" had so loudly separatist a ring that Doubt, in view of his own situation, tried to calm him down. Now that Polish partisans from Tuchler Heide had begun to infiltrate Kashubian territory, police patrols were making the rounds at night. On two occasions shots (without consequences) had been exchanged near the Klostersee.

In order to squelch Stomma's revolutionary fervor, Doubt debunked the career of Count Egmont. From a historical point of view, he explained, Count Horn, who does not appear in the play, was more important; the real Egmont was up to his ears in debt and had eleven children. Doubt deflated the hero. Stomma wouldn't listen. His blood bubbled; he grew violent. Punishment (after a long surcease) was due. Because Doubt had acted out of character and prevented Anton Stomma from

---

* The heroine of Goethe's *Egmont*.

liberating Kashubia, the leather belt swished from its loops:
Behind the sheet, in among the hats, Stomma counted twelve to
his guest. But all in all, what with the play-acting and the
thrashing, the evening provided exercise and helped to attenu-
ate the chill of the northwest wind.

No, children, I can't act it out. Not even in our cellar. I lack
the extreme situation: Doubt's bundle of fears.

After the performance Lisbeth stayed on. . . .

Nor can I remember any of the other plays that Doubt may
have acted out in front of the sheet, behind the sheet, because
the election campaign and the unrevalued mark . . .

While trying to coax a little warmth out of her body, he told
his mute beloved the story of Luise Miller and her Ferdinand. . . .

And because I saw the snail backside forward on horseback . . .

Doubt made Ferdinand and Luise visit cemeteries with a
view to active love; but eloquently and feelingly as he exchanged his beach-grass mattress for ivy-covered graves,
nothing, not the least little sigh, emerged from Lisbeth.

Because actually.
Actually you
It's actually.
Knock a dent out of a ball.
The dent remains, moves around, and apes itself.
But we don't want the other ball.
We're afraid that it, too.

The old ball is better.
Because actually, actually.
(And because the others and others' others.)
Because actually
and, to wit, it's proven: no ball without . . .

In Constance, actually, where after the meeting we had a good laugh on the Lake Constance ferry to Meresburg because Bentele, with his chronic hunger, actually . . . And when the proprietess of the Hotel Rothmund said to Jäckel senior: "Actually, I'm from Danzig myself. . . ." And in Waldshut election district, where actually Kiesinger is running, and I was so blissfully excited in Säckingen, because Anna and Franz were actually in the hall with friends from Lenzburg and Wettingen. And in Reutlingen, where actually I didn't spend the night but left for Tübingen, stopped at the Hotel Krone, and in the wee small hours fled into my waste book, because Augst was from Tübingen and actually Augst—if only in footnotes . . .

While mending bicycle tubes, Doubt had succeeded in proving the affinity between stasis and progress. They are related respectively to clinging and mobile snails. The Roman snail is not the only one that reproduces by autoinsemination. "The human race," wrote Doubt in his diary, "is becoming increasingly hermaphroditic, because . . ." His pet idea. Self-sufficiency. The reciprocal assimilation of the sexes. The end of all history. A state of permanence. The hermaphrodite duct. Happiness.

Because Lisbeth on Doubt's mattress (despite purgative hellebore and theatrical experience) was still cryless, alien, and dry.

■■■■■■■■■■

And if Augst's grandmother hadn't made him practice the piano, he would have . . .

Men, men all over the place. This limited richness: Baring the hothead; Gaus for whose fingers no cut is too trifling; Ehmke with his undercover mysticism; Jäckel senior, when his efficiency frays around the edges. And all I (now on the road) wanted to do was sketch snails in (slow) motion (and crawl away somewhere).

Our memory stores up blackness until we grow heavy, sag at the knees, barely go through the motions of holding our felt pens, our toneless telephone, our compasses, and no longer envy each other's shadows.

And so Doubt wondered if Lisbeth Stomma couldn't be kept busy with bicycle tubes: Melencolia mending bicycle tubes.

She's with me after Säckingen: twosome.

And Lisbeth passed the tubes through water, as Doubt had taught her: but she saw no bubbles rising, couldn't see the damage, because. . . .

Which dent do you want to knock out?

Let Franz tell you what happened in Säckingen after we'd visited a factory in Laufenburg, seen the usual deplorable conditions, talked privately with a few of the shop stewards, swallowed a little dust.

At first we were embarrassed. The meeting went off normally. There being no A.P.O. in Säckingen, some extraparliamentary oppositionists had come over from Lörrach. When father and son see each other with detachment. The A.P.O. from Lörrach had a speaker blessed with apostlelike beauty. Anna noticed our embarrassment; possibly she thought we were funny. The apostle from Lörrach mixed a socialism of his own invention with Alamannic anthroposophy. (Started right off with Rosa Luxemburg and Rudolf Steiner—revolutionary spontaneity and eurhythmics.) He took the floor unignorably while I was still speaking and had the voice of a prophet. (Between the Black Forest and the Swabian Alb mingling brooks have always beclouded each other.) I saw how Franz was listening to the orator, who diffused a Pentecostal mood. (Augst was no orator, all wild confusion.) Sitting there in the hall with Anna beside him, Franz thought the apostle was great. ("Kind of long-winded, maybe, but the way he looked and talked and the things he said—you know, about self-liberation and stuff—if you ask me, he was great.") Maybe I was jealous. (Later on, Franz said, "And, besides, you had the mike. Doesn't matter who was right. If you ask me, discussion is great.")

Early Christian in sandals: now soothingly mellifluous, now aggressively prophetic (and with it all sexy, with several Magdalens in tow), he preached global harmony to the burghers of Säckingen. Just like that, in his ecstasy and grandiloquent beauty, with his full red beard and flowing hair, I'd have liked to sketch him, tinkling beads, Azteco-Germanic amulets and all; but my hands weren't free. I had to take notes, cumbersome earthly stuff that proved unconducive to harmony and inspired no counterecstasy. (But beautiful he was with his peddler's tray full of baubles and German idealism. Franz is right: "He looked terrific.")

And that in the Säckingen-Waldshut election district, where blackness is the law of nature. Our candidate, a timid young clerk in the tax office, didn't have a chance against Kiesinger. (Shortage of funds, no campaign headquarters of his own, only a few helpful Young Socialists.) When Heinz Offergeld wanted to distribute leaflets with his wife in the afternoon, he had to get his mother-in-law to mind the baby. (All right, Franz, you try to campaign under such conditions.)

In Säckingen I said very little about Kiesinger. Before me, Offergeld had spoken of regional matters: the opening of the Rhine to navigation as a means of promoting the economic development of the Waldshut-Säckingen region. Like the burghers of Säckingen, our friends from Switzerland, who had come with Anna and Franz, took an interest in regional matters. It was possible to regard the meeting in Säckingen as a success: lots of women and young voters. . . .

Suddenly (and while the discussion was going along quietly, no longer geared to redemption), I looked right center and saw Franz sitting small and excited beside Anna: an image I took with me and kept. (I still have it. Even though the background has grown blurred and the distance greater than it was, I think I see that Anna sees me as I see her beside Franz: very close. . . .)

■■■■■■■■■

Take a look at yourself.

Get a pound of detachment.

I wish I were standing in the hall, not behind an upended crate; I want to interrupt myself.

I wish I could see (and sound) myself when hewn in stone I become too sure of myself.

I wish I could be there before I arrive.

Wave at myself.

I wish I could sleep, sift sand, play dead, and speak soothingly to myself while reeling off opinions (and kneading questions into answers).

I wish that while shaking hands I could keep both hands in my pockets.

I wish that just briefly, just for a second, the time it takes to do it and not so long as to attract attention, I could step behind myself and slip away (hidden by the boxwood) to one side.

I wish I could refute myself and cancel myself out.

(I wish I could go to the movies.)

I wish—yesterday in Säckingen and today doubly so in Reutlingen—I could trip myself up and leave myself lying flat; then at last I'd be able to unburden myself behind the upended crate, unburden myself without interruptions from hecklers:

About lapses of time and displaced phases,

About Augst after he and when I,

about intervening time, Anna and myself,

about the cellared Doubt and his quiet visitor

(also about snails and their fear of flying)

And about distances, the detachment they give.

/

22 I took no notes. Announced, I arrived with set ideas, which I began to cast off in the cab from the station to Wendelinstrasse: Let yourself be surprised for once. Just look and listen before you. You've been clothing Augst in changing trumpery for too long. Augst lends himself to disguises. A man who holds still. Augst is exemplary, not a mere footnote. (Take Doubt with you.)

For an hour on the train I was struck by the compulsive way Swabian towns have of calling themselves Esslingen, Plochingen, Nürtingen, Metzingen, and by how persistently (absolutely) the Swabians prevent landscape with one-family houses. When the train stopped at Reutlingen, I remembered: I'd been there after Constance and Säckingen; afterward, Drautzburg and I had covered the Verden and Cloppenburg election districts. We'd gone to Osnabrück, where it was raining—and to Lünen, where the Ruhr begins, ends. But in Reutlingen Augst was closer to me: broken down into notes and fragments of varying length. He left written remnants, speculations, and his family: Frau Margarete Augst, three sons, a daughter, Ute. (No dog or other domestic animals.)

The cellar bug turns up, joins in the conversation, has taken notes. Says I should put in the date, and that he (then) put in the date: "February 20, 1943, cold letting up. Worried about the winter potatoes . . ." Consequently, I, too, should put in the date, especially as I'm anticipating, getting ahead of time.

Cautiously (because the following adjective often compensates for gaps), I called it funny that I should find a relinquished place at the Augst family table, which, out of habit, as it were, I occupied: between the three sons and the daughter. (This I did on December 16, 1969, when Willy was already Chancellor.)

After a protracted attempt to dispose of him as a footnote, I had written a letter, and on December 4 Frau Augst had answered: "Your desire to learn something about the background of my husband's suicide does not strike me as unreasonable . . ."

So I took the train.

The Augst family lives as we do, in a one-family house. The house belongs to Frau Augst and her brothers and sisters, an old local family, as Dean Noetling, who spoke at Augst's funeral—Psalms 23:4—"And though I walk through the valley of the shadow of death . . ." had said.

It is said that in every Swabian family music is cultivated from infancy. So it was with the Augsts. Since I didn't take notes on the spot, I can't say for sure which of the sons plays the flute or blows the trumpet, and which one only sings. To all the Augsts music is important; even so, Frau Augst did not speak of a punctually consoling religion. She said, "We enjoy our music."

All except Augst. The family agreed that the late Manfred Augst had been unmusical and as father and husband had positively detested music. "It was foreign to him. Unlike the rest of us, he didn't get anything out of it. He felt excluded from music. Maybe that was why he hated it."

....

Doubt, who always takes notes (on the sly), underlined the last sentence and expanded it into a footnote: in giving this explanation for his hatred of music, Frau Augst is also thinking of Augst's grandmother in Thuringia who brought him up and made him take piano lessons at the age of nine.

Only one of the sons tried to retrieve his departed father for music. He reminded his brothers and (more particularly) his mother that when during Advent of the previous year the family had played some Christmas pieces for children (Leopold Mozart) their father had joined in; he had played not only the rattle, a rasping instrument, but also the hubble-bubble.

I've at last found the motive: the trouble he took with musical instruments. A (briefly) satisfying feeling. (Will ask my friend Aurèle Nicolet, who after playing too much Bach and Telemann to a Bach-and-Telemann audience claims to hate music, about secondary motives.) For Augst refuses to be or become simple. I wish I could sit them both down at a table: the excluded ones . . . But in the meantime Doubt has had a quiet visitor.

In March, 1943, after it became necessary to evacuate Rzhev on the Volga loop, the winter potatoes in the cellar diminished visibly. And once, when the mute Lisbeth came down the stairs with a basket for potatoes, Doubt, who actually wanted only to see Lisbeth climbing the stairs with basket on hip, saw time moving on more than one track. No sooner had the trap door fallen back into place with a dull thud than at the edge of the mound of potatoes, where Lisbeth had rumble-tumbled her basketful, he caught sight of a slug, which on closer scrutiny he identified as a specimen of the great slug

(*Agriolimax maximus*). (Torose breathing aperture at hind edge of mantle, carinate posterior.) A gastropod (a real one) in the midst of speculations.

On Wendelinstrasse I alluded only briefly to the fact that my book has snails in it, exemplary, legendary, theoretical, and actually existing varieties.

Doubt squatted beside the potatoes. He didn't touch it. His gaze encompassed the roughly four-inch-long mollusk, the tapering carinate posterior, the dark lengthwise bands, the spotted mantle and the eye tentacles. He heard its characteristic sound. He saw the eye tentacles grow shorter and longer, saw the lower tentacles reconnoitre the area in front of the creeping sole. He saw the breathing aperture at the back and to one side of the mantle come to life, saw the glassy body mucus, and saw the colorless sole mucus, as it marked a track away from the potatoes and across the stamped clay floor: a track neither straight nor tangled, which was obviously purposive. And still he squatted. Long absent, happiness came to him. He wept; he was able to weep. Happily, Doubt wept and laughed a shrill falsetto laugh.

"What about Augst? Did he ever?" Maybe in the past and maybe once again during the Christmas music when he as father managed to join in with his rasping rattle, but happiness . . . (And even Dean Noetling, after the consoling Psalm, was obliged to say: "And so we ourselves as we stand at his graveside, are the defeated, the questioners.")

When, later on, Lisbeth brought Doubt his rye-flour soup, he showed her the great slug. She saw, but it is unlikely that she saw what Doubt saw.

After the meal Stomma came down with the newspaper and

his pipe tobacco. Doubt didn't show him the slug. Slowly he read the daily Wehrmacht communiqué to his host. The bicycle dealer's pipe sent up smoke signals. The *Vorposten* reported heavy fighting, varyingly successful defensive actions, in the Lake Ilmen sector. In the Izyum area, still according to the *Vorposten,* enemy spearheads had been contained. Doubt asked Stomma to stop filling his pipe and coughed by way of explanation.

When Stomma and his daughter had gone, Doubt was no longer alone. After brief ventilation—the cellar window wouldn't open more than a hand's breadth—he lay on his mattress in the dark and knew that its eye tentacles were playing in space.

Frau Augst remembered: "That's right. Just once, before Christmas it was, he got a little pleasure out of music."

The three sons are twenty-two, twenty, and eighteen, and have turned out passably unlike. Toward each other they take an amiably didactic tone and toward their mother a pronounced attitude of precocious responsibility. Each of the three sees, explains, forgets, and judges his father differently, often in direct contradiction. They also correct their mother's recollections from three angles; Frau Augst looks for help and confirmation from one or the other of her younger sons when, with strict attention to detail, she wishes to correct her eldest son's portrait of his father.

None tried to whitewash or embellish. No game of father construction, no family court of justice at the living room table. Each son let the next keep his (admittedly) distorted picture. All were agreed that they hadn't known him, that he had been a (strange) stranger in their midst, and that they had begun to think about him only recently, only since the pressure had let up.

I asked questions cautiously, preferring not to take notes. At present I'm not sure whether the eldest son (who is supposed to take after his father) said that Augst had looked upon Hitler as his model to the end, or whether the eldest son contradicted the youngest: "Hitler as an individual, no. What fascinated him was the so-called leader principle." With greater certainty I can say that the second son disagreed with his brothers: "Hitler could have been someone else, as far as he was concerned. He was against the personality cult." But on one point all three brothers saw eye to eye: "What was important to him, of the first importance, was the idea of community, and that's why the theological concept of fellowship meant so much to him."

Nor could Dean Noetling exclude the possibility that for Augst Protestant fellowship was a substitute for the lost national community. (At the graveside he said, "All through the years he was a seeker, driven by hunger!")

One of the sons spoke of Augst's hunger for public meetings: "That's why he attended discussions and tried to join in, even though he was a poor extemporaneous speaker and was afraid of being laughed at."

"It's obvious, Raoul: he had to ventilate because snails don't like pipe smoke." Something I'll have to insert is that when Lisbeth came down the stairs for potatoes Doubt always watched her with a vague expectancy. (Since potatoes were dished up daily in West Prussia, especially in wartime, Doubt was expectant every day.) He expected something of her heavy gait, of her sighs as she bent over, of the rumble-tumbling potatoes, of Lisbeth in general; but perhaps he didn't dare to form an intimation of what finally turned up.

This power to communicate in public, to speak out. (Doubt needs a pause to enable his trembling happiness to catch up.)

This license to call into question, this wanting-to-point-out-just-once-more. (I refuse to look when he's upset and possibly—because he's moved—makes faces.) Every discussion gave Augst a small advance toward the community he was looking for. (I can imagine Doubt confessing buckets of hopes to his long-awaited snail.) To stand shoulder to shoulder, to belong, to have the right to pledge allegiance. (Let him speak out, as Augst tried to do: Doubt in his cellar, Augst publicly.) Sit them both down at a table? Not even Dean Noetling with his Twenty-third Psalm would have the tongue for it.

For a time Augst's eldest son had been a member of the S.D.S. ("Then I got out. They were getting too intolerant to suit me.") Sometimes he must have understood his father, because the S.D.S., more than other student groups, was (for a time) something of a conspiratorial community. The need to be led. The desire to obey. The spirit of self-sacrifice, the principle of selling off doubt as an unnecessary luxury.

Because the snail was now there, impeding all speculations, he would have liked to get religion.

"My husband," said Frau Augst, "was a member of five or six associations, organizations, working groups. I could show you papers; we haven't had time yet to put most of them in order. His attempts to express himself. Of course I had to cancel all his memberships, if only because of the dues."

Worship a snail? Why shouldn't Doubt have done just that? So much patience. Its Passion. (Protected by their mucus, they can glide unharmed over razor blades.)

Augst's deepest involvement was with the Free Christians, or Free Church, an offshoot of the German Christians, who under their Reichs Bishop Müller had sought Christianity in National Socialism. (They still meet: die-hards.)

In addition, Augst attended conferences at the Ludwigstein where the Free Academy held its meetings. In Augst's papers I find, along with pamphlets about fellowship and the meaning of selfless comradeship, signs pointing in another direction, names and book titles: Dorothea Sölle, *Political Evening Prayer*; Enzensberger's *Kursbuch*, No. 14; *The Question of God*; Tillich, Jaspers . . .

On the day of his suicide he had actually intended to take the early morning train to the Ludwigstein, because the Free Academy was in session (from July 18 to 24), but Frau Augst had forgotten to wake him up.

"And because the train had left and I knew he'd be miserable at home, I said: 'Why not go to the Church Congress in Stuttgart, where several discussions are going on at once?' "

The second son, who worked at the pharmacy where Augst, too, had worked, contradicted his mother: no, his father had already decided for the Church Congress and against the Ludwigstein the day before. "In any case, he went to the pharmacy with me early in the morning and took something, probably that."

I asked if Augst had been a collector. Apart from organizations and public discussions he had collected nothing. (Not until late in the afternoon did someone say in passing that Manfred Augst had often gathered mushrooms.)

When, as at vacation time, you see me walking the beach at low tide and searching the clumps of seaweed that have been washed ashore, or when Franz takes my picture with the sun on my back and neck, bending down and picking up, rejecting and comparing, then, to be sure, you are photographing me, but not my motives. Collecting is an answer to a state of dispersion, regardless of whether uniform buttons, Art Nouveau glasses, miniature car models (Raoul's Oldtimer), my sea shells, Augst's memberships, or Doubt's snails are collected. Almost everyone collects something and says that other collectors are nuts. Collecting also disperses the time that collects second by second: when Doubt dispersed the compactly burdensome time for his Lisbeth and for Stomma, his host, with stories he made up; when I gather stories that lie dispersed and tell them to you. (For instance, one that keeps crossing my path: two musicians—a pianist and a singer of Schubert lieder—travel all over the world and see nothing. Their collected medium-sized concert halls. Their postcards from this place and that, sent home where they are collected. Their unvarying quarrel, which they drag from Lisbon via Tokyo to Caracas, about the tempos of the *Winterreise*. Their Godforsaken life. Their hotel rooms. The expense vouchers they collect . . .)

Since for melancholics the world has narrowed down to something that can only be endured as an ordered whole, collecting is an active manifestation of Melancholy; in her dwellings are found complete collections embracing all the species of some genus: all ferns, prepared; all titmice, stuffed; all the Central European beer mats of the twenties . . .

When Doubt in the cellar showed his mute beloved the great slug, Lisbeth Stomma, who endured her narrowed world by collecting cemeteries, may have sensed how much snails meant to Doubt; for when spring came, she brought him, in her watering can, as many as she could find in the graveyards of Karthaus district: brick-red rufous slugs and yellow slugs, which she found under the fallen leaves that she raked from between graves. But Lisbeth also brought snails that carried their houses: large spotted Roman snails, red-brown hairy snails, and the fine-grained lapidary snails that she harvested from under the ivy on graveyard walls. (She even brought home leaves, moldy wood and moss-covered stones.) Soon Doubt had a collection that, however, could not be complete, because Lisbeth looked only in warm, damp bottomland and not on heaths and sandy soil. Doubt kept only two specimens of each variety of live snail or slug; Lisbeth carried the rest back to the graveyards in her watering can. (Once she brought small bones to his cellar.)

And Augst, who in Tübingen seems to have been consulted as an authority on mushrooms? Would he and Doubt have been able to talk shop? (After all, there are plenty of snails that feed on mushrooms.)

At first Doubt tried to hide his collection from Stomma, but when his host caught him tidying up snail shells, Doubt showed him what with Lisbeth's help had become a collection; and Stomma, whose bicycle repair shop couldn't help attracting and, as it were, collecting all sorts of accessories, laughed good-naturedly when he saw the snails: "Well, at least they won't make noise." (Actually, land pulmonates, considering their size and molluscan character, are rather noisy creatures. Not only in motion but also in a state of rest, they produce a characteristic sound: their foamy crackling.)

Stomma donated tin boxes that he had used for collecting valves and bicycle bells, screws, nuts, and miscellaneous junk: Doubt's new terrariums.

Higher values, deeper meaning. "That's what he was always looking for," said Frau Augst. "In 1933, when he was still a student, he joined the General SS, the Black SS as it was then

217

called. Later on, he volunteered for the Waffen-SS, several times in fact, but they wouldn't take him. He wore glasses, but that wasn't the only reason. When the war broke out, he was assigned to the Air Force, but not to the flying personnel. He never got to the front much. Only for a short time in North Africa. The climate down there was too much for him."

To that Augst's sons said nothing. Only Frau Augst spoke: "In '44 they made him a lieutenant. We didn't marry until '47. . . ."

"What did Doubt do during the war?"
"Collected his snails."
"What did he do with the snails?"
"Observed them."
"What snails eat and that kind of thing?"
"How they move."
"And when he wasn't observing?"
"He took notes on what he had observed."
"What about the war?"
"It got along without him."

After 1945, Manfred Augst began to be many things at once: a proponent of soldierly comradeship and—without having to change his glasses—a convinced pacifist, untiring in his urge to make converts. (At first he did social work for the Evangelical Church, then he became a pharmacist's assistant.) Later, he started joining. Up to the mid-sixties he belonged to the "War on Atomic Death" movement. As cashier and organizer he helped with preparations for the annual Easter marches. Regardless of the weather, Augst was on hand.

I see him under the rain, attacking atomic death in the shock troop of the Tübingen section. As Easter marcher,

Augst is entitled to wear insignia: the runic symbol. More foes of atomic death might have turned up if the weather had been better, but the little band is enough for Augst. His canvas jacket rubs against the next man's loden coat. Human contact. Despite the sustained heckling of the rain, Augst voices a collective will. At long last he had a goal again. From the curbstones jibes and hostility. (Perhaps Augst was happy as a rain-drenched pacifist, because in peacetime soldierly comradeship shed its skin and put on a new one.)

Later the Tübingen section seems to have been torn by strife because the antiatomic-death movement drew its membership from mutually exclusive political groups. The goal got the wobbles, the felt of community lost its warmth: again Augst was alone with himself. (Now a pharmacist. He had got his pharmacology degree in '61 at the age of forty-eight.)

It's not true that all snails move with equal slowness. As an experiment, Doubt began to mark out lanes with the help of a compass he had found among Stomma's junk.

"Could your husband laugh? About anything?"
"Laugh? Never!"
"But he could be ironic."
"Even cynical."
"Right. He could be downright sarcastic."
"But he couldn't laugh."
"That's why he was cynical."
"And often hurt other people's feelings."
"Without even wanting to."

After drinking from it, Augst showed the little bottle to a girl student who sat next to him in Hall 1 at the Church Congress. His last words (without microphone) were: "That, young lady, was cyanide."

"But he enjoyed working in the garden."
"Only sowing and transplanting."
"And we were stuck with the weeding."
"But he really knew about mushrooms."
"We'd gather them on Sundays. The whole family."
"He even taught: micology."
"People showed him the mushrooms they had gathered."
"And we ourselves ate mushrooms for supper."

(In October: not only chanterelles, the tasty goat's lip, honey agaric, and paxillus; also delicate puff balls, green white-spored agaric, chestnut boletes.) We fell silent for a while in the family living room. "We can only be thankful," said Frau Augst, "that he didn't take us with him when he went."

Over his grave Dean Noetling said: "And so I am glad that in this hour you yourselves have suggested the words of the Twenty-third Psalm, that hymn of perfect faith and trust."

Yes, Raoul, as a father he seems to have been tolerant: he helped his two eldest sons, who were conscientious objectors, to formulate their reasons; he did so as a well-informed pacifist. The one thing he couldn't do was laugh.

When Doubt had measured off all his lanes and distances with his compass, he set up tables in his diary. His project was hardly new: Egyptian hieroglyphic inscriptions tell us that in the days of the Pharaohs snail races were a common form of entertainment in the Nile delta. . . .

23 In so many places: at the Bergischer Hof, at the Hotel Burggrafen, the Hotel zum Gutenberg, the Hotel Heimer, the Hotel Hohenzollern am Bahnhof, the Parkhotel Lünen . . .

My hotel rooms jumbled together.

Keys on their tags interchanged.

(Room 32 is still with me: a tube with an escape valve, while plumbing moans through partitions and gurgles arise . . .)

And the candy bars on pillows full to bursting, where bittersweet flirtatiously they wait: Suchard.

Each night Vitagel, vitalizing and vitamin-yellow: the crackling bubble bath revives the exhausted and heals discussion wounds. The changing views: air shafts, garages, squares, warehouses, building sites, railroad tracks, the city park, the restored Old City: swans and shingled roofs as in the prospectus. (Late Gothic coated with pigeon shit.)

In the early morning, that special noise when the streetcars, garbage cans, coughing cooks, and wide-awake jackhammers come to life. (Cocks only rarely; but once in the gray of dawn—where?—a motorcycle didn't want to start.)

I should have kept a gauge, I should have set up tables (like Doubt).

If I could classify the decorations in the rooms: indigenous water colors of ramparts and gabled houses; hand-colored medicinal plants; the bell-shaped digitalis, or mallow blossoms for cough syrups; reproductions of art works—Dürer, van Gogh, Paul Klee—and merry-vagabond scenes by a painter named Hummel.

I ought (for my table) to have consulted a compass; for if I knew where I slept with my head to the east . . .

And what I've left where: often toothbrush, felt pens and ball-points, socks pamphlets addresses, never my tobacco.

Firm resolve to remember the wallpaper.

(I should have taken samples.)

Design a wallpaper with a mythological landscape—the Fehmarn bridge, the Autobahn traffic circle in Frankfurt, scattered airports junk heaps parking lots—peopled exclusively by slugs, moving in endless repetition.

Where I've said amen.

Where I've wanted to shed my skin.

Where seven-line curses, because the heat—in May—couldn't be turned off.

Several times (heaven knows where) I stuck footnotes on Doubt and Augst, comments on penal-law reform, chiseled polemics, confessions about myself (what I'm like, not like) into the Bible—right beside the phone, and in the morning (after random openings: Job) found only the barest traces of them. And this and that.

What wall-to-wall carpeting swallows.

What makes hotel rooms so sharp of hearing and tomblike.

What doesn't appear on the bill.

What's lacking.

On waking, the locality is missing. It will turn up after a while, at the latest with the newspapers at breakfast: soft-boiled eggs.

In case you didn't know, children, a writer these days is just a fug measurer. What they call stable smell. Back from Ver-

222

dun, Cloppenburg, Osnabrück, Lünen. Fug-filled bell jars ring in the evening. Last stop the Scholl High School. For my table: Catholic fug. (That was on August 29, a month before the elections.)

Because this time I haven't brought home a thing except the sniffed insight that it smells everywhere, and not only in quaint one-family houses, that sometimes frankly and pungently, sometimes lavender-sweetened, here masked by refrigeration, there streaked with mold, and next door unspeakably, it stinks, because here, there, and next door the cellars harbor corpses which, elaborately hushed up and filed away in seven offices, no nose can locate, because corpses stored from the very start in all these cellars, not only in those of old houses, but also in the new ones with the paint hardly dry, diffuse an aroma you can cut with a knife and that passes as a working climate: pluralistic fug which only in its centers of concentration threatens to blow out the pressure valve.

No, children. Not an explosive. Since everyone knows that everyone's cellar contains something that contributes public-spiritedly to the climate, all have agreed to take the presence of undefined corpses for granted and to speak not of corpses but of conditioning factors that anyone who starts poking into other people's cellars will have to reckon with.

As Moses divided the sea, so here on dry land we have to divide the fug.

Look for the corpse in your own cellar and give it a name. A writer, children, is a man who loves fug and tries to give it a name, who lives on fug by giving it a name; a mode of life that puts calluses on the nose.

. . . .

Describe the slow displacement of an empty lot; how in broad daylight it's put on rollers, how under more private lighting it rolls into a zone where land brings higher prices, how without growing it gets fat, how one good turn deserves another, how the displacement of an empty lot is baptized "of public utility," how the affair is exposed and after giving off a bit of its smell covered up again by those who had regarded themselves as impartial; how the Bremen, Hagen, Gelsenkirchen people point their fingers at the people in Moers: the same all over.

Sometimes a little too fast. "Do we have to speed like this?" Drautzburg curses his way through the back country. He's taken the wrong road. Misinterpretations of scholastically disputing church steeples between Münster and Osnabrück. ("Why shouldn't snails greet each other with the word "Speed!"? Think of all the people who call each other "comrade.") Drautzburg is getting more leftish by the minute. Everywhere, even in cow pastures, he unmasks fascists.

I try to calm him down, call the landscape friendly and flat. It worries me when he frets inwardly, outwardly fills in word balloons, and meanwhile drives too fast, though still reliably. (Snails are often fascinated by gazelles.)

Maybe the sight of flat country promotes a desire to make a radically clean sweep. "Look here, Drautzburg. It's already been done. In October, 1917."

It worries me when the revolution, no sooner proclaimed, sticks in the craw. I can see it from the back seat: two-way dissatisfaction colors his seersucker ears yellow. "But fifty years after the October Revolution . . ."

"I know. Everybody knows."

"Do I have to remind you . . ."

"Slow down at least."

"They have their revolutionary fug, hard to move and almost impossible to divide; we have our reformist fug, hard to divide and almost impossible to move."

"So what?"

"You've got to make up your mind between fug and fug, or they'll mix: the mixture will be impossible to divide and nothing in the world will make it move."

It worries me when the yellow of his ears starts fading from the edges in, when—the moment he slows down—the seersucker smoothes out.

"Shit!" he says. A word that has enjoyed a bullish market in the last four years even outside the universities. (Raoul has sold it to Bruno.) Though lately it seems to be leveling off.

"All right," I said. "But where we're going now, it's worth the trouble. Vechta, Cloppenburg! Except for the eggs they send to market, everything's pitch black. I was there four years ago. A region with a future. Things can only get brighter. There's 5 per cent to be gained. The people there want something, the only question is: Do they want what they want? . . ."

Now Drautzburg is looking forward to Cloppenburg. "I see. One of your usual snail stories."

On paper or into the empty air: I write. On the road between cars and trucks, laned in on the Autobahn, stopping and starting in bottlenecks, I write in our Volkswagen bus: fug shorthand, lead-containing footnotes, evocations of Doubt, hymns to Laura, snail stories . . .

When Doubt put a rufous slug on a bicycle seat . . .

When he designed a treadmill for snails . . .

When in the summer of 1944 Stomma gave his cellar guest a magnifying glass to help him count the spirals of the tiniest shells and enter them in his tables as homespun truths . . .

When . . .

Always and everywhere. (Turned backward riding forward.)

On cigarette paper, beer mats.

In my hotel rooms, which quickly cancel each other out, as
soon as the two plain-clothes gentlemen have shown their
badges and looked in the cupboard, under the bed, et cetera,
for ticking objects, whatever comes to mind: incidentals without decimal points.

"Look here, Anna, it won't be long and even if it takes
longer it will be sooner than we had reason to hope because
actually the distance between partial aims . . ."

Also names, such as Sorryweather or Fussbudget.

Exclamations in parentheses: Augst lives!

Also in Bonn, toward 7:00 A.M. when the underground railway builders put an end to my sleep with their jackhammer, I
write beside my packed bag: What's making Willy hesitate?
What Ehmke lacks and Eppler has too much of . . .

What bugs me on the road.

The mike that refused to work outside the foundry gate in
Herne.

In Lünen more schoolchildren than voters.

When, after too much discussion and a good deal of beer, I
drove from Vechta to Cloppenburg with Lemp, our candidate,
I ceded to pressure, asked Lemp for a pee stop and while
passing water at the edge of a typical South Oldenburg scrub
forest, wrote a long-winded diatribe, replete with fresh beginnings, against Barzelish quadragenarians.

Their slippery, well-lubricated confessions,

their fumbling for spectacles,

their sidelong Catholic glances at abodes of sin,

their middle-aged industriousness,

their tax-free skier's tan,
their hermaphroditic self-sufficiency,
their lukewarm hermaphroditic natures . . .
(Is that what Doubt wanted when he took the Roman snail as an example? Now, seen through the magnifying glass, his utopia has moved palpably close: mutual assimilation of the sexes. Self-sufficient individuals. Doubt fills in his tables: short steps in the direction of happiness.)

"Whatcha writing now? Do you always have to? You writing about horses or my bunnies? Or is it still the same old S.P.D.? Couldn't you just stop?"

(Look here, little girl.) Everywhere all the time. I write while I talk listen answer.

I write while I chew a cutlet, run on gravel, sweat in crowds, attack chanters with silence, cook beans with smoked shoulder of pork, invent myself somewhere else. . . .

Watching the furnace tap at the Oberhausen metal works, in the midst of silos at Wacker Chemicals, in a glass factory that spits out Maggi bottles, in Dortmund while the shop stewards pickle the acyclic Schiller in quarts of beer, I wrote what turns up.

Often nothing but adjectives: disgruntled gloomy grumpy.

Beginnings of sentences: A young man who threw eggs at me four years ago in Cloppenburg, apologized because he . . .

When, while drinking coffee with the Osnabrück voters' club, I saw Fritz Wolf, the caricaturist, sitting opposite me, I understood why melancholy takes refuge in jokes. . . .

Or at Leo Bauer's: while he was telling me his story, I read in his face—calm built on lava—the meaning of the words "solitary confinement," for his Siberian stomach ulcers . . .

227

(It's true, Laura: often I write only to prove to myself that I exist, that it's me who's writing words on slips and throwing them out the window.)

Also when my plane is late in taking off, whistling away fatigue, skyward while swimming on my back, negated by noise, while peeling onions, while (like Doubt on his mattress) trying to crawl into a woman, always and everywhere, even when I'm dejected, condemned to silence, I make words.

What is not written.

Sentences that lie around, run after me, torment me and demand to be cast in lead.

Before this there was that, got stuck in Iserlohn.

A cold-rolling mill squeezed into the valley: thinner and thinner sheet metal.

I write on rain-splattered slate roofs, in puddles of beer, on a conveyor belt: I I I.

Even if I have to go back to Tübingen now and pass through Doubt's cellar on my way to see Augst, I'm thinking about myself, and how everywhere, even while writing this or something about the asparagus fields around Bruchsal, I'm always writing about fug and nothing but fug.

Doubt had attached his magnifying glass to a shoelace that he wore around his neck: his tables and mine.

24 "We've set a place for you at the dinner table," said Frau Augst. "Really, it's no trouble at all." After a short visit to Dean Noetling—I was curious to know on what occasions the Twenty-third Psalm is trotted out—I was back on Wendelinstrasse.

All right, Raoul, maybe you'd sooner train fleas, but I stick to my story. When during the war the schoolteacher Hermann Ott was obliged for political reasons to hide in the cellar of a crude but good-natured bicycle dealer, he revived an ancient Egyptian snail game and developed the pastime of the fellahin (and of the Israelite foreign workers of the Egyptian Empire) into a kind of sport. In his cellar he organized races between snails of like and unlike species. A game in which silence was permissible. Often the snails stopped in their course and had to be set in motion by purposive wishing. A game against time and its sounds.

On Wendelinstrasse I inquired almost obsessively about Augst's knowledge of mushrooms. Had he collected systematically and kept tables? For Doubt tabulated the performances of his racing snails.

He never lacked for equally full-grown or equally half-grown rufous slugs, common field slugs, or great slugs, or for shell-bearing strawberry snails, Roman snails, or grove snails, which Lisbeth Stomma brought home from her cemeteries. Sportsman enough to try for records.

The table top measured four feet by two feet eight; a surface sufficient for qualified snails to engage in every track event from the (in snail measure) hundred-yard dash to the two-mile run, and after a while in the exciting hurdles, which even Augst, though against his will, would have found exciting.

Not that the snails met the new demands from the start. At first they were disoriented, strayed from their course, failed to stop at the table edge, and reared molluskwise. When Doubt was obliged to intervene, he touched the eye tentacles, waited until the snail had withdrawn into its shell or (in the case of slugs) shrunk, lifted it with a lateral pressure of the thumb that never injured the creeping sole, and turned it around. Doubt had a knack for handling snails firmly but circumspectly.

I ought to ask Augst to join in, just for a try; for the dull, indifferent, and even between the legs unfeeling Lisbeth Stomma joined in and (like Doubt) handled the snails circumspectly. Strangely enough, when Lisbeth touched the eye tentacles, they were retracted much more hesitantly, ever so slightly and sometimes not at all: Doubt noticed this extraordinary insensibility. (There was an understanding between the mute Lisbeth and the snails.)

A slice of raw potato or an apple core served as the goal. Butter fungus and puff balls were also found suitable. Doubt and Lisbeth started their racing snails at the opposite edge of the table and observed devoutly how the rufous slugs, at first contracted into tentacleless hemispheres, stretched to full length, how the breathing aperture in the mantle widened, how they extended first the black-lacquered eye tentacles, then the short lower tentacles, marked time while taking cognizance of the goal with their tentacles, and then (Lisbeth's first) started off, unrolling their mucus-coated feet and rather quickly prolonging their tracks.

Honestly, Raoul: speedy animals. I think I'll do a sketch, with pencil charcoal ink: greyhounds unsuccessfully chasing snails. (Yes, I know: Augst.)

It soon developed that the Roman snails were unable to perceive vegetable goals (salad, carrots, slices of potato) more than two feet distant, while the yellow slugs' sense of smell, though Doubt himself could not have said for sure which of its organs transmitted olfactory stimuli, registered goals over three and a half feet away. Doubt measured and remeasured the course and began to classify his track events according to snail varieties: systematically and tabularly, it goes without saying.

He took little sporting interest in the races but watched them with the curiosity of a scientist. (With all his slugs he obtained improved performance by soaking bread crusts in sugared milk and using them as goals.)

And Lisbeth? Her cemetery-based melancholy did not reveal whether she saw anything creeping beside snails, or whether she even recognized snails as snails. Nevertheless, Doubt detected changes in her. He noted rudimentary forms of infantile joy when her Roman snail or rufous slug finished first and, eating vigorously (with retracted eye tentacles), set about digging craters in the mushroom or slice of potato. Since Lisbeth (apparently) had an understanding with snails and could wish harder, she almost always won. Her faith was rectilinear, undeviating. She watched her snail dynamically.

··········

231

Before dinner: "He completed his studies much too late. Interrupted by the war. Then finally he got his degree in pharmacology. The achievement of his life. But even that didn't really satisfy him." I should have asked Frau Augst for photographs, for the family album: Augst as lieutenant. Augst on the Ludwigstein. Augst as an Easter marcher. Augst gathering mushrooms, sorting mushrooms.

Doubt still had the pocket watch that had been given him at the age of fourteen by his uncle, the treasurer of the Praust drainage co-operative. And with that softly-sweetly ticking watch he timed his racing snails. Food for his performance tables.

He arranged elimination races. When on one occasion two Roman snails broke off their race, pressed their creeping soles together, raised them up, secreted calcareous darts—known as love arrows—thrust them into each other's soles, and played their hermaphroditic game, he disqualified them both, although clearly the hermaphroditism of Roman snails gave promise of happiness, utopia. Athletics were one thing and love-making another.

"My husband," said Frau Augst, "never compromised. For him everything was black or white, yes or no. Sometimes he'd talk all night with my eldest son, who was still with the S.D.S. at the time and also detested compromise. But it never got to be a real conversation. They always talked past each other."

Doubt's utopia did away with the sexes and the battle of the sexes: equalized and harmonized, free from hatred of father's suspenders, free from hatred of mother's apron.

When Manfred Augst spoke at the Church Congress, someone from Dean Noetling's congregation heard him speaking into the microphone. "There's our Herr Augst again with his crazy *idée fixe*."

"But he wasn't able to speak freely and fluently, because he belonged to the war generation, and his grandmother had brought him up and made him take piano lessons."

"So," said Frau Augst, "my husband attended several elocution schools. We still have the tapes. But I don't want to hear them. It's too soon. As his wife, I'm too deeply involved. It will take time for . . ."

It was already summer. Already the last German offensive had collapsed in the Kursk sector. Already Stomma had become more friendly to his guest than according to the Wehrmacht communiqués he should have been; he moved his lumpy, faded-burgundy wing chair down to Doubt's cellar. Already the snail races had become more complicated, more varied as to difficulty. Wishing to make increased demands on his gastropods' visual sense, Doubt formed the briquettes that Lisbeth Somma had piled up in the cellar into a labyrinth whose narrow passages and light sluices had to be located and negotiated by the sliding snails.

These, too, are no more: pungent-smelling men's societies, sharp-tongued women's right movements. No more hormone injections for Russian shotput championesses. And—dear Herr Augst—no more grandmothers . . .

Impassively as Lisbeth Stomma won race after race, her father was an active audience. "Faster!" he would shout at his favorite snail. "Get the lead out of your ass!" He kept his fingers crossed. Though Stomma almost always lost, he donated generous prizes. The victorious snail was rewarded with white bread soaked in milk. To Lisbeth, the mute winner, he gave a small bag of glass beads (she had an odd way of playing with them) and to Doubt, the inventive organizer of the races, sweets, peppermint drops for instance. (Remember, children, it was wartime, and in exchange for his rare merchandise—bicycle pumps, seats, tubes and rear reflectors—Stomma could get anything he wanted, even Lübeck marzipan and French liqueurs.) It got to be very cosy in Doubt's cellar, cosy and cheerful.

When I visited Dean Noetling, he said in his study: "A great weight has been lifted from that brave woman's shoulders. All those years with such a man: it wasn't easy for her."

Later on, Doubt gave his utopia a name. "On the Happiness of Hermaphrodites": such was the title of his treatise, which he (unfortunately) never finished, on the relationship between snails on the one hand, melancholy and utopia on the other. In Doubt's hermaphroditic society giving and taking were one. No one went away empty-handed. No more threats: if you don't, I won't . . . No more hatred . . .

Frau Augst was often afraid: "Not because of the fights followed by door slamming and leaving the house. That happens in most marriages. But he was hardly ever at home. Something was always going on: conferences, discussions. But three weeks before it happened, he said . . . I didn't say a word, I was afraid. He was a sick man after all, and you never can tell." (Augst never struck anyone. Only once, at the end, did he become aggressive: against himself.)

Look what I'm drawing for you, children: an archer; there's a slug on the shaft of the arrow that he's fitting to his bow.

■■■■■■■■■

Doubt knew how sensitive the front edge of the foot is and knew how snails react to chemical stimuli. With a chalk solution, to which a dash of ammonia had been added, he marked off straight lines on his table top. None of the competing snails ever crossed the dividing lines. It goes without saying that they achieved better times between chalk lines than on the blank table top. They kept rigorously on course: between acrid-smelling lines twelve field slugs or nine Roman snails advanced as a body, though now and then a contestant would rest his foot, and only its tentacles would strive toward the goal. (Forward amid stimulants.)

"He had to do it. He knew it all along," said Frau Augst. "If I said, 'It's high time you bought a new pair of trousers,' he'd say, 'You're right. But it wouldn't pay.' He had closed his books. It was just too much for him. He even stopped going to his elocution classes. When I said, 'But you've been doing pretty well,' he said, 'Yes, but what's the use?' He wouldn't go to the doctor either. He was undergoing treatment; he was very sick. To tell the truth, I wasn't surprised. But it came as a shock all the same, especially to Ute. Now we're all pretty well adjusted and now we play a good deal of music. My husband, unfortunately, wasn't musical. The family was too much for him, too. He was always looking for fellowship. We couldn't give him that, no we couldn't." (Frau Augst might also have said, He was still in the race, but without competitors. Time must have hung unbearably heavy on his hands.)

Doubt was never bored. Every day until well into the fall, he timed his competing snails with his softly-sweetly ticking pocket watch. And though her snails won race after race with monotonous regularity, Lisbeth Stomma wasn't bored either. Only Stomma was impatient. "Get a move on," he'd shout at a snail. "Go on. Get the lead out of your ass!"

At the Augsts there was tea, sandwiches, and meat salad for supper. By then the daughter had joined us. No more was said about August. I said, "We also have four children: three boys and a girl. But they're all a lot younger. It's louder in our house: 'Go on! Get the lead out of your ass!' "

In the winter of 1943–1944, all Lisbeth brought home was a few snail shells she had raked from under the snow and moldering dead leaves: no more races. Evidently Lisbeth was distressed at her inability to bring Doubt racers, for when the last lapidary snails fell from the damp north wall and the rufous slugs shriveled like leather and lost their mucus and sheen, she began to move the newly stored winter potatoes; but although the great slug likes to hibernate in cellars, there was no slug to be found.

As though in leavetaking Frau Augst said, "Professor Bloch lives right around the corner. We see him now and then when he goes for a walk. We'd like to talk to him and ask him. But we don't dare."

Lately, Stomma had taken to shaving before visiting his guest in the cellar. And his tone became more and more respectful. "What I'd like to know, sir, being you're a genuine Jewish doctor, is . . ." Doubt's efforts to prove his Aryan origins. He sketched a family tree with Mennonite roots twining back to the sixteenth century. He reminded Stomma of his passport, which Stomma (to be on the safe side) had been keeping for years. But since he had first, out of habit, introduced himself by his nickname—"Just call me Doubt, that's what my pupils called me"—Stomma refused to believe in the Mennonite ramifications or in what was written in the passport. (Years before, in Dirschau on the Vistula, he had known a Jew by the name of Gläubig, the owner of a trucking business.) Moreover, the daily shortenings of the front in the Wehrmacht communiqués confirmed the newly courteous Stomma in his belief; he was proud of himself and thought of himself as a hero for hiding a Jew in his cellar: "I'll stand up for him. At the risk of my life."

Not until March, 1944, when the divisions of the Narva army group were forced to retreat to the Lake Peipus-Pleskau line did Lisbeth Stomma find a few reddish-lipped strawberry snails that had wintered in the piles of beech leaves in the Brenntau cemetery. In Doubt's cellar they emerged from their shells. Hesitantly, happiness repeated itself. But there were no more races. Instead, renewed attempts at tenderness toward what was present of his beloved: playfully Doubt set the strawberry snails on downy-blonde flesh and was affectionate by proxy; but Lisbeth remained distant—not even revulsion.

This motif is already to be found in Persian miniatures. And also the Hittites are said to have put snails on their women, to have taken their time about love.

Write a monument to Augst.

When in April Doubt celebrated his thirty-ninth birthday, Stomma gave him a brass letter scale on a glass pedestal; now he was able to weigh his snails.

The three Augst sons took me to the station. I returned via Reutlingen Nürtingen Plochingen, noting little in my waste book: wore glasses. The pacifist. The rattle. Micology and elocution school. The Twenty-third Psalm. Only four months in the Afrika Korps: the climate didn't agree with him. Fellowship. The war generation. The Ludwigstein. Seems to have read a good deal of Kant. What else Dean Noetling said over his grave. His grandmother and the piano lessons. Degree in pharmacology at forty-eight. Wouldn't buy a new pair of trousers. Took trips with the children: once to the Tyrol, once to Alsace, where they visited the former Struthof concentration camp. Debts until shortly before the end. His memberships . . .

I got out in Esslingen and visited the childless Jäckels. "Tell us about it," they said. And I began: "He wore glasses and was a pacifist. Wanted to enlist in the Waffen-SS but they wouldn't take him. Gathered mushrooms and didn't like music. They all tried hard, his wife and children. Belonged to the Free Church. Under treatment for depressive state: probably Tofranil. Supposed to alleviate endogenous melancholia . . ."

Suppose I sat the two of them down at a table after all? Now that Doubt has his letter scale, it ought to work. Augst has forgotten his glasses; that evens things out. It's already May in Karthaus and the rest of Kashubia. The rain has brought lots of rufous slugs: brick-red peat-brown rust-red mustard-yellow . . . one of them could mediate between them. There'd be plenty of food for exchanges. (Hermaphroditic happiness is at least conceivable.) The rufous slug would be present for both of them: fellowship. (Raoul, too, can imagine the two of them at a table.)

Afterward, the Jäckels, alternately and simultaneously, related travel experiences they had brought back from India. Even if I laughed at comical episodes and seemed to take an interest in India, I was far away.

25 It forms wherever they get together and give each other the floor, wherever they bicker wrangle argue and sit in shirt sleeves, where in tête à têtes they understand each other better (a little better), where they're all in the same boat and dog refrains from eating dog, where they try not to think about themselves but to fix their (blinking) eyes on the over-all picture, where protests are (chronically) sharp and objections emphatic, where they negotiate with each other before voting, where compromises are worked out in advance and as a precaution stated (clearly) for the record, where expenses are investments, where agendas are compared and postcard greetings to absent members passed around, where in the course of many sessions men have learned to appreciate each other, where it stinks . . .

Leaf back: Münster, room with view of the zoo. Our candidate in Lünen a parson. Universal fug on many levels. Osnabrück in the rain shortly after Willy. A golden hamster belonging to Franz has disappeared. *Local Anaesthetic* is being panned. The Münster and Osnabrück voters' clubs are working with large and small ads. Overlapping fug zones. Krefeld where I at the Königsburg and Kiesinger at the Niederrheinhalle. The golden hamster belonging to Franz lay dead in the pantry. Despite unfavorable forecasts, 2,000 at our meeting. People call for air. Dropped in on Girardet & Co. in Wuppertal; talked with the editorial board, printers, and type-setters. (Quote from Heinemann's September 1 speech.) The golden hamster was found in an empty earthenware jar. Though I detest exclamation marks, give an explanation. Anna (with her sensitive nose) had traced the smell. She said, "Just take it out to the garden and . . ." But then she couldn't help seeing the fur crawling with worms. Franz knew how much a new one would cost. Drautzburg, the ear witness, went to hear Kiesinger: "Boyohboy! A solid hour about the yellow peril. China China China, till they're all shitting in their pants: they're coming, 700 million of them, every last one of them to Krefeld." At the burial of the golden hamster once belonging to Franz no one made a speech. Now the election campaign is in full swing all over. Mobile smog pockets. Beginning tomorrow, five times daily with loudspeakers on the top of the Volkswagen bus. No more skat with shop stewards, only talk-talktalk . . .

Wearing his cable-stitched knitted jacket, Doubt is sitting in the wing chair, his arms on the upholstered rests. (I'll try to dig him up, children. Too many other things passing through my head. Landscapes, for instance. When Doubt in his cellar felt the need of a landscape, there was always the north wall with its splotches of mold and fungus growth: he had a good imagination. So many undefined details.) Well, anyway, he's sitting in the wing chair. Outside, it's supposed to be summer. The newspaper reports defensive actions in Kurland, the eastern front is coming steadily closer. By now it almost looks as though Doubt were safe in his wing chair. On the table he has built up a still life: beside the brass letter scale lies the softly-sweetly ticking pocket watch, whose chain points in a roundabout way at the open razor, on which the magnifying glass (without shoelace) is leaning. Along the watch chain, over the glass pedestal of the scale are moving or hesitating two rufous slugs (brick-red peat-brown), two Roman snails (one of which will later glide unharmed over the open razor), and a yellow slug. Now the other Roman snail, carrying its shell, is resting on the dial of the softly-sweetly ticking pocket watch. Now the yellow slug is climbing up the brass rods of the letter scale, which it will soon tip. Free delivery of guidelines. Doubt is guided by the engraving (to the right of the cellar window); he's enjoying his *Melencolia*.

Change it. But it would be a mistake to look for fug exclusively in organizations, working groups, town halls, seminars, Republican Clubs, and athletic fields: loners also smell of insular attitudes, and even the despisers of fug sometimes meet in small circles. You can hear their little dry coughs: victims of demonstrative ventilation.

In August, Lisbeth Stomma, after bringing Doubt a good many easily namable snails, produced a slug that he, who knew all the mollusks belonging to the order of gastropods by name, was unable to identify. It resembled the great slug in length but was not carinate. Its red was not the rust-red brick-red fire-red of the rufous slug; purple-red, it had a grayish-black-spotted mantle. Like the rufous slug, it had a yellowish sole, but the mucus was vitreous and greenish. Its breathing aperture, like that of the yellow slug, bulged around the edges, but instead of being situated at the hind end of the mantle was more in the center, as in the rufous slug. (It looked like a cross between a rufous slug and a great slug.) Systematically as Doubt leafed through the specialized literature in thought, he could not identify it. No point in asking the mute Lisbeth where she had found it. Nevertheless, he questioned her methodically and finally grew harshly impatient. He wanted to know whether the soil had been dry, sandy, or shady-damp, whether she had found the unidentified slug clinging to the cemetery wall, on rotten wood, or on moss. He came close to striking her. (Or, when Lisbeth remained mute, did Doubt, though I can hardly believe it, rap her on the knuckles or on the crown of her head with the ruler he used for laying out tables?) Later, it became known that the unidentified slug was attracted to conifer needles but also to dead leaves, though it showed none of the characteristics of the rufous slug, which is found on heaths and in mushroom-rich pine woods.

A town in which mysticism and small-scale industry have settled uphill and down: efficiency induced by unfaltering spiritual illumination. Doubt didn't have to strike. Lisbeth recovered her tongue without benefit of violence. Slowly and hesitating at thresholds, she began to stammer whenever Doubt put the unidentified slug on her forearm, on the back of her hand, or on her knee. He had no purpose in mind, for he had often put snails or slugs on Lisbeth, and this surrogate tenderness had never brought about any change in her; but the unidentified (miracle) slug restored her speech. From day to day, Lisbeth's stammering and palatal grunting became more like intelligible words. Soon she was muttering and mumbling. And a week after Lisbeth had found the unidentified slug, she was able to say where: "It was with little Hannes."

Wuppertal takes in two election districts that were won in '65 with a safe 44 and 44.5 per cent. The comrades are too sure of themselves, too involved in the fug of local politics. To shake them up would require a (another) miracle: but when the time came, we climbed to 48.6 and 49.6 per cent—almost unbelievable.

■■■■■■■■■

For a time there was no further change. When the unidentified slug's foot crept along Lisbeth's forearm, followed the
crook of the elbow, and proceeded along the upper arm,
smoothing the blonde fuzz as it went, Lisbeth began to talk
about her son: what she had said to Hannes, what Hannes had
told her about his rabbits and hedgehogs, what had happened
while the other cemetery children were playing with Hannes—
quarrels about lost and found bones. But Lisbeth spoke only as
long as the slug clung to her. Sometimes Stomma, with cold
pipe, sat looking on. Of course he was surprised, but since he
had always known Doubt to be a doctor and what's more a
Jewish doctor, he was not immoderately surprised. "Now she's
talking again," he said, and on his next trip to town he procured a lovely blank copybook in which Doubt noted the
progress—delayed by relapses—of Lisbeth's cure.

When, after a side trip to Rheydt, we stepped into the
Krefelder Hof for a bite to eat, Kiesinger drove up to the door.
A few guests left their tables to watch him drive up. Our
waitress (who was just taking our orders) left us, although
Silvertongue could hardly have meant anything to her. I could
see by her back that she found Drautzburg more amusing, that
she followed the suction to the front window only reluctantly.
Consequently, though there was nothing to pepper yet, I called
out: "Would you kindly bring us some pepper?" The waitress
detached herself from the window front, smiled as though
liberated, brought the pepper, and, while Kiesinger drove up
and the applause of the Junge Union went off without a hitch,
finished taking our orders. So don't be in such a hurry to say
"typically authoritarian" when I call you, Franz, away from
the television screen and your UFO's, or lure Raoul away from
the suction by guile. Because suction is my enemy. It creates

groups that I'm afraid of. It ends with a single will with a single mouth letting out a single cry for redemption salvation miracle. (A writer, children, is someone who writes against suction.)

When the students got sick of their own smell, they left the lecture halls, linked arms, and, carried away by the suction of their slogans, aired themselves on the street. Despite violent motion and miraculous unanimity, this often photographed attempt at radical defugment was a failure, because the students didn't mingle; when it grew colder, they discovered a zone of warmth in their jargon and moved into it, many of them on long leases. (And now it looks as if sweet Jesus were going to help the cause with leftist parlor tricks.)

Anyway, without believing in miracles, we took the Krefeld election district from the C.D.U. Climbed from 40.2 to 45.2 per cent. And that although Silvertongue had implored high heaven and thrice cried out China at the Niederrheinhalle.

And laid his hand on her. And touched her. And said: Arise. And performed a miracle. And those who beheld it believed from that day onward. And Stomma, too, though Doubt kept contradicting him in elaborately scientific terms, said, "A regular miracle!"

Actually, it was nature that took away or gave back and healed. "Except," said Doubt, "that we don't know what substances take, give, and heal." In the tables of his diary he entered many uncertain particulars; and I, too, children, manage to pass through this and that local smog zone, but as soon as I leave Wuppertal or Krefeld, the fug closes behind my back, provoking a still unidentified sound.

While Lisbeth was being cured and changing more and more rapidly, the curative slug was also changing and discoloring; its purple turned to violet, darkening along the gray mantle, and finally to blue-black. The previously yellow creeping sole turned brown, while the mucus on which it glided lost its vitreous brown and became at first milky-white, then gray. It was as though the unidentified slug had sucked up Lisbeth's melancholy, possibly her black bile; for while discoloring, while drawing in the substance of melancholy with irresistible suction and storing it up, it grew to a span's length, put on weight, and became more and more leaden: a development registered daily by Doubt's letter scale. The bulge around the breathing aperture developed nodosities and proliferated, pushing the mantle upward. From the first days of November on, Doubt referred to the unidentified slug in his copybook exclusively as the suction slug. Step by step, he recorded its discoloration and ultimate darkening.

Samples from Bavaria and Münsterland: the oldest fug is the religious variety. A condensation of incense, plaster dust, stupidity, and the sweat of poor sinners. Communism, for instance, might have a future as a religion. I already have a foresmell of how, after a hermaphroditic encounter with Catholicism, it will breed a superfug from mysticism and materialism. No more atmospheric disturbances. Times untroubled by motion. No room for doubt. Only regularly scheduled canonizations and, issued by the Central Committee, proclamations of miracles.

At first, when it was still possible to call the suction slug unidentified, beautiful, and perfect, Doubt had more or less playfully set it down on his beloved's flesh. And once the

creeping sole fastened on to her and took action, Lisbeth had
begun, quite matter of factly, to stammer her old cemetery
tales. Later, when the suction slug acquired its name, began to
grow, discolor and darken, she talked more about what was
going on in the house, kitchen, barnyard, and rabbit hutch.
And still later, when the cure could be termed advanced, Lisbeth spoke not only when she had the suction slug on her, but
copiously in between. About the customers in the repair shop,
about her father's barter deals, about things that had happened
in the neighborhood. As soon as Lisbeth (both during and
after the treatment) began to spin her stories, her hunger for
small-town gossip and the down-to-earth news that neighbors
exchange across garden fences found expression.

We call it drivel. I always come home with a bellyful of the
pluralistic drivel that proliferates like knotgrass in fug centers
that are hard to pinpoint. Mixed commissions representing
doubly stitched interests. Hotbeds of regional embroilment. A
fug that spontaneously restructures itself. Tail-wagging idiom:
"We made a bit of a stink." "Let's stir up a little trouble."

The cellar witnessed relapses, which Doubt noted. Occasionally when the slug was applied, it induced intense pain.
Lisbeth whimpered, squinted, and rolled her eyes; she was
shaken by spasms. Doubt, who had counted on quicker progress, was obliged to break off the treatment more than once,
and then to space it, for—so it appeared—the suction slug also
had to be handled with care. When Lisbeth was doubled up
with pain, the slug also doubled up and reared. Its eye tentacles stiffened and vibrated. Even Lisbeth's whimpering had its
counterpart: the breathing aperture with its proliferating rim
emitted foamy bubbles, which crackled as they burst. (Slow
progress. You know, children, what desperately short steps we
take. And Raoul asked me recently if I knew that even the

Chinese minister of transportation goes by the name of Long Dee Leh.)

Since with my distracted nose I might neglect to describe my native vapor, I will now name the reform fug and explore its verbal field: amended project, partial model, step-by-step program, comparatively speaking, development. Something is always lacking. (What's lacking?) Serviceable foundations, an improved framework law, formulations of goals. A data bank is lacking. (What, apart from consciousness, should be changed?) Not everything at once, in point of fact the system. Sentences beginning with the word "somebody": somebody ought to, somebody should . . .

Rufous slugs in the rain. In wet weather they swell, take on a brighter coloration than in books, breathe visibly, pump promisingly, glide more easily. And their track becomes blurred.

A dry autumn. (Even with the window closed, Doubt heard the chestnuts bursting in the yard.) As long as Lisbeth's melancholy was transferring itself to the suction slug, he had little time for Stomma. He even had to neglect and later stop the lessons in ancient Greek, remarkable as had been the progress of the still unlettered Stomma and comical as it sounded when the bicycle dealer spoke of Agamemnon and Clytemnestra in his broad Baltic accent. (In Doubt's opinion, Stomma's pronunciation of ancient Greek conveyed an idea of the regional coloration with which the shepherds and peasants of Aeschylus's day may have purveyed gossip and rumors.)

Our reformers speak as the snail moves. In an area too vast to fathom: medium-term considerations based on a long-range program. Since they are always on the move, they hope to escape the stagnant smell—but drag it along with them.

Because Stomma, who ordinarily regarded every word as a trap, followed his daughter's cure as though looking on at a miracle, he asked Doubt to heal him as well and to apply the suction slug to his gout. After the slug had paced the length of his back for exactly five minutes, he regularly said, "I feel better now. Pretty soon I'll be wanting to dance the polka like a young whippersnapper."

With the project makers. Everywhere the battle over the velocity and direction of progress (as it should be called) is eating its way through projects, resolutions, supplementary motions, and minutes.

On the first day of Advent, 1944, at a time when winter, the last of the war, determined the situation on all fronts, Lisbeth Stomma went to the hairdresser's in Karthaus and came home with a permanent; a young and terrifyingly normal woman. Doubt noted this change as he had noted all preceding changes, just as in his schooldays he had observed the vision and breathing of pulmonate snails, the reproductive process of the hermaphrodite Roman snails and their mode of locomotion, and framed his observations in elegantly formulated notes. On May 28, 1944, he wrote in his diary: "Just after application (left thigh) L. St. began first to hum, then to sing, though the tune was unrecognizable. Only toward the end of the treatment did the formless la-la-la develop into the melody of the popular song "Rosamunde," though the text, except for the title and the words "savings account book" was not clear. According to my own observation and the testimony of her father A. St., this was the first time L. St. had sung since the death of her son Hannes (on September 2, 1939!). And by way of comparison, this entry: "Today, on September 21, 1944, both the suction slug's eye tentacles showed impaired reactions. When subjected to shade or to touch, they did not retract. After an hour their insensibility began to wear off. But it was almost evening, eight hours after treatment (back of neck) before the suction slug's visual and other reactions could be termed normal."

When the snail met itself coming in the other direction, it regarded itself as refuted.

"This won't do!" it cried out. "I say that up front is up front."

After hesitating in its own way, it changed direction and soon met itself again.

"So I was right after all. Up front is up front."

It turned and moved away from each other: a tragic and also—seen from a distance—comical cleavage.

How Lisbeth became a normal woman. (Several Swiss have confirmed that not only in Zurich-Niederdorf but also in the rural cantons, "the snail" or "you cunning little snail" is a vulgar-affectionate term for vagina; more graphic than twot or cunt.) You're lucky. Laura will guard her snail, Franz and Raoul will go looking for snails, and Bruno will move into lots of snail shells.

Normalization. Under November 6, 1944, Doubt wrote in his copybook: "Immediately after inception of treatment (pelvic region to edge of pubis) L. St. entered into a state of excitation, culminating after four minutes in orgasm. After a ten-minute pause (with application of suction slug) brief intense excitation was again followed by orgasm, during which the patient twice cried out the name of Roman Bruszinski (father of her deceased son Hannes), who was killed at the beginning of the war. The swollen vulva and copious emission indicated normal sexual behavior. When the suction slug moved across the pubis, the patient again entered into a state of excitation: heaving, rapid breathing, swelling of the vulva, raucous groans. (It became necessary to suspend treatment because the suction slug's breathing aperture began to emit bubbles.) At last Doubt had a woman.

You'll find out about that, children. I beg you to be tender and not to lose patience. And don't leave anything out. Be avid for new feelings. Keep looking for new places. Be satisfied, but not surfeited. Learn from the snail, take your time. . . .

26 . . . and congratulate you on your birthday. Both turned twelve at the same time. (Neither in the lead.) Raoul has got his record player after all. Once September starts in, it's hard to be consistent: something persuasive about the light.

I've retracted myself on the terrace with my tobacco: when I was twelve—though I don't mean to draw comparisons—the war was six years old and Poland had long been. I had no room of my own, but only the niche under the righthand window sill. You've each had one since we broke up the fight, because when twins are so radically different. And my sister, whom you call Gotte in Swiss German (and who has become a midwife since then and brought some 7,000 children into the world) had the niche under the lefthand living-room window sill. Now Franz is banging on the partition wall because Raoul and his metal file. Otherwise there was only one bedroom where we and our parents. "All right," I said. "Let them each have a room of his own." And my father said on Sundays: "He'll be better off when the war is over and a three-room apartment in Schidlitz." Because when I was twelve and my sister Waltraut nine, I lay awake in the dark and heard everything: quarrels and their sequel, the sound of love in bed, my parents sleeping. You have what I didn't have: a rectangular room where you can think yourselves out, imagine yourselves. (But under the window sill I, too, thought myself out, imagined myself.) When I now drop in on Franz and order, on Raoul and chaos, in Franz I recognize the products of boredom and myself in every detail, while in Raoul's room I'm overwhelmed each day by a new shambles. Both collect: Franz to arrange and classify, Raoul to disperse what has been arranged. Because something is always falling apart, and the world, this workshop and work in progress, is unfinished. (In my niche I collected beautifully jagged shell fragments.) Franz saves travel souvenirs from real and imaginary countries. We have plenty of room.

Now the new record player stands amid the chaos, dreading the curiosity of its owner, who is still working off energy outside. Franz is rolling and pitching in his cabin. I, just back, am catching up on my notes about Münster and Lünen, occupying the terrace with my tobacco: wisps of dust, peace and quiet, Doubt . . .

Raoul and objects. Here he comes, lamenting; he's bashed his right shin playing hare and hounds in the backyard (he was the hare). "No, Raoul, not your fate. It was the sharp edge of the cellar wall." Everybody wants to see the thin leg and the juicy wound. Bruno gives Anna advice. Franz is embarrassed. Laura discovers that something hurts her, too. I line up sayings: "It'll pass. Bad luck on birthdays brings good luck. Cross my heart; you'll see."

(They want chicken for lunch, those repulsively pale hormone birds. No meat, all pap.) In the afternoon we took Franz and Raoul and their seven or nine friends to the movies in Steglitz (Allegro) to see a Western: *Bad Day at Black Rock* with Spencer Tracy. "It was great!" That wasn't the end of the doings. Bettina's birthday cake, the new record player, claims of ownership upstairs and down. A family of this size knows no respite. Always something growing, something erupting, something healing up, somebody interrupting, something getting lost, part of something missing, always something going on. Often when the noise in the house and at the table becomes self-sustaining, Anna and I sit in a bell jar under two bell jars. Flight in different directions. Years of compromise. Dissimilar memories. Each in love with his refuge. Jointly absent. Sometimes within calling distance: "You still there? Any mail from Prague? When do you have to? What's the matter? Speak up. Tell me about it."

We went to see him in his special train, just before it pulled out: 12:12 A.M., Hamburg Central Station. He'd spoken himself hoarse in the market places of Schleswig-Holstein. Nothing new: he did it before, in '61 and '65, talked himself hoarse both times, both times with inadequate results. Will he make it this time? We sit in a semicircle: four or five dispensers of concern. A masseur, who is at the same time a security guard (and a butler on the side), kneads his shoulders and the base of his neck. So this is what the drawing room of a special train looks like: like the waiting room of a high-class private dentist. In our semicircle we learn how and where massaging balls of the thumb are applied. He begs each one of us on his little chair not to be put off by the therapeutic process. His program is checked off: seven times, "Dear Fellow Citizens . . ." Now he's pleased with our visit, smokes hoarsely, and tells a joke as if he were telling it for the first time.

Though I think I now know him, he remains a man who has come from far away, who though sitting here isn't here yet, who though recognizable in outline is indistinct in detail, who has an amazing supply of jokes, but in telling them seeks (as in school and playground days) refuge behind them. For

253

behind his laughter—and he can laugh, brittlely contagiously—well-tied bundles are piled. Who would want to touch them, to undo them?

A man with a background.

A man who in the course of his rise has collected defeats at every turn, bundled them up and carried them with him. (But even after victories, which were never more than partial victories, he was never willing to unload, to drop ballast.)

With every step he takes, he moves the past, his, our national rocks. A packhorse that runs only when overloaded. (In his knees there's something that creaks and wants to be bent; and a year later in Warsaw, he did indeed go down on his knees instead of dispensing words.)

When he speaks, his sentences push each other. Each pushes the next and is pushed by the one behind it. Shunting sounds. Where is the push when nothing pulls?

He doesn't like to call things by name. (Often when he knows something perfectly, address and all, he talks around it until the thing itself becomes a vague circumlocution.)

Phases of hesitation, dispersion. He sees the important issues and relationships down to the smallest granule, but persons (even important ones) in a blur, through frosted glass. (When the frosted glass is removed and persons he had favored turn against him, he is silent and hears his silence.)

A man who hesitates to say "I" and yet cannot disregard himself. (If there were a Sisyphus in Nordic legend, his name would have to be Willy.)

A man of the tribe of Doubt.

And smokes and is hoarse. Our advice about using a mike for speaking out of doors; for sometimes he believes without speaking. Footnotes about the strikes in the Ruhr and the

Howaldt shipyards. The usual worries, the findings of not so recent opinion polls. Leo Bauer has some new figures that are too encouraging. I say something slow and insistent about deficiencies in Upper Swabia. He nods, agrees, collects deficiencies: another bundle. In the high-class drawing room of the special train that will shortly pull out, the security guard massages his neck.

Yes, children, I'm friends with him. This came about belatedly. For years (at intervals) I've been talking to him and writing to him; we've listened to each other, formed sentences together, never had time enough. I don't know if he knows more about me than I tell him. Before we get to ourselves, we always talk about the cause. Because we're so different, we need a cause that we call ours. (Revolves around a bluish future, is counterbalanced by oxidized past, forms a grayhatched present.) A planned friendship. Not enough accidents . . .

A man who gives his melancholy deadlines.

A man with his feet on the ground, incapable of presumption.

A man whose escape hatches are blocked, who retreats forward.

Many have agreed to help themselves by helping him. He accepts their help.

And this in a whisper: I'm worried about him. I'm afraid that he's a target. It could happen any day. (If only because he's so relentlessly loved.) I'm almost afraid to hope that he'll win and become even more conspicuous to the hatred of our enemies.

■■■■■■■■■

With Sontheimer, Jäckel senior, Gaus, Linde, and who else? When we went to see Willy Brandt shortly before the special train pulled out of the Central Station in Hamburg, we were chary of suggestions. Gaus, whom I often try to think of as Doubt in his cellar, spoke analytically. His voice carried. He was right in the first to fifth place. (Only Stomma with his simplicity and guile could have refuted him.) On the round table lay newspapers and the *Bild-Zeitung*. A few lines underscored. Evil in mass circulation. (But no more matches, no labyrinth game.) Will he? Will we? Is it conceivable that? Behind the S.P.D. candidate and the massaging security guard a closed window offered a view of Platform 4: in the yellow light a couple kissing. Both of voting age. Both far away.

The special train was ready to leave. We politely wished ourselves good luck. When we left, a man remained behind whose loneliness draws large crowds.

Presents: mine and yours.

Franz contributes a snake skin.

"Where'd you get it?"

"From the store."

He's referring to the animal shop—bird food, aquarium accessories, guinea pigs—next door to the "Sweet Corner" on Friedrich-Wilhelm Platz.

"He shed it. It was just lying around. A ring snake. Listen to the way it crackles."

In return, Franz wants to give the shopkeeper two newborn golden hamsters.

"When mine get babies. Any minute now."

Change a snake skin for what?

If I could shed my skin.

Be outside myself.
Sticky-new.

On the day after your birthday, right after the meeting in Marktredwitz, somebody I'd been to school with (I don't know which one) slapped me on the back: "What do you say, old-timer?"

27 As her cure advanced, the simple-minded Lisbeth
Stomma became a young woman with a permanent and other
needs. She was now twenty-four and knew (of late) when her
birthday was. (She could also say Monday Tuesday Wednesday
and five after seven and the day after tomorrow and the day
before yesterday.) The more the suction slug took away from
her, the more she laughed. No girlish giggle, a loud snorting
laugh, too big for the cellar. On Lisbeth's laughter floated an
invitation to laugh with her.

She went more and more rarely to the cemetery where her
Hannes lay. Sometimes (while taking potatoes from the pile)
she said, "I ought to go because it's so dry. Well, maybe the
day after tomorrow." To faraway, out-of-town cemeteries, in
Brentau or Oliva, for instance, she stopped going altogether.

Lisbeth began to live; eagerly she collected proofs of being
alive. When she came to Doubt—and soon she was coming
every night—she held him and squeezed him; she didn't just
lie there under him, she took him in. Her step on the cellar
stairs announced demands. She was coming and wanted something. Her melancholy flesh had submitted to Doubt's thrusts
with dull indifference; before the suction slug changed Lisbeth, Doubt had tried vainly, with frenzied fumbling and
industrious thrusts, to wrest a little tenderness from her. But
now she responded lavishly, gave in return. Lisbeth Stomma

became curious, capable of astonishment; she had to touch, to grab hold of. She wanted to know what's done how and where, and learned all about it. And wanted more, wanted it crosswise, astraddle, from the side, from behind, and then again from the front. She was yielding and tense, she sucked herself fast when sucked; she had claws and gently caressing fingers. They licked each other like dogs and left nothing out. No longer dry and tight, open and moist she let herself come, panting when she came and when he came. And in between, her gasped syllables and rutting cries.

Love moved into Doubt's cellar with a pungent smell: sperm cheese, steaming double flesh. Never enough. The mattress too narrow. Under the two (who were one) the mound of potatoes gave way and spread out. On the stamped-clay floor. Spread-eagled in the wing chair. Standing until their knees gave way, against the damp north wall. They performed gymnastic feats as though there were prizes and medals to be won. Everything that could be done, until at last (so it seemed) they had enough and the only resource was sleep. But even in their sleep, children, they reached out for each other and trembled with exhaustion because they were so empty.

Often Lisbeth stayed till morning. Doubt was sheltered from the cold: the breath beside him. Sometimes they whispered between sleep and sleep: hachured little words, tiny murmurings, close-knit why-chains. Since Lisbeth was now a woman who had a man, she began to ask (and Doubt liked to be asked). Before the suction slug cured Lisbeth and changed her, she had never wanted to know where Doubt came from, what had brought him to the cellar, why he never left it. For more than three years she had come day after day without a question, and even when Doubt told her, in words such as children use, about himself and his man-crazy grandmother, about his books and pupils, about the village of Müggenhahl among the drainage ditches, and his ancestrally furnished apartment, about Laban the bald vegetable dealer and the emigrant ship *Astir*, about the sale of the synagogue, the warehouse on Mausegasse, about hope, about Mount Carmel in Palestine, and even about the heavenly Jerusalem, Lisbeth Stomma had been a mere hole, which Doubt could talk into without ever filling it: it sent up no answer. But now Lisbeth wanted to know every teeny-weeny thing.

From Marktredwitz to Wunsiedel, where it was raining and we had to take refuge in the Golden Lion—from Wunsiedel to the casino garden in Bad Berneck, where under the trees the old people, weary and laden with cares—from Bad Berneck to Bayreuth. We managed four meetings a day (plus press conference and hasty organization of voters' clubs). Drautzurg stabilized the top of our bus with a platform and hitched up two loudspeakers. In Lake Constance Swabian, Bentele announces: "In fifteen minutes you will be addressed in the market place by . . . on the casino terrace the well-known . . . the world-famous author will answer your questions. . . ." We arrive to the tune of a musical number concocted by Drautzburg and Bentele: "Oh, happy day." Usually I'm still lying flat in the back seat when it starts booming out on top. The moment we stop, the little aluminum ladder is snapped into place so the various candidates and I can climb up on the platform. Short speech. "Ladies and gentlemen"—while the public gathers into a semicircle, prepared to be amazed. Down below, Drautzburg, through a megaphone, invites participation in discussion. Inside the bus, Bentele controls the volume and sweats during breakdowns. I up top have to take care that my microphone doesn't get tangled up with the loudspeakers: a battle wth technology, the weather, lifelong prejudices, and smug ignorance. An N.P.D.-prone region. (In Wunsiedel two long-haired youngsters, this time right-wingers, who had learned to call me not "revisionist" but "seller-outer.") In Bad Berneck a vigorous lady, who seemed to have incorporated the microphone in her anatomy, was determined (with my help) to save the aboriginal population of Australia. Everywhere the woes and fears of the pensioned old people. Their careworn faces. The confused (officialese) way they talk. Pushed aside, put off, wizened. Though uncomprehendingly C.S.U.-fixated, they look only to the Social Democrats for help. (Children, if you want to help yourselves, help the pensioned old people. They have plenty of bitterness to offer.)

Society of achievement—that's what it calls itself. Wherever I went, regardless of whether capitalism proved flexible or Communism ramrod stiff and well fed, everywhere production quotas and superquotas ruled, and the old people sat useless because they'd been pushed aside (or pushed aside because they were useless) and talked of past achievement.

Next day: Eibelstadt—wine sampling with invited guests—Ochsenfurt in the market place—then Würzburg, city of many churches.

Hard hard work! Still, it's fun to share the wobbly bus top with varying candidates, to look out at baroque façades, to be interrupted by church bells, to stand as though free-floating beneath the sky and its sparrows, to speak at last without an upended crate and, in variable weather with an invariably dry reform program, to be so near the crowd, right in their midst.

In Munich we were out to win the midtown election district. (We won it.) There as in Würzburg, Nuremberg, Erlangen, voters' clubs are operating with small and large ads, with lists of prominent persons, with statements by professors, with floods of leaflets, and with telephone advice. On Leopoldstrasse, Schwier, the comedian ("There's no law against laughing") and I sell our campaign paper *dafür*. Night meeting at the smoke-curtained Löwenbräukeller. Vestiges of morose A.P.O. Off-the-cuff speech: "On the unknown voter." Sick of reading. I know the questions by heart, my answers, too. It's more fun in the country.

Bavaria makes you hoarse. In Bavaria a man can talk himself hoarse. (A blue-and-white hoarseness.) Next morning, after talking for a whole hour without a mike at the Gasthof Bräuwirt in Miesbach, I was as hoarse as Willy. Afterward, Klaus Hardt, who built up the Munich voters' club, gave me something sharp that dulls the pain to gargle with. It helped instantly; it's called Idon'trememberwhat. It wouldn't do to go on being hoarse. Sounds too laboriously pathetic. Only Willy has a right to be hoarse and strained. In him it has credibility.

Nothing easier than trampling a snail; snails ask for it. You nod, children. You've had that impulse in your shoes.

It began when Lisbeth refused to gather snails for Doubt and his collection. In the late summer of '44, after the suction slug had imbibed all the blackness and battened on Lisbeth's melancholy, she stopped taking her watering can when she went to the cemetery. But then she might go out into the garden after all and come back with a few rufous slugs and grove snails. "All right. If you really want me to."

For Lisbeth was a woman who liked to do her man a favor (though not always in a hurry). She washed and mended his shirts and socks, his long underdrawers and matted cable-stitched knitted jacket; she swept his cellar, covered his

262

hitherto naked beach-grass mattress with a fresh sheet, changed the pissy quilt for a feather bed, set down a bunch of asters beside his letter scale, and patiently took care of him when he caught the flu in October; she just didn't feel like picking up any more snails, not even those who had withdrawn into their shells under the autumn leaves.

Now don't be angry with Lisbeth or save all your sympathy for Doubt; for Lisbeth Stomma was—all in all—a good and even good-natured woman, who, once cured and changed, had become so normal that she began to be revolted by snails.

This beauty crawls into its shell.

This beauty insists on mucus.

This slow beauty doesn't want to be touched.

Eloquently as Doubt praised the gloss, the hesitant charm, the harmonious play of the tentacles, the traditional revulsion was quicker. He wrote in his copybook: "The beauty of snails cannot overtake disgust with snails. Normalcy wins out and remains stupid."

Quite possibly, now that the suction slug, grown black, bloated and ungainly in the course of the healing process, lay idle (as though pensioned) on its bed of sand and pine needles, it aroused Lisbeth's disgust, first with itself, then with all other gastropods; be that as it may, she began, as soon as Doubt fell or pretended to fall asleep on his mattress, to hiss curses, now in Polish, now in Kashubian, at the bloated, motionless slug, which had lost every vestige of purple and was now covered with bumps, knobs, and warts. Doubt heard her spitting at the slug. Then he saw that Lisbeth's accumulated saliva had struck home and begun to discolor. These reactions he also noted in his copybook, as indications that the cure was complete. "Evidently L. St. is trying by means of spitting and cursing to keep her sickness, which is now accumulated inside the suction slug, at a distance. Fear of relapse. Hatred of compact blackness. Catholic-pagan motif, comparable to the sign of the cross. As though the devil had gone into the slug: evil in the form of a slug."

At the end of November—it was the first Sunday of Advent and Lisbeth had had her second permanent the day before—shortly after the evening meal, consisting of fried potatoes with bacon and scrambled eggs, as Doubt was reading the paper to Stomma, his host, and explaining the developments on the Kurland front, everywhere planned withdrawals and shortenings of lines—Lisbeth with her right Sunday shoe trampled the unidentified slug, first tentatively named purple slug, then from its function suction slug. It burst from the breathing aperture to the end of the keel. It burst with a full-bodied report. On the inside, too, it was black. Inky-black and odorless, it drained. Stomma was about to hit his daughter. Doubt stopped the blow and asked Stomma to leave. Lisbeth wept after trampling the slug. When Doubt drew her down to him on the mattress and under the feather bed, she was still crying: "I couldn't stand it any more."

Nail the slug to the cross. A quiet happening. The eye tentacles fastened at the sides. No blood, only mucus at the foot of the cross.

That night, when the two of them (each desperate in a different way) had loved each other dry, Doubt began, because the slug had been trampled, because the northwest wind was blowing, because Lisbeth wouldn't stop asking questions, to tell her about himself and where he came from, about fear and flight, until Lisbeth knew all and too much; but nothing worried him as yet.

■■■■■■■■■

After the meeting in Miesbach (Upper Bavaria) the Social Democratic mayor took me aside to inform me, on behalf of the Munich police, of a threat to murder me. I say, "Sure. I've been getting a lot of them lately. Usually there are two plain-clothes men inconspicuously looking after me." But the mayor was still worried, and I, too, felt uneasy when he told me about a midnight phone call in Berlin: "Your wife reported it this morning. . . ."

When words cast shadows. Should Doubt not have told her anything? Should he have kept it all to himself? Thus, under a blanket, exhausted, one flesh, enlaced by arms and legs, bedded in warmth (as though in trust), he spoke and left nothing out.

Anna and two plain-clothes men were waiting for me at Tempelhof. In the cab they told me: at midnight Franz had heard the sentence, "The bullet's ready," and asked politely— he can be polite—for further details, but the only answer had been the monotonous repetition of the sentence. Then (still in all likelihood half asleep) he had gone back to bed. At breakfast he had reported the midnight phone call. He had called it disagreeable, kind of funny, kind of spooky: "You know, the voice and all. Sounded like a tape. Like something in the movies. How's anyone going to believe that . . ."

I, hoarse in Miesbach, was scared, children. We seem to be getting somewhere. Somebody has let hate off the leash. If we win, he'll mark up targets. (Doubt should have stuck to his disquisitions on hermaphroditic happiness and not said anything about himself.)

28 They stand in the doorway, invoke justice, claim to know somebody that we know, knock after entering, ask without waiting for an answer, disguise themselves as doormat spittoon toothpick (used).

They're known as complainers. Their words are: remission of residual costs, motion for reversal of verdict, pretrial investigation, decree reducing war victim indemnities, district court decision, land office, reimbursement of costs, in respect of, hereinafter, compensation, repeatedly.

After every meeting, just as it's starting to break up and I'm autographing (inwardly saying amen)—they make a beeline for me and reel off their case. Right up close. Their usually fusty breath. They talk loud and fast, as if they were in court, afraid the judge will shut them up. Or with quiet urgency or rasping passion. Obsequiously. Hunted men, tidily dressed.

They press me to leaf through photostats that have often been leafed through and are falling apart.

Correspondence with lawyers and (in the meantime) deceased department heads. Dismissal notices, negative replies, medical certificates (fistula of the rectum). Clergymen's testimonials and medical affidavits are set before me. Limp papers. The obstinate pursuit of justice. Kohlhaas and his horses. (When Doubt in his cellar told this tale that is always new, Stomma, his host, said, "Damn it, he was right!")

266

I leaf forward and backward. Cramped writing that overflows margins. Underscored in red: "For an alleged right of access . . . after refusal to comply with the Poor Law . . . fear of facts . . . shamelessly hushed up . . . a state built on injustice!"

They beg and threaten. I say, "On the spur of the moment I couldn't." They say, "Always the same excuses . . ." And I say, "I'm sorry, I haven't time. . . ." They say, "I thought you were for justice. . . ." I say, "But right now I have to . . ." They say, "From courthouse to courthouse for the last nine years . . ."

Faces you'd take on trust. (Ever since the snail was indicted, all lawsuits have been long drawn out.) Permanent-emergency faces. Superannuated faces. (My travel souvenirs: fossilizations of the system.)

Kohlhaas marginal group. (Now he's running and serving himself with summonses.)

It's overlapping hearings and overheated rooms.

Gray-hatched carbon copies of negative decisions.

It's the formula for addressing helplessness: We regret to inform you.

The universal, now habitual constipation.

It's the permanently unusual circumstances: We're all overburdened.

And other hardship cases that can't be attended to: After all, we're not magicians.

Time, say its consumers, is getting scarcer and scarcer.

Replies on printed forms: retroactively on schedule.

But there must be . . .

What gives us headaches is that so many and more and more people are running in different directions and always pointing forward. (In Porz am Rhein, when something entirely different was being discussed, a woman shouted without raising her voice: "I've been deprived of my rights! I've been deprived of my rights!")

And Lisbeth Stomma also began to ask about the four acres of farm land in Kokoschken, which after her mother's death had been farmed by her stepbrother (Clemenz Czapp), although Lisbeth might have presented a justified claim, especially since Stomma and his daughter had become ethnic Germans in the meantime, whereas Czapp had not had himself Germanized.

And Lisbeth went to the land office in Karthaus and came home with papers: forms that Doubt had to fill out. They revolved around inheritance and justice, four acres of farm land and two dozen sour-cherry trees. . . .

A Westphalian peasant wedding had been in progress at the Hotel Schloss Berge since early in the afternoon, and was still going on. Gelsenkirchen makes its Hotel Schloss Berge available for peasant weddings all year round. Next morning, before going to Cologne with its four election districts and ninety-nine foolish virgins, talked with Alfred Nau about Social Democratic necessities. (His Bebelian memory retains everything down to three places after the decimal point.) At the Päffgen brewery I meet somebody I'd known as a stonecutter, a fellow Danziger what's more. But we were unable to reminisce in dialect, because I had to ply the megaphone on Neumarkt, then at the Karstadt department store with shop stewards, and later on the bus top with all four candidates by turns. But that evening at the Satory Hall various things went wrong, and I got to thinking about them at the Hotel Schloss Berge, though the Westphalian peasant wedding was so ramified that its family trees grew into my room. I've become hardened in the course of time, but I felt rotten when an A.P.O. maiden from Cologne gave poor Marchand hell for editing *dafür*, our campaign paper. Oh, how they pull the rug out from under each other's feet. Oh, how they love to liquidate. Oh, how—unbeknownst to them—Goebbels peers through their Stalinist buttonholes. . . . I sighed in my bed, which brought me no sleep, because downstairs the intertwined families of Westphalian peasants and in my head the evening's discussion refused to stop. Next day Wanne-Eickel, Wattenscheid, and in the evening Gelsenkirchen (Hans-Sachs-Hall). But even in Huckarde near Dortmund, while I was visiting the Hansa Coke Works, and the comrades (during the change of shifts) showed me their pay slips and even words intended to be friendly were colored wth anger, half of me was still sitting with the miners' wives and mothers in Wanne, who were sitting over coffee and crumb cake, which crumbles backward and makes a man homesick. I'm willing to admit that in my unprofitable bed I heard and hummed various popular songs that made me pretty mournful when I was young (nineteen) and rutting: "Ramona" . . . "Raindrops" . . . Forget it, I'm here again and ready for use. But don't let anyone tell you that campaigning is all routine. I come in with my carefully worked-out manuscript and see a hall full of miners' wives: unfriendly, indifferent. Instantly, my written matter strikes me as ridiculous. I sit down on my written speech, I'm sweating; in a second (right now) I'll have to jump into cold water, speak off the cuff while I'm sweating internally, say whatever comes to me in my distress: "Like our Gustav Heinemann, who loves not the state but his wife . . ." And keep it up until the miners' wives and mothers in their chairs turn away from their crumb cake, because up there behind the upended crate . . . (The *Westfälische Rundschau* reported: "The women took him to their hearts. . . .") At about five in the morning I must have hummed myself into a kind of three-quarters sleep. Of course I was proud when the miners' women applauded for quite a while. For a writer (and pedant) tends to stick to his manuscript as though bewitched, and now all of a sudden to do without, like the Apostles when the Holy Ghost . . . Anyway, I've got better at it since then. For instance, what it says about Dortmund in my waste book: addressed shop stewards with Karl Schiller, etc. (This time Erdmann Linde was there. Stricken because someone had died and he didn't know how he could carry on.) Late, after another speech—Small Westphalia Hall—and before finding the sleep that the peasants in Gelsenkirchen, as stingy as peasants can be, had refused me, someone turned up from the *Sonntagsblatt,* who had attended the meetings in Cloppenburg and Osnabrück, but on this occasion was interested only in subordinate clauses about literature. That was far away. I had to pinch myself, to remember myself in a roundabout way; but not even Doubt in his cellar wanted to chat about snails and be witty.

"Tell me, doesn't it fragment you?"
"Yes, it does."
"Then I can say you're fragmented?"
"I am."
"Isn't that regrettable?"
"Why?"
"Because you used to be all of one piece, if nothing else."
"Not really. Just a bundle of fragments."
"What are you going to do now? In part."
"Sleep!"
"What would you like to do if you could?"
"Crawl into my shell."

I'll leave you now.
Your shell reminds me.

In motion you were understandable.
I've taken lots of notes.
Never hesitating to deviate from thought-out lines.
No swallow's flight: a snail's track.
A feeling for gaps and suchlike virtues.
Without accidents, except for the one . . .

On the forehead of a recumbent woman, who has found her breath again, the snail rests before she once again finds everything. (Yes, it's bestial the way she takes him in. "Now!" she cries. "Now!")

It became a habit and carried them through till they woke up. In the daytime strife took over; a new subtenant in Doubt's cellar. For now that she was healthy and normal, now that she wanted to inherit farm land and own sour-cherry trees, Lisbeth Stomma became quite normally cantankerous. Because she knew everything and while peeling potatoes made it clear how much, thanks to Doubt, she knew about Doubt, also because she knew that no one was supposed to know what she knew, Stomma, who thought she knew too much, began to fear his daughter and out of fear to beat her. This was after the Soviet armies broke through at Baranov. Insterburg in East Prussia had fallen, the last German offensive in the Ardennes had collapsed. Doubt and Stomma, his host, could have awaited the imminent end of the war with an easy mind if an excess of health had not made Lisbeth Stomma, who wanted to inherit and knew too much, so cantankerous. Anything—Doubt's habit of cracking his knuckles, Stomma's habit of emptying his pipe by knocking it against the table leg—was pretext enough for long-drawn-out nagging and endless backbiting. At first she merely bandied her knowledge as an obscure threat, but beginning in January, 1945—as the front came closer, pushing vague hope before it—her threats became more blatant: "If

271

you think I'm going to put up with all this, you've got another think coming. Not if I have to report you to the police."

When Stomma raised his fist to strike, but close to the ceiling it hesitated, his daughter laughed in quickly successive stages: a malignant raucous giggle was followed by volleys of ear-splitting laughter; she snorted, lost control, panted between short-winded screams, guffawed, pressed her thighs together to hold back her water, gurgled, gave up in exhaustion, and recovering her good humor, let it tinkle.

Dürer is said to have had a cantankerous wife. His friend and boon companion Pirckheimer tells us that Agnes Dürer, née Frey, broke his heart with her nagging. Day in day out, she scolded and grumbled, though he always gave in, hastily selling off his engravings and woodcuts, the *Lesser Passion* and the *Greater Passion,* the *Life of the Virgin* series, and countless separate works (including the *Melencolia*) at bargain prices. Possibly Doubt recognized Dürer's Agnes in Lisbeth Stomma, and in both the woman who, amid bric-a-brac and household articles, sits symbolized as an angel of wrath, doubly smitten by Saturn, the tutelary deity of loud scolding and dull melancholy.

Even after the Russians had rolled over Poland and East Prussia, after Elbing had fallen and the Vistula Army Group had been cut off, even when shattered German units retreating on the Karthaus-Langfuhr highway projected the sound of tank treads into Doubt's cellar, Lisbeth kept on scolding and brandishing threats of Gestapo and military police. To make matters worse, she was pregnant. "The kike has knocked me up." Two days before Karthaus was evacuated and occupied by units of the Soviet Second Army, Doubt tried to explain to Lisbeth Stomma on the one hand that he wasn't a Jew but that as a Jew he would soon be able on the other hand to make himself useful. Whereupon she worked herself up into such a screaming fury that Stomma, who was afraid of having soldiers billeted on him any minute, hit her until she lay on the clay floor, bleeding from her right eyebrow to her hair line: he had hit her with a bicycle pump.

Well, children, what more is there to tell? Doubt bandaged Lisbeth Stomma and took care of her. When the Russians arrived, Doubt conferred with Soviet officers. Doubt prevented the pregnant Lisbeth from being raped in spite of the bandage on her head. In the course of long drawn-out questioning at the Kommandantur, Doubt was able to identify himself. Doubt, whose name was once Ott, interceded successfully in behalf of Stomma, his host, for Stomma, who had become an ethnic German, would otherwise have been sent to a camp in Thorn. Doubt paid off. When Soviet troops were replaced by Polish troops, he was even entrusted with administrative duties. Stomma, too, went about town with a red armband and was soon generally feared.

Maybe this can be added: for a long time Doubt refused to give up his cellar. The minute he got home from his office—he had to register all the German nationals in the district—he descended the stairs and lay down on his mattress, though Lisbeth had a bed waiting for him in her attic room. Doubt, now Hermann Ott, found it hard to live upstairs and out of doors, where everything was real and terrifying. Not until summer—by then he was married—does he seem to have left the cellar as though for good and to have moved (as though for good) into the attic room with Lisbeth, now in an advanced state of pregnancy. But Doubt had undergone a change. In the first days of spring he began to look, not for snails and slugs in general, but only for the one unidentified slug whose purple had turned black as it swelled, which Lisbeth had trampled with her Sunday shoe, which had become a sponge for melancholy and transformed Lisbeth into a woman with needs: laughing and cantankerous, good-natured and terrible.

For two whole years Hermann Ott, who for a long time had been known only as Doubt, seems to have looked first everywhere, then only in cemeteries, for the unidentified slug and for proof that melancholia is curable; in so doing, he seems to have succumbed little by little to melancholia. In the late summer of '47, on the strength of a petition by his wife Lisbeth, who had borne him a son Arthur, he was committed to an institution (near Oliva): there, at first muttering over the jumbled handwriting on his papers, then utterly mute, he seems to have lived for twelve years. Toward the end he seems to have feared every sound and—when fish was served—fish bones.

You doubt me, children; you say Doubt doesn't and didn't exist. All imaginary and made up, and only the election campaign is real. But wherever I talktalktalked—in Kaiserslautern and Saarlouis, in Merzig and Dillingen, in Weinsberg Neckarsulm Heilbronn, in Ebingen Biberach Augsburg, in Schongau and Garmisch, in Murnau, Bad Tölz, and finally in Weilheim—talked and heard myself talk, I wasn't sure whether I was really talking and whether the market places and little postcard towns, our Volkswagen bus and the Saar Neckar Riss rivers, the candidates Kulaweg Eppler Bayerl, whether Drautzburg and Jäckel with his hair so neatly parted, Bentele (and I

274

myself) were not imaginary and made up. Naturally, you'll say, with fever and flu it's no wonder. Doubt of Doubt. As though the election campaign with its moods and air holes, its word traps and pauses for applause had left no room and offered no occasion for Doubt. As though he hadn't everywhere (first in Kleve and last in Weilheim) been silently present at every speech. For in sentence after sentence, if Jäckel hadn't watched so vigilantly over every period and comma, the fever that was my traveling companion would have bent all my fervent exclamations into question marks: the curlicues of Doubt's signature. Only when on the last day—two days before the elections—we apostrophized Franz Josef Strauss without detachment (in Weilheim, his election district), did Doubt take a vacation. . . .

"And what about this Doubt you made up?"
"And the snail that you only made up a little?"
"And Augst who really existed and wasn't just made up?"
"What are you going to make up now?"

Election night, children, when we barely won and my travels were (for the present) over. . . .

29 When, early in election night, the incorrectly programmed computer came up with totals strongly in our favor, when later on the first returns painted a black victory on the television screen, when at our headquarters (on Adenauerallee) no beer wine schnapps but only lead was drunk, when the recidivism of history seemed to be demonstrated and out in front the C.D.U. was issuing torches to their Junge Union, when Jäckel senior and I jotted down words of consolation for Marchand, Drautzburg, Gisela Kramer, and for ourselves as well on napkins, when (once again) we were all set to bear defeat as something we were used to—"It won't kill us . . . Next time we'll"—when we were all trying to crawl into our shells, only Erdmann Linde said, "Something's wrong; let's wait and see"—the television screen began, first jerkily after the decimal point, then firmly before the decimal point, to show those changes that seemed to refute the recidivism of history, that doused the black torches, moved (cautiously) first Schmidt and Wehner, then Schiller onto the screen, finally— after some purposeful phone calls—lured the whole big snail from its shell—and Willy said, "I will . . ." But none of us (on Adenauerallee) was willing to believe in victory; we had already attuned ourselves to dejection. (When a prize was to be given for hesitation, the snail hesitated on its way to the platform.)

■■■■■■■■■

Here are the figures on our close victory: on September 28, 1969, the black vote fell from 47.6 to 46.1 per cent. The Liberals slipped from 9.5 to 5.8 and were able—since the N.P.D. drew just under 5 per cent—to join with us, who had risen from 39.3 to 42.7 per cent, in forming the Social Democratic–Liberal government, which (contrary to all predictions) is still governing and has since then accomplished more than it realizes. Because the Social Democrats, children, are people who believe not in their own accomplishments but, radiating a diffused light, in their more ambitious resolutions. (With their tentacles they are always ahead of themselves.)

Somebody counted it up: ninety-four times I talktalktalked.

In the end, some sixty voters' clubs seem to have huffed and puffed.

Drautzburg says, "Exactly 31,000 kilometers without an accident."

I lost only four and a half pounds.

In retrolistening I hear a jumble of halls: casinos, meeting halls of every description. ("Drautzburg, what was the name of the hall where that schoolteacher wanted to win the First World War retroactively for the C.D.U.?") In Verden on the Aller, Höltjes Gesellschaftshaus has room for 850 people. Although the C.D.U. had more secondary votes, a bare 7,000 more primary votes put our candidate across. ("We'll go and sing there again," said Drautzburg. "We can do even better.")

The Münsterlandhalle in Cloppenburg is normally devoted to the egg business. (Sometimes I dream about it and wake up hoarse.) A region so dyed-black-in-the wool Catholic that even sacks of coal cast no shadows. Nevertheless, we managed, with the help of St. Francis, to creep from 14.9 per cent, past our dream goal, to 20.1 per cent.

The municipal meeting halls include: the Josefhaus, the Municipal Fruit Exchange (Kaiserslautern), and the Satory-saal (Cologne), where Katharine Focke, in the second election district, neither crawled nor glided, but in defiance of all regulations jumped from 37.8 to 48 per cent, defied the force of inertia over all the objections of nature, and established a Central European snail record.

In Reutlingen, however, where the Friedrich List Halle proves how hard of hearing money is in Swabia, the C.D.U. rose from 46.5 to 48.5 per cent while we inched our way from 34.1 to 37.6.

Ah, and the flop in Augsburg . . .

But that's enough about before and after the decimal point.

We won Catholic workers, working women, young protesters who were disillusioned with leftist splinter groups; and in the middle we won dentists, civil servants, schoolteachers, medium-level white-collar workers, and old ladies who were frightened by Strauss, were beginning to find Kiesinger embarrassing, and wanted to do something useful for their grandchildren.

Ah, yes, the municipal meeting hall in Kleve. That's where it began; in a drizzle . . .

"Well, Drautzburg, what do we do now?"

He's opened an art gallery and is living communally: Drautzburg has settled down.

Erdmann Linde is studying like mad, so he says. Sometimes he's mentioned in *Der Spiegel*, because he's a Young Socialist and a member of the radio council.

Marchand has got his degree with a thesis about Josef Roth. (At the moment in India as a university instructor.)

Bentele is still spherical but more compact. He's studying in Constance.

I haven't heard from Holger Schröder for ages; I'm told that he's married.

278

Gisela Kramer is still our secretary. The work goes on, and the time is coming closer, we'll soon be starting in again. Veronika Schröter, who with Christoph Schröter, built up the Erlangen voters' club, has prepared maps of the election districts and has bought pins with colored glass heads. Gaus and Jäckel senior (and now Jäckel junior as well), Baring and Troll, Böll and Lenz are still, again, finally with us. (It's hard to break snails of a habit; they foresee no end.)

"What about your Volkswagen bus?"
"Is it still around?"
It's on the road again, but in private hands. Drautzburg sold it. I'm told that somebody drove it all the way to Turkey.

"But what about Doubt?"
"Did he really die of a fishbone in the nuthouse?"
"Tell the truth: Is he really dead?"
"Or did you just make him up to be dead, because you're coming to the end?"

All right: he's alive. (But Stomma has died in the meantime.) In the late fifties, Hermann Ott (cured) left the People's Republic of Poland with his wife Lisbeth and his son Arthur. And Ranicki, the critic, who lived Doubt's story somewhere else, came to West Germany at about the same time. It wasn't easy for Doubt to get used to life in the Federal Republic; the same with Ranicki. He had to change newspapers several times. In the early sixties, Dr. Ott was living in Kassel as a cultural affairs official, like Dr. Glaser in Nuremberg. (I have his correspondence, dating from that period, with a snail collector in Uppsala, who sent him a copy of his book *On the Vaginal Form of Marine Snail Shells*, with the dedication: "To the friend of the gastropoda . . .") Today Hermann Ott is

279

perfectly normal and lives in retirement with his Lisbeth: an elderly gentleman who occasionally lectures at people's universities. On the snail as ancient fertility symbol and its medicinal properties; on sentimentality and hypochondria; on Forster and Lichtenberg in relation to the French Revolution; on the Lichtenbergian element in Schopenhauer . . .

"You're just making it up again."
"Whadda you mean, Lichtenberg? I thought this name was Lichtenstein?"
"He really exists, he isn't just made up."
"I saw him one time. In our kitchen. His wife, too."

They came to see us on Monday, September 6, 1971. We talked about our impending trip to Israel and his book of documentation, *The Exodus of the Danzig Jews*, which was soon to be published by Mohr in Tübingen. Then we talked about my snail book. Though I had intended to ask questions only on my arrival in Tel Aviv and after adequate preparation—who, for instance, had put the bomb on board the *Patria* in Haifa harbor: "Was it the Stern gang or the Haganah?"—I began to ask questions (rather disjointedly) right here in Friedenau. "When David Jonas was deported from the warehouse ghetto in Mausegasse to Theresienstadt in 1943, did he have a successor as chairman of the Jewish community?"

Erwin Lichtenstein named the lawyer Fürstenberg, who, as he told me, died two years ago in Hamburg "at a ripe old age."

"And how many of the people on Mausegasse survived?"

Lichtenstein informed me that in the battle of Danzig, when the Old City, the Right Bank City and the Lower City were destroyed, the warehouse ghetto on Mausegasse had been burned to the ground. Only twenty members of the Jewish community survived.

"And who succeeded savings-bank director Bittner as Commissioner for Jewish Affairs?"

"One Robert Sander, formerly sports editor of the *Danziger Neueste Nachrichten*. David Jonas and Sander had known each other for years as sports fans. Come to think of it, it was Sander who had arranged for the Bar Kochba Gymnastic Society to use the gymnasium on Schichaugasse and the track facilities in the Lower City. He did what he could. He's still living in the German Democratic Republic."

I asked Erwin Lichtenstein to announce our visit to Ruth Rosenbaum and Eva Gerson. "When we go to Israel in November. I'll have some more questions . . ."

Frau Lichtenstein asked Franz, who sold her some bent silver wire as jewelry, whether he liked school. (His answer— "Of course"—can be explained.)

That was in the winter after the September elections. We went to Britz to take a look at your new school. The two of us took the Number 25 bus, then the Number 67, as you would have to do. (Anna got there first in the Peugeot, with Raoul Laura Bruno.)

Sitting on the top deck, we rode through Tempelhof and Neukölln, past cemeteries and small factories, through remnants of the Bismarckian era and housing developments of the thirties. Seen through the front window, the new, austerely conceived complex of high-rise buildings came toward us.

Pasted against the sky. Still growing. The filigree cranes frozen in Sunday idleness.

The Walter Gropius School was closed. From outside we peered into ground-floor rooms: congealed English on blackboards, scissors-and-paste work, moon shot, botany. Short-term silence.

I liked the school. You said, "Not bad."

In the expensive gymnasium, Zehlendorf girls were playing Faustball against a girls' team from another neighborhood: for your benefit, there was one with long frowzy yellow hair.

On the far side of a newly excavated building site abandoned during the cold weather, we (the whole family) visited a stone windmill with a revolving cap, still used as a silo among growing high-rise buildings. I explained wherein it differed from a post mill. Only Raoul was interested.

Then we watched the majority of the family drive off in the Peugeot. We rode back on the Number 67 and Number 25 buses. (Franz at the bus stop: when shivering, he's thinner and more affectionate.) With Raoul's wrist watch—you had lost yours, I don't own one—I timed the trip back to Friedenau: forty minutes between home and school. (Now that the new subway is running, only thirty-five minutes.) And that for seven years, there and back. Figure it out, Franz, how much time just for you . . .

When the snail stopped to rest, it heard its track drying. A jellylike track that soon becomes papery and wavy. In Sweden and in the province of Hesse there are more consolidated schools: airy, as though playfully designed institutions, where the teacher no longer occupies a raised platform and the pupils no longer sit in symmetrical order. The snail couldn't bear listening to its drying track for very long. The consolidated school is an experiment; it's up to you, Franz, to make it succeed! So the snail continued on its way, making sounds that drowned out the crackling of its drying track. In the course of the election campaign, I spoke about the consolidated school. "It's the prerequisite to student participation in decision making," I said; trade unionists prefer to look at it the other way around. The snail is afraid of its next resting place, of the crackling sound of its track. We've barely managed to win one election, children, no more, children, no more . . .

"But all the same it was hot stuff."
"It was fun, wasn't it?"

Yes, I'm glad that a change has come about in a perfectly normal way, through elections. But one thing the C.D.U.–C.S.U. don't know how to do is lose. They'll put fear into circulation: small lies on foot, a half suspicion with a cold, false hope drawn by four horses, and running backward on rails; the great Nothing (as such) . . .

And will we, for a while at least, resist the temptation to make leaps, the dream of jumping, common to all snails?

I fear (and hope) we won't. All over the country, they're dying to cover ground, and on principle in a hurry. It's their eagerness to get ahead of each other that makes snails so swift. The respectable snails (bent on holding office) and the heave-ho snails, the Young Socialist bigger-and-better snails, the provincial fug-and-system-bucking seminar snails, and even the system-attuned, pragmatic, reformist house snails—all are condemned to creep, talk (dream) of the great leap. . . .

Will they get ahead? A little way.

Will they deviate? They'll always try.

Will they quarrel? At all costs.

Will they change anything? More than they themselves know.

Will they go wrong? As per plan.

Will they turn back? Seemingly.

Will they get there? Never.

Will they win? Yes (in principle).

....

"What about you? Will you keep on?"
"Writewritewriting—talktalktalking?"

A few weeks ago I was standing at the bar at the Bundeseck (Friedenau), playing with beer mats. Some young writers approached cautiously, as though fearing a rebuff. They spoke gently. (Yes, of course my commitment was important, but didn't it interfere with my writing?) They spoke anxiously of their talents, as though they needed to be sheltered from drafts. Worried about me only a moment before, they grew belligerent when I demonstrated my daily life with two beer mats: "This is my political work that I do as a Social Democrat and citizen; this is my manuscript, my profession, my whatchacallit." I let the distance between the beer mats increase, moved them closer together, leaned one against the other, covered one with the other (then the other with the one) and said, "Sometimes it's hard, but it can be done. You shouldn't worry so much." But the young writers insisted on worrying about me and expected me to flip one or the other beer mat off the bar. They got downright angry because I indulge in two beer mats. (The next day I went to Bremen to talktalktalk. Many partial goals: this, that, and the other.)

Yes, children, now I know Dr. Glaser. On May 7, 1971, Anna and I converged—I coming from Gaildorf in Swabia, Anna from Friedenau—in Nuremberg. In the evening I delivered my lecture on Albrecht Dürer's engraving *Melencolia I* at the Kleine Meistersingerhalle. I'll make you a present of it.

When I'd finished speaking—maybe you'll read this later on as an appendix—there was applause. (Hermann Glaser was pleased.) The next day Anna flew to Berlin: to practice ballet steps with children. I went to Amberg in the Upper Palatinate: to talktalktalk.

Now Franz and Raoul are fourteen, Laura ten, Bruno six. You insist on my writing that in the meantime all four have not only grown, but changed completely. (In July, 1971, the Friedenau section of Schöneberg celebrated its hundredth birthday. At the festival (free beer) Laura and Bruno danced on Breslauer Platz).

In April, 1972, we're planning to drive to Danzig in the Peugeot and look in Gdansk for places where I was six, ten, and fourteen years old. Maybe we'll find traces of Doubt. . . .

On Stasis in Progress

Variations on Albrecht Dürer's engraving *Melencolia I*

On a summer day in 1969, ladies and gentlemen, shortly after the spaceship Apollo 11, in elliptical orbit around the moon, released the lunar module Eagle and in it the two men in their enormous suits with their offerings, something happened that no newspaper saw fit to report. Even television hid behind the excuse of "static" when the two astronauts—immediately after landing the plaque, the flag, and the sensitive instruments—unpacked archaic household utensils. Edwin Aldrin set up the scales, the hourglass, and the bell, laid down the magic number square, and stuck the open compass, which cast a normal shadow, into the ground. With his gloved finger Neil Armstrong traced, large and as though for eternity, the initials of the Nuremberg master: between outspread legs the A took the D under its protection in the moon dust. All this happened on July 21 in the Sea of Tranquillity. Here at home people were talking about the war experiences of the suffragan bishop Defregger. The mark was wasn't going to be revaluated. Saturn looked on and was well pleased with his children.

When, in March, 1969, I was invited by the city of Nuremberg to contribute a lecture to the celebrations marking the Dürer year 1971, which has now come around—right after the Lenin centenary, as chance would have it—I found myself on uncharted political ground, engaged in preparations for the forthcoming parliamentary elections. From March 5 to September 28 I was on the road campaigning, yet all the while on the lookout for material for my lecture on Dürer.

Words, words, words, hot and cold by turns. On the one hand, I was buoyed up and kept moving by the lusty appeals of progress, on the other, weighed down by the lead content of this lecture, because I soon decided to talk about Albrecht Dürer's engraving *Melencolia I*, done in 1514.

My creeping sole traveled the pathways of a society on whose fringes groups were beginning to take desperately extreme attitudes of resignation or euphoria. Daily flights into utopia found their counterpart in relapses into melancholic withdrawal. From these vanishing points I tried to derive the tension that seems to be man's burden and is often—despite better knowledge—called his fate; the name of its ancient deity is Saturn.

He presided over melancholy and utopia. Here I shall speak of his twofold rule. Of how melancholy and utopia preclude one another. How they fertilize one another. The area between the vanishing points. Of the revulsion that follows one insight and precedes the next. Of Freud and Marx, who should have sat for a double portrait by Dürer. Of superabundance and surfeit. Of stasis in progress. And of myself, for whom melancholy and utopia are heads and tails of the same coin.

First the engraving, which in picture-postcard form I carried with me through Swabia and Lower Saxony, to Biberach and Delmenhorst: a nocturnal, batlike animal, a Saturnian creature like the dog in the picture, holds the banderole with the title. A transferable motif. For just as this heavy-set young woman surrounded by instruments turned bric-a-brac lends a melancholy expression to all humanistic learning, so the grounded angel is susceptible to any number of popular interpretations. There sits a female iceberg, all dressed up and nowhere to go. Constipated from overeating, she despairs of traditional laxatives. A mournful clod, a bluestocking who had studied too much. And much more.

This state of mind provokes ridicule. People trying to evade it often take jokes as their vehicle. We laugh ourselves sick at something profoundly sad. We recognize a glass eye because its glance is so human. The sad clown. The comedy of failure. A state of mind and its escape valves. In regard to this state of mind language has a good deal to offer: black bile or gall—in the sixteenth century also a name for ink—bilious, atrabiliar, bitter as gall. The probably untranslatable German words *Schwermut, Weltschmerz, Trübsal, Wehmut, Grübelei* come to mind. Someone is, looks, or feels peevish, morose, sick of it all, lousy-rotten. Moods while raking leaves, reading old letters, cleaning a comb, moving bowels. Find their embodiment in kitsch or poetry: poetic kitsch. In railroad stations, on foggy waterfronts, in shantytowns, wherever something is meaningless or moribund, she turns up. She sulks, eats her heart out, stews in her juice; she has become a burden to herself, insufferable. Everything is shallow, empty, calculable, mechanical; one and the same article passes by in heartbreaking uniformity. . . .

So I put Dürer's Melencolia in a cannery, a poultry farm, on a conveyor belt at the Siemens plant. Supported by her left hand, which no longer supports a head, her right hand, which a moment ago held the compass, is stamping sheet metal, packing eggs, helping parts to find parts. Melencolia is wearing a scarf over a permanent. For eight hours a day she's a stranger to herself, because she's lost. True, she's doing something, but *she* doesn't do what she's doing. The conveyor belt does it. She reacts only partially. Her manipulations are timed to the second, to the fraction of a second. I could remove both her active hands and bend her arm stumps back into the Dürer pose. I could put a new article on the conveyor belt: for instance, an exact replica of Albrecht Dürer's *Melencolia I*, cast in lead as a cute souvenir. A mass-produced article that might well find a market on the master's five hundredth birthday. Sitting by the conveyor belt, she, the Melencolia of today, would only have to snap the wings of the mass-produced Melencolia of long ago into place and press the tiny compass into the crook of her hand. Manipulations as units of time. Profit becomes myth: impalpable. I haven't invented this work process, only varied it.

By the conveyor belt the Melencolia of rationalized production finds her everyday expression: a state of mind guaranteed by the legal wage scale. No self-doubting erudition. No dire astrological constellation, no predetermined, inscrutable fate. Nor is this forced labor a punishment for the responsible parties. No inventors or subtle perfectors, let alone stockholders or directors, but girls and women sit wingless and as though sexless at the conveyor belt for eight hours a day.

Melancholy has ceased to be an individual phenomenon, an exception. It has become the class privilege of the wage earner, a mass state of mind that finds its cause wherever life is governed by production quotas. The timekeeper is watching. A silent Melencolia reduced to silence by the noise of production. You have to listen carefully to hear how in a factory, wherever piecework rules and productivity is the dominant principle, rage accumulates, particle by particle, takes up space, finds no outlet as yet, but looks for one.

What utopia might provide a counterworld to the melancholy-producing conveyor belt? Is more leisure, resulting from increasing automation, already a reality, or is it still a utopia? And how is leisure to be organized, in accordance with what guiding principles? For leisure wants to be regulated. Leisure has its timekeepers. What conveyor belt will take care of the workers' free time?

Just as Albrecht Dürer's humanist Melencolia was at the same time Geometria, so in a portrait of our times tourism—or, if she existed, "Touristica"—might serve as Melencolia's alter ego. Herded in groups at attractive prices by our leading agencies to sunny beaches, to fields of educational ruins, to the Piazza San Marcos of the world, wherever the sightseeing conveyor belt chooses to operate, Touristica as Melencolia snaps her pictures, until suddenly, or gradually, the click of the shutter release, the idiotic mechanism of the exposure meter, and the foretaste of ridiculous results rise to consciousness. Now she's sitting slumped amid picturesque scenes. Exhausted, fed up, she refuses to absorb any more. Sweating, preoccupied by her own effluvia. Sick of beauty in wide format, repelled by so much numbered history, bored by competing marvels, she has lost her feeling for regulated, organized leisure. As long ago Geometria–Melencolia held the compass, so Touristica–Melencolia holds her camera and has no desire to put in another roll of film.

If in the world of labor, at the conveyor belt and so on, melancholy as a social state of mind is a reality, if in touristically organized leisure melancholy barges in and—though not mentioned in the prospectus—insists on its place, if work and leisure are soon to be subordinated to this one utopian principle—absolute busyness—then utopia and melancholy will come to coincide: an age without conflict will dawn, perpetually busy—and without consciousness.

Mere speculation? An arbitrary variation on the Melencolia theme? In love with the present and constantly surrounded by moods of semipolitical dejection, I found it hard to gain the detachment needed to keep my perspective cool and my subject matter dry. Because, learned ladies and gentlemen, I was so closely beset by the heralds of leapfrog-playing utopias and because, whether in Franconian or in Rhenish surroundings, I was constantly entangled by melancholy, I found little time to consult Aristotle or Ficino, Burton or Shakespeare, Kierkegaard or Schopenhauer, Benjamin or Marcuse. Neither Panofsky nor Saxl passed me notes. It wasn't until after the campaign that I compared left-wing melancholy with right-wing melancholy on the basis of Wolf Lepenies and Arnold Gehlen. Only then was I able to corroborate, question, and amplify my own view by reading. My own view is that where melancholy comes into being and endures, it is not aware of itself.

Wherever I went, enthusiastic people succumbed in a highly uneducated way to resignation, and those who were already melancholy failed, without a thought of Hegel, in their last attempts at high-jumping. Uncertain of themselves and hence also of their related origins, the maidens Utopia and Melancholy jostled their way to the same microphone and fought for priority. For this reason I shall not comb the existing literature for quotations—if I quote, it will be only in passing. Instead, I shall tell you how often and in what form, both naked and in disguise, the leading representatives of melancholy have crossed my path, stood in my way, and affected me: heavy-heartedness is not just a word; it tips the scales and can't be outweighed, except perhaps by utopia.

Frankly, my manuscript, which has been growing and shrinking for the last two years under the title *From the Diary of a Snail* has been weighed down by my lecture and the work of art on which it is based; for obstinately as I noted and measured the snail process known as progress for my children—and perhaps for other people's children—I was unable to dismiss Dürer's motif from my mind. So I tried, for the benefit of my own and other people's children to interpret the stasis in progress. The quickly drying track. I played with the accumulated bric-a-brac, transposed its components. Scales, hourglass, and bell, number square and compass found parallels. If Melencolia can sit at the conveyor belt, turn into a pillar of salt on photosafari, or ride an empty snail shell, then she can also find a place in the control room and enter into Einstein's formula for the present-day world.

Often on the road, during jams on the Autobahn, besieged by exhaust fumes in my jerking waiting room, laned-in as though forever and engulfed in the creeping process of rush-hour traffic, I saw her sitting glumly at the steering wheel: Melencolia with a driver's license. When Albrecht Dürer engraved his Melencolia on copper, he was forty-three years old; that is my age now. This lecture comes at the end of a snail's balance sheet.

An engraving with a historical background. In 1502, still committed to medieval allegorism, hence to the four stereotype temperaments, Dürer cut Philosophia in wood for the title page of a book and in the four corners portrayed the choleric, sanguine, phlegmatic, and melancholy temperaments as the four winds. Boreas, the cold north wind, symbolizing the old, earth-bound man, blows icicles into the twining foliage around Philosophia and bears witness to winter. The four Apostles in two oils on wood also owe their characters to the doctrine of the temperaments; as Dürer's theoretical writings show, it was also his guide as a portraitist, crucial for his conceptions of anatomy and proportion. Only *Melencolia I* is marked by new influences contrary to allegory, though the new element is still uncertain, affected by medieval habits of thought, and therefore appears in mummery.

In the 1470's the Italian philosopher Marsiglio Ficino wrote to a friend: "In these times I don't, in a manner of speaking, know what I want; perhaps I don't want what I know and want what I don't know."

Ficino attributes this profoundly melancholic state of mind, which thus summed up reads like an anticipation of Schopenhauer's prize essay *On the Freedom of the Will*, to his Saturn, striding malignantly backward in the sign of Leo. As a humanist and scientist, however, he was dismayed to find himself believing in the power of the planets and looking upon melancholy as a Saturnian calamity. Finally, on his friend's advice, Ficino stuck to Aristotle, probably the first thinker to recognize and justify melancholy as a source of outstanding artistic and scientific achievements.

And so it was with Dürer, who, in the course of his travels in Italy, was made acquainted by his friend Pirckheimer with Ficino's principal work, *De vita triplica*, a book about Saturnian man.

Saturn still rules; but his reign is no longer exclusively disastrous, for it secures the area of melancholy as a place of contemplation. St. Jerome in his study engraved on copper in the spring of the same year was an occasion for practice. The quiet study, the hermitage—that is where Utopia, in freely chosen seclusion from loud reality, carries on her experiments.

With this, melancholy became ambivalent. Still an inadvertible calamity to the ignorant common people, it gave the knowing an elitist aura. Already, the eighteenth-century genius cult is foreshadowed; and so is the subterfuge of our modern conservatives, who decree that change is impossible and vindicate inertia as a melancholic heritage. Melancholy as the privilege of an elite who pass their time in sophisticated inactivity, and arrogance as its conservative expression.

From time immemorial, the dead weight of things as they

are has been played off against progress as the possibility of change. For wherever progress is frustrated by premature aims or utopian flights from reality, wherever its advances are so slight as to be ludicrous, the conservative who "knew it all along" triumphs. His melancholy gestures signify that nothing can be changed, that all human effort is vain, that an imponderable fate rules: human existence as doom. Only order, a universally respected system, offers security. It consolidates hierarchical structure and the power of the powerful. It gives permanence to things as they are. Of the common people it demands earnest fulfillment of duty and resigned contentment. Melancholy is reserved for the knowing, the leading elite, the holders of power.

For, like all rigid systems, the conservative order classifies the masses as ignorant and denies them the right to be melancholy, that is, to reject the existing order and its conventions. Power is sacrosanct. Satisfaction with the existing order is compulsory. Melancholy arouses suspicion the moment it ceases to be the privilege of an elite and colors social attitudes. Suspicion of melancholy as a preliminary to interdiction of melancholy has always been based on the identification of melancholy with disease.

The sick Dürer. The melancholy Dürer, melancholy because he was sick. At the Bremen Kunsthalle there is a pen-and-ink sketch that experts date before the *Melencolia*. It is believed that Dürer did this sketch as an aid to a doctor he wished to consult at a distance. Dürer's nude self-portrait with its pointing forefinger. Roughly in the area of the gall bladder, liver, and spleen, a yellow spot indicates the seat of the disease. He appends the words: "Where the yellow spot is and where the finger is pointing, that is where it hurts."

We know that Dürer complained of a swollen spleen even before his journey to The Netherlands. Down to the last century, peasant calenders referred to Saturn as a peevish, sick planet that caused disease of the liver, gall bladder, and kidneys. Since these inner organs were under Saturn's jurisdiction, they induced melancholy.

Did Dürer's diseased spleen make him a melancholic? Is the equation melancholy equals disease still valid? If Dürer was sick and, being a humanist, was also melancholy, must he necessarily have been sick because he was melancholy?

Physicians have used the word and concept since the fifth century B.C. Since then, word and concept have been ambiguous. Though modern science distinguishes between endogenous and reactive depression, between schizophrenia, anxiety neurosis and paranoia, the comprehensive term "melancholia" is still widely thought to stand for a disease similar or related to insanity.

Up to the eighteenth century, in keeping with the doctrine of the temperaments, a disturbance in the mixture of the four humors was regarded as the cause of "black bile," which in turn was the cause of melancholia.

Entertaining as a description of the medieval treatments for melancholia might be, I shall spare you and myself a list of absurd mixtures. It was Paracelsus who first ceased to rely on purgatives and—a pioneer of shock therapy—prescribed pills that provoked immoderate laughter, which, when it reached its climax, he countered with pills inducing sadness. Physical exercise was also recommended. Even then: fresh air for stay-at-homes. Music, especially played on a lute, was said to have an appeasing if not curative effect. Melancholics were advised not to eat cabbage, because it made for flatulence. For 2,000 years a purgative decoction of hellebore was used as a household remedy for oppressive gloom and dark melancholy. Today Tofranil is used for the alleviation of depressive states. Advertisements speak of a "milestone in the treatment of melancholia."

I'm not a doctor. I shall not venture to judge whether—quite aside from the humanist's knowledge-induced nausea—the pain in his spleen darkened Dürer's disposition. I don't know when melancholy can be called endogenous. I find it impossible to call social states of mind, demonstrable in individuals as well as groups, pathological merely because the utopian principle of health, regardless of whether it invokes "healthy national sentiment" or "socialist man," absolutely forbids melancholy in the systems that it dominates.

The depressive states recorded in the case history of the endogenous melancholic have their counterpart in euphoric phases, just as in normal cases of reactive melancholia utopian flights of fancy have their reversal in a state of narrowed consciousness.

The depressions of many students, whom only yesterday a social utopia fired with enthusiasm, are not only reflected in statistics. A new vocabulary has taken hold of melancholy, overhastily stigmatized as a disease: something is frustrating; someone is frustrated; frustration is spreading like wildfire, encompassing groups and ultimately the whole of society.

At this point, perhaps, the much and variously interpreted "Suburban Widow," who has been leading her marginal life for years now, after having been generated on the drafting boards of architects and city planners, might be brought into the picture. Spirited away from the city, settled in the green belt, the jobless housewife is bored sick in her flat-roofed bungalow. It is easy to surround her with the products of sterile perfection. Naturally she wears her hair in rollers during the latter part of the morning. What comes to mind in place of the compass? My choice is an object made of India rubber, supplied by certain mail-order houses. For, removed from its more restrictive sense, masturbation has become an expression for everything that has proved, for lack of human contact, to be void of meaning. We have communication problems, suffer from egocentrism and narcissism, are frustrated by information glut and loss of environment; we stagnate despite the rising G.N.P.

Not Geometria as Melencolia, but the beautiful, frustrated woman, also known as the "Suburban Widow," is sitting there. High Fidelity: piles of phonograph records ward off silence. In a moment she will open her little box of Librium or inject herself with something or other. Is she sick? I say her behavior is normal and in keeping with her state of mind, which is social. Consequently, I shall not speak of neuroses. My subject, Dürer's engraving, presents not a manic-depressive state but the state of reactive melancholy prevailing in the age of humanism.

When thought is at an end and melancholy has set in, annulling what has been thought, an allegorical figure sits brooding with shaded face and sightless eyes. The Middle Ages are still present—Saturn is there, documented by dog, stone, and bundle of keys—but perspective and geometrical instruments express the new era as seen by the learned humanists. Technically this piece is rather stodgy, lacking in boldness. Among the engravings the *Lesser Passion* and the *Life of the Virgin* and any number of drawings as well tell us more about Dürer the graphic artist than the *Melencolia*. Nevertheless, we are struck by this anatomical translation of a state of mind. Engraved fourteen years after the Christian world expected to be destroyed and seven years before Luther's appearance in Worms, it holds meaning for us—more than as a work of art—as testimony to a period of transition whose effects are still at work today.

Shortly before the curtain was torn away. A time of great projects and unreflecting ecstasy. Copernicus and Columbus: a time of discoveries that shatter all conventions. The Fuggers and Thomas Münzer: social and hence religious tension. Foreshadowed by hair-thin cracks, cleavage is in preparation, already implicit in faith, society, and consciousness. Medieval introverted mysticism will turn outward and find its counterpart in social utopias. Falling sickness and the heights of exaltation come so close together that they overlap. Parlor games with hieroglyphics. The Emperor Maximilian's circle of humanists: a grandiose disappointment. For a meager fee: the emperor's Gate of Honor, crawling with allegory. Apart, detached, and untroubled by friction: reason and its limits. True, thought lost its scholastic curlicues, ceased to be cyclical, and began to run in one direction, forward, progressively, but at the same time the new experience of stasis in progress set its stamp on the new era. Dürer put it into a picture.

Phases displaced individually and in relation to each other. Progress overtaken. Inactive amid instruments. As though geometry had outmeasured itself. As though the latest knowledge had bogged down in doubt after its first attempts to walk. As though science had canceled itself out. As though beauty were an empty fiction. As though only mythology would endure.

Saturn, who does things on a large scale and is used to ruling with Kronos, manages quite well in the new era. His "Golden Age" shows no sign of ending. Not only is he the god of the peasant's earth and seed; numbers and geometry, the distiller's art, and, in the sign of Capricorn, philosophy, and all earthly power come under his jurisdiction. Consequently, what finds expression in our engraving is no dull atrabiliar *Schwermut,* but a melancholy that grew from knowledge and understands itself.

Amid rigid immobility the propped left arm and the clenched fist supporting the head become a gesture signifying thought after so much futility. Once the void opens and words lose their meaning in vast echoing spaces, the head demands to be supported, the fist clenches in helplessness.

Not a new motif: in artistic representation, Apostles and

Evangelists, God after creating the world, Hercules after completing his labors, Kronos and Saturn, tend to prop up their heads; but in Dürer bent arm and clenched fist hold a more central position than in any of the models that may have been known to him. Brightly lighted, they delimit, and actively contrast with, the traditionally shaded face, whose gaze, directed at nothing, corresponds to the slack right hand holding the compass.

The prevailing mood is not one of vagueness. Incongruously, as mythological relics of antiquity mingle with the instruments of the new era, so creating the immoderate disorder which—like immoderate order—gives rise to melancholy, the soberly balanced composition and the still-life quality of the detail make it clear that the clutter is not an unfortunate accident; in Dürer it is a symptom of science's self-doubt, hence of melancholy.

Stasis in progress. Hesitation, halts between steps. Thought about thought, until the only remaining certainty is doubt. Knowledge that engenders disgust. All this is applicable to us.

Our Melencolia sits brooding between ideologies and stunted reforms, impoverished amid inertia. Tired, disgusted by long-drawn-out snail processes, dejected amid timetables, she, too, like Dürer's Melencolia, props up her head and clenches her fist, because in hermaphrodite fashion stasis in progress begets and gives birth to progress from stasis. In a moment she will rise to her feet, reform some bungled reform, appoint a provisional goal, set some important deadlines and—on the sly—plan a simon-pure utopia, in which cheerfulness will be compulsory and melancholy strictly forbidden.

There used to be a tear-jerker that claimed: "We were put in the world to be happy. . . ." People enjoyed listening to that sort of tra-la-la and still do. Wherever utopias have been realized as systems—whether by the state in the Soviet Union or by TV commercials in the U.S.A.—happiness is either ordered by the Central Committee or aggressively taken for granted. The insistence on happiness in the American way of life and the American conception of happiness embodied in the say-cheese smile are nothing other than a convulsive reversal of the Puritan sin-and-damnation ideology and its attendant melancholy. On the other hand, where the utopia of Communism first became reality and has learned to exert power, it has become enslaved by its own conceptions of happiness. Since Lenin, punishment has been imposed for offenses that go by the name of skepticism and nihilism. Revealingly enough, intellectuals in recent years have been punished for critical attitudes by internment in psychiatric clinics: in the strictly ordered home of Communist socialism Melancholy as Utopia's sister is under house arrest.

Healthy women in love with childbearing, pure and joyful young people, serenely thoughtful old people, and grave-faced but energetic men advertise a society that is not allowed to become conscious of its reality. Under a layer of ideological window dressing, socialist daily life languishes in melancholy, bureaucracy demonstrates its presence by waste motion, revolutionary gestures have ceased to be anything more than crumbling plaster, language has been reduced to phraseology, and melancholy—since the slightest critical statement is subject to punishment—has turned inward: no longer stasis in progress, but progressive, soon absolute, stasis.

All those who are willing to think about the thousands of Communists who in despair and resignation met their death under Stalin, who are likewise willing to consider the additional melancholy that has weighed on all Communist countries since the occupation of Czechoslovakia, will need another variant of Dürer's model.

I exchange the Saturnian angel with her accessories for a

much-quoted socialist woman. Instead of the compass that doesn't know what to do with itself, she is holding hammer and sickle. At her feet the exhibition pieces of the Revolution are assembled: Lenin's forward-pointing finger, the spiked caps of the Bolsheviki, in miniature the cruiser *Aurora*, Trotsky's pince-nez, a bust of Karl Marx. Let the *Communist Manifesto* —the title page of the first edition—take the place of the number square. Let the geometrical body give way to a diagram of the Hegelian dialectic. And let the *Weltgeist* in the form of a plug crowd out the mournful dog.

The much-quoted socialist woman also props her head on her clenched fist. She has eyes in her shaded face, but where she is looking nothing is opening up. What has become of her spontaneous socialism? Under her old-fashioned broad-brimmed hat, she is a woman of today. She was born a hundred years ago. The Dürer year and the engraving *Melencolia I* suggest that we doctor a photograph of Rosa Luxemburg and, after our three four variants, print a new engraving, a *Melencolia V*.

Because 450 years after she came into being, humanist melancholy has found a parallel in a quarter where—a cynical absurdity if there ever was one—it has become customary to invoke humanism.

A variant that can easily be amplified. Where shall we put Kirov, where Bukharin? At this point it would be easy to move a George Lukács into the picture in place of the nicked sword. How highhandedly he has relegated philosophers and theoreticians, to whom melancholy and resignation were neither alien nor forbidden, to a residence which he—who undoubtedly felt sure of his knowledge—called "Hotel Abyss"; but it would be pointless to list all the ignoramuses who with Hegel hurry past Schopenhauer and to lodge them in a "Hotel Hubris."

1514: the death of his mother, the date in the number

square. Seldom, since Dürer, has anyone assigned a place to melancholy and demonstrated its necessity with such an air of the self-evident. The Renaissance is commonly regarded as the age when the individual was discovered or rediscovered. But, along with the liberation of the individual, his right to melancholy was asserted. This right has been disputed, has been lost time and again, and is still called into question. True, where melancholy has taken demonic forms, it has been accepted as a professional quirk of genius. When benighted genius proclaimed the rule of barbarism and the monstrous forces of the irrational were unleashed, this melancholy, interpreted as creative madness, could count on the applause of aesthetes and the sacred awe of the public at large. Melancholy has been a privilege granted to "solitary eminences"; as a social attitude, however, it has seldom been legalized.

Usually with contempt or philo-Semitic commiseration, melancholy has been regarded as innate in the Jewish people of the Diaspora—not in the citizens of Israel, however—or as their fate since the destruction of Jerusalem, as though the deaths of millions in the gas chambers were merely the tragic consequences of the Diaspora.

Auschwitz has become a museum, "incapacity for mourning" a much-bandied phrase. This ability to get used to genocide has its parallel in a premature readiness to shrug off the crimes of the National Socialists as momentary insanity, as an irrational aberration, as something incomprehensible and therefore forgivable. Perhaps the wordless action of a statesman, who shouldered the burden and knelt at the site of the Warsaw ghetto, has given belated expression to a people's awareness of undiminished guilt. Repentance as a social state of mind would then be the corresponding utopia; it presupposes melancholy rooted in insight.

Foreseeing disintegration and disruption, war and chaos, the humanists despaired of their impotent knowledge and of the ignorance of the powerful. Conscious of their helplessness, they took refuge in formal, controlled melancholy. Not until the following century, during the Thirty Years' War and in its wake, did baroque language find its way to tragedy—Andreas Gryphius—did baroque poetry treat of grief—Quirinus Kuhlmann—did hope springing from chaotic disorder become a principle; its locale was the vale of tears, its goal redemption.

I don't mean to say that Dürer, bent over his copper plate, intended to predict such extremes of misery and darkness. Only this much: very much like ourselves today, he saw the limitations of his epoch, saw the new rising up unformed, and was oppressed by the inadequacy of thought, its impotence to forestall evil.

In their work on Dürer's *Melencolia I*, Panofsky and Saxl do not exclude the possibility that the ladder leaning against the house might stand for an unfinished building. The abandoned construction site. The rough brickwork. In the course of building doubt cropped up. Useful tools, precise calculations, proved ability lost all vigor and meaning, grew weary of themselves. Before it had ever come into being, the projected building saw itself not as a torso, not as a valid fragment, but as a ruin.

This modern insight, which anticipates today's city planning, its utopian projects and high-rising melancholy, was gained at the beginning of the new era.

It is at home in every field of endeavor. While I was on the road, yet all the while jotting down notes for this lecture, my own experience brought me into contact with melancholy group attitudes, with biographies steeped in melancholy, with the fug-warm backrooms of resignation. The never-resting treadmill of reason. Often while speaking, while my speech automatically delivered itself, I was overcome by leaden discouragement. I fell silent while speaking. While—like many others—active for small reward in the service of enlightenment, I sat dejectedly, surrounded by paper arguments and mutually contradictory projects for reform, crushed by the conflicting opinions of the experts, as though under a glass bell: absently present.

Or after speech had talked itself to pieces and been drained into speech balloons. My jottings for this lecture came to me in meeting halls and school auditoriums, while discussions were dragging on and chants bringing forth their utopian appeals in jingles, when the high of revolutionary exaltation enabled me to foresee the low resignation. Nowhere did the prophets of a "Pacified Existence" as ultimate goal and the ascetic taskmasters of the "Great Refusal" drown each other out more stridently than in the political arguments of those days.

It might be called a sociological bad joke that the disciples of these two doctrines—the one utopian invoking redemption, the other neomelancholic counseling refusal—kept citing the same Herbert Marcuse. I incline to see a unity in such philosophical contradictions. Even if a predominantly youthful audience interpreted Marcuse in two radically different ways— each camp taking what it wanted—it must nevertheless be recognized that here for the first time a thinker established a relationship between the great individuals Freud and Marx, understood the correspondence between melancholy and utopia, and created inspiring unrest by developing from the dialectic of despair the coincidence of the melancholic and the utopian attitudes: the great refusal leads to pacified existence.

With its echoes of Early Christian and ascetic conceptions of salvation, such a utopia of resignation was bound to draw crowds from all sides. Our times favor sectarianism. Religious youth groups, loners in search of community, sons and daughters of the insulated bourgeoisie momentarily ashamed of their privileges, pacifists, hippies, rockers, protesters against the war in Vietnam, against the military dictatorship in Greece, against the occupation of Czechoslovakia, plus large numbers of disoriented fellow travelers have taken from Marcuse's teachings what met their individual or group needs: a massive dose of "Great Refusal" and a pinch of "Pacified Existence"—or contrariwise. Often quotations from Marcuse merely served as trimmings for the quoter's own ideas, which could be Christian or bourgeois-antiauthoritarian, socialist or pacifist, group-dynamic or individualist-egocentric in nature.

A spontaneous movement, whose lifeblood was spontaneity, helped at first to change the society that it was trying to write off as incapable of change. While still being heralded, "Pacified Existence" was forgotten. Revolutionary verbalisms became part and parcel of the advertising jargon of the consumer society that the movement was trying to combat by refusal, that is, refusal to consume. The movement dwindled. Certain groups joined the political parties; others tried their hand at social work. The radical minority, taking a leaf from the book of socialism, broke down into innumerable splinters.

A year later, when the resignational-utopian protest and refusal movement had scattered, I went to Stockholm to meet with trade unionists and discuss a project of aid to underdeveloped countries, in which the Swedish, Yugoslavian, and West German unions were to participate. An idea as simple as it was complicated. The deliberations were of the same order.

During an intermission I took advantage of the good weather—sun and sea breeze—and went looking for a park bench. When I found one, Swedish history, combined with the Swedish present, gave me an opportunity for free-wheeling comparison.

Under a clump of trees that had been planted to provide the Charles XII monument with a background, some young people were sitting loosely grouped around an open-air snack bar. Girls busy with their hair. Strangely contemplative saints.

Flute-playing Vikings. Adherents of sects unknown to me, wearing Indian amulets side by side with the runic insignia of the antiatomic-war movement. Here and there, touristic mummies and daddies snapping pictures of Charles XII in bold foreshortening and—without making a dent in their relaxed melancholy—of the young people, each separately, since the distance and elevation of Charles XII made it impossible to squeeze Sweden's warlike history and a segment of the peaceable Swedish present into the same picture.

I jotted down what I saw, what came to mind, and what, quite independently of photography and its optical limitations, could be seen as related or contradictory: the cautious steps of bare feet on gravel. The iron chains around the granite pedestal of the monument. The yarmulkes, Indian headbands, and ponchos. The wind in Nordic hair and, inviting to meditation, the wind-blown notes of the flute. The sleepy solo dance of a buxom maiden.

I noted and sketched: how on an arm too long for his body Charles XII's hand points eastward. The unimpressed seagulls. Distant traffic, its sound. The socially circulating joint. Gestures of playful love and waning love in the tree-filtered light. In the background the ox-blood-red church. Someone in a long white shirt seeing miracles through eyeglasses and leading a white goat.

Also words. Poltava. Orange juice. Disguise. Dandelions. Frederikshall. Sorrow out of doors. Narcissus. Shampoo.

I saw: far away in an air bubble, power and impotence. The expectation of a meaningless messiah. Mao's Little Red Book and older breviaries. Dürer's complex collection in fair weather.

And I understood why all in all these young people were cheerful: Saturn has released his children from history.

For this, too, forgetfulness of history at the foot of a

306

monument—seen in Stockholm and seen again elsewhere—is a melancholy expression of utopian flight from reality. When was the battle of the Narva? What was the war with Norway about? What was Charles XII doing in Turkey? No more dates. No development. History without consequences.

If we put a Stockholm-style Melencolia into the picture, history with its secretions will no longer be present. Surrounded by piles of consumer goods, beset by superabundance in cans, nonreturnable bottles and insulated bags, she will be sitting on a deep-freeze chest. Surfeit and disgust will determine her expression. In her right hand, which spurns activity, she will hold a can opener.

Supply without demand. Landscape whose horizon is marked by mountains of butter and hogs, plateaus of cars fresh off the assembly line and imageless television sets.

Compulsive overproduction, a growth rate driven to utopian heights by the principle of maximum productivity have taught Melencolia a corresponding attitude: there sits a young lady, not glutted but refusing to eat and overeat, emaciated, perhaps deriving her last pleasure from hunger, weaned from all amusement, from love and its vicissitudes, from curiosity and even from fashions. Her dress is cut like a monk's habit: coarse linen. Only asceticism can overcome her melancholy and inspire her with a new utopia: an existence pacified by stern discipline.

But we've seen such an existence before. The Puritans' catalogues of vices, their Stalinist, Old Testament severity are known. Known is happiness by decree. Known is the pejorative use of the word "defeatism." As formerly under feudal-absolutist systems the bourgeoisie stagnated for want of an alternative and turned its back on the world in boredom, so absence of alternative weighs on totalitarian socialist states and societies, giving rise to resignation renunciation refusal.

I have spoken of compulsive consumption in the capitalist countries of the West and its consequences: surfeit and disgust. The young people of the ideological dictatorships, so joyful in photographs, know a different kind of surfeit. It springs from the duties imposed by revolutionary phraseology, from a directed will, no longer free to make decisions, from a decreed socialism, in which the concept of freedom has ceased to be anything but an ornament of scholastic casuistry. Like Saturn in his day, the revolution has marked its children with melancholy.

For instance, a late-acquired friend. Essentially a cheerful man, optimistic on principle, a picture of imperturbable Saxon-style bustle: always brimful of projects. But his biography belies appearances. A long, consistent development—youthful Marxist, Communist, Communist refugee, after the war Communist deputy in the Hessen Landtag, then editor in chief at Radio Deutschland in East Berlin—followed by a break in the early fifties. To keep pace with the show trials in Budapest and Prague, the German Democratic Republic wanted a show trial of its own. Like Rajk and others, like Slánsky and others, Bauer was accused of espionage, high treason, and collaboration with the CIA. Partial confessions were obtained by methods inviting comparison with those of the fascists. Sentenced after long solitary confinement and finally deported to Siberia, he was released in the mid-fifties before the end of his term, his health broken and his faith in Communism irrevocably destroyed. He now lives in the Federal Republic. Condemned to endure the ridicule of the know-it-alls, the indulgence of the blameless, and at present a deluge of slander: the Strauss mentality.

He, too, is not an isolated case. A biography among thousands. Abjuring faith, Leo Bauer has become a Social Democrat. The distrust of his new comrades, the hatred of those he has lost, and the baseness of his political enemies have put their mark on him. You would expect him to give up, to drop out. But a will such as only men who have many times been broken and given up for dead, men whose consciousness of guilt springs from their own inner resources, can summon up, enables him, if not to go on living in the fullest sense of the word, at least to be active. Only late at night, when everything had been said, when the daily drudgery seems to be over, does my friend turn to stone. He sits strangely absent in our group of political detailmongers, themselves tired but still present in their eagerness for information. Then whatever it is that keeps his will running falls away from him. He seems to be listening to the sound of time, to have taken up lodging in the void. His eyes seem to fix on nothing. A gray shadow curtains his face. I realize, of course, that Saturn's favorite organs—spleen, liver, and gall bladder—are still imprisoned in Siberia, but what hits me even harder is the words "in vain" cast in lead. Revulsion after old and before new insight. To this socialist the concept of justice has become doubtful, invalid, and absurd, just as in times gone by geometry seemed to the humanists.

When Albrecht Dürer set to work on his engraving *Melencolia,* he sketched glumly seated Melancholy after his cantankerous wife Agnes. A copy of a sketch of the sleeping dog has also come down to us. It helps me to understand how, late at night, after the last of the utopias has extinguished its bedside lamp, my friend Leo Bauer crawls into the picture of melancholy: grown heartsick after so many false starts.

But how is it that Leo Bauer will go on until it kills him? How is it that so many whom I have met on my way, so many who, like myself, know stasis in progress, start afresh, pick up their lead balls and from their burden of Saturnian boulders strike the sparks that kindle our utopian lamps.

While writing—for my own and other people's children—a

309

book in which progress is measured by snail standards, I also described what makes the heart heavy. I have tried to put in a good word for melancholy. I have shown its modern variations, in order that we may see it as the social reality it is, and no longer as a suspicious eccentricity.

Only those who know and respect stasis in progress, who have once and more than once given up, who have sat on an empty snail shell and experienced the dark side of utopia, can evaluate progress.

Günter Grass
The Rat £3.95

Through the thoughts of a caged female rat we learn the history of the world from the rat perspective, interleaved by Grass's narrator with tales old, new and fantastical of the protagonists of earlier writings. The result is a chilling insight into what the future holds: the human race stands condemned by wasteful consumerism and an urge for self destruction, to be supplanted by its logical successor in the evolutionary chain: the rat.

'Grass has written an apocalyptic novel which goes further than any of his work in plumbing the dangers of our nuclear age; the book is dark, bitter, witty and somehow warming. It asks the obvious fundamental questions – Who controls the world? Who controls the imagination? – but, instead of anguished romanticism, does it with the realism of its own convictions and the convictions of its own imagery' NEW STATESMAN

'The narrative is seamlessly welded together and lent power by the brown rat that the author has been given for Christmas . . . Reading his prose, as always superbly translated by Ralph Manheim, is like being wakened from the sleep of reason by acid rain' NEW YORK TIMES

'Massive and magnificent' DAILY TELEGRAPH

'A magnificently organized howl of anguish' INDEPENDENT

Elias Canetti
Auto Da Fé £4.95

This extraordinary novel, set in Germany between the wars, tells of a distinguished scholar, Peter Kien, whose eccentric temperament leads him to destruction at the hands of a grotesque society. On one side stands his illiterate and grasping housekeeper who tricks him into marriage; on the other, a brutish concierge who is typical Nazi material. Kien is forced out into the underworld of the city, a purgatory where his guide is a chess-playing dwarf of evil propensities. Eventually restored to his home, he is visited by his brother, an eminent psychiatrist who, by an error of diagnosis, precipitates the final crisis . . .

'A novel of terrible power' C. DAY LEWIS

'Disturbing . . . terrifying . . . ferociously funny' WALTER ALLEN

Gregor von Rezzori
Memoirs of an Anti-Semite £3.50

'These haunting stories portray history unwinding within a single skull, a
cultivated, often charming mind being betrayed by a single catastrophic
flaw' TIME

'Here is a work that tackles – without reproof, without illusions and without
shallow moral judgements; by turns engaged and detached, funny and sad,
tender and heartless; often in a tone of merciless self-flagellation, and
always from the most oblique angle one can imagine – the phenomenon of
anti-Semitism, and its correlative anti-Goyism, the double tragedy of banal
misunderstanding that changed the face of Europe and the world'
BRUCE CHATWIN

The Death of My Brother Abel £4.95

*'I cannot exist in a world that haunts me with its rubble. I would rather do
without the European heritage . . .'*

The year is 1968. In a Paris hotel room a famous, successful scriptwriter is
sitting at a desk, trying to write. Before him are boxes and folders crammed
with material he must assemble into the one great novel he has always
promised himself and his agent he would write. But is it possible, or even
worthwhile, to write such a book in a world ruled by mindless mediocrity, a
world that refuses even to remember its past, so thoroughly annihilated by
war?

At its heart, *The Death of My Brother Abel* is concerned with the ultimate
paradoxes of destruction and rebirth, with the way these forces affect our
literature, our art, and the flaws and glories of our own humanity. Gregor
von Rezzori's exuberant, dazzling novel stands alongside the works of
Musil, Mann and Grass as a landmark in twentieth-century literature.

All Pan books are available at your local bookshop or newsagent, or can be ordered direct from the publisher. Indicate the number of copies required and fill in the form below.

Send to: **CS Department, Pan Books Ltd., P.O. Box 40, Basingstoke, Hants.   RG21 2YT.**

or phone: 0256 469551 (Ansaphone), quoting title, author and Credit Card number.

Please enclose a remittance* to the value of the cover price plus: 60p for the first book plus 30p per copy for each additional book ordered to a maximum charge of £2.40 to cover postage and packing.

*Payment may be made in sterling by UK personal cheque, postal order, sterling draft or international money order, made payable to Pan Books Ltd.

Alternatively by Barclaycard/Access:

Card No.

Signature:

Applicable only in the UK and Republic of Ireland.

While every effort is made to keep prices low, it is sometimes necessary to increase prices at short notice. Pan Books reserve the right to show on covers and charge new retail prices which may differ from those advertised in the text or elsewhere.

NAME AND ADDRESS IN BLOCK LETTERS PLEASE:

Name————————————————————————

Address————————————————————————

3/87